DISCARD

DISCARD

EMPRESS OF ETERNITY

TOR BOOKS BY L. E. MODESITT, JR.

THE SAGA OF RECLUCE

The Magic of Recluce
The Towers of the Sunset
The Magic Engineer
The Order War
The Death of Chaos
Fall of Angels
The Chaos Balance
The White Order
Colors of Chaos
Magi'i of Cyador
Scion of Cyador
Wellspring of Chaos
Ordermaster
Natural Ordermage
Mage-Guard of Hamor
Arms-Commander

THE COREAN CHRONICLES

Legacies
Darknesses
Scepters
Alector's Choice
Cadmian's Choice
Soarer's Choice
The Lord-Protector's Daughter
Lady-Protector (forthcoming)

THE IMAGER PORTFOLIO

Imager
Imager's Challenge
Imager's Intrigue

THE SPELLSONG CYCLE

The Soprano Sorceress
The Spellsong War
Darksong Rising
The Shadow Sorceress
Shadowsinger

THE ECOLITAN MATTER

Empire & Ecolitan
    (comprising The Ecolitan Operation
    and The Ecologic Secession)
Ecolitan Prime
    (comprising The Ecologic Envoy
    and The Ecolitan Enigma)
The Forever Hero
    (comprising Dawn for a Distant Earth,
    The Silent Warrior, and In Endless Twilight)

Timegod's World
    (comprising Timediver's Dawn
    and The Timegod)

THE GHOST BOOKS

Of Tangible Ghosts
The Ghost of the Revelator
Ghost of the White Nights
Ghost of Columbia
    (comprising Of Tangible Ghosts
    and The Ghost of the Revelator)

The Hammer of Darkness
The Green Progression
The Parafaith War
Adiamante
Gravity Dreams
The Octagonal Raven
Archform: Beauty
The Ethos Effect
Flash
The Eternity Artifact
The Elysium Commission
Viewpoints Critical
Haze
Empress of Eternity

EMPRESS OF ETERNITY

L. E. MODESITT, JR.

TOR®

A Tom Doherty Associates Book
New York

This is a work of fiction. All of the characters, organizations, and events portrayed in this novel
are either products of the author's imagination or are used fictitiously.

EMPRESS OF ETERNITY

Copyright © 2010 by L. E. Modesitt, Jr.

A Tor Book
Published by Tom Doherty Associates, LLC
175 Fifth Avenue
New York, NY 10010

www.tor-forge.com

Tor® is a registered trademark of Tom Doherty Associates, LLC.

Library of Congress Cataloging-in-Publication Data

Modesitt, L. E.
    Empress of eternity / L.E. Modesitt, Jr. — 1st ed.
        p. cm.
    "A Tom Doherty Associates book."
    ISBN 978-0-7653-2664-5
    1. Technology and civilization—Fiction.   2. Canals—Fiction.
3. Climatic changes—Fiction.   4. Revolutions—Fiction.   I. Title.
    PS3563.O264E47 2010
    813'.54—dc22

                                                            2010032572

First Edition: November 2010

Printed in the United States of America

0 9 8 7 6 5 4 3 2 1

FOR CAROL ANN,

because she refuses to accept life without meaning

Knowledge for the sake of knowledge bars understanding.
When knowledge becomes a weapon, all lose.

PROLOGUE

Green tendrils of the aurora borealis swept southward across the night sky, and the ground beneath the city groaned and grumbled. Even the towers, from the lowest to those white spires proud against the stars and against the darkness between those points of light, began to sway, more wildly with each set of tremors.

Any eyes that had time to look would have seen a swollen puffy yellow-gray-white circular mass dominating the sky like a sightless eye surrounded by a haze of dust. The first of all-too-many tsunamis to come crashed across the city from the western ocean, inundating all but the highest spires before it retreated, and those towers in turn crumpled into the rest of the rubble.

Small streaks of fiery white scarred the sky, followed by more and larger streaks, and by an increasing set of sounds like roaring thunder. Waves of burning red and smoldering purple flowed across the sky to blot out the white point-lights of the stars.

Amid it all, with the very earth rupturing, and flaming debris cascading down through the shattered tendrils of the aurora, a gray-blue arc shimmered into being, spanning the midsection of the tortured lands of the continent . . .

. . . and rising from that stone solidity, the only solidity upon the Earth in those terrible moments, climbed a brilliant rainbow, its colors brighter than any sun, accelerating heavenward to do battle with the moon . . .

1

6 Eightmonth 1351, Unity of Caelaarn

The man in a working singlesuit and a thermal jacket, both of aristocratic silver, stepped out of the door, letting it slide closed behind him, a wonder that he had become used to over the past many months. He paused and looked up into the early night sky, his breath a pale white fog in the bitter air, although it was but early autumn. Above and below the Selene Ring the handfuls of time-scattered stars glittered faintly. Farther to the north, less than a few score points of light were scattered across the darkness. The same, he knew, was true far to the south, if well below the horizon he observed.

He needed to hurry. That he felt, and he strode westward, his right arm and hand almost brushing the wall, toward the point overlooking both the ocean and the canal. Even with his long strides, his steps were careful, for patches of thin glazed ice were scattered along the smooth and unmarked blue-gray stone that stretched the entire length of the canal. The ice patches would melt, of course, but stepping on ice floating on the thinnest layer of cold water could cause a nasty fall. He didn't look to the south, which only held the pine barrens and the swamps of the Reserve. Instead, he glanced to his right out across the dark waters. There the line of white rising above the gray wall marked the north side of the midcontinent canal . . . and the ice looming beyond.

At the end of the point was a dark redbrick structure, set in the angle between the coast wall and the canal wall, rising no more than five yards above the flat top of the two walls. While the seamless blue-gray stone of the canal walls looked pristine, the bricks were anything but, with the mortar needing repointing almost everywhere. From within the glassine dome above the last circle of bricks, the faceted fresnel lens focused the light from the electric arc into a beam that swept seaward, marking entrance to and the south side of the canal, not that there was nearly so much shipping since Edelburg had been abandoned to the ice two years earlier.

He stopped just short of the lighthouse and waited, ignoring the bite of the bitter breeze on his face and ears, as well as faint whining of the wind turbines along the cliffs farther to the south. Shortly, a faint *crack* announced that the unnamed glacier that dominated the north side of the canal had calved another white-silvered iceberg. After watching the odd-shaped block of ice fragment and plunge over the canal wall and into the water, he waited until the silent tsunami raced across the four kays between its impact and where he stood. The mass of dark water surged up the gray eternal stone, if only ascending half the height of the canal wall, sending spray skyward. The waters crashed back downward, foaming in places. The ice-mist rose in turn, condensing into fine frozen droplets before settling on the stone that comprised everything from the protective chest-high wall to the canal itself and the ancient station structure, and adding more to the intermittent ice-melt patches. He could see the tiny points of ice settling on the silver-sheen fabric of his jacket, then sliding off.

Before long, he saw the water from the smaller rebound wave break on the north wall of the canal, loosening a few more fragments of over-hanging ice.

He waited, wondering if he would sense more, but he was alone with the wind, the cold, and the arc-light reflected down on him and the blue-gray stone from the glassine dome. In time, he turned his careful steps back toward the ancient station structure he euphemistically called his manor house, not that it was his, or even anything close to a manor house or a house at all. In size, large as it was, it was nothing compared to what had been crushed by the advancing ice a generation earlier and three hundred kays to the northeast. He still held lands and rent-holds to the south, purchased cheaply enough when the ground had been marginal grasslands, if that, lands that now provided an adequate income, with the slight increase in rainfall that had come with the ice to the north of the canal, and his prudent investment in a range of fibreworms, some of which had doubtless produced the threads of the silversheen jacket he wore.

Yet . . . so little compared to what Great-Grandsire had enjoyed, but times and climates change. His lips curled. *So must you.*

When he reached the position of the door facing the canal, not that there was any sign of an opening, he reached out and barely touched the unmarked surface, neither warm nor cold to his fingertips, and the stone slid into itself to form the doorway. Tiny icy pellets followed him inside, clicking on the smooth stone of the floor and the Voharan carpet that covered most of the floor of the chamber they called the study, before the wall re-formed, leaving no sign that there had been an opening there.

"Maertyn . . . why do you always go down to the lighthouse when a berg breaks loose? It was a berg, wasn't it?" Maarlyna asked, looking up from the ancient armchair that had once graced the estate at Norlaak.

Before answering, Maertyn smiled fondly at his wife, taking in her clear skin, her amber hair and eyes, once more silently grateful that things with her had turned out so well as they had. So much could have gone wrong, so much of which she was unaware. "You know it was. You know more than you ever tell me."

She shook her head, the corners of her narrow lips turning up just fractionally in the expression of amusement he always enjoyed.

He'd tried to explain when he'd first become aware of the feelings, the sense that the eternal seamless stone of the canal talked to him somewhere in the recesses of his mind. Maarlyna had smiled indulgently then, nodded, and said, "You must be hearing ultrasonics or the like."

He'd just shrugged. Letting her think that was better than having her think he was not quite right in his mind. And yet . . . she hadn't been exactly skeptical . . . more likely amused in some strange way, as she was now, but he was still wary about questioning her in any way that might spur unnecessary introspection. Perhaps . . . in time.

"How long will they keep you here?" she asked, as if she did not already know.

"You don't mind the isolation that much, do you?" He smiled at the game.

"No. You know that. I'm not looking forward to leaving."

"I told the Ministry that a complete study would take three years."

"At least, that will give us another year and a half."

"A year and five months," he said with a light laugh, "unless we wish to remain and devote ourselves completely to maintaining the lighthouse."

"They really don't need a lighthouse-keeper, either. There's not that much shipping anymore."

"There are enough long-haul freighters running between Saenblaed and Xantippe that they won't close the lighthouse in my time."

"They could mechanize it completely."

"When you consider the overall costs, people are cheaper, and that even includes deputy assistant ministers who are impoverished lords. Mechanization and microthinking devices are saved for places where putting people is infeasible or impossible."

"Like deep current monitoring?"

Maertyn nodded. "Besides, the Ministry finds my observations about the building and the canal wall useful . . . or perhaps amusing."

"They find your absence from the capital even more valuable."

"Speaking of which, I will need to return next month to make another periodic report to the Ministry."

"When?"

"Around the twentieth. I'll take the canal-runner to Daelmar and the tube-train from there to Caelaarn."

"Isn't that when they rotate the Reserve guards?"

"It is, but that's not why I'm picking that time. It was stipulated by Minister Hlaansk some time back. There's also the possibility that I may need the Ministry to approve a request for the additional equipment."

"How long will you be gone? Two weeks?"

"Ten days to three weeks, depending on whatever difficulties arise, and they will . . . and other matters."

"Are the advocates still sparring over the bones of your grandmother's estate? Trying to revalue the Martian antiquities to demand more taxes? Or is it some other endless legality?"

"They may be, but I haven't heard any more about that, not recently." *Unlike a few other complications I can't exactly share with you, dearest.*

"What is it, Maertyn? You looked so sad for a moment, there."

"Call it melancholy. There are times when it would have been nice to retreat to Norlaak. I can't help thinking about it, sometimes."

Maarlyna raised her eyebrows.

"I know. I know. It was gone beneath the glaciers before I was born, but I've seen the representations and the paintings. They're real enough, and I can still think about it."

"Representations aren't the same," she pointed out reasonably.

He smiled gently. "It would depend on the representation, I would think. In some ways, aren't we all representations of a mere biologic plan?" And with all the ages of humanity stretching behind them, who knew how much of that plan was evolutionary and how much genetically planned far in the distant past?

"That makes us sound more like pieces in a game of life, created and played according to this or that formula. We're more than that . . . aren't we?"

He stepped toward the armchair, stopping before it, reaching down, and taking her hands. He guided her to her feet and embraced her, murmuring in her ear, "So much more, especially you, dearest." Closing his eyes, holding her tight to him, he was more alive than ever.

Her arms went around his waist.

2

❖   ❖   ❖

5 Quad 2471 R.E.

T*ick, tick, patter, patter . . .*
        The grains of sand swept westward over the midcontinent canal and its walls like microlocusts, their silicon edges nipping futilely against the stone of the meteorological station. Sharpnesses blunted by the surface that had been designed to outlive eternity itself, each grain sighed and sleighed downward, creating miniature dunes against the land-side walls of the canal and the ancient structure.

Inside the first-level instrumentality and environmentality center that occupied the ancient station, Eltyn pulse-linked to the geosats. Before his eyes—virtie eyes rather than bio-orbs—appeared an amorphous not-quite-wedge-shape of orangish brown, a fantasy color whose wavelengths averaged somewhere around 630 nanometers, an approximation of a triangle that stretched back southward to the foothills of the Second South Range.

2SSR, confirmed the link.

MetStation sole unit structure inhabitable south side MCC west of desert research station. Interrogative estimated habitation/equipment viability duration? The query came from the geosat continent monitor chief, Laembah.

Drama excessive, Eltyn return-pulsed. *Greater probability of solar flare instant-now than silicon inundation in 10^3 cycles.*

Humor/sarcasm unappreciated.

A flash of superheated air washed over Eltyn, then diffused as the door closed as quickly as it had opened to let Faelyna enter. The sand granules picked up by her softboots clicked on the stone floor before they were absorbed into the soles, but others cascaded off her coverall as she peeled back the face shield and detached the hood to reveal short and curly brown hair, hazel eyes, and a slightly pointed chin too strong to be considered elf-like. Then she stripped off the coverall to reveal a dark gray formfitting singlesuit.

Stet, he returned to the geosat.

Dubious humor, Faelyna pulsed through private-link, the unmonitored local freq.

Dubious probabilities for serious and officious[5] chief.

Both Eltyn and Faelyna laughed.

He lives for weather ops, added Eltyn.

He's a Ruchocrat, scheduler, and grid-locker. Faelyna projected a headshake. *Bureaucracy ill serves the Ruche.*

Ill serves any efficient society.

They both knew that TechOversight's covert placement of their project under Meteorology had been the only way to hide its implications from RucheControl. That cover would not last the triad, Eltyn had calcjected—unless no one from The Fifty or the upper Ruche bureaucracy had looked beyond the project title: "Meteorological Endothermic Implications of the MCC."

Routine summer met status-reps ready for Ruche-Centre? she asked.

Sixday. 1000. Eltyn opened the link and let her riffle through the past week's observations. *Analysis incomplete.*

Too many hotspots exceeding baseline projections. Met correlation will compare to reconstructed Searing data.

Probability of comparison exceeds point seven-three, he agreed. *Reconstructed data more conjecture than solid[2].*

Irrelevant. Fear factors associated with Searing and post-Caelaarnan period over-rebound have excessive impact. Her words held the overhued crimson-green of cynicism.

Illogical[5] . . . but likely. Even The Fifty—the Administrative Council of the Ruche—veered toward emotion if the councilors perceived any possibility of Seared Earth or Iceberg Earth, remote as the second possibility might be in the near future.

Query. Structure survey probe status? Cool urgency underlined her question.

Red[3]. Electron probe negative. Fermion beam feedback fused focal assembly. Negative on all laser applications. He follow-frequed his comments with a hint of frustration.

Equipment requisitions?

Submitted. Approval pending, likely.

Account subcategory deficiency?

Negative this triad. Next triad . . . ???

Novel approach possible?

Approach(7) already attempted. Working on approach(8). Eltyn snorted, knowing Faelyna was nanoneedling him. The equipment scheduled for arrival in six days had a special configuration. If it didn't work . . .

Approach(9) . . . my shadow retrogression? she pulsed.

More like retro-nonexistent imaginary future tech. He shrugged. She could certainly try if his next discernment attempt failed. He'd have to re-tech radically and take another tack.

You have a better alternative?

He didn't. Not yet. Not if his next effort failed. *Yours?*

Shadow polariton retrogression [deep image] one ready to commence setup by fiveday next.

He projected a nod as she made her way to the antique ramp leading to the upper level and her laboratory and equipment. He watched her, admiring her walk, and her assurance. To have said more, or pulsed more . . . that would have been improper . . . most unRuchelike.

Yet . . .

Tick, tick . . . patter . . . patter. . . .

Outside the all-too-ancient structure, the sand flailed futilely at the smooth unblemished surface of the gray stone, and to the north other granules drifted across the waters of the canal before sinking, their surfaces wetted, into the unchanging depths.

3

❀   ❀   ❀

9 Siebmonat 3123, Vaniran Hegemony

Kavn Duhyle glanced northward across the canal. His eyes studied the thin line of silvery white that marked the ice less than twenty kays to the north, beyond the swampy green and scattered trees. Nearer, but on the far side of the canal, he noted that the icy runoff from the all-too-brief summer had dwindled to three narrow waterfalls over the blue-gray stone canal wall. The canal was a massive engineering work that stretched two thousand kays, almost precisely. It predated the Old Ones of legend who had survived the second time of Iceberg Earth by close to half a million years. The precision of the canal's engineering never failed to impress him, day after day. Its permanence emphasized, in his mind, their greatness far more than their scattered records that referenced civilizations yet even older—and much more than the fragmentary and decayed ruins of more recent civilizations.

At times, strange artifacts washed up on the sandy shores of the Jainoran Ocean south of the canal along the coast, fragments of fossilized animals wearing equally fragmented and fossilized collars. More intriguing were the strangely designed artifacts that appeared to be replacement parts. Most appeared unchanged by age. Some had what passed for circuits on the nanetic level. Some even channeled energy flows, but for what function and at what levels of current and amperage it was impossible to determine without larger assemblies.

In the late afternoon, Duhyle stood behind the wall that topped the canal near its western end. Ten yards to the east stood the ancient structure that was an integral part of the canal and now served as Helkyria's laboratory. To his left, beyond the shadows, the summer sun warmed the air above the pale blue-gray stone, but not the stone itself, that anomalous adamantine synthstone that formed the walls of the canal and the building. The material was impervious to weather, and even to nucleonic cutters. The canal walls extended down four point three kays, widening as they did. Duhyle's own observations confirmed the few studies that suggested it had been engineered on the fermionic level. That technology had vanished with the Old Ones. Over the years, structures had been built on the wide canal walls, but none had lasted. Records stated that more than one lighthouse had been built where the ocean side of the wall met with the canal side. Now there was not a trace of any structure. A solar filament collector, integrated with the landscape over more than five square kays south of the canal, as well as a small tidal pump, provided power to the lab and to the extensive backup battery/capacitors.

In places, land had formed inside the canal. There were more than a few lakes or swamps behind the canal walls, especially on the north side. Nowhere had the walls broken. In some locales, the walls appeared to curve, but surveys and satellite images had indicated that the canal remained unbowed. The surveys also indicated a semicircular depression—an underwater meteor impact crater one point seven kays across—that extended seaward from the underwater end of the canal. That crater, now mostly filled with sediment, and the fact that the impact had not had any effect on the canal itself, confirmed the canal's indestructibility.

To Duhyle's right appeared Helkyria, also looking out over the canal. He glanced toward her. "What are you thinking?"

"About the ostensible purpose of the canal."

"Ostensible purpose?"

"It's obvious that it was designed to stop glaciation from spreading farther south on the continent . . . or extreme desertification from spreading northward. But why would the Old Ones really have bothered? That couldn't have been its only purpose."

"You've said that before. Besides, in full glaciation, the water would freeze the entire way across the canal."

"If we had had a recurrence of Iceberg Earth, that would have been true, but for periodic ice ages it should have worked. It apparently did. It also slowed desertification from the south side more than once, and certainly during the time of the Hu-Ruche." She glanced across the dark gray-blue waters. "The canal walls go down kays and then rejoin. In almost no place is the water in the center less than a kay and a half deep. It's wide enough that it's effectively as salty as the Jainoran Ocean and the Great Eastern Sea, and the walls are impervious so that the salt water doesn't penetrate the water table. It's almost, but not quite, an ecological barrier. Why just almost? *They* had to have known that."

"They didn't know enough to preserve what they learned."

She smiled faintly, and the tips of her short-cut silver-blond curls shimmered golden for a moment above the creamy brown skin of her neck and forehead. Duhyle wondered what he'd said that amused her so. He had enough sense to wait for her to speak again.

"That's not necessarily true. All we know is that we haven't found or recognized any repository of high-tech knowledge, except for the canal itself."

"Those of the lost times did?" He shook his head. "We've found the artifacts and ruins of two differing cultures on Mars and on some of the asteroids. There's no hint of the Old Ones, or any technology that could have built the canal." He glanced skyward, his eyes avoiding the glare of the midday sun and settling momentarily on the Mist Ring, a silver line that arched from horizon to horizon, like a bridge across the sky.

"That makes my point."

Duhyle had no idea what her point even was.

"Don't you understand, Kavn? If you were one of the Old Ones, would you have wanted us to know all that now? How many times have technological civilizations arisen and fallen?"

"All the more reason to leave the knowledge," he pointed out.

"With odds at a thousand to one against me, I'd still bet that no preceding civilization, even that of the Old Ones itself, collapsed for lack of technology." She offered a broad smile.

"The Tech Paradox?"

"It makes sense. You can see it at work in our own culture. More technology requires greater interdependence. Greater interdependence creates greater vulnerability, which in turn requires the greater application of technology and more concentrated energy sources—"

"Now," he interrupted, "is when we could use help. The ice is advancing an average of four-fifths a kay a year. That rate is projected to increase. We're losing forests, and the lands that support our biologics. Directed solar energy is too concentrated for effective climatic balance. No one trusts us engineers to deploy greenhouse gases and other large-scale geo-engineering."

"Not after the Searing. Besides, I'm not certain knowledge always provides an answer."

"Then why are you trying so hard to find it?"

"Because the alternatives appear worse. The Aesyr are pressing for building breeder reactors and filling the atmosphere with greenhouse gases—anything to stop the glaciation in the short term. We're here in a desperate attempt to find another alternative before the political unrest turns into chaos and possible revolution." Her voice held an edged humor. "Even so, I worry. What if the ancients knew their technology wouldn't be good for us? Technologies don't always graft to the cultures that didn't develop them. We don't even understand some of the biologic records from the Caelaarnan Unity, and they never advanced beyond near-space and a few out-system remote sensing stations." Her silver irises darkened to almost black, and Duhyle could have sworn that chill radiated from her. "The Hu-Ruche Technocracy rose and almost fell before it rebuilt itself. Along the way they measured everything and left incredible records of those measurements on anomalous permaplate, but almost nothing of their technology, and what little remains is so condensed and cryptic that no one yet has made sense of it, except that after that near fall, there are continuing and puzzling references to what appears to be the rainbow. Neither the Amberian Anarchists or the Saenlyn Federation even attempted colonization or out-system planetary modifications, not so far as we can tell."

"You think the Old Ones meant to doom everyone who followed

them, unless any successors were bright enough to duplicate what they did? Or did they expect us to find the mysterious technology trove that no one has discovered in millions of years? That assumes it exists."

"Then why did they build the canal—the only indestructible canal on Earth?"

"Maybe that's all they could do, and the effort wrecked their civilization."

"Or maybe the canal itself is the key. Perhaps it's a bridge."

Duhyle laughed. "Don't you think thousands of other scients have had the same idea over all the millennia? They must have tested every possible approach to determine if there is a key. If it even exists."

"Then I'll have to find another way." Her curls glittered silver from root to end, if only for a moment.

"What do you want for dinner?" he asked.

"Whatever you're cooking," she replied, straightening so that her eyes looked down on his. "How long will it be?"

"Tell me when you want it. Redgrass soup, and fowl with cream pasta and shrooms."

"Give me a stan and a half. I'm deep-linked to Vestalte, with a side link to Vaena."

He nodded, then watched as she reentered the ancient structure. It now held the most advanced technology that the Vanir had yet developed. His eyes returned to the canal and its deep waters.

4

❖　❖　❖

17 Eightmonth 1351, Unity of Caelaarn

Late into the fall evening Maertyn pored over the results of his latest observations and calculations in his "temporary" laboratory. He'd hoped to have been able to report some significant progress to the Ministry of Science when he returned to Caelaarn, but all the measurements he'd taken and all the calculations he'd made had not proven as helpful as he would have hoped.

He studied the screen before him, and the energy/position/gradients displayed there. They confirmed that, in a real way, the canal and its walls were not built of any discrete material. From what he'd been able to determine, the entire canal was a unit, created/fused/bonded on a subatomic level.

He paused. That wasn't necessarily so. Certainly, that finding was true for any part of the canal he had been able to study. But was it the same throughout—or did a thick layer of that adamantine material cover what lay within just to a depth that precluded any energy from reaching through such an outer layer?

Yet . . . from his instruments, the canal walls were a uniform width everywhere, thirty point seven one Caelaarnan yards. And there were only two structures protruding from it along its entire length, both identical in exterior shape—one at the eastern end and the other, where he was, at the western terminus. But the eastern structure remained sealed, with no evidence that it had ever been entered. For the canal and the structures to have endured at least half a million years, and possibly many times that, it would seem that it should be composed of the same material throughout. If that material were neutronium or of a similar nature, it would mass more than the entire Earth, and major gravitational irregularities would be more than obvious. In fact, the earth probably wouldn't exist except as debris. But what if the canal's gravitational effects happened to be shielded?

Maertyn knew of no way that was possible. He also knew of no way that the canal could exist. Which impossible possibility was more likely?

He smiled. Reality trumped theoretical science on any day of any year. Maarlyna's presence was more than proof of that.

The other problem centered on the doors and ducts. No form of scanning or focused energy that he had been able to deploy revealed their presence or triggered their opening. Only a living human touch did that. He'd spent two full days running his hands over every part of every surface in the structure, both inside and outside, and while he'd discovered what appeared to be two lower-level storage closets or rooms that had not been discovered by previous researchers, as well as five unused ducts/conduits, no other doors, even in the "new" storage areas, responded to his fingers.

Then he'd tried the same method on the top of the canal walls, first between the western end of the structure and the ocean wall, then along the narrow space between the structure walls and the chest-high retaining walls, and finally for a good hundred yards to the east. He'd discovered nothing new. There well might be other entrances to spaces within the canal walls somewhere along its two-thousand-kay length, and, in fact, he had no doubts that such must exist, but who had the time or the manpower to feel every span of a structure that stood a hundred yards above the water and spanned a continent?

He took a deep breath before, useless as he suspected it to be, he slowly considered, yet once more, the numbers, facts, figures, and equations on the pale green screen.

He wasn't even aware that he was no longer alone until a soft voice intruded.

"Maertyn? Will you be coming to bed soon? You've worked so late so many nights, and you do have a long journey ahead of you before long." Maarlyna stood in the archway that separated the largest main-floor chamber from the slightly smaller room that served as his work-room and laboratory.

"I'm sorry." He turned the swivel chair to face her, but did not stand. "I was just trying to see if I could make any sense out of the latest ob-servations. I'd really like to be able to report something new. But the more measurements and observations I take, the more it's clear that the midcontinent canal is perfectly uniform."

"Has anyone else taken that many measurements and observa-tions?" Her smile was warm and indulgent, yet not critical.

"Not in our history. Perhaps the second dawn cultures did. There aren't any records. In fact, there's not much of anything left, except some large holes filled with ash, sand, and the detritus of millennia that is still faintly radioactive."

"There are fossilized remnants of the ancients, aren't there? Is the canal that old? Or is it older yet?"

He smiled. "I'd judge so, but there's no way to tell with great accuracy. I don't know of any way to date the stone of the canal, and the stone and bedrock on and in which it rests doesn't seem to follow crustal move-ments, or not in any way that we would think as probable. The rock and soil layers farther away from the canal itself suggest far more than a million years."

"Isn't that new information? For the Ministry?"

"New? I don't know. It tends to confirm past incomplete data." His smile was crooked. "The Ministry is looking for somewhat more than that."

"You'll find it. I know you will."

Maertyn was touched by her faith, uncertain as he was about whether he could live up to it. "That's what I'm working toward." If he could only figure out how to discover a means by which he could discern more about the canal. The biologic sciences of the Unity weren't suited to deal with the subatomic level physics, and the records of older civi-lizations were too fragmentary . . . and enigmatic.

She smiled. "I won't keep you. I hope you won't be too long."

With her smile, and the clinging gown she wore, Maertyn knew he wouldn't be looking at his screens for much longer. "I need to save this format of the data to the backup system. Then I'll join you."

Maarlyna turned.

Maertyn watched her move through the archway and out of sight, taking in the gentle sway of her hips, neither constrained nor exaggerated, but all of a piece with the woman that she was, then swung back to face the paired pale green screens. He had the unshakable feeling that the data revealed something . . . but he couldn't put a finger—or his thoughts—on exactly what that might be.

He shook his head and initiated the backup sequence. He did wish that he had a cable interface to his own system in Caelaarn, or even a private comsat link, but the Ministry saw no reason to lay cable to the end of the canal, and he and his work didn't have priority enough for a comsat link. Nor did he have the boost-antenna necessary, either.

Once he finished, he stood and stretched, then flicked off the lamps powered by the turbine-powered unitary system that the Ministry had grudgingly installed for him, since the area was too chill for an efficient biosystem. He frowned, because every time he turned the lamps on or off, the same recurring thought came to mind. What powered the "doors" of the old building, and what power allowed the "windows" to pass light?

Even his most precise equipment failed to detect any energy flows. That confirmed, unsurprisingly, that the material comprising the canal and the building in which he was living and working was totally opaque to all energy flows. Yet the doors and windows had worked for the hundreds of years that the Caelaarnans had observed them, and doubtless for thousands and thousands of years before that.

He left the workroom and crossed the main room, then paused at the foot of the ramp that led up to the overly expansive second-level room that served as their combined bedchamber and private sitting room. Had he heard the wind howling, the precursor of an early storm or blizzard? His lips curled in amusement. How would he know? The oblong sections of the walls that approximated windows only transmitted light, not images or sounds—unless they were actually set in the open position, a position that they'd only hold for a third of an hour before automatically sealing. The walls blocked the sound of even the loudest of storms, and no outside vibration was ever transmitted to the interior of the station.

With a shake of his head, he started up the ramp to rejoin Maarlyna. When tomorrow came, and the days to follow in Caelaarn, he would deal with what they brought. What other choice did he have?

5

❈   ❈   ❈

Eltyn's virties focused on the external readings on the sandstorm that raged outside, another of the seemingly unending silicon tempests that continually assailed the station. Inside the ancient dwelling, he felt nothing, heard nothing. His bio-eyes took in the information on the local net not linked to RucheCom. The data readings on the small console showed no change in the surface temperature of the outer wall of the station or of the midcontinent canal walls at one-kay intervals over the fifteen kays to the east.

Interrogative storm dust/sand density? came the question from the geosat continent operations monitor.

Sampling sensors shuttered. Last data matched Category 8, Eltyn pulsed back to the GCMC. There was no point in leaving the samplers exposed, not with the wind velocity and sand/dust concentration bombarding the station and the southern walls of the MCC. Unlike the stone of the station, the unsealed sampling sensors would have been damaged by the sand granules propelled at storm velocities. The other—sealed—sensors continued to report temperature and pressure.

Interrogative rationale for shuttering?

Ruche MetCentre wanted a reason? They had the data.

Eltyn pulsed back, *Air mass velocity exceeds 400 kays. Estimated deposit 5k tonnes/hour/K^2. Temperature stable at 64° S.* Just a "mere" twenty-seven

degrees above blood temperature, with enough fine sand to bury the
southern side of the station halfway up the wall in a few hours. Farther
than that if the storm remained in the area more than the projected six
hours.

The ancient building had conduits that accommodated cables and
plumbing. There might be hidden passages. Neither he nor Faelyna
had found any, but they had discovered and charted the ducts in the
walls and floors that opened if human touch pressed against them, provided the outer wall wasn't buried in sand or snow. The stone of those
conduits flowed around cables and pipes to provide a seal against the
weather . . . or any other intrusion. The western MCC MetStation hadn't
seen snow in centuries. There hadn't been significant precipitation in
the area for decades, despite the Ruche's priority efforts on climate
mods. As for the structure presumed to be the eastern station, no one
had ever been able to enter it.

Faelyna glanced toward him. *Idiots.* That was a private pulse, on
the direct freq that Eltyn continually checked to assure it remained
shielded from RucheCom monitoring. That was vital, given their
project.

Concur^3.

For a moment, neither looked at the other or pulsed. Then Faelyna
asked, *Progress on approach(8)?*

Testing of new installation to be complete by 1330 tomorrow.
?????

Eltyn had kept the details to himself, very unRuchelike, even if no
one from RucheCom was able to monitor his work that closely. Still . . .
Faelyna might save him trouble by going over matters now that the system was in place. *SysConfig . . . here.*

[Appreciation/understanding].

Eltyn tried to ignore the feathery touch of her inspection by recheck-
ing the latest data on the sandstorm. Even her comm touch was . . . He
shook his head. That would have to wait. They couldn't afford anything
that would jeopardize the project. They were TechOversight profes-
sionals, working for the good of the Ruche.

After several moments, Faelyna pulsed, *Inquiry?*

Acceptable.

DNA substrate positioning suggests fractionally post-pressure. Sensi-

tive response system would register DNA prior to or simultaneous with contact pressure.

Eltyn had considered that, but he hadn't been certain of what interval might be best. The idea was to create an artificial method for opening the doors and ducts of the station. If he could accomplish that, it was logical that the results would provide guidance toward a more comprehensive system for uncovering other means of access to what lay beneath the eternal blue-gray stone. *Suggested mod?*

A flow/power/response schematic appeared before his virties.

Prelim, offered Faelyna.

Eltyn considered it, then traced out the key elements, admiring its elegance as he did. *200 nanosecs closer? Measured response time on current doors . . .*

The hint of a frown hung behind the non-pulse before Faelyna replied, *Point taken. 500 might be better.*

Mod will require rework of decision cortex.

[Apology].

Not required. Good observation. Still, accurate as her observation was, that meant another hour or so rebalancing the flows.

As he set to work, he found himself humming under his breath. Perhaps he should have adopted sliding parameters based on the DNA substrate positioning time . . . but then . . . how much would the pressure change, and would the canal's systems detect that differential?

Possible differential required for each activation? Faelyna's suggestion was pulsed oh-so-gently. *Precise human pressure gesture not replicatable on nanoscale, even microscale.*

He couldn't help but nod. She was absolutely correct. Even in the best of circumstances, even with the best of Ruche training and education, the precision of human entities lagged far behind that of their tools and systems.

He hummed happily as he continued to improve the system. He did glance at Faelyna more than once.

6

❖ ❖ ❖

10 Siebmonat 3123, Vaniran Hegemony

Duhyle and Helkyria sat across from each other at the small table on the lower level. That was where he served all their meals. He preferred the wall-diffused more natural light of the main and upper levels, but not to the extent of carrying food, dishes, and utensils up the ramp . . . and then back down.

He took a methodical swallow of the bergamot tea, then set down the silvered crystalline mug. When Helkyria didn't speak, he did. "You worked late last night. You didn't come to bed until past midnight."

She lowered her mug and nodded. She'd been holding it just below her chin and savoring the scent and vapor of the tea. Her irises remained their natural silver.

"The environmental parameters . . . or the treasure hunt?" he pressed. "Or something else?"

"The first drives the second. The latest reports from EnvCentre in Vaena aren't good," Helkyria admitted. "With essentially no compensating feedback on any subsurface systemic level, there's just not enough planetary core radioactivity remaining. The solar cycle is at a minimum, and the projections are that it will be another ten thousand years, at a minimum, before received solar radiation returns to past estimated baselines."

"Past estimated baselines? How reliable are they?"

"Not so reliable as we'd like. You know what happened when the Jhaenists tried entangled fermionic solar manipulation from Mercury . . ."

"That's still a theory. We don't know."

"The results of whatever they were trying seared half the planet and disrupted the deeper solar processes enough to reduce the amount of solar radiation emitted," replied Helkyria. "They succeeded, by chance or accident, or the sun just obliged them on its own, but that fractional reduction of radiation left us with less than we need for a stable envirosystem, and for the millennia since then we've been teetering on the edge of ice age after ice age."

"Where is global warming when we need it?" Duhyle added quickly, "Isn't that what the Aesyr would ask?"

"They've asked it enough, without any real understanding. You know that, Kavn. Most important, the ancients burned so much of the Earth's fossil fuels that we couldn't replicate that even if we wanted to and if we could deal with the polluting by-products. The greenhouse gases that we could create are too long-lasting, and we'd be back where the Jhaenists were. A compounding greenhouse effect is almost always a runaway process over any length of time—something the most distant ancients didn't understand, even with the obvious example of Venus. Neither did too many of their successors. That's why the Jhaenists were so desperate. Life in the universe appears to be balanced on the edge of a very sharp and unforgiving blade, and in the end entropy will always win." She offered a sardonic smile, enhanced by a momentary flash of green in her eyebrows. "But only eventually, and not until after the sun becomes a red giant."

"Not before Earth freezes solid again."

"That probably won't happen. Unless we can discover something less catastrophic, the advocates of enhancing the greenhouse effect will win out, backed by the Aesyr, and our descendants will face another seared Earth. This time, there's not likely to be any way to recover."

"Haven't scients said that before?"

"When the clock finally stops, it's usually the wrong time."

Duhyle didn't ask about the applicability of that metaphor. She was convinced that the clock was all too likely to stop when it melted in the furnace of a runaway greenhouse. From the recent comm-system disruptions staged by the Climate for People and the Warm Clean Earthers, both Aesyr fronts or sympathizers, it was also clear that too many humans wanted the ice gone—now. They wanted it to vanish without any untidy or unpleasant complications. That had never been possible, and it wasn't likely to happen this time, either. That also was why his tech status had been reactivated and why Helkyria had been called up, again, as a scient-commander. He had asked if she'd really been assigned, but she'd always evaded the question.

"What about terraforming Mars again?" he asked after a moment.

"With what? It takes water, and the previous efforts scoured the easily available ices from the Kuiper Belt. Those remaining are farther out and smaller. That takes time, resources, and energy. We're short on all three."

"Even if . . . ?"

"Enhancing thorium for a breeder program would require massive energy concentrations as well, and it's politically unthinkable, except for the most radical of the Aesyr. Besides, even if we could do that, we don't have the resources to move four hundred million people."

"The distant ancients numbered billions . . ."

"When everything fell apart, most of those billions died. You've seen enough of the fossils and all the evidence of total societal collapse. The Hu-Ruche apparently evaded one collapse, and they're the only ones who did . . . and that only postponed the inevitable."

"Are you certain?"

"Every simulation I can run predicts Iceberg Earth. So does every other simulation attempted by the Department."

"With no rebound?"

"I wouldn't say that the probability of no rebound is unitary, but it's so close that . . ." Helkyria offered a sad smile, and the tips of her silver-gold locks flickered the off-blue of disappointment. Her eyebrows did not shift hues, suggesting that her discouragement was perhaps not so deep as her words conveyed.

"That it might as well be," Duhyle finished.

"That's why I'm here. The Stats center has calculated a ten percent chance that detailed study of the canal will reveal data or information not presently known."

"Based on what?"

Helkyria smiled. "An array of inputs that would take far too long to even summarize over breakfast."

"How about one?"

"The fact that the apparent density of the canal, as measured by indirect gravitational distortion, suggests a structure that could not hold itself together for more than fifty years, let alone millions."

"Indirect distortion?" He already knew the answer.

"Do you know a direct way to measure something embedded in a planetary crust?" A faint twinkle of gold glittered from the tips of her eyelashes and eyebrows. "We did work out an even more indirect method, since the traditional means showed nothing at all."

"Indirection is everything," bantered Duhyle.

"No one's ever measured the material of the midcontinent canal before," Helkyria continued as if he had said nothing. "How could you measure or determine the properties of a substance you can't sample? It's essentially impervious to all forms of energy. It either reflects or scatters anything focused on it, or both, depending on the wave form and amount of energy involved."

"What did you discover?"

Both her irises and the tips of her hair turned a blackish purple.

Duhyle had never seen that, and he swallowed.

A crooked smile followed. "The results were . . . mixed. It has no mass; it has the same average mass as the Earth's crust; its mass is independent of the Earth." She rose from the table.

"How is your scanning project coming?" He also stood.

"I'll know when the last equipment arrives. It might work . . . and it might not. I'll need your help with the equipment."

"You're worried."

"They're sending a spec-ops team and weapons with the equipment. They should be here tomorrow."

"Why?"

"Several days ago, the Aesyr extremists launched a stealth submersible from Urda—that isle under the northern ice. They've learned about the project, and they're afraid our probing will unlock immense forces and devastate the entire globe." Her laugh was soft, ironic, and bitter, and the tips of her curls flickered cold silver. "That's a cover.

They think that we're doing weapons research. As if the ancients would have made all the effort to create and plant the canal into the crust just to leave a doomsday weapon for the future. If they'd wanted to destroy the world, they had far better options."

"The Aesyr don't understand," he temporized.

"Extremists never have. That's because they don't want to." She shrugged. "Time to get back to work."

"Refining the control programming while you wait for the rest of the equipment?"

She nodded, offered a brief smile, and turned.

As she left, Duhyle wondered if he'd ever understand more than the basic theory of fermionic ghost diffraction imaging. He certainly had had more than a little trouble when Helkyria had tried to explain quantum ghost imaging and the differences between it and fermionic diffraction imaging. As for fermionic ghost entanglement . . . and he was an electrical engineer. He shook his head and picked up her dishes.

He'd have to take a midday meal up to her. She forgot to eat when she immersed herself in the depths of her work.

Still . . . an armed stealth submersible sent to attack or infiltrate and take over a research installation on an ancient canal that hadn't ever done anything to anyone or anything over the millennia?

7

❈   ❈   ❈

35 Eightmonth 1351, Unity of Caelaarn

Once more, Maertyn read over the dispatch that had come with the canal-runner that morning.

From: Minister of Science
          Unity of Caelaarn

To: Maertyn S'Eidolon
          Deputy Assistant Minister

Subject: Pending Research on Climatic Impact of MCC

I am looking forward to your presentation on the twenty-first of Ninemonth.

You will be addressing the internal Ministry council. Your project has taken on a particular import, as you may have learned from the by-elections in Aracha, especially in Saenblaed. Difficult as it may be for some in the government to accept, there is growing popular pressure to resort to physical geo-engineering to deal with the situation. In this light, any insight you can offer on how the ancients may have employed the canal to avoid such extremes would be especially valuable, particularly in light of your request for additional equipment.

Saenblaed, reflected Maertyn as he lowered the dispatch for a moment, was where the bulk of the refugees from Edelburg had settled. They always voted for the Returnist party and any scheme, no matter how improbable, that offered hope of reclaiming their lands. What the short dispatch had not said, but clearly implied, was that the strictly biologically based projects and research, always the strength of the Unity, were not turning out as planned, because of either star-high costs or technical problems, if not both.

He couldn't say that he was surprised. Biological means of providing the concentrated energy required by technological societies tended to be inefficient or to require significant additional processing and/or infrastructure to increase that energy concentration, effectively diluting the end-use efficiency. Also, efficiency declined in extremes of heat or cold, and the earth was definitely cooling.

His thesis had been relatively simple. After scanning of the records of temperature observations taken at the east and west end of the canal and at selected points in between and cross-matching them, as best he could, to comparable observations within a kay or more away from the canal, but still within the same climatic area, there seemed to be a definite indication that the canal moderated temperatures more than could be accounted by all the known factors. In the year and a half since he and Maarlyna had been at the station, his own measurements had made that clear. He had yet to figure out why. The impervious blue-gray stone—although he doubted it was stone in any chemical or compositional sense—never changed temperature, regardless of how much sunlight fell or how chill the winters were. Did it somehow regulate its temperature instantly, or did its very composition insulate it from temperature changes?

He'd originally hoped that determining the basis for that definite temperature differential might lead to developing possible means for pushing the ice back from the northern side of the canal. The more he studied that aspect of the problem, the more he doubted that he could develop even a viable theoretical approach. While he was not about to tell the Ministry that, not yet, there were other aspects of the canal that offered better prospects, including his growing awareness of what might almost be called "messages," such as the understanding of when a berg might calve or when a tsunami might reach the station—

although that had happened but a handful of times. He couldn't very well put those into a research paper or presentation. Even Maarlyna, who loved and trusted him, had hardly given him any indication that she believed what he sensed. Yet . . . he had the feeling she sensed something as well, although he had not pressed her on that, not when she was neurally so vulnerable.

Now he had to give a convincing presentation on a thesis in which he no longer fully believed in order to retain Ministry support to allow him to pursue a research alternative he couldn't logically justify or quantify. And Minister Hlaansk's dispatch had made it more than clear that he had best be very convincing.

There was also the question of whether that was even the real purpose of Hlaansk's politely worded demand. Was it as simple as what he had stated, or was Maertyn's presentation designed to provide political cover for the minister against the appointees who were loyal to other political figures, or was it to make an example of Maertyn by showing that even lords were accountable . . . especially if they requested more equipment? Or was it something else entirely?

Finally, he pushed the chair back and stood, turning from the pale green screens that held meaningful but irrelevant data. He stretched, then, after several moments, walked from his workroom into the main study. He did not see Maarlyna, and he turned toward the ramp that began just inside the main entrance on the canal side of the station building and headed down to the kitchen, located in the chamber below his work space.

Maarlyna was not there, but Shaenya was standing before the cooktop.

"Might I ask what's for dinner?"

"Carplet stew, but with a pinenut glaze, and spiced potatoes in yogurt with some greens I gathered from the sheltered garden."

"The panels have kept it from freezing?"

"Them and the water walls. For now. In another two weeks . . . who could say?"

"If there's time next week in Daelmar before I catch the maglev to Caelaarn, I'll see if I can stop and have a side of lamb sent over from there on Haarlan's freightrunner."

"You'd not have to do that, Lord Maertyn."

"I want you, Svorak, and Maarlyna well-fed in my absence." He grinned. "If I do, don't you dare save it for my return."

"Not if you'd be telling me not to, no, sir."

"You haven't seen Maarlyna, have you?"

"Lady S'Eidolon?" The cook shook her head. "She came down an hour ago, but not since then."

"Thank you." Maertyn turned and walked back up the ramp and then outside onto the narrow space between the station and the canal wall. He glanced around before catching sight of Maarlyna. For a moment, he just looked, taking in the glint of light off her amber hair and the way she appeared so much a part of the canal and the lighthouse.

She stood in the weak late-afternoon sunlight to the left of the lighthouse, looking out at the cold gray waters of the ocean. She did not turn as he joined her.

"It's peaceful here." Her voice was quiet, so low he could barely make out her words above the hum of the wind turbines, the rush of the wind, and the intermittent muffled crash of the waves below hitting the enduring blue-gray stone.

He understood. "Not that many people around."

"They didn't used to grate on me so much."

"Times change."

"So do people. I've changed, Maertyn."

"We all change as we grow."

"You're humoring me."

"Perhaps a little. Isn't that the husbandly thing to do?"

She finally turned to face him. "You never used to do that. You never were so solicitous before . . . before . . ."

"No. I should have been, but almost losing you made me realize how much you meant to me." His eyes looked into hers, a shade of amber that matched her hair almost perfectly.

"I know. I don't pretend to understand, but I know."

He leaned toward her and brushed her cheek with his lips. "I'm glad you do."

"The longer we're here," she mused, "the stranger the station seems, and yet the more like home. I have the feeling that I won't want to leave."

Maertyn nodded. He wasn't certain he felt quite that way, but then, he'd never felt as though any place had ever been home. In those moments as he stood beside her under the high gray clouds, his thoughts returned to the station itself. As Maarlyna had said, there were so many prosaically strange aspects to the station. There were no vermin, no pests, and, according to the records, domesticated animals howled and moaned if they were kept inside. Yet the old records showed that the former lighthouse-keepers had had fewer accidents and lived seemingly healthier and longer lives than their contemporaries. Had some of them sensed what Maertyn did? At least subconsciously?

The functionality of the doors bothered him. They had from the beginning. According to the older records, they didn't respond to animals, only to people, and that included children, and generally only to bare skin. Did the "windows," doors, and ducts respond as much to mental intent as to human touch? Did the windows admit light if no people were present? How could he easily test the effect of presence or intent?

"You have the oddest look on your face, Maertyn . . ."

"I was just thinking . . ."

"About what?"

"The station." He paused. "Would you do me a favor, dearest?"

"If I can." Her voice was puzzled.

"I'd like you to touch parts of the station wall as we walk back, but I want you to close your eyes after the first touch, take several steps, and touch the station wall again. You remember when I was doing that? I didn't think about doing it with my eyes closed when I couldn't see the wall."

"Would that make a difference?"

He laughed softly. "I don't know. I just never thought of it."

"If you think it will help," she offered, smiling.

"One way or the other, it will," he promised.

As they walked back toward the station, she grasped his arm with her left hand a trace more firmly than usual.

"Where do you want me to start?"

"Right at the corner, here. Then you close your eyes and take several steps. I'll tell you when to touch the wall again. Keep your eyes closed, but reach out and touch the stone. Then, we'll do it once more . . . several times more."

Maarlyna reached out and touched the rounded square corner of the stone, then closed her eyes. "How many steps?"

"Try three."

Maertyn let her lead him.

"Here?" she asked.

"That's good."

At the third stop, where, on the inside, Maertyn thought there was a window, there was no change in the opacity of the stone. Maertyn hadn't expected there would be, but the confirmation was slightly satisfying.

After the fourth stop, he said, "Just two steps this time."

Maarlyna took the two steps, then stretched her arm and touched the smooth gray stone.

Maertyn watched intently. For a long moment, nothing happened. He counted silently. *One, two, three.*

Then the door opened, the stone sliding/folding into itself as it always did.

He almost nodded. "You can open your eyes."

"We're back. What did you find out?"

He gestured for her to enter the study, following her inside, before replying. "The door opened more slowly when you weren't thinking of it as a door."

Behind them, the door re-formed into the smooth stone wall.

She nodded. "I can't say that surprises me. I couldn't tell you why, though." She smiled. "I wonder if it would refuse to open if someone hostile tried."

"I'd rather not have to try that experiment." He returned the smile. "I need to think about some things before dinner."

"I'll just read in here, if it won't disturb you."

"You never do." Maertyn returned to his workroom through the open archway and settled into the swivel, thinking.

Had that long hesitation meant what he thought? Exactly what else could he do? He nodded. He should have thought about it earlier. He could certainly measure the light levels in the main rooms just by leaving a recording photometer behind. That would tell him about the windows. He leaned forward and began to list the equipment he needed.

He'd have to modify some of it to get the accuracy he desired, but it wouldn't take that much work.

When he finished, some time later, he straightened and considered the situation.

The first and most obvious question was why had others not discovered what he had. The first thought that came to mind was that they might well have, but how would he know, given the fragmentary nature of the records remaining? If they had discovered only what he had observed so far, then the results would only have been a curiosity. To discover more would have required higher-level technology, and human records tended to become more and more impermanent with such technology, not to mention that humans seemed to have great difficulty hanging on to civilization—and records—once technology reached a high level.

Maarlyna's question raised another line of thought. Determining hostile intent suggested more than mere mechanical response. Could the stone hold an entire intelligence of some sort?

Yet, if it did, why had it remained detached, or at least passive, over all the years? Was there some sort of test involved? Or was the test simply to discover what the canal truly was and how to best use it?

He frowned. Then again . . . could anything as enigmatic as the canal truly be "used" by anyone?

As always, what he discovered was raising more questions than answers, and he needed some sort of answers to keep the Ministry off his back . . . and to keep Maarlyna away from Caelaarn—indeed anywhere near Unity spies and functionaries—for as long as possible.

8

10 Quad 2471 R.E.

Outside the station, the late-spring midmorning temperature hovered around 39° Standard. The wind speed was negligible. That lack of meteorological instability allowed Eltyn to return to evaluating the results of the latest attempt to delve into the unseen and unknown systems controlling the station. His virties scanned the records of the device's attempts, but only confirmed what the very first attempts had revealed—that the DNA-infused pressure probe was effective in opening conduit covers, but not in operating doors and windows.

Pressure[DNA] novel (8) ineffective in gaining interior/exterior access.

Suggests [system?] awareness of consciousness/intelligence? Faelyna pulsed back from her work space.

Interrogative possibility of incorporating replica brain-wave patterns? Would estimate probability of failure to approach unity.

Interrogative integration/facsimile of higher functions? pressed Eltyn.

Equivalent result probable.

????

Your earlier observations. Windows only pass light when humans present/ awake. Suggests that full-body-brain construct required. Clone offers theoretical possibility, but to what end? [disgust] Replica human equivalent to FFH.

Eltyn considered her point . . . and the associated probabilities. Even before a rational and quick calcjection, he knew she was right. *Agree/accept. Interrogative your basis for approach(9)? [polite inquiry, non-intrusive]*

Replication of sensorium . . .

?????

Basis for reception . . . [observe] . . .

Eltyn appreciated the easy access to her protocols, even as he marveled at the ingenuity involved. Then he paused. *Interrogative access to polariton generator/imager?*

Loan from IPS. ETA on fourday.

She'd wrangled that from the Institute for Physical Science? *Excellent. [marveling admiration] Duration of loan?*

Two months. Maintenance while restructuring fusion laboratory.

Probability of shadow/dark energy imaging?

Real time/space interfaces fully examined. What remains?

Faelyna definitely had a point. The stone doors and windows reacted to human presence and acts, and intent. Yet under a complete range of observable energies, no form of radiation passed the stone's surface, nor was there any diminution of energy upon impact, nor any observable reaction from the stone. *Shadow entanglement?*

One possibility.

Interrogative follow-up approaches? he pulsed.

Possibilities . . . Assistance appreciated.

[grateful thanks] Eltyn had the feeling she was being kind. He could accept that. They'd succeed or fail as a team, and he'd not been that successful.

You spurred thought.

Had he unconsciously private-pulsed her? Or she understood what he was feeling? *From my failure . . . your success?*

Unsuccessful efforts leading to success are not failure. Our success. [apprehension/hopefulness]

At that moment came a white pulse, followed by, *MCC MetStation (W). Request b/up data, confirming sandstorm intensities, past year. Absent from report.*

?????, Eltyn private-pulsed to Faelyna. *Idiots[5]! [contempt]*

[fatalism[2]] You expected competence?

[rueful shrug] She was right. Their project had been buried in

Meteorology because RucheMet was known not to be aggressively self-examining. He pulsed back, *MetControl. Data sent. Possible transmission loss. Appendices 2 & 3. Resending this time.* It took him several seconds to locate, link, and resend the report.

MCC MetStation (W). Request b/up report transmission for future reports. CommNet capacity interference increasing.

MetControl. Will comply.

Eltyn paused, frowning. CommNet capacity interference? When RucheCom had been touting more than adequate capacity for generations to come? He keyworded/concepted the term and pulsed Ruche reference, tagging for current news.

All he got was a definition. *Loss of data in transmission resulting from unbuffered packet interruption.* The image at the top of the virtie-screen, above the words, was one of the standard ones—an image of Ruche Central, the golden-domed hexagonal structure at the center of Hururia, shimmering in the cooler sun of its northern latitude.

He pulsed Faelyna. *Capacity interference?*

Raelyn noted same at IPS. [skepticism] Full-band monitoring could reduce net capacity 40%.

Eltyn pondered that for all of ten seconds, until he received another MetCom transmission.

All dispatches/reports to RucheCom and Meteorology require complete impersonality. Failure to comply will result in disciplinary action.

Complete impersonality??? offered Eltyn on a local pulse to Faelyna. *Rationale? Rationality? [ironic not-quite-disbelief]*

Excessive individualism is the root of societal collapse and the bane of the Ruche. [sarcasm][snort]

The "new" tenet of The Fifty?

???? Old tenet. Very old. Resurging with the possibility of another Searing, replied Faelyna.

IPS not solar meddling?

After the discovery of the ruins at Jheana? Not likely. Sandstorms and drought equate to Searing for most workers/drones. They vote-post. The Fifty reacts.

Unfortunately. [wince]

They may not react enough. [sadness/cynical worry] Fear reinforces worst of tradition.

Great³ Wonder. After a moment, Eltyn added, *Suggest we work on additional approaches for use of polariton generator/imager. Intensive uses.*

[complete agreement]

Outside the station, under the smoldering sun, the temperature crept higher. The blue-gray waters of the canal held little more than ripples, those generated from the low ocean waves, ripples that subsided into stillness a handful of kays to the east of the station.

9

✤   ✤   ✤

Duhyle stood by the chest-high section of the protective wall that topped the main canal wall for the first kay eastward from the ocean. He watched as the sleek biosolar transport approached the station from the east. The transport eased to a stop on the blue-gray stone ten yards east of the station. The driver positioned the vehicle three yards from the protective wall. That left a good thirty yards of clear flat stone on the south side of the transport.

Duhyle waited for a moment, then walked toward the shimmering craft, whose dark exterior soaked up every possible photon.

The tall officer who stepped out and toward him wore the single silver bar of a subcaptain and the black beret of special operations. She had silvered black hair and the creamy tan skin of a transplanted norther. Her deep black irises matched her hair, except for the flecks of silver scattered around her pupils. The equipment belt at her waist held a stunner on one side and a sidearm on the other. "You must be Tech Duhyle," she offered. The tips of her hair and eyelashes remained dark, unemotional.

"Yes, ser."

"Is Scient-Commander Mimyra Helkyria here?"

"She is. She's in her laboratory. Could I announce you?"

"If you would. I'm Subcaptain Symra. We'll be unloading her equipment."

Eight other well-muscled techs emerged from the transport. All wore the dull deep green singlesuits and boots of spec-ops. Five were women, and three were men. The shortest of the women was Duhyle's height. Duhyle was taller than the three male techs.

"I'll tell her." Duhyle turned and headed back toward the station.

He had just reached the foot of the ramp up to Helkyria's lab when he saw her hurrying down. "There's a Subcaptain Symra and a spec-ops squad here. They have the equipment . . ."

"I thought they were close. I picked up a burst transmission a moment ago on our freqs." She frowned as she rushed past Duhyle. "There was also another squawk on a shielded freq . . . not shielded enough."

Duhyle trailed her outside.

"Subcaptain!" called Helkyria as soon as she stepped through the stone doorway. "Move the transport up here as close to the south side of the station as possible. Right now!"

When Helkyria used the full force and command in her voice, it reminded Duhyle why her military-security rank was commander. The demonstrations against the planetary government headed by the Vanir had increased a year earlier. Then, he had been surprised that she had not been recalled to deal with the unrest. Her assignment to the canal project—and his recall and promotion to chief tech—had confirmed that her project was far more important.

The subcaptain hesitated not at all, but gestured brusquely. The techs sprinted toward the station, and the subcaptain trotted beside the biosolar transport. Both the officer and the transport were directly beside the station entrance where Helkyria stood when the first rocket exploded—exactly where the transport had first come to rest. Shrapnel—or heavy ceramic flechettes—deluged the east end of the station. Some of the projectiles struck the rear of the transport.

Duhyle had sensed several flashing by him. Three of the techs staggered. Two straightened. One pitched forward.

"Shields!" the subcaptain snapped at the transport driver.

Only the faint distortion of the midafternoon light revealed the shields—that and the high-pitched humming from the transport.

"Get the equipment inside before the shields fail," ordered Helkyria.

One of the techs knelt to check the fallen man, while the others immediately opened the transport's rear doors. Duhyle hurried to join them. He could carry equipment.

Another rocket arched down and exploded above them. The shrapnel fragments rattled against the transport's shields, then dropped like dark hail to the stone surface, clattering irregularly. Some flechettes dropped onto the brush and grass to the south beyond the stone.

A third rocket followed, but the result was much the same.

"Tracking complete," reported the driver. "Relayed to SecCon."

Helkyria, standing beside the subcaptain, nodded, then said to Duhyle, "Have them take the equipment directly up to the workroom."

"Yes, ser." Duhyle took one of the crates as another tech handed it out of the transport and then stepped back, waiting for a moment before leading the way into the station and then up the ramp to Helkyria's workroom.

He had just returned to the transport to carry another small crate into the station when he noted that the figure of the fallen tech had been shrouded and sealed.

The spec-ops tech with the shrouder stood. "Flechette caught him in the temple."

Duhyle nodded. Their uniforms provided a considerable amount of protection, but not against head wounds.

The booming echo of a loud explosion rumbled through the afternoon air. He couldn't help but glance over at Helkyria.

"SatCom located the Aesyr submersible. The debris pattern suggests that the retaliatory strike was successful."

"No more rockets?"

"For the moment."

Duhyle moved to the rear of the transport. There he picked up the last crate and followed the other techs inside and up the ramp. Helkyria trailed them. As he walked up the right side of the ramp, he passed the other techs coming back down, but not the subcaptain, who had remained outside with the driver.

"How long will it take us to set up?" he asked as he set down the last crate beside those already carried in by the spec-ops techs.

"A week . . . if nothing's broken and everything goes right. Another few days for testing and calibration, and then we'll see."

Duhyle stepped back as the subcaptain walked up the ramp.

"Commander, ser. All the equipment is out of the transport."

"Thank you, Subcaptain." Helkyria glanced at Duhyle. "If . . . if you'd show the techs to their quarters on the lower level. The subcaptain will have the smaller main-level chamber."

"Yes, Commander." The situation was now definitely security-defined.

Once he had the remaining seven techs and the driver settled into the long chamber that served as a barracks of sorts, Duhyle made his way back up the ramp to the main level and then toward the bottom of the ramp to the workroom. He listened.

"They were waiting, ser," offered the subcaptain.

"Why do you think I had you move behind the station so quickly? If we had entries here large enough for vehicles, there wouldn't have been any problem at all. But then, without the attack, Security wouldn't have been able to find and neutralize the Aesyr submersible."

"Ser . . ."

"You don't like being a target, Subcaptain? Neither do I, especially when it takes away from research that just might have a possibility of averting more unrest and more deaths in the years to come."

"What about the reports? Won't they bring more attacks?" The junior officer's voice was lower, but tighter.

"Unless I'm mistaken," said Helkyria, "there won't be any reports at all, even on the subnets."

"Ser? What about Tech Maruk?"

"I'm certain his death will be reported as an accident. Aren't all spec-ops' deaths accidents? As for the rockets, the Magistra of Security won't report the attack, and Security will be waiting to hacktrack any reports of the attack. The Aesyr know that. They won't risk trying to leak it, not after the destruction of the submersible. That would compromise their nets. They might try to get some naive idealist to do it, but after what happened to the Sudaarn Student Activists who became a WCE front . . . I don't think that there are many idealists stupid enough to want to announce a part in an offense involving attempted premeditated homicide and treason."

Duhyle understood that, but how long could Security keep tightening the pressure on people while rations were being stretched thinner and thinner? Or could they keep doing it for just that reason? How long before the Aesyr forced a plebiscite on the Vanir government by causing more and more unrest and blaming it on the Vanir?

He shrugged, then turned and headed back down to the kitchen. He'd be feeding more mouths, and he needed to plan the meals based on what he had in the storeroom . . . in addition to assembling and testing all the new equipment.

10

20 Ninemonth 1351, Unity of Caelaarn

When he stepped off the canal-runner outside the tube-train station in Daelmar, Maertyn scarcely glanced back at the vehicle that was little more than a steamer powered by a solar flash boiler and a biofuel boost, with a single long car attached to the antique engine. The front half of that car served for freight and the rear for passengers, both freight and passengers almost entirely destined from or to the various Reserve posts along the canal. How much longer the Unity could afford to maintain those posts was open to question.

Maertyn carried but a shoulder bag, since he had a full wardrobe at the town house in Caelaarn, in fact a far greater wardrobe there than at the station. He hitched the strap higher as he crossed the street and walked toward Haarlan's Victualary, the third narrow front to the east opposite the tube-station arch. The first front he passed was the Outfittery—closed, as it usually was. Maertyn wondered how long the owner would even keep up the pretense of the business.

The girl sitting before the screen and behind the counter at Harlaan's looked up as Maertyn entered.

He recognized her as Harlaan's niece, although she was a white-blonde, so unlike her grizzled uncle. "Eylana . . . I'd like to order a side of lamb and a half score of fowl to be sent to the canal weather station on twoday, along with an assortment of whatever greenery and vegetables are the freshest."

"Yes, Lord Maertyn." While it was clear from her initial glance that Eylana hadn't immediately recognized him, she was bright enough to deduce his identity from the order and destination, as well as his maroon and silver-gray travelsuit. "Would you like anything else?"

Maertyn considered, then nodded politely. "The same order two weeks from next twoday."

"For the two, sir, it will be one hundred thirty-seven, including the delivery charge."

"That will be satisfactory. Thank you." Maertyn pressed his personal credpass against the old-style recorder. A faint chime sounded.

"Thank you, sir. We do appreciate your patronage."

"You're more than welcome." He smiled politely, but warmly, before turning and leaving the victualary.

The street was nearly empty, as always, except for a steamcart headed eastward in the direction of the methane extraction works, and the associated power-generation facility. He strode across the broad expanse of composite, once necessary to handle a long-vanished rush of vehicles, to the wide sidewalk on the south side and then through the entry archway and down the ramp toward the single platform under the station, carpeted in what amounted to a form of hard-surfaced, and slow-growing, self-repairing, deep gray lichen. From the top of the ramp he could see that the left-hand side of the platform was vacant, while the three linked shimmering sleek gray cylindrical cars on the right awaited passengers.

For all that he knew Maarlyna was far safer at the canal station with Shaenya and Svorak, and the nearby Reserve guards, than in the capital, he still worried about leaving her for so long—and the fact that once he was in Caelaarn, even more unforeseen circumstances were likely to arise and delay his return. Yet he couldn't have ignored the summons of Minister Hlaansk, pretext as it mostly likely was, not when he needed the additional equipment to have even a chance of discovering anything meaningful about the canal.

Just short of the entry kiosk and the gates that blocked unpaid entry to the trains, on the side of the platform awaiting the late-afternoon inbound train, Maertyn saw a figure in a scarlet singlesuit. He couldn't recall when he'd seen brilliant scarlet as the sole color of apparel. The wearer looked to be a woman with short-cropped hair, either silver or white-blond, and an angular face that still appeared close to androgynous. Was she an ice-sport who'd crossed the canal to tempt some unfortunate from the dwindling population of Daelmar?

He shook his head. Despite the lore, the Unity had proven long ago that there were no ice-sports, rumors and reports to the contrary. Yet the unfounded rumors persisted.

Still . . . his eyes lingered on her slim figure, with only the hint of curves, just enough to suggest femininity.

In her hands was a metallic rectangle that caught light from some source he could not see . . . or generated its own. Her head lifted from the metallic gleam, and her eyes focused on him. For the briefest moment, her eyes seemed to linger on him before she turned and retreated back into the shadows to the north of the ramp and kiosk.

What was that about? It was almost as though he were the ice-sport . . . or the oddity, rather than the lord of a distinguished, if financially diminished, line.

Maertyn hurried to the kiosk and swiped his credpass through the beam beside the gate.

"Car two, third compartment," the kiosk announced as the deep green gate-bars recessed.

He quickly stepped through, but he couldn't help looking back to make certain that the gate had closed behind him. There was no sign of the woman—or ice-sport—in red.

Walking deliberately, he made his way along the empty platform toward the second car.

"The train will be leaving in fifteen minutes, sir," came the words from overhead as he stepped from the platform through the open portal into the car, a conveyance whose interior walls were brushed pewter with silvered fixtures and a piled carpet of sea green. The faintest scent of evergreen infused the air.

He moved forward until he reached his compartment and slid the recessed pewter-finished door open. The high-backed couch, upholstered in a green two shades darker than the carpet, could have seated two comfortably and three less so. The small corner desk held a built-in wall screen capable of interfacing with any dataport. There was a faux-window, displaying a view of the Reserve as seen from the west side of Daelmar. The view would shift once the train got under way, showing what passengers would have seen had they been conveyed on the surface.

Maertyn set his shoulder bag on the end of the couch farthest from the compartment door, then sat down. He wouldn't have been surprised if he had the only occupied private compartment on the train— at least until Brathym, the first stop of five on the way to the capital. There would be a handful of Reserve workers or officers in the seats of the first compartment, although most of them would depart at Brathym, where most of them had dwellings.

He turned back to the compartment door, then slid it shut. After a moment, he pressed the lock bar. He glanced to the corner desk. That could wait, although he did need to go over his presentation to the internal ministry council. Instead, he sat down in the middle of the couch, trying not to think about Maarlyna as he waited for the train to depart.

11

Eltyn virtie-scanned the MetSat images of the massive storm headed westward, well to the north and east of the MCC. Enhancements displayed points of violent weather across much of the midsection of Primia. He couldn't do much about that, and he turned his attention to that area of the continent to the southeast and below the MCC. While the canal did have a moderating effect, the massive northern low pressure was still causing a wind shift to the south. All the indicators were that another sandstorm was already beginning to form and would sweep toward the canal station.

He thought to pulse Faelyna, but refrained. She was running the last set of tests on the equipment necessary for her approach(9). As she'd predicted, the polariton generator/imager had arrived on fourday, and the two of them had set to work reassembling and testing the equipment piece by piece. Even with both of them working, it had taken more than a week before the PG/I was ready to test, and another three days after that before the entire assembly was ready for its initialization.

He had the sense, backed by probability calculations, that they were running out of time before their TechOversight project came to the attention of someone at Ruche Meteorology, if the overseers at Ruche-Control didn't ferret it out sooner. How long would that be? Days? Or a few weeks? The project was designed to discover ways to use the station to mitigate climate warming. It was something to benefit the entire Ruche. Yet it had been turned down ten years earlier as too "individualistic," and it had taken TechOversight years to change the approach and wait for MetCom personnel to change before recrafting it.

He continued to scan the continental met-data, and the alternative weather projections ranked by probabilities, hoping that it wouldn't be too long before Faelyna finished the last set of initialization checks.

Interrogative estimated formation of sandstorm, duration, and intensity? The query came over the geosat monitor chief's link, but without the petulant intensity of Laembah. The duty monitor was likely making the request for the chief.

Margin of error for estimates at this point in time exceeds half unity. Currently project Category 7, two days at full intensity, four days from now.

Report appreciated. Request updates.

Will comply.

Eltyn took another quick scan of the already fully developed northeastern storm. He shook his head. The sandstorm-to-come would be nothing compared to what was already happening across the northern midsection of the continent.

As if to punctuate his assessment, a white priority pulse seared across the command level. *URGENT NOTICE. Intense regional tornadoes across NRS have resulted in destruction of more than 28.5% of midcontinental atmospheric turbine stations. Cyclone Betar has disrupted Primia continental tidal bore stations. Nonessential energy usage is hereby declared an offense against the Ruche . . .*

Emergency energy curtailment? That made sense in Hururia and other more populated areas, but except for comm-links, MCC MetStation (W) had no connections with any population centers either in Primia or, through the undersea links, to Secundia, and no links at all to the power grids. So how could the station's failure to reduce energy usage be declared an offense? The local solar grids and tidal pump couldn't be connected to anything else, and what was the point of cutting down monitoring when better observations might help?

All stations must certify compliance with RucheCom directive to appropriate authority . . . and list steps to eliminate nonessential uses . . .

Idiots[6], pulsed Faelyna, irritated at being interrupted, since command-level links overrode all privacy barriers.

Frightened/worried idiots[6], returned Eltyn.

Idiots, nonetheless.

Definition of nonessential??? [dry humor] To what, The Fifty's sense of propriety and equalization?

Don't even inquire, replied Faelyna. *Especially on RucheNet.*

She was right about that, too, although he was anything but that foolhardy.

MCC MetStation (W) certifying reductions, Eltyn pulsed to Met-Control. *No power downloads from grid this time. None required in immediate future.*

Report and certification received, MCC MetStation (W).

Eltyn waited for any further reply. There was none.

After several moments, he returned his attention to the meteorology screens. The station was still receiving satellite feeds. That made obvious sense, since shutting down orbital solar collectors wouldn't help the planetary power grids in the slightest. At least someone in Meteorology had some intelligence and understanding of reality. So far.

He leaned back, for only for a moment.

Pulse anomaly detected and blocked, the local system announced.

Supply specifics, Eltyn immediately shifted full attention to the local-net defenses.

Pulse on GeoMet tertiary . . .

The single pulse had been a probe, not a snake or a full-spectrum assault, and it had not been followed by any other activity. Who even cared about an isolated MetStation system . . . unless they knew the true reason why Eltyn and Faelyna had been assigned? Only TechOversight knew that, or so Eltyn hoped.

Or had the pulse been one of many triggered by the announcement of power reductions across the RucheNet?

Eltyn pulsed Faelyna. *Local net intrusion probe . . .* He flashed the details to her and waited for her response.

Possible RF snoop?

Why would the fanatical and secretive RucheFirst want to probe an isolated MetStation? *You think they've infiltrated TechOversight?*

Negative. They wouldn't need a probe then, she pointed out.

They must have found out something. Or RF is using power-down as opportunity.

[affirmation . . . regret/sadness] Shows fear level within commonality. Negative on reporting attempted intrusion.

Eltyn appreciated her quick understanding, both technically and politically. He did enjoy being with her, but in pulse-linked situation, the barriers against mental closeness were all too necessary. Lowering them . . . He pushed that thought aside. *[agreement . . . affirm regret . . . apprehension] Interrogative system tests for approach(9)?*

Complete by 1540. All green so far.

Was there a wistfulness behind her pulse? *Time required to run initial protocol?*

One point five hours. After that . . . ????

Interrogative possible modifications?

Sufficient^2 for the eventualities foreseen to date.

Neither mentioned that there were always more eventualities, or that the most optimistic prognosis could only bear a low probability of success. None of that included the increasing climatic chaos that swirled around them and the station. Or the cracks and stresses in the Ruche Commonality, cracks that TechOversight was trying to patch with improved techniques and systems, and that fundamentalists like RucheFirst were trying to exploit in order to turn society toward a lower-tech, lower-environmental footprint . . . at least until the sand buried everything.

12

❖   ❖   ❖

12 Siebmonat 3123, Vaniran Hegemony

In the dim light of dawn admitted by the wall-windows, Duhyle finished pulling on a duty techsuit. He glanced at his consort. She wore one of the ice-blue singlesuits, rather than a uniform security singlesuit.

"You'll call when breakfast is ready?" she asked.

"It'll be a bit. Preparing for ten takes longer."

"You'll manage. You always do. It's one of your graces." She smiled, and for a brief moment, gold flickered at the tips of her short-cut hair and across her eyebrows. "I'll be in the lab."

"Working on . . . whatever you're going to call it? The fermionic entanglement and ghost diffraction imager? The FEGDI?"

Helkyria laughed. "That sounds like an Aesyr curse or some killed-animal pie. We'll have to think of something better . . . if it works at all. Oh . . . I'd like you to depower everything you can after breakfast."

"The FEGDI's a power-glutton?"

"More than I'd calculated. That's something else I'll have to track because it's not showing up as excess heat, either."

"Inadvertent battery or capacitor effect?"

"I hope not. All I'd need is a discharge in the wrong place or at the wrong time . . . or some sort of magnetic effect." She frowned. "I don't think so. My scanning monitors would have registered an energy buildup."

She turned and walked across the top of the ramp to the laboratory on the other side.

Duhyle followed her to the ramp, then turned downward. That there were no internal doors in the entire station hadn't bothered him when there had just been the two of them, but now . . . ? He shook his head. He'd get used to that as well.

While Helkyria started work in her laboratory, Duhyle continued down to the area he had made the kitchen. There he began to assemble a breakfast for ten. Doreat—one of the male techs—entered the kitchen area as Duhyle was whisking the eggs for omelets. Scrambling eggs would have been the easiest, but for him scrambled eggs were always a last resort. He hated to do anything as a last resort.

"Can I help?" asked the other tech.

"You could grate the cheese and slice the shrooms." Duhyle moved to making the drop-biscuit batter.

Half an hour later breakfast was ready, with two large pots of tea and crystalline mugs at each place. Everyone except Helkyria was seated around the two tables that Duhyle had linked together. He could hear her boots on the stone ramp. The other techs stiffened.

"At ease," offered Helkyria dryly. As she settled herself at the head of the table, she looked somberly at Subcaptain Symra.

"Ser?"

Helkyria sipped from the crystalline mug before replying. "There's a heavy cargo-sailer headed inbound for the canal. Vestalte doesn't have any records on the vessel, and the profile only matches the *Skadira* or the *Gullveig*."

"The giant cargo-carriers?" asked Duhyle. "They'd be hard to miss."

"There's only one problem. The *Gullveig* has been verified as in the Great Eastern Sea, bound for Muspelhome, and the *Skadira* was reported as vanished five years ago, ostensibly lost in a storm in the Jainoran Ocean."

"Then she's reappeared under Aesyr control," suggested Symra. "What other possibility is there?"

"I've contacted SpecOps headquarters. There aren't any patrol vessels within half a day's travel, not any with weapons sufficient to deal with that large a ship. They're sending a company from Saarland by airship, but they still won't get here until early afternoon. SatCom estimates the *Skadira* will be off the point by noon local."

"How many airships?"

"Two."

"They won't be bringing that much in the way of heavy weapons, then. They're only rated for a half-company without support."

"That's what's available in the time frame we're looking at. Security still has three companies on containment duty around Scefing. Just a coincidence, of course." Helkyria's voice held the faintest trace of irony.

Duhyle glimpsed the faintest flicker of green across her eyebrows, but no one else did. He could see that.

"Can't SatCom take out the ship?" asked Symra.

"Not until she demonstrates hostile intent, and the Aesyr will have an attack planned with that in mind. They'll expect to lose the vessel, but by then everyone will be clear. They'll jam all comm with a facsimile CME and visual with a pseudo fog. We may *know* that the sailer is filled with Aesyr beserkers, but it would be just like them to fill it with holidayers, create what SatCom interprets as an attack, and sacrifice innocents. Both the Aesyr and SecCon understand that. If we sank a pleasure ship because it might contain Aesyr 'irregulars,' just how long before an immediate plebiscite overturned government and we had emergency security decrees everywhere while Baeldura the Beloved implemented Operation Greenhouse?"

Several of the techs winced.

"We'll discuss how to proceed after breakfast." Helkyria smiled politely at the subcaptain, took another swallow of her tea, and then a bite of the omelet. "Very good, Kavn."

"Thank you."

"It is indeed," added Symra.

Duhyle detected a trace of darkness glooming from the tips of the subcaptain's hair, but he nodded politely and addressed his own platter.

With the help of the other two male techs, Duhyle had the kitchen cleaned and powered down in less than a quarter hour after everyone had eaten. The two officers had departed for Helkyria's laboratory and makeshift comm center.

The techs hurried outside, presumably for drills or recon. Duhyle decided to check all the energy-using applications in the larger main-floor chamber first. He might overhear something of interest, although Helkyria would tell him later. That assumed she had time.

He began in the corner away from the ramps. He disconnected the holojector, since the standby function did drain power, albeit a minute amount. Next came the emergency lighting pack, which he had to switch off and then disconnect, since power interruption actually turned on the light. From there, he picked up some of what drifted from the laboratory.

". . . cargo-sailer that size could carry three companies and weapons support . . . Even with the company from Saarland . . . can't expect to hold them off . . ."

". . . for a research installation?" replied Helkyria.

". . . is not normal research, Commander . . ."

Helkyria laughed.

". . . be difficult to defend . . . certain you can't block the entrances?"

". . . always opened to any human . . . don't see why that would change . . . but they'll have trouble entering except in twos . . ."

". . . two entries makes it harder . . ."

Especially if the attackers used an energy beam through one entry at the back of any defenders on the other side, mused Duhyle. They'd have to get the bulky equipment up the western cliffs or up the sheer wall of the canal, but the cargo-sailer was big enough to carry a ratchet-climber or the equivalent. Still, if the defenders put their backs against the wall beside each entry . . . Then, too, the upper-level "windows" would open, if briefly, and that would allow defensive fire from points that couldn't be stormed.

He hoped that the fighting didn't get that close and personal, but the way the two officers were talking, it was all too likely.

He moved to the second emergency lighting console.

13

20 Ninemonth 1351, Unity of Caelaarn

When the tube-train slowed to a halt, the compartment speaker announced, "Arrival in Caelaarn. You are on platform twelve, second level. All passengers please exit."

Maertyn rose, picked up the bag, slipped the strap over his shoulder, and opened the compartment door.

"Have a pleasant day in Caelaarn, Lord Maertyn," the car speaker offered politely.

He did not respond, knowing that the system would merely offer another programmed response.

A dark-haired woman of indeterminate age, wearing the solid blue trousers and jacket of a senior Ministry functionary, opened the door to the next compartment as Maertyn neared, but she immediately paused. "You first, Lord."

Maertyn smiled politely. "I'm in no hurry. Please . . ." He gestured for her to proceed.

After a moment, she did, and he followed her at a discreet distance to the train car door and then through it. As in Daelmar, the platform was of deep gray, lit indirectly. Unlike Daelmar, the living surface showed signs of wear in places, and it was far from empty, with two hundred or so passengers slipping quietly from the long cyclindrical cars and walking swiftly toward the moving ramp that led up to the main concourse. As befitted the world capital, the tube-train station in Caelaarn was substantial, with two levels of twenty platforms each. The indirect lighting was bright enough to banish shadows, but not intense enough to create reflections off the brushed pewter-like finish of the cars of the tube-trains and the walls and fixtures of the station.

As he let the ramp carry him upward, Maertyn pushed aside his worries about Maarlyna, if with difficulty, and concentrated on what lay ahead of him, and not a moment too soon, because when he reached the top of the ramp and stepped out onto the pale golden surface of the main concourse, he caught sight of a slender older man, attired in maroon and silver-gray, but in the more formal maroon jacket over silver-gray shirt and trousers, with a simple black cravat.

Seeing the familiar figure of Ashauer standing between two Ministry guards—in khaki singlesuits with black belts and boots—Maertyn couldn't help thinking, *Lord Ashauer S'Detemer, to be precise, conveying so effectively polite and measured menace.*

Ashauer stepped forward, smiling warmly. "Maertyn!"

Maertyn noted that the other still wore the small pewter pin of the Transport Ministry on the thin lapel of his jacket, indicating that the older lord continued to hold a position as Deputy Assistant Minister for Regional Liaison. Doubtless Ashauer also kept up his reputation as a bit of a gambler and wastrel, all of which served as a cover for his real position—what amounted to the director of lordly intelligence operations for Executive Administrator of the Unity . . . and probably far more than that, Maertyn suspected.

"Ashauer. You're looking as dapper as ever." Maertyn offered a rueful smile. "I hadn't expected an escort."

"How could we not provide an escort to one of the few hopes remaining to the Unity?" Ashauer added cheerfully, "Minister Hlaansk has been most vocal in singing your praises." He turned and began to walk toward the high pewter arch that led to the transit corridors. "He has not been restrained in the breadth of those praises."

"He sings everyone's praises," replied Maertyn with a soft laugh, walking beside Ashauer, but not too closely. "That's one reason why he's effective in dealing with scientists."

"Ah . . . but you're the only lord in our generation to also be a fully qualified scientist, and that does make you special."

"Different, perhaps, but hardly special."

"Special enough that he would not want you taking public transit to your town home. That is where you're headed this evening, is it not?"

"It is indeed, but I doubt that Minister Hlaansk would trouble himself over it. Others might, as you well know, but why would any concern themselves with the obscure research of an even more obscure lord? Or his brief visit to Caelaarn?"

"You have always been modest, Maertyn. I've never been certain whether it was the modesty of arrogance or the arrogance of modesty." Ashauer led the way through the arch and past the local tube transit corridor to the covered portico over the small circular drive of the northernmost transport corridor.

Two vehicles were waiting there, the first a two-seat patrol vehicle with a single hard-faced patroller standing beside it, her dark uniform emphasizing the angularity of her face. She nodded politely but not effusively as the two lords passed and made their way to the second personal transit car, its gleaming finish the dark blue solar-metallic of the Transport Ministry. It was designed to hold but four, the driver/guard and another guard in front, and two in the shielded rear, with a small boot for luggage. The locks clicked open as the guard touched the door plate.

Knowing that Ashauer would insist he enter first, Maertyn took the cushioned seat behind the driver, noting as he did that the privacy barrier was up. Ashauer took the other seat.

"You would not have heard that there is dissension in some outlying districts," offered the older lord once the car pulled away from the station.

"Doubtless somewhere in Galawon or and especially in Saenblaed."

Ashauer nodded. "And in places in Occidenta."

"What has the Gaerda found as the reasons for such unrest?"

"The Gaerda? How would a mere Transport functionary know their judgments?"

Maertyn smiled faintly. "How indeed?"

After a moment of silence, Ashauer said conversationally, as quietly as if idly musing about the regularity of the tube-train schedules, "There are reasons why you've been recalled to the capital, Maertyn, and not merely for a routine report or because a few ultra-capitalists protest the science behind Unity regulations."

"Besides my research? Or besides my charms and nonexistent wealth?"

"You're not so poor as you have let others believe. The Gaerda—rather Gaerda chief Caellins—tasked the Finance Ministry with assessing the holdings of all lords currently serving in the government. Yours are far from the least substantial. They are, however, among the most, shall we say, dispersed, so much so that even the Finance Ministry reported it was unlikely that all of them had been identified."

"The Finance Ministry does me far too much credit."

"Far too little it would appear. Now . . . would you like to know why it was suggested to Minister Hlaansk that he request a report in person from you? Or rather that he remind you to come to Caelaarn to make your report in person?"

"I would be most interested in knowing that." *Not that I'll trust most of what you're about to impart.*

"Knowing you, I'm certain you'll be skeptical, but there are those who would prefer that you succeed in your research. The leadership of the Gaerda is not among them. Any indication of progress on your part will require more attention be paid to you, and, obviously, will leave fewer resources and emphasis on the scrutiny of others. Your recent request for more equipment suggested that your research might actually result in useful information."

"As opposed to being a mere cover for a sabbatical for a lord who dabbles in research? Even so, why would our vaunted security forces be interested in my research or even in my nonexistence? I certainly pose no threat to them." Ashauer's words and presence definitely confirmed, in Maertyn's mind, that the Executive Administrator of the Unity, to whom Ashauer reported, assuredly directly, was engaged in a struggle of some sort with the Minister of Protective Services, who also controlled the Gaerda."

"Your request for equipment confirmed, among some, that more lies within the great canal than you have reported. They are also convinced that you are unlikely to turn that information over to them."

"If they're so convinced of that, why haven't they just appeared at the station and demanded that I turn over all my research?"

"Besides the fact that it would represent overriding the authority of the Minister of Science? Or that it would require a written order of either the Executive Administrator or the Minister of Protective Services?"

"Which the Council or the Judiciary might well overturn."

"The Council could be finessed, with the proper timing. The simpler answer might well be that they don't believe you will turn over what they wish. Or that you could be forced to do so. It's rumored that you're an Indurate Master."

"So that I can't be mentally coerced? If I were, and there's certainly no evidence of that, it still wouldn't mean I couldn't be killed or otherwise . . . neutralized."

"Your existence, or lack thereof, is of little concern. The knowledge you might possibly recover is of great concern." Ashauer shrugged. "All men have their weaknesses, and you know yours. Mine, as you know, has always been my vanity. I did think that it might be wise for me to suggest that those few matters that surround you and your work are receiving more scrutiny than might be otherwise obvious to you . . . since you have not been in Caelaarn that recently."

"I do appreciate your concern." Maertyn paused, letting the silence draw out.

"Oh . . . it's nothing personal, Maertyn. I'm certain you understand that."

Maertyn did. The Executive Administrator of the Caelaaran Unity—the most honorable Estafn D'Onfrio—did not wish that whatever Maertyn might discover should fall into the hands of the Gaerda, but he also didn't want the struggle becoming public, not with unrest in both Galawon and Occidenta. That also suggested that Minister Hlaansk had other agendas . . . and other supporters that neither the EA nor Minister of Protective Services Tauzn wished to cross. And all of that left Maertyn very much alone—and that was before he'd discovered something that everyone thought he would. *I would that I had their confidence in my capabilities.*

"It's never personal to others, Ashauer, but it's always personal to those it affects, and yet through the ages, men have persisted in insisting that actions adverse to others are not personal."

Ashauer laughed. "You do retain a philosophical bent, Maertyn."

"It's the best way of viewing government. You should know that." Maertyn offered a brief chuckle in return.

Ashauer nodded, but did not say more, and in a few minutes, the vehicle came to a silent and gliding stop. Maertyn glanced through the glassine side window toward the gates that blocked the entrance to the front courtyard of his town home.

"I wouldn't worry yet," said Ashauer. "No one would want anything to happen to you now."

"I do appreciate your concern. Thank you for the transportation."

"You're most welcome."

Maertyn opened the car door and slipped out, then closed it, offering a polite smile to Ashauer before the vehicle eased away in the twilight.

He glanced up at the Selene Ring, somehow less bright over Cae-laarn, then back at the house. The three-story town dwelling was on the hillside overlooking the greenbelt, with the front gates on the perimeter road where Maertyn had alighted. The vehicle gates were at the west end of the property. He stepped toward the iron grille and tapped the combination into the security pad, then let his fingers rest on the sensor. The gates recessed to let him step into the brick-walled courtyard, then closed behind him. The exterior biowood panels of the house were a deep green, except for those framing the corners, which were dark gray, as were the window casements and door frames. The front of the house was twenty yards wide, roughly as wide as the canal station, with a centered main entry a mere two steps above the antique sand brick walk that led from the gates. Maertyn's boots clicked slightly on the bricks.

As he stepped under the entry portico roof, the door opened, held by a muscular figure in black trousers and a deep green jacket.

"Lord Maertyn, welcome home." The man bowed slightly, then stepped back

"Thank you, Rhesten." Maertyn smiled. "It's good to be here." *Safely.*

Rhesten closed the door and turned to face Maertyn. "Will you require dining, sir?"

"I'll have a light supper in the study. Just bring it in when it's ready."

"Yes, sir."

"Thank you."

Maertyn walked through the modest two-story entry hall and took the second door on the left, into the study. The lights eased on as he closed the door, revealing the desk with the comfortable swivel behind it, the side windows, now blanked for the evening, and the settee flanked by two chairs, each with a now-concealed reading screen.

Stark—that had been how Maarlyna had always described it.

He shook his head. Simple, he would have said, but he never had, at first because it hadn't mattered, and then, later, because it had mattered too much.

He set the shoulder bag on the narrow shelf to the left of the ebony panels that concealed the working screens, then turned to stand beside the wide and empty desk, a desk, for all its polished ebony finish, that felt ever more alien each time he returned.

As had doubtless always been the case, nothing was quite as it seemed on the surface, or perhaps it was better said that nothing was all that it seemed, either on the surface or beneath.

14

Eltyn stood to one side of the "window" in the upper chamber that served as Faelyna's laboratory. After one glance, he did not look toward the corner that held her pallet bed. He tried not to shift his feet from one side to the other as she went through the checklist for the array of equipment centered on the modified and overpowered polariton generator/imager.

Estimate three minutes before initial probe. Faelyna made some adjustments that Eltyn could not follow.

Second time you've said three minutes. [irony]

You want me to focus unshielded PG/I on you? [humor]

Not possible . . . before I move. [wide grin]

Her response was a feminine snort.

What Faelyna had earlier hoped would be several hours, or less than a day, had turned into two days and then three, before she had judged that the equipment was properly set and positioned. Then she had discovered a need for an additional modification. While she had worked on that, Eltyn had made some changes to the station equipment and power system, particularly in the reporting monitors—in reaction to the totally irrational periodic demands for station power reductions. He'd also isolate-blocked the internal net against probes from outside, but in a way that simply indicated that the entire comm system had been shut down except for emergency comm. All incoming probes and messages were quarantined so that he could view and analyze them without contaminating or compromising the station systems.

Two minutes.

Ready. Eltyn looked at her, trying to maintain a calm and unworried expression while not showing any sign of what he had begun to feel about her. To do otherwise would be unRuchelike.

The command comm level seared a white priority pulse across all CommNet channels. *URGENT! URGENT! All stations! Mandatory reduction of power usage to minimum. Discontinue all routine and [low] priority usage. Nonessential energy usage will result in disciplinary action . . .*

Faelyna glanced at Eltyn.

Eltyn triggered the shield-system he'd developed in reaction to the power hysteria coming from Hururia, a hysteria he suspected was being generated by the RF fanatics among The Fifty.

????? questioned Faelyna.

System shields activated, Eltyn private-pulsed. *[concern] Possible RF takeover.*

Fanatics[4], idiots[7]!

The screens that had just shown the satellite images of continental weather blanked, followed by momentary light-static, and then blackness.

MetCom out/down, observed Eltyn.

Troubled times = fanaticism. So much easier than thought. As if political control will change the weather.

Eltyn waited, then inquired, *Wish to continue?*

No logical reason not to. Even more reason to continue. One minute.

Eltyn moistened his lips, trying not to look too nervous while he waited. Her equipment could project enough power to fry his fingers. It wasn't supposed to, but it could.

Now . . . touch the "window" to open it.

Eltyn did so, pressing his fingertips against the stone where human touch actually created an opening to the outside. He suspected that prolonged touch was unnecessary, that intent was primarily required, but some sort of touch/movement was nonetheless necessary. A gust of all-too-hot air dried the perspiration of anticipation—and fear—almost instantly.

Close it.

He did so, aware that even that momentary blast of air had raised the temperature in the laboratory where he stood significantly. He took a moment to smooth his hair, short as it was.

Power to standby, announced Faelyna.

Eltyn took a slow deep breath, then pulsed, *Results?*

Something registered on the PG/I tracker. [satisfaction/anticipation]

What??? Eltyn couldn't help but display some impatience, unRuche-like as that was.

Probable shadow entanglement. Parallel shadowing.

Eltyn couldn't help smiling. Did he dare? After a brief hesitation, he added, *[admiration . . . affection]*

He could sense her embarrassment.

Thank you. [appreciation]

Not wanting to dwell longer in the uncomfortable area of expressed emotion, he pulsed, *Detection sufficient?*

Indications suggest tracking by ???? within or behind the stone of the canal and station without actual energies being radiated or deployed beyond the surface of the stone.

Eltyn frowned. *How???*

Unknown this time. One step at a time. Doors next, then conduits. Pattern check. After that . . . [shrug]

Pattern replication?

Possible alternative. Except . . . what if replication freezes command structure?

Eltyn winced. He certainly didn't want to be trapped inside the station. Yet . . . being trapped outside in the heat and the wind-whipped sand wasn't likely to be much better.

The white emergency indicator pulsed three times before an announcement followed. *In response to the urgent needs of the Ruche, The Twenty have superseded The Fifty, in accord with Prime Emergency Authorization Number One. The Twenty are already restoring full communications in Hururia . . .*

Prime Emergency Authorization? questioned Eltyn. When Faelyna did not respond, he added, *????*

Unlikely to have ever existed. RF invention. But it will appear in the records of The Fifty's proceedings. Very proper.

Already in place. [cynical acceptance]

They turned and looked at each other, as if neither quite knew what to say when it appeared that the very structure of the Ruche was either crumbling or being supplanted from within.

A single cyan pulse flared through the comm system. *TechOversight Contingency Three. Contingency Three.*

The two exchanged glances.

Contingency Three? That's . . . retreat to Chiental redoubt, Faelyna observed.

How do we comply? Transport? A thousand kays from the north side of the canal.

In the middle of the Fhranan Peaks. [ironic disbelief]

All the contingency plans had been designed more for climate or weather disasters, or for a breakdown in civil order, reflected Eltyn—not an internal coup and takeover. Still . . . it might work. Then he shook his head. There was no way they could even consider crossing the canal, let along making their way that far to the northeast. They had no boat, and who knew what was happening in Apialor, where there was a ferry?

Another comm pulse followed. *Disregard all other transmissions. Ruche security has already placed all comm and power-generation systems and facilities under immediate supervision. Over the next weeks, all independent and outlying installations will be inspected to assure compliance with the emergency procedures promulgated by The Twenty . . .*

That's to give everyone time to give the impression of compliance, Faelyna observed.

Sorting out noncompliers . . . isolating those who support The Fifty. He paused. *TechOversight?*

Total creation of the less "traditional" of The Fifty. That's why the cyan alert.

They exchanged knowing looks.

Eltyn pulsed, *Interrogative possibility of gaining control of shadow system to prevent "inspection" by the RF usurpers?*

Time before arrival?

????

Shadow system appears to exist. Existence = controls. Control protocol unknown. Control language unknown . . . A faint smile crossed her thin lips.

[understanding . . . reluctant acceptance] [hope?]

Suggest we move equipment to lower door. Soonest. Depowering system this time.

Eltyn nodded and moved toward her.

Their project was taking on very personal importance, with The Twenty in control of the center of the Ruche in Hururia, especially since there was no way to cross the sands to the south and east, and they had no watercraft for the ocean and canal . . . and neither time nor equipment with which to build one. There certainly wasn't any way that they could make their way to Chiental without encountering the minions of The Twenty . . . or any certainty of what they might find there if they could.

15

❀ ❀ ❀

12 Siebmonat 3123, Vaniran Hegemony

The suspicious cargo-sailer did not attack. Instead, precisely at midday, the vessel anchored to the south-southwest of the station. Before long, several individuals began using giant kites to surf the waves. Then two other groups launched sea-canoes and began a series of races, stopping just short of the outer surf line before turning and paddling northward, if slowly.

Duhyle stood at the corner of the ocean wall and the canal wall in the chill breeze. He studied the vessel, its sails furled, the picture of an ancient holiday cruise vessel, except for the heavy cargo booms securely fastened and immobile . . . and the cool temperatures out on the waves.

Subcaptain Symra stood to Duhyle's left.

"What are they doing underwater?" asked Duhyle.

"Preparing to attack," replied Symra. "Most likely using an underwater lock to transfer gear and equipment to an undersea installation being assembled as we speak."

"SatCom won't do anything?"

Symra gestured toward the apparently innocent scene playing out on the deep blue-green waters of the Jainoran Ocean. "Someone doubtless has images of what we see. Can you imagine . . . ?"

Unfortunately, Duhyle could. "There's no way to see what lies below? No evidence at all?"

"What *may* lie below. The water's deep enough, and sonic monitoring isn't descriptive enough, especially if what they're using is largely nonmetallic, which is what any smart operator would do, I'd judge."

"At present," suggested Duhyle.

Symra only nodded.

Duhyle turned and walked back into the station. He made his way up to Helkyria's laboratory to see what she might need. She didn't even look up from the screens when he came up the ramp and waited. So he hurried down to the larger supply room and began to inventory what was there and what might be useful in unforeseen ways when they were actually attacked.

He'd actually created about a kilo of biotherm and colored it to match the stone of the station when he received a private link from Helkyria.

The airships are less than ten minutes to the southeast. They may need assistance in unloading and moving supplies.

I'll take care of it. Is there anything there for you . . . or that you need?

No. Thank you. I'm working on something else. The link blanked.

Duhyle packed away the score of innocent-looking circular lumps of biotherm so they wouldn't dehydrate. The detonators would have to wait.

By the time he was out on the stone to the south of the station, the first airship had arrived and trailed disembarking lines. The black cylindrical craft hovered ten yards above the ground, its bulbously asymmetrical nose pointed into the wind out of the northeast, its dark and nonreflective solar-film finish soaking in every possible photon for the four engines and ship's systems. Security troopers slid down the lines. The soft and almost swampy ground to the south of the canal muffled the sound of their boots hitting the surface.

Duhyle could not see the cargo-sailer from where he watched the troopers leaving the lower airship. But above him and to the south, the second airship had taken station to monitor the *Skadira*.

Large as the two airships looked, at more than one hundred yards in length, Duhyle had earlier checked the specs. He'd found the payload to be something around twenty-five tonnes. The average security trooper, with full gear, weighed in at around 130 kilos. Theoretically, the airship could easily have carried two companies, yet each only carried half a company. That should have left mass for heavy equipment as well. Or did the payload refer to the entire gondola and crew?

He couldn't tell from the airship specs.

After the troopers came the pallets of food, ammunition, and other supplies, lowered on cables and quickly detached by the troopers on the ground. Given how organized the troopers were, Duhyle just stood by, in case there was something else that needed to be done.

A lanky security captain, in one of the shimmering security single-suits that changed shades depending on the environment and the needs of the troopers, trotted toward Subcaptain Symra.

Duhyle couldn't make out what the two women said, but almost immediately about half of the first troopers moved toward the cliffs to the west and took up positions overlooking the ocean.

In minutes, the remaining troopers from the first airship were on the ground and had carried and stacked the cargo pallets on the stone of the canal wall next to the station. Then they turned and trotted toward the cliffs to join the first contingent. The first craft lifted, the engines whining gently as the airship circled skyward to cover the other ship. The second airship made a circling descent and deployed disembarking lines. The second half of the security company scrambled down the lines, following the same procedures as had the previous troopers.

In minutes, all but ten security troopers were in position on the cliffs. The ten stood in a relaxed line before Symra.

"Tech Duhyle, here, will show you where all the supplies will be stored." After a brief hesitation, Symra added, "The station is effectively proof against any known form of explosive. Its one drawback is that access cannot be blocked, except by troops with weapons."

Duhyle thought quickly, then nodded, stepping forward. "The pallets with ammunition need to be stored in the main room just inside the south doorway. Put them against the wall."

One of the troopers looked pointedly at the featureless stone wall of the station.

Duhyle smiled. "There is a door. I'll show you."

He turned to move toward the point where the door was, but was spared that by the fact that the stone opened, and Helkyria stepped out into the weak sunlight.

"Right there." Duhyle gestured. "If it closes, just press your hand against the stone at the side. It won't close if you're in the doorway. The ration stores can go below inside in a secondary storeroom. I'll show you."

"You heard the tech," came the voice from a senior ranker at one end of the ten. "Hyldgard . . . you and Bhriony . . ."

Before heading into the station, Duhyle glanced back and skyward. The two airships climbed on a southeast course. He looked at Symra. "They're leaving? Already?"

"They're too vulnerable," Symra pointed out.

"Hardened air transports have historically been a waste of resources," added Helkyria from behind them.

Waste of resources? For whom? Duhyle neither spoke nor commpulsed that thought. Instead he walked toward the station door.

In a quarter hour, every item that had been on the pallets was stacked inside the station, and Duhyle reemerged into the afternoon sunlight. He strode toward Symra and Helkyria.

". . . have to wait to see what they do."

". . . makes me uneasy, ser," replied the subcaptain.

"It makes us all uneasy, but the Aesyr haven't done anything that could be construed as unlawful or inciting violence. We might as well take a closer look at what they're up to." Helkyria turned and began to walk westward toward the end of the wall.

"No one's firing." Duhyle took several quick steps to catch up.

"Not yet," added Symra from behind them.

When the three reached the ocean wall, Duhyle immediately looked for the cargo-sailer. From what he could tell the *Skadira* stood slightly farther off the cliffs and the narrow beach below them, but he did not see any wake.

"She's easing away," suggested the subcaptain.

The *Skadira* slowly moved southward, then more toward the southwest under engine power, since the sails remained furled.

"The deck's vacant," mused Symra. "Those boats are as far away as they've been all day."

Duhyle could barely make out the four sea-canoes, so far south had they traveled, and there were no kite-sailers anywhere in sight.

A long whining scream ended with a brilliant gout of fire, flaring from where the cargo-sailer had been instants before.

THWHUMP!

Debris flew in all directions, with pieces raining into the ocean wall of the canal—a good fifty yards below where Duhyle stood, open-mouthed.

"Frig!" exclaimed Symra. "I thought—"

"That wasn't SatCom. The Aesyr did it themselves. They've got a sky-eye somewhere. They'll beam the images worldwide and claim it was an unprovoked attack by the government," observed Helkyria. "Tell the security company captain to be ready for an attack, Subcaptain. I need to inform Vaena and SecCon." She turned and ran toward the station.

Symra sprinted toward the rear of the troops arrayed along the top of the cliffs, although Duhyle caught no comm pulses.

Without contrary instructions, Duhyle decided to follow Helkyria.

16

✧ ✧ ✧

21 Ninemonth 1351, Unity of Caelaarn

Maertyn did not sleep well. But then, he hadn't slept all that well in Caelaarn for years, and certainly not since Maarlyna's illness. After breakfast, he finished dressing, choosing a silver-trimmed green jacket with maroon cuffs, designed to deflect shocker bolts and resist projectiles. Then he made his way to the garage and the small personal vehicle retained at the town house, both for Maertyn's use when he was there, or for Rhesten when Maertyn was not.

The building that held the Ministry of Science was to the north and west of the greenbelt that Maertyn's town home overlooked, less than a ten-minute drive. Once there, without incident, Maertyn pulled into the open-topped area that allowed solar recharging, if into a space reserved for those of his Ministry position and higher, where he stepped out and locked the vehicle. He carried only a thin portfolio. Most of what he had to say was in his head and not in any set of records, except at the canal station.

The distance from the car park across the narrow bridge to the entry walk was less than a hundred yards, and when Maertyn stepped through the outer doors of the Ministry building, he saw two guards in the dark green and black of Unity Protective Services, but behind the security console. When he'd left, there had been no guards stationed in the building.

Maertyn proffered his hand to the scanner, which announced, "Deputy Assistant Minister Lord Maertyn S'Eidolon, cleared to all levels."

One of the two guards looked intently at Maertyn as the gates opened, but said nothing as he passed them and headed for the ramp up to the second level. Once there, he walked down the corridor some ten yards, where he reached the bottom of the ramp that led to the third level. He again had to have his hand scanned, but there was no announcement as the entry gate to the ramp irised open, and he made his way to the third and top level, and then down the central hallway.

The office of the Minister of Science for the Unity of Caclaarn was at the rear of the building, with a view of a gardens below that amounted to a private park for those who worked at the Ministry headquarters.

Maertyn had no more than stepped into the outer anteroom of the minister's suite than a muscular young man in a green singlesuit and gray jacket, with a professionally cheerful face that Maertyn didn't recognize, stepped forward. "Lord Maertyn, the minister hoped you'd be here early. Let me tell him you've arrived. If you'd care to take a seat, I'm sure it won't be long."

Maertyn nodded politely. "Thank you." He didn't bother to seat himself. Hlaansk didn't bother with petty gestures like making subordinates wait unnecessarily.

The young functionary had barely entered the minister's private office when he emerged.

"Lord Maertyn . . ."

Maertyn walked into the office, noting that the door closed behind him, softly but firmly.

Minister Hlaansk Ovisor was black-haired, perhaps a few centimeters shorter than Maertyn, but slender, with a warm open smile that extended to the corners of his intense blue eyes. He wore the green jacket of the Science Ministry with a gray shirt and trousers and a pale green cravat. "Maertyn . . . it's good to see you. You're looking healthy and more rested than the last time we met." Hlaansk gestured toward the chairs in front of the amberwood desk, a desk that was bare of anything except a single thin file that lay at a slight angle.

"Thank you." Maertyn waited until the minister started to seat himself, then followed.

"You've been working at the canal now, what, for not quite a year and a half . . . ?"

Maertyn wasn't in the slightest deceived by the apparent casual opening, knowing that Hlaansk knew Maertyn's time at the station down to the nearest hour, if not the exact second. "Something like that."

"We haven't seen much in the way of detail in your reports, and when I received your request for equipment, I thought a more detailed presentation to the senior staff here at the Ministry might be useful, especially anything you have discovered about the old quarters there."

"I have reported on the temperature discrepancies and the resultant impact on climate and weather—in some detail, as I recall. As for the quarters . . . what could I possibly add to years of observation by light-keepers and others?"

"Come now, Maertyn," offered the minister jovially, "the light-keeper's station has to be more than that. That's one reason why you were allowed to pursue your research there."

"One reason?" Maertyn's words were quiet, almost matter-of-fact.

"In terms of your scientific inquiries and your research, as well as the policies you administered while a deputy assistant minister, you've always been above reproach."

That wasn't an answer, true as the words were, and Maertyn waited.

"I've read enough reports from scientists to understand one aspect about your proposal about the MCC." Hlaansk leaned back in the overstuffed swivel chair, offering a broad smile.

"Oh?"

"You know as well as I do, but I'll spell it out so that you'll understand where you stand. The compact underlying the Unity is most clear about one aspect of both research and commerce. It's clear about many, but the one that applies to us is the absolute prohibition on the use of or research into any energy generation or concentration system that creates toxic or nonbiodegradable wastes or that creates or enhances radioactive by-products or end-products. Given the duration of the great canal, its imperviousness to all known energy forms, and its isolation from all forms of energy, it has to embody a higher-level energy usage and generation system. Once upon a time, when Earth had a moon, tidal power was a greater source, but that diminished eons ago. Now, in these times, when we face severe limitations on bio and solar power, discovering a more unique power source could prove critical, especially to the Ministry that rediscovered such a system."

"That's . . . rather far-fetched, and a long ways from my initial proposal, sir. Besides, I'm a single scientist. Would not a team prove more likely to discover such a source, rather than a lone researcher?"

"Teams are useful in discovering ways to implement and build upon discoveries, but at times, insight is more important than collaboration . . . and more practical."

In short, you need the Ministry of Science to make the first breakthrough here. "You're expecting a great deal, sir."

"You've shown that you have a streak of insight and innovation matched by few, Maertyn, and I'm counting on that. So should you."

Maertyn nodded politely. "I will do my best. You know that."

"I know you will." Hlaansk cleared his throat. "I must bring up one distressing aspect of the present situation. The Executive Administrator's Council has taken note of your reports, although how they obtained them is a matter of some question. It has been suggested that . . . if you cannot discover the secrets of the canal within your research term, or at least make significant progress, Protective Services will likely turn to more . . . forceful means."

"Oh?"

"The Gaerda will be allowed to test its new nucleonic weapon there."

"Isn't that a violation of the energy compact?"

"The nucleonic weapon was not built or created on Earth. The compact does not apply to weapons or energy systems above the outer atmosphere." Hlaansk shrugged. "It doesn't leave any radioactivity, I've been assured, and while it might raise the local temperature for a slight while, that will be considered acceptable, more than acceptable given the continued progress of the northern ice. It will be registered as an off-planet trial of means to arrest glaciation, and no one is likely to object too much to that. The Minister of Environment and the Minister of Protective Services have both suggested that, while pure research is valuable, we also need results in the foreseeable future, and that, at the very least, the reaction of the canal to a nucleonic weapon might reveal what more . . . prosaic methods cannot."

"That is certainly possible," replied Maertyn calmly. "It is also possible that it would destroy forever anything embedded or concealed there."

"Truly said." Hlaansk shrugged. "But knowledge, if even potentially of great value, that cannot be accessed and applied when it is most needed, such as now, is knowledge of little use."

"You would deny that to future generations?"

"I would deny nothing. The Gaerda has already noted that our various forebears were less than accommodating in that respect."

"The Gaerda does tend to focus on immediate results, with sometimes less than desirable results, although as its ultimate supervisor, the Minister of Protective Services seems often to have to offer his regrets. Too often, some have said."

"He is good with regrets, but regrets can be of little consolation, especially in such small matters as, shall we say, an unregistered cloning . . . or more precisely a majority cloning registered as a partial regeneration. Not that such is illegal, unless, of course, legal personage is an issue."

Maarlyna . . . sooner or later . . . but more than a few senior ministers have "unregistered" clones of some sort . . . "As you say, Minister, regrets offered after the act are often of little consolation."

"But . . . we needn't talk of such irregularities. I'm certain that your presentation to the senior staff this afternoon will prove most enlightening. You need not go into all the details, but perhaps an indication of the potential—suitably and cautiously presented, of course—would indicate to them the reason for your continued efforts there." Hlaansk smiled broadly.

"I think I can manage that, sir."

"I knew you would." Another smile followed. "And how is your lovely wife?"

"The climate there has been most beneficial to her continued recovery, sir, as I'm certain you knew it would be, for which we are both grateful."

"I'm glad to hear it. Very glad." With a smile, Hlaansk stood. "Until this afternoon, Maertyn. We're all looking forward to your briefing."

Maertyn stood. "I'll do my very best to provide the information everyone needs." He inclined his head.

The minister returned the gesture.

17

❈   ❈   ❈

27 Quad 2471 R.E.

Two days had passed since the priority pulse announcement of the government restructuring—or coup—by The Twenty. While general announcements continued, no comm pulses had been directed specifically at the station or at Eltyn or Faelyna, and certainly not one of the cyan frequencies of TechOversight. Neither had the satellite transmissions from MetCom nor any geosat resumed, and MetCom did not acknowledge any transmissions. From the station there was no way to determine whether MetCom had been shut down or destroyed.

While Faelyna worked on modifying the shadow-tracking equipment, Eltyn had checked the emergency solar-powered three-wheeler. It was operable, but the narrow tires restricted it in practice to the top of the canal, since they would quickly bog down in the sand to the south and east of the station. There was no way to widen the footprint of the tires. Even if he could have, the extra weight and the need to carry water—and the lack of a viable destination—would have turned flight through the sand near suicidal. The supply wheeler had not arrived on its scheduled oneday delivery, unsurprisingly, given the coup and a moderate sandstorm, but they did have over three months' worth of dried rations, barely edible as they were. The solar still and the independent power system insured that they'd have more than enough water and energy.

What else could they do but pursue the TechOversight project? Pursue that project, and see what defenses they might mount beyond the stunners and the two projectile rifles that were their sole protection against feral sandcats and anything else wild that might appear outside the station.

Slightly before midmorning on threeday, Faelyna adjusted her equipment, now focused on one of the unused and closed ducts on the station's lowest level. They had already scanned and shadowed-tracked all of the main doors and windows in the station, discovering essentially two patterned "shadow" responses, one for doors and one for windows.

How long before scan? Eltyn knelt on the hard stone, hands on his thighs, bending his head forward to stretch tight neck muscles, then waiting.

Two minutes, replied Faelyna. *Interrogative probability of airlifted team inspection?*

Low. If priority, the team would already have been here. Most likely a canal wheeler or an SEV from Apialor.

No supply run on oneday or yesterday. Suggests problems for The Twenty in Apialor. She recalibrated a setting on the focal head.

More² problems for us. Armed team likely to conduct "compliance inspection" . . . if they even bother.

Sooner/later they'll bother. Stand by. One minute.

Standing by. Eltyn forced himself to wait. While Faelyna had always been precise in each examination, he still found it unsettling to know that his hand and fingers were within centimeters of both high power and an enigmatic and ancient control system that certainly had the power to remove both fingers and hand. Although there was no record of anything like that, there were stories about disappearances. Also, no one had probed the station walls with equipment nearly as sophisticated as that which Faelyna was using. Not that they knew, but from what records remained, the Unity of Caelaarn's technology had been more biological in nature, and other earlier civilizations had left few indications of such capabilities, at least since the ancients who had built the MCC.

EEEE!!! The white emergency pulses signified the first announcement in more than a day. *All outlying or isolated installations—beware of those approaching. In several locales, enemies of the Ruche have fled from populated areas to avoid treatment for antisocial and contra-Ruche tendencies. Such self-proclaimed refugees are often armed and dangerous. They should be reported to appropriate authorities as soon as possible.*

TechOversight—enemy of the Ruche? asked Faelyna.

Eltyn knew that the seniors in MetCom—if they'd even survived—weren't the kind to oppose the RF or The Twenty. *Possible. TechOversight didn't wait to announce Contingency Three. Chiental's under a mountain.*

Third general announcement about "refugees," noted Faelyna. *More than a few unhappy with the new government. Besides TechOversight.*

Few? Anyone who doesn't agree with The Twenty is now an enemy of the Ruche.

Including us. [dry cynicism]

Eltyn nodded without pulsing.

Touch the conduit cover.

He reached out and pointed to where the stone had flowed around the heat-exchanging line, not quite touching the surface. The stone flowed back onto itself. A musty and slightly rancid odor drifted up, and he couldn't help but wriggle his nose.

Close it.

Eltyn barely moved his finger, concentrating on thinking about the conduit cover closing. The stone sealed itself around the composite piping, and he released his breath, if slowly.

Power to standby, announced Faelyna.

Results?

Need to analyze. Different pattern.

[hopeful] ???? Eltyn straightened and stretched.

It's a beginning. [doubt/hope] Possible key to command structure.

Linguistic basis?

Structured basis required. Linguistics . . . ???

Isn't all structure based on language?

All structure we know, Faelyna pulsed back. *Since no one yet has figured out what lies behind or beneath the station . . . ????*

How would we know? They might have figured it out and still left the station alone. Knowledge can't always be translated into acts.

For our sakes[3] . . . best hope we find a way.

Eltyn's response was a wry smile.

Vehicle approaching! pulsed the local alarm system.

Faelyna turned, an inquiring look on her face.

Eltyn virtied the scanner and pulled an image. *Supply wheeler.* He watched for a time, extending the image to Faelyna. A woman driver eased the vehicle up to the station's south side.

That's Rhyana. She sometimes does the deliveries, Faelyna pulsed. *Seems like a good enough person.*

Might as well see what she has to say.

The two of them left the equipment and walked up the ramp to the main level. Eltyn picked up one of the stunners before he pressed the stone to open the southern door. Then he led the way.

Rhyana had pulled the wheeler up close to the door, in the area that Eltyn and Faelyna kept clear of the sand. That was both to keep sand from flowing into the station and to make it easier for those who delivered goods, parts, and equipment. The delivery woman stood beside the wheeler, her hands empty. Her eyes flicked from Faelyna to Eltyn and the stunner. Her orange driver's cap was slightly askew over her short and curly brown hair.

Eltyn couldn't tell if the covered cargo bin of the solar-powered wheeler contained anything. Whatever it might be wasn't that massive, because the vehicle wasn't resting heavily on the narrow tires.

"What is it?" Faelyna asked.

"I had to leave Apialor. I saw what they were doing. They didn't see me. No one looks at manualers. The Twenty sent a team with a scanner. They're brain-scanning everyone. Those who aren't loyal are force-conditioned."

Eltyn winced inside. Brain-scanning was bad enough. If done less than expertly, the process created permanent damage and learning problems. Force-conditioning wasn't much better than an ancient lobotomy or a Caelaarnan partial brain transplant. The body was the same, but mental functions were greatly diminished, and initiative was almost non-existent. "Why?"

"They claimed there were secret agents of The Fifty everywhere, especially anyone associated with TechOversight." Rhyana glanced back eastward.

The level surface of the canal wall was empty of figures or vehicles.

"I did bring some supplies . . . had to be those left in the wheeler. Would have liked to have brought my rifle. Couldn't risk going back into the depot," added the driver. "Would have liked to have used it."

Too bad she couldn't, Eltyn private-pulsed.

Agree[3].

"You think I could stay here?"

"You're welcome to." Faelyna smiled. "It's severe. No entertainment, except a few cubes we brought."

"Brought my own favorite cubes, the ones I carry with me for when I have to wait," admitted Rhyana. "Couldn't see staying. First thing they did was grab Kealyn and force-condition him to tell everything about anything. Heard that, and I sneaked off and took the wheeler."

"Kealyn's just a driver," said Eltyn. "Why would they do that?"

"Said drivers know what everyone does."

"How soon do you think they'll be headed here?" asked Faelyna.

The delivery woman shook her head. "I don't know. They came in from the north side of the canal on an old SEV. I took the only wheeler they weren't using. They had the others carry stuff from where they tied up the SEV, down on the floating dock. Their team was armed. There weren't that many, maybe twenty." She paused, then added, "I thought you might have some way to hide or defend yourselves."

"We're working on it," replied Faelyna. "The station is impervious to explosives and energy weapons, but the entries can't be blocked." *Not at the moment*, she private-pulsed to Eltyn. "You should know that, but you're welcome to stay. We do have food. It's mostly dry-condensed, but not bad."

Rhyana shuddered, looking southward at the sandy dunes and scattered cacti and sagebrush and mesquite. "No place else to go." She forced a smile. "I can help . . . do things . . ."

"We'd appreciate that," replied Faelyna. "Do you need help unloading?"

"I wouldn't want to be a bother . . ."

"That's not a problem," said Eltyn. "The sooner we get everything inside the better. We might even be able to squeeze your wheeler inside."

"That'd be good."

Very good, pulsed Faelyna to Eltyn.

He nodded.

18

❖   ❖   ❖

13 Siebmonat 3123, Vaniran Hegemony

Duhyle stood at the ocean wall of the canal, looking out over the patches of late-morning mist that drifted across the low waves of the Jainoran Ocean. There was no sign of anyone who had been on the cargo-sailer. A day after the destruction of the vessel, the sea-canoes and kite-sailers had vanished. The narrow beaches below the western cliffs were empty of all human presence, without any prints in the intermittent patches of sand between the pebbled shingle. Seabirds swooped and landed, and skittered along the edge of the waves. An occasional crab scrabbled sidewise to avoid or to engage the water.

"You won't see anything, Kavn." Helkyria stepped up to the ocean wall beside him. "Not yet. Not until just before they decide to attack—if they decide to attack." She half-turned.

Duhyle heard boots on the stone. He glanced back to see Captain Valakyr and Subcaptain Symra approaching. Both wore professionally grim expressions on faces that might otherwise have been attractive.

"Ser?" offered Valakyr as she stopped a yard from Helkyria. "What have you heard?"

"Outside of the reports of political chaos, the violent demonstrations in Asgard and all across Midgard, the more muted counter-demonstrations in Vaena, the political maneuverings among assistant

magistras, the blanket condemnations of Security? Outside of those?"
Helkyria's eyebrows lifted, and highlights of green and dark gray momentarily appeared there, while the tips of her hair darkened into
nearly pure black before fading to gray and then resuming their silver-
blond hues. Her eyes remained silver.

"Ah . . . yes, ser," replied Valakyr.

Symra nodded, the tips of her hair darkening the slight bit that was
possible.

"All the Aesyr representatives to the Assembly have left Vaena, and
so have the magistras in charge of Environment, Transport, and Finance and Commerce."

"Those were all the departments headed by Aesyr, weren't they?"
asked Captain Valakyr.

"That's my understanding."

"Why the condemnation of Security?" asked Duhyle. "At least half
the security companies are primarily Aesyr."

"The Magistra of Security didn't deploy those companies." Helkyria's
voice was dry. "For rather obvious reasons."

"Some of them might be down there, hidden out of sight." Valakyr
gestured toward the ocean and the empty beaches. "Seventh Company
all requested leave at the same time. Major Gemli granted it."

"What else did she grant? Access to unlimited lethal weapons? Use
of company vehicles or government transport?"

"I wouldn't know, ser."

"I wouldn't have thought anyone would go that far, but . . . these days,
who could say?" Helkyria nodded. "If you will excuse me, Captain, Subcaptain, there are matters to which I need attend. Please don't draw any
power from the local net without checking with me or Duhyle first. Let
me know if you see any sign of activity from the Aesyr . . . or anyone
else."

"Yes, ser."

"I'll let you know if I hear anything else from Vaena." Helkyria inclined her head to Duhyle, then turned. He immediately joined her, but
did not say anything until they were inside the station and walking up
the ramp to her laboratory.

"You're going to try something with the fermionic entanglement
and ghost diffraction imager?" After her earlier reaction to the FEGDI

acronym, he wasn't about to use the term in speaking. He still thought of the odd assemblage of equipment that way.

"Yes. It's the next logical step beyond implementation of a matching protocol system."

"You've made sense out of those ghost patterns?"

"They're more like shadow patterns, created by some sort of entanglement. I can use them to open and close the doors and windows without being near them. That's interesting, but not terribly useful. I need—we need—some way to lock the entries. Beyond that . . ." The corners of Helkyria's lips lifted, if for a moment.

"Beyond that?" prompted Duhyle.

"There's more beyond the stone than meets either the eye or past instrumentation and equipment. The question is whether I can find a way to view and control what else is there. It's unlikely, but not impossible, that anyone has done so since the station was first used by the early Vanir. Before that, who knows?"

"Isn't it possible?"

"Possible? Yes. Probable, no. The potential power of the canal is so great that had its secrets been rediscovered and used, it's unlikely Earth itself would be anything but fragments."

"Like the Mist Ring?"

"I wouldn't be surprised if the two were linked, but right now I have no way to even prove theoretically that is possible. We do know that the Mist Ring constitutes what remains of Earth's moon, and that ancient tidal patterns confirm that it was an unusually large satellite in comparison to Earth itself, so much so that some scients have doubted those findings."

"If the science shows it . . . ?"

"Even in those with an education in science, belief can dominate education, facts, and proof. That's why not all who are educated in science are actually scients." She laughed. "It's the same everywhere. Not all who study music turn out to be musicians. Not all students of economics end up as competent economists . . . If unfounded belief is stronger than discipline and knowledge, then the practitioner is seldom a true professional in the field, whatever that field may be." She stopped short of the equipment. "It will be a bit before I'll need your help. Is there anything you need to do?"

"Not now. I do have some biotherm ready."

"Save it."

"In a while I'll need to think about fixing lunch." Duhyle moved to the second stool and settled onto it.

Helkyria turned her attention to her assembled devices.

Outside the station, the security forces patrolled, watched, and waited.

19

❖   ❖   ❖

21 Ninemonth 1351, Unity of Caelaarn

After his short morning meeting with the minister, Maertyn walked to the front of the building toward the small office he retained in the Environment Research Subministry. He stopped outside the office of the assistant minister.

"Is Josef in, Marcent?"

The young-faced aide looked up from his console. "The assistant minister will be out until the twenty-third. He's touring all the science universities on Conuno that receive Unity Science Grants—the environmental ones."

"Who's going to tour the science universities in Occidenta?"

"There are only two that receive grants there."

Maertyn knew that, but he'd asked the question to make a point.

"Or Galawon?" Maertyn persisted gently.

Marcent did not reply for a moment, then said, "Oh . . . sir. Assistant Minister Cennen said that you were to use his office while you were here."

"That was kind of him . . . or has he given mine to one of his . . . protégés?" "Protégé" was a polite term for the string of unusually handsome male graduate students on whom Josef lavished special attention . . . and doubtless more.

"Only until you return permanently, sir. He . . . well . . . you don't return to Caelaarn that often these days."

"That's true." Maertyn smiled politely, then made his way into the assistant minister's office, a space roughly six yards by eight, overlooking the gardens on the east side of the building. It held a desk with full built-in comm capabilities and a conference table that could be used as either another desk or as part of a remote, full visual and sound, conference facility.

Josef's absence and the effective reassignment of Maertyn's office strongly suggested that Assistant Minister Cennen did not believe that one Lord Maertyn S'Eidolon would be returning to his previous position, and that the good assistant minister did not wish to be linked at all closely to Maertyn.

"Not surprising," he murmured to himself as he settled himself at the small conference table by the window. He really didn't want to use Cennen's desk, and he didn't have to in order to review his presentation, or even to answer any comms that might come his way. He doubted there would be many, and certainly not before all his peers evaluated what happened at his briefing.

He opened the folder. What was so obvious that he had forgotten to explain it? What could he present more effectively? Those questions always helped refine a presentation.

Just before midday, there was a rap on the door, which Maertyn had left slightly ajar. He looked up to see Amirella Lihusan, easily recognizable for her straight gray hair, a result of a gene that couldn't be modified because it was linked to another defensive gene whose absence would have created an unacceptable risk of a score of different carcinomas or whose modification was impractical, if not impossible. "Amirella!" He rose from the conference table.

"Would you like to join me for lunch?" She smiled. "Or, more properly, might I join you so that we could eat in the junior ministers' dining room?"

"You're of deputy assistant minister rank . . ."

"But not with the title. Besides, it sounds better if I can tell everyone you asked me."

"You're incorrigible." He walked to the door and stepped out to join her.

"With what I do, how else could I be?"

"I am hungry."

"Good."

They walked out of the assistant minister's suite and into the corridor that led to the ramp. Maertyn could sense Marcent's eyes on his back.

The junior ministers' dining salon was located on the second level in the middle of the front section of the building, overlooking both the narrow line of greenery and the car park.

"Lord Maertyn . . . it's good to see you back," offered a woman in a dark gray and formfitting singlesuit.

"A corner booth, if you please, Cariena." Maertyn noted the increasing warmth of the hostess's professional smile at the use of her name.

"I think we can manage that. This way . . ."

The two followed the hostess to the booth in the farthest window corner on the east. They had barely settled into the natural green leather of the booth when a server appeared.

"Might I get you something to drink?" Her smile was polite and solicitous.

"A glass of white shiraz," replied Amirella.

"Just iced tea, please, unsweetened," said Maertyn.

"The day's menu is on the sheets. I'll be back with your drinks and take your selections."

Maertyn nodded and picked up the single thin flexible sheet and scanned the options. Every morning, each sheet was fed through the repermer with the new menu. Most sheets lasted close to a year before they had to be recycled.

"What will you have?" he asked.

"The quail. You?"

"The pheasant. The biologics up north are mostly limited to lamb and beef and chicken. Not enough people to support a full-scale bio-replication facility. I also like the fact that the wild rice is actually marsh-grown."

"It's a bit . . . wild . . . for me."

The server eased up to the table and set the goblet of clear wine before Amirella and the tall glass of tea before Maertyn. Amirella ordered first, then Maertyn, and in moments they were alone at the table again.

"How have things been with you?" asked Maertyn.

"In what I do very little changes." She smiled mischievously. "I understand you're giving a presentation on your research on the canal to all those in the Ministry—at the level of deputy assistant minister and above. All those in science and not staff positions, that is."

"Except for my own superior. He's out touring the science universities in south Conuno."

"Just far enough away to be unavailable and close enough to return in a hurry, if necessary."

"You'd think that of the honorable Josef Cennen?"

"I think worse of him than I'll ever say. What would you say?"

"I'd say that his behavior is excessively prudent."

Amirella laughed.

Maertyn couldn't help smiling.

"How's Maarlyna?"

"Better. The quiet is good for her. She's not looking forward to returning to Caelaarn. I think she's counting the days with trepidation."

"I can understand that," Amirella said sympathetically, then paused before going on. "What can you tell me about your research? In simple terms. I'm a numbers person, not a researcher."

"I noted from temperature reports and scattered observations that the temperature around the canal was never as extreme as in the adjoining areas. Also, the temperature of the stone never varies no matter how much sun strikes it or how much ice piles on the north side—except it doesn't stay piled there. It builds up right behind it and then topples over it and into the water. In simple terms, I'm trying to find out why."

"Are you having much success?"

"I've found out a few new things about the canal. Some suggest possibilities, but I haven't yet figured out how to devise the follow-on experiments to investigate or quantify them."

"That's very cautious . . ."

At that moment, the server arrived with their meals.

Over the rest of lunch Maertyn steered the conversation away from specifics, and Amirella was kind enough not to object. They went their separate ways from the salon, and Maertyn wondered exactly why she'd asked for him to take her to lunch. He'd have to keep that in mind while he was in Caelaarn.

All too soon, it approached two in the afternoon, and Maertyn made his way back to the minister's conference room with the long table that could seat close to thirty. When he entered, he smiled politely as he tallied those present—a "mere" sixteen, without Hlaansk.

"It's good to see you, Maertyn," offered Daelaz Cuivot, the Assistant Minister for Transportation Research. "Is it as cold as they say up there?"

"Colder . . . especially when the icebergs are calving and they drift south. Or when the deep winter winds blow." Maertyn set the portfolio he would not need in front of the empty chair at the foot of the table, the space always reserved for the one doing the briefing, but he did not seat himself, knowing what would come next.

As he expected, the side door from the minister's suite opened, and Hlaansk stepped into the room, nodded to all those at the table, and seated himself at the end with his back to the west window, darkened to reduce the light and glare coming into the room. Then he looked toward Maertyn. "If you would begin, Lord Maertyn?"

"Thank you, Minister." Maertyn paused for a moment, then raised his voice. "For those of you who have not read the initial précis of the project and for those of you who have been so inundated by the demands of your own responsibilities that your recollections may have blurred, I'll summarize the rationale for the project. Analysis of current and historic temperature reports and scattered observations over more than a century before systematic reporting indicated that the temperature around the midcontinent canal was never as extreme as in the adjoining areas. More intriguing was the fact that the surface temperature of the stone never varied regardless of the intensity of solar radiation or the lack of such during the depth of winter . . ."

From there Maertyn went on to describe his initial baseline research, which included localized directed laser and high-energy bombardment of the stone in contained areas, as well as temperature and pressure reductions in the air or in other substances in direct contact with the stone. ". . . not only was the surface totally unmarred by these, but there was never any variation in surface temperature, even for milliseconds. After confirming these facts, the project moved into the second phase . . . the investigation of possible control and temperature stabilization methodologies . . ."

After speaking technically, and slightly elliptically, several minutes more, he finished quickly. ". . . and that is where the project stands at this moment." Maertyn inclined his head. "I'll be happy to take any questions." He wasn't all that pleased to take questions, suspecting what might well be coming, but there wasn't any help for that.

Vergena Stett, the Deputy Assistant Minister for Research Applications, whom Maertyn recalled as an anal nitpicking scientocrat, smiled brightly and said, "As I understand it, Deputy Assistant Minister, your original proposal was to determine whether the specific properties of the midcontinent canal did in fact retard or eliminate the purported advancement of glaciation and, if that could be demonstrated, whether there was any way to replicate that effect. Is that a fair statement of the goals of your research?"

"That was what I offered a few minutes ago. Your restatement is a fair summary," Maertyn admitted.

"That's all you have to say?"

Hlaansk frowned, but did not speak.

"Those were essentially the goals I advanced."

"I may be missing a critical point here, Deputy Assistant Minister," persisted Stett, "but if the point of the research is to find ways to duplicate the effect of the midcontinent canal, why has the focus of your research shifted from that to the purported control systems, when, so far as you have indicated, there is no linkage between the control systems in the station and the properties of the canal itself?"

"I apologize, Deputy Assistant Minister Stett. I had thought the linkage was explicit. By the fact that the material comprising the station is the same material comprising the canal and by the fact that it responds to human intent, and only to a limited human intent, it appears highly likely that the same control mechanisms apply to both. Since the material cannot be moved or manipulated—except through those controls—it would appear that the key to duplicating and using the properties of the canal lies in mastering the control systems."

"How likely is your research to discover the basis of the system?" That question came from Alaser Fancoyn, the Assistant Minister for Protective Services Research.

Maertyn allowed a wry smile to cross his face. "If I knew the answer to that question, Assistant Minister, we'd be more into application than research. So far as I've been able to determine, no earlier research has actually separated human touch from human intent. That is promising. That's all I can say at this point."

A flurry of questions followed.

"Assuming you indeed discover the basis of this so-called effect, wouldn't the wide-scale implementation have disturbing environmental effects?"

"Aren't you concerned that, if you are successful, you may change the properties of the canal and create other difficulties, either geologically or climatically?"

"Your description of your next steps was sketchy at best, to say the least. Could you give a more detailed description of how you plan to proceed from here?"

"Have you been able to measure or discern any radiation or form of signaling from within the canal structure or the station that suggests how the station measures, as you call it, 'intent'?"

"While your findings are certainly the most detailed involving the canal, and indeed fascinating, are the goals of this project not rather fanciful and far-reaching?"

"Do you honestly believe this is a worthwhile expenditure of Unity funds at a time of financial hardship?"

After another twenty-five minutes, Minister Hlaansk rose. "I think we're seeing rephrasing of questions that Deputy Assistant Minister Maertyn has already addressed. I thank all of you for coming and for your insightful questions."

As the others rose to leave, Hlaansk gave a quick sharp look to Maertyn that indicated he was to wait until the others had departed.

As he stood nodding and smiling as the room emptied, Maertyn considered the briefing. He'd managed to avoid making any major errors—he thought. More than a few of the pointed questions had come from Stett, and there hadn't been what Maertyn could have called a scientific consistency behind any of them, but a political agenda that suggested they had been drafted almost more by someone working for the Ministry of Environment . . . or the Ministry of Protective Services.

Once he was alone in the conference room with the Minister of Science, Hlaansk nodded. "Very well handled, Maertyn."

"Thank you, sir."

"There is one other matter I wished to discuss with you."

"Yes, sir?"

"Since you are already here in Caelaarn, I've requested that Josef tour the other science universities, especially the two in Occidenta, and those in Galawon as well. You'll be acting Assistant Minister for Environment Research in his absence. That shouldn't hamper your research, since it's not as though that equipment you requested will reach the station immediately, either. I also must say that it was truly a shame Josef couldn't have been here to view your presentation. Quite masterful, I might add, especially in dealing with the environmentally slanted inquiries. I understand your concern about your wife, but I'm certain that, under the circumstances, she won't begrudge us your expertise for another few weeks."

"I'm most certain that she will understand, sir. She's always been most supportive."

"And you, I know, have done far, far more than anyone could ever ask, even of the most devoted husband, in her cause." Hlaansk offered a warm and sympathetic smile.

"I've always done what I thought best, sir, for her, and for the Ministry, and the Unity," replied Maertyn.

Hlaansk nodded. "I'm certain that you have, and I look forward to your oversight of Environment Research in the next few weeks and any recommendations you might make for improvement. It's always good to have a different perspective." Another smile followed. "We'll have to have lunch sometime next week." With that, the minister left through the side door into his suite.

Maertyn picked up the portfolio he had never opened and then walked back toward the front of the Ministry building. He strongly doubted that the half-proffered luncheon invitation would actually be forthcoming.

Hlaansk had accomplished three objectives with his last decision: punishing Josef for avoiding Maertyn's research briefing, suggesting potential irregularities within Environment Research and forcing Maertyn to look into those possibilities, and reminding Maertyn that his entire project and Maarlyna were at Hlaansk's suffrage.

Maertyn didn't see matters getting any easier . . . or better. Nor did he see any alternatives . . . unless he could discover something truly unusual about the canal, and he was enough of a realist to suspect that was most unlikely. Still . . . with the additional equipment, it was theoretically possible.

20

⸙   ⸙   ⸙

Fourday began without any communications from Apialor, or anywhere else. Fearing the worst, based on Rhyana's reports and both his and Faelyna's reading of the delivery woman, Eltyn decided the only way to deal with anyone from The Twenty, presuming that they didn't arrive in great force, was simply to capture or remove them. Neither Rhyana nor Faelyna disagreed. The three of them effectively faced losing their intelligence, if not their minds . . . or their lives.

Before more than a moderate number of inspectors showed up, Eltyn and Faelyna—mostly Faelyna—needed to master the command structure in order to keep outsiders from opening doors or windows. The stone would stand against anything in the Ruche arsenal. If large forces camped around the station, that was another question. In the meantime, he moved their weapons, power packs, and ammunition to the upper level, next to the "window" overlooking the south entrance. Then he went back to work.

During a moment when Faelyna stopped to take a brief break, in early afternoon, he pulsed, *Possible duplication of shadow-tracking?*

Possible. Need to restructure detector and build equivalent of transmitter.

Interrogative schematics?

Blue-orange folder [here].

Eltyn studied the details for close to half an hour. If he substituted here . . . but changed the power flows there . . . He nodded, then pulsed Faelyna. *Possible alternative transmitter.*

??????

[here] He expanded the rough virtie diagram.

For several minutes Faelyna studied his proposal. *Approach should work . . . Total one-time power draw? System capacity?*

Eltyn considered. She was right. *Spare storage discharge capacitors? Banked there . . . surge draw??*

[cautious approval]

I'll begin work. Eltyn headed for the storeroom.

After a good two hours of digging and organizing, he proved that the inventory was accurate. His memory was not, and that meant developing a work-around for the control circuits handling the surge power required. Still, he was well on the way to solving that problem when he finally had to give up from fatigue that evening and collapse into a thankfully dreamless sleep.

Fiveday did not begin in nearly so accommodating a fashion as fourday had.

Before eight in the morning, another priority comm blast shivered in. *All local installations on both sides of the midcontinent canal will be inspected in the next several days. The inspectors are fully authorized agents of the Ruche, acting with the full authority of The Twenty. These inspections are merely to assure compliance with power requirements and continued loyalty to the Ruche so that the proprieties of social order and structure are maintained. Once these formalities are concluded, the process of returning to normal activities will resume. No changes in operations are planned at this time.*

Eltyn's lips quirked. *No changes in operations, but what about changes in operators . . . or their minds? They're not mentioning other apparently permanent changes. MetCom and the satellites are still down.*

Permanently down. Probability = unity³.

How did RF manage it?

The Ruche is based on unity and security. The Fifty wasn't successful enough in fostering a sense of security, not with the sand covering most of the south half of Primia, and temperatures rising every year. TechOversight viewed as too liberal.

Too liberal?

Too open to nontraditional approaches.

Force-conditioning the most intelligent will provide solutions and security?

Punishment for failing to provide. [ironic laughter]

"What is it?" interrupted Rhyana, standing at the top of the ramp. "Begging your pardons, but I don't know what that buzzing meant."

"It means that, fairly soon, The Twenty will be sending inspectors out here."

"They'll get in over my corpse."

"Over all of our corpses," Eltyn agreed. "We're not exactly in the best of graces with The Twenty."

"All that fancy gear going to help?"

"It won't be finished before the first inspectors arrive," Eltyn said. "It might be ready in time for the second group . . . if we can handle the first."

Optimist[5]!

Agreed . . . Why not?

Faelyna smiled.

"I'll be doing my part," stated the delivery woman.

Eltyn managed to finish his control-circuit work-around in the next hour and was assembling the power banks when the local alert system buzzed.

Transport wheeler approaching. Distance four kays. Arrival time in six minutes and fifteen seconds.

Eltyn immediately virtie-linked to the local system, taking in the composite view of the dark gray vehicle from the system's scanners.

Speed and wheeler depression suggest five individuals, plus or minus one, given cargo, added the system.

????? inquired Faelyna.

As planned. "Rhyana!" Eltyn yelled, having the internal system sound-cast his words inside the station. "Up to the upper-level south side!"

Faelyna remained on the main level, with one of the stunners, to cover the doors, since the upper window wouldn't open wide enough to allow three people space to fire accurately. Also, that position provided her with a quick exit from the station on the canal side, either for escape or for a rear attack on the RF enforcers.

Behind the upper window, still closed, Eltyn continued to virtie-monitor the approach of the heavy-duty wheeler, as did Faelyna from the main level.

Eltyn glanced to Rhyana. "When the window opens they'll be below us, some five yards out."

"I'll be ready."

The vehicle stopped short of the east end of the station. For a time, nothing happened. Then six individuals, all in gray-blue uniform singlesuits, stepped out of the wheeler. Each wore a crimson shoulder patch with the intertwined letters "RF." All carried long stunners, discharge barrels slightly down.

RF uniforms, pulsed Faelyna.

Thought they just wore those for ceremony. Humble servants of The Fifty, they called themselves. [snort]

Eltyn waited until the six were closer, then murmured, "Ready," and touched the window, willing it to open wide.

Before he could even squeeze the firing stud on the projectile rifle, Rhyana had fired twice, and one of the "inspectors" had dropped. Eltyn fired, and one of the men staggered. He fired again, and the man dropped.

Eltyn could sense Faelyna hurrying out of the canal-side door. He didn't like her exposing herself, but he was in no position to do anything about it.

Rhyana fired twice more, and another inspector—a woman— toppled.

"Back to the wheeler!"

The man who had given the order turned and ran almost ten yards back toward the dark gray vehicle before falling—dropped by Faelyna's stunner.

The other two inspectors darted back, then turned and sprinted almost due south, heading toward a low dune. Beyond them, he could see the black shimmering pools that were but heat mirages.

Eltyn didn't fire again. He doubted he could hit anyone at that distance, and they didn't have that much ammunition. Besides, the two RF inspectors were angling back toward the canal, but in a way that suggested they weren't about to return to the station. Not soon, and not without reinforcements.

Eltyn had his doubts about whether the pair could make the more than sixty kays to Apialor on foot in the heat, the wind, and especially if a sandstorm came up in the next day or so. He watched for a moment, then keyed a command into the local net to inform him of any movement approaching the station. Only then did he turn from the window and head down toward the south door. He did switch magazines, as did Rhyana, before he opened the door.

Three figures in RF uniforms were dead. That left the one Faelyna stood watching.

"He'll be out for hours."

"We'll need to make sure he's firmly restrained."

"I can take care of that," announced Rhyana. "Take care of it good."

"You took care of most of them already," Eltyn said.

"I had to. They're the ones who were turning poor Kealyn into little more 'n dribbling mal-brain. That one there was, anyway." She pointed to the body of a slightly taller man with skin a shade darker than either Eltyn's or Faelyna's.

"What do we do with their vehicle?" Rhyana paused. "I suppose it doesn't matter. Satellites have probably picked it up already."

"Not necessarily," replied Eltyn. "The sat-links seem to be down. They'll have minidrones coming this way, if they aren't already. Can you camouflage it?"

"I'll see what I can do, after I take care of His Mighty Rucheness here, and the bodies. You two need to get back to what you were doing. You let me know if anyone's coming? Or if any of those RF types head back here?"

"Absolutely," declared Eltyn.

Faelyna nodded.

As the two left Rhyana, Eltyn couldn't help but ask, *Did they just think we'd let them walk in?*

Why not? Everyone else has, it appears. Except TechOversight. No way for us to get there. No way to know if Chiental has held them off.

It's a covert location . . .

The RF types seem to be everywhere.

Eltyn shook his head as he entered the station.

21

⊛　　⊛　　⊛

14 Siebmonat 3123, Vaniran Hegemony

The next morning dawned clear and bright . . . and without any sign of the Aesyr. The security company had gone to stand-down. One squad remained on alert, stationed around the por-tahut on the grass just south of the canal wall. Duhyle stood outside the south station door talking with Subcaptain Symra, since Helkyria was buried in her workroom, trying to track "ghost" patterns within the station proper.

"What will the Aesyr try next?" asked Duhyle.

"Anything that will catch us off-guard. It's likely to be an attack that doesn't look like one. Or it could be a peaceful protest designed to look like an attack to get us to make a mistake. The Aesyr and half the government are already demanding the resignation of the Magistra of Security over the sinking of the *Skadira*."

"Security didn't sink the ship. The Aesyr sank it themselves."

"That may be, but how do you prove a negative, especially when people saw a ship exploding from what looked like a satellite-launched missile? If you deny it without evidence, people think the government's deceiving them, but the more evidence the government produces, the more people believe the government is fabricating it all and that it's a cloaking job."

"Doesn't anyone ask why the government would want to destroy an innocent ship? Or that it might not be so innocent?"

"Throughout history, people have feared government, and mostly they've been right to do so." A faint pink of sardonic humor colored the subcaptain's eyebrows.

The distant muted sound of horns caught Duhyle's ear, and he and Symra turned. From out of the low evergreens to the south of the canal and the station emerged a handful of men playing brass horns of various lengths. All wore leathers, leggings, and horned helmets. Duhyle squinted. There were short battle-axes in leather cases attached to their wide belts.

"Security!" snapped Symra, clearly on a tactical net. "Full alert."

The hornists were almost a kay away. So far they were alone, but that didn't mean they'd stay unaccompanied.

Security troopers began mustering south of the portahut, and two other Aesyr walked out of the woods. Each carried a long pole, with a banner stretched between the poles. Against the banner's gray background, the four-word message in fluorescent crimson stood out— *Aesyr Against Secret Research*. The banner-bearers, also with battle-axes at their belts, followed the hornists by around fifteen yards.

Captain Valakyr appeared, her eyes darting toward the demonstrators. "Sonic axes! Two can play that tune." She hurried toward the portahut.

"Sonic axes?" asked Duhyle.

"They look like toys or ancient replicas, but they project tightly focused sound. They can be far more lethal than a real axe. They don't have to strike physically to kill. In fact, if the edge actually impacted your arm, it might malfunction, but they look like toys, and they're very light."

Two hundred or more demonstrators emerged from the trees behind the banner. All wore Aesyr costumes, with short leather cloaks, leather belts crossed over their chests, bound leggings, and horned helms. All were swinging the sonic axes in some sort of rhythm.

Duhyle frowned, then asked, "Is the advantage to the sonic axes that Security can't use longer-range weapons because they can't prove hostile intent until they're actually within yards of being killed or injured?"

Symra nodded. "You can't tell if it's a sonic axe or a toy until it's used. They can march up to the security troopers and turn away . . . or attack at the last moment. Oh . . . and the axes also have another capability. They disrupt several different forms of nonlethal restrainers, such as loopers and body foam."

"So . . . if the axes are lethal . . . ?" pressed Duhyle.

"They used toy axes last year in Asgard. Security cut down the first line of Aesyr demonstrators with high-strength stunners, and several died. The captain in charge was cashiered, and brain-conditioned. Even after a public trial, there was an uproar about Security overreacting."

Duhyle recalled seeing the media on the incident, but there hadn't been any mention of the resemblance between toy axes and sonic axes.

"That's why there aren't any Vanir security companies stationed anywhere in Midgard any longer," added Symra. "They're all Aesyr."

"They're trying to create their own separate government for Midgard."

"Trying?" Symra's single word was sardonic.

Duhyle looked back at the approaching Aesyr. More than half a kay away a number of other things struck him immediately. Most of the so-called demonstrators were male; all the men were bearded; and the majority of them were not only taller than he was, but considerably taller and broader than their few female compatriots.

The security troopers formed up in a staggered triple line along the flat stone at the southern edge of the canal wall. All carried circular shields and short stunners.

"Are the shields sonic blockers?"

"Yes. They're not always entirely effective." Symra's voice was clipped. "Excuse me, Tech Duhyle." She strode briskly toward the vehicle that had brought her, where the seven remaining spec-ops techs had formed up.

Once she reached them, there was a quick exchange, and then one of the techs slipped into the vehicle and drove it forward toward the middle of the line of security troopers. Symra and the other techs trotted alongside the vehicle, until it came to a stop in the middle of the line.

Duhyle nodded. Symra would use the vehicle's shields.

Captain Valakyr joined the subcaptain and the two talked for a moment before Valakyr turned away.

By now, the hornists were three hundred yards away from the security troopers. They did not continue toward the troopers, but turned east-ward, marching until they were even with the easternmost troopers. Then they stopped, about-faced, and resumed playing. In the meantime, the banner-bearers had turned westward, heading parallel to the security forces. When they reached the western end of the troopers, they swung around so that the banner faced the hornists. They stopped and set the banner poles on the ground.

More and more Aesyr marched forward, and the group took on a semi-military appearance, with spacing neither that of a crowd nor in the ranks of an overtly disciplined force.

Valakyr issued an order, and the security troopers immediately re-formed into a front only slightly wider than the approaching Aesyr demonstrators, now all swinging their axes in a coordinated pattern, as if in a drill, and chanting, "No more Vanir secrets . . . no more Vanir se-crets . . . no more Vanir secrets . . ."

Symra's voice rang out across the space between the two forces. "This is a reserved and protected area! Demonstrations are not permit-ted here, by order of the Assembly. You have made your point. Disband the demonstration or face restraint and incarceration."

The Aesyr did not respond, but kept marching toward the canal and the troopers, their chanting ever louder and more rhythmical, as was the swinging of the sonic axes—or were they merely toy axes?

In the distance, Duhyle could hear a high-pitched whining coming from behind him. He glanced over his shoulder, but the structure of the station blocked his view to the north. He turned his eyes back toward the advancing Aesyr, now less than a hundred yards from the security troops.

"You have been warned!" Symra announced. "Halt immediately or face restraint and incarceration!"

Duhyle had to wonder what Symra had in mind, because the demonstrators easily outnumbered the security troopers by three or four to one. Exactly how did the security troopers or the spec-ops techs plan to restrain a force four times their size, especially if the axes were indeed sonic weapons? He looked back at the station. Since there was no way to lock the stone entrances, there was little point in retreating inside.

The Aesyr were close enough that Duhyle could make out individual expressions. Those varied from outright laughter to broad smiles, many of them cruel.

The whining became even louder, accompanied by a thunderous roar.

Then Symra gestured, and the spec-ops vehicle somehow shimmered and vibrated, and the air seemed darker . . .

. . . and Duhyle could hear nothing, nothing at all.

What he saw and felt was a single security ramjet pass less than a hundred yards overhead before climbing out to the south. With that single pass the Aesyr crumpled—every last one of them, until they all lay on the uneven partly grassed ground south of the station. Several of the security troopers staggered, but they did not fall.

The spec-ops vehicle returned to normal, and Duhyle could hear once more.

This time Valakyr's voice was the one amplified. "Restrain every single Aesyr. Some may be dead, if they fell on their own axes, and for some the axes may have intensified the effect of the sonic stun. You have less than a quarter hour. Move!"

The security forces hurried toward the fallen figures, loopers and foamers out.

Duhyle turned to see Helkyria emerging from the station, but she was headed toward the spec-ops vehicle and the two junior officers. He followed.

"The airships are on the way, Captain," Helkyria announced to Valakyr. "They'll be here in less than two hours to pick up the demonstrators. We'll need a count of any casualties."

"I'd like it if there weren't any," replied the captain. "That's not likely. The way some of the Aesyr were swinging those axes, they were already projecting."

"We have some recordings of that." Helkyria nodded. "Even so, the media will be demanding your removal. I'll be taking the liberty of releasing an analysis of the axes, along with a schematic and a cutaway of the weapon. The Subministry of Public Safety will pick up the axes from the airships and will make them available to the media. That might prove to be of some assistance."

"They'll claim that we switched the axes."

"I know. Almost anything we provide, they'll find a way to twist or refute. We stunned peaceful demonstrators, and killed some of them."

"Few healthy humans die from stun-shock, especially prime physical specimens like those."

"It doesn't matter." Helkyria's voice was suddenly resigned . . . or tired. "You take care of the demonstrators and get me some axes quickly."

"Yes, ser."

Helkyria turned.

Duhyle followed her, but waited until he and Helkyria were back inside the station before he spoke again. "They've planned this all out."

"They have, and there will likely be another attack, but not until the Aesyr have fully exploited the idea that the Vanir government is excessively brutal and cruel when the most reasonable Aesyr are only asking for an end to secrets." She kept walking, making her way up the ramp to her working area.

"Most of the Aesyr were men, and they were huge."

"Most people don't know," replied the scient-commander. "The Aesyr have been using genetic engineering to reemphasize sexual dimorphism. It's been tried before. The last documented usage was during the last years of the Amberian Anarchists. The women reacted violently to that not-so-disguised attempt at resubjugation, and that led to the fall of the culture, but those traits have persisted in a diluted form. The Aesyr have been isolating and gene-splicing them for close to three generations."

"Isn't that against the Assembly principia?"

"It is, but genetic material is private and legally privileged. How can one prove that if those who are 'benefiting' from the traits refuse to have their genetic material analyzed?"

"The Aesyr are perverting the laws and protections to their own ends, and no one can say anything about it?"

"All fanatics and all those with great wealth have always done so. Why would that change now?"

Obvious as that was, Duhyle had nothing to say.

"If we of the Vanir pervert the laws to stop them, then how are we any different from them? Where do we stop?" The deep blue of sadness suffused her hair and eyebrows. "With each crisis, it becomes easier and easier to justify the erosion of principles, until we have none, and, in the end, principles and a common belief in them are all that hold a civilization together." After a brief pause, she said, "Excuse me, Kavn. There's so much I need to do. I'll see you later." She turned.

Duhyle walked back down the ramp.

22

❀ ❀ ❀

26 Ninemonth 1351, Unity of Caelaarn

After not quite a week in Caelaarn, Maertyn hadn't yet discovered what else Minister Hlaansk had in mind for him. He judged it wouldn't be long before he did. Marcent, Josef's longtime assistant, had been scrupulously polite, and so had everyone else. That worried him as much as Hlaansk's decision to have him act as assistant minister.

At just after ten on the twenty-sixth of Ninemonth, Maertyn finished reading the routine memoranda for the morning and turned to scan the news. The second story caught his eye.

> . . . crop yields, even with biologic stimulation, continue to decline on a worldwide basis . . . largely as a result of the shorter growing seasons in the northern hemisphere . . . trend has historically been countered by expansion of croplands, but further expansion threatens the ecologic balance . . .

As he finished reading, the message indicator chimed. He frowned. The chime indicated that the message was from Hlaansk and urgent. He touched the screen panel once more, and the first sheet of the message appeared in the surface of the desk.

From: Minister of Science
          Unity of Caelaarn

To: Maertyn S'Eidolon
          Assistant Minister [Acting]
          Environment Research Subministry

Subject: Funds Redirection

In the absence of Assistant Minister Cennen, you are charged with the
preliminary draft of recommended redirection of all unallocated and
undisbursed funds under the operative control of the subministry. The
draft recommendations are due to me no later than the third of Tenmonth. Attached are the accounts and subaccounts currently showing
those funds as of yet unspent or unallocated. Please correct the figures
to reflect funds allocated since preparation of this document, and then
submit planned disbursements and recommended reallocations.

The screen indicator showed more than a hundred pages of supple-
mental documents. Those would have to wait until later that day, perhaps until evening, although that would require him to remain at the
Ministry. He wasn't about to study figures with people and messages
coming and going, especially not with the political implications behind
every account.

He'd barely leaned back in the desk chair when Marcent spoke, his
words projected from his console outside the office. "Assistant Comptroller Amirella, sir."

Maertyn couldn't say that he was surprised. Amirella hadn't stopped
by the subministry to see him the week before just on a whim, and he'd
been wondering just how long before he heard from her again.

"Have her come in." He stood and moved away from the desk toward
the conference table. With Amirella, sitting behind the desk would only
make matters harder.

The dark-haired accountant stepped into the office. She closed the
door herself.

"It's early for lunch," he offered with a smile, gesturing toward the
small conference table, where he seated himself at the same time as she
did.

"Two lunches in a week? Come now, Maertyn." She shifted her weight and well-formed curves in the chair, then smiled. "Sorry. Habit. That doesn't work with you. It never has."

Maertyn laughed softly. "And you know that, but still did it to make a point, and, yes, you are attractive, and, as always . . . no." He paused for just an instant. "Are you here in your official capacity as a senior comptroller?"

"Why else? You've been away for over a year. Times have changed."

"Don't they always?"

"The draft excess funds reallocations are due in a little more than a week."

"I've been informed that they'll be my responsibility. You knew, didn't you?"

"No one told me, but it had to be that way."

"Why? Because Josef wouldn't reallocate the way Hlaansk wants? What difference does that make? The minister always has the final say." Maertyn had a good general idea why, but he wanted to see what Amirella would tell him.

"Josef is very close to Minister Tauzn. Josef really wanted to work in Protective Services, but Tauzn persuaded him to accept the research position here."

"I'd heard that Josef wanted to head up Military Research, or at least be the principal deputy assistant minister."

Amirella nodded. "D'Onfrio stalled matters so that the other positions were filled first, and then had Hlaansk offer Josef the Environment Research Subministry, where he could do less damage."

Not for the first time, Maertyn considered that Amirella knew far too much to be just an assistant comptroller. "From Hlaansk's point of view, then, it almost doesn't matter what I do, so long as I don't reallocate in the way Josef did?"

"The minister appointed you because if any deputy assistant minister would have a different view from Minister Josef, it would be you."

"Exactly what's his problem?"

"It's not his, Maertyn. He's making it yours. If anything happens to you, the minister will either have to make the reallocations himself or appoint Olason Tedor. Olason's the next senior deputy assistant minister. He's also married to Tauzn's youngest niece."

"Olason's been here longer, much longer."

"You're a lord, remember. The charter gives lords seniority—"

"That hasn't been invoked in decades."

"It's never been repealed."

"So I make the draft reallocations, presumably to every other sub-ministry but Military Research . . ."

"It is called Protective Services Research, Maertyn."

". . . and Minister Tauzn arranges an accident for me, and then Hlaansk and the EA reaffirm what I do, and block Tauzn to some degree, and Maarlyna has to return to Caelaarn for my state funeral. I can't say that I find that terribly appealing."

"You're less likely to have an accident than anyone else. People look harder when things happen to lords, especially after they've happened to other officials."

Maertyn didn't find her words reassuring in the slightest, particularly the mention of accidents to other officials. Still . . . he smiled. "This will bear some thought. It may take me a while to address the draft redirection of funds." He paused, then mused, "Protective Services Research . . . I've never seen their expense ledgers."

"You wouldn't have. Even Josef hasn't. He only sees the environmental research for Protective Services. The other Protective Services research is eyes only for the Executive Administrator, the Minister of Science, and the Minister of Protective Services. Three months ago, the Unity's comptroller inspector had a fatal vehicle crash. That was right after he began looking into the use of funds by the Minister of Protective Services . . ."

Maertyn thought of Ashauer. "Which ministries are behind the EA, and which support Tauzn?"

A faint smile crossed Amirella's lips. "You always have a surprise or two, Maertyn."

He waited.

"No one knows. It's getting too dangerous to express opinions publicly. The Assistant Minister for Weapons Improvement suffered a fatal allergenic reaction to shellfish two weeks ago, and an assistant minister in Finance will be hospitalized for months while they regrow most of his lower body."

"Why does Tauzn think he needs better security weapons? The reports I've seen don't show that much of an advance of the ice. Or is it the shorter growing season and the lost of high- and low-latitude fertile land? Things can't have gotten that bad in a year."

"There's an election coming up in a year. Tauzn is likely to be the candidate to succeed the EA." She paused. "You tell me how bad things will be in ten years. Crop yields are falling, and biofoods production is more expensive. The numbers of those resettled from the ice-lands keep growing, and they're less and less happy with the Unity. Tauzn is trying to strengthen Protective Services, especially the Gaerda, to deal with civic unrest. Saenblaed is always a problem, and there are already demonstrations on the out-continents."

"Galawon and Occidenta? I do hope something doesn't happen to dear Josef."

"That kind of sarcasm doesn't become you . . ." Amirella broke off. "You were serious, weren't you?"

"Indeed. With what you've described, if anything did happen, I'd likely be acting assistant minister for far longer than I'd prefer. I might never get to finish my research project."

"Is it a real research project?"

What she was asking was whether it was merely an excuse for him to help Maarlyna recover. "Actually, it is."

"That does make matters more interesting. It might make your position stronger."

"With Tauzn, perhaps, or Hlaansk, but not necessarily with others."

"I'm confident you can deal with the others, Maertyn." She eased her chair back, as if preparing to rise and depart.

"Does the Comptroller of the Ministry of Science have any recommendations for reallocations for this subministry?"

"Comptrollers are only interested in making sure that proper procedures are followed, Maertyn." Amirella stood.

So did Maertyn. "It was good to see you again."

"It was good to be here." There was the slightest emphasis on the word "here," and her eyes flicked in the direction of Marcent.

Maertyn smiled. "You do deliver messages well, dear lady."

"Only one of my many talents, Maertyn."

After the door closed behind her, he walked to the window and looked out at the gray sky that threatened snow. Ashauer and the EA certainly opposed any more funding or power—or even anything that Maertyn might discover about the canal—going to Tauzn . . . or his tacit minions. So did whoever Amirella was acting for, as did Hlaansk.

Even so, Maertyn didn't see that being a lord or even an acting assistant minister was likely to dissuade Tauzn and the Gaerda if he gave any indication of blocking their access to anything they wanted.

"Assistant Minister Tidok, sir."

Tidok Bienn, physician and Assistant Minister for Medical Research, was close to the last person in the Ministry that Maertyn wanted to see, especially at the moment. He walked over and stood behind the desk that was his only temporarily. "Have him come in."

The angular physician stepped into the office. Behind him, Marcent closed the door.

"What can I do for you, Tidok?" With a smile, Maertyn gestured toward the chairs in front of the desk and seated himself.

The angular physician laughed ironically as he took the center chair. "Not much of anything. I just stopped by to pay a friendly visit. In your position, there's not too much you can do, even if you were inclined to do so. I'm sure you know how I feel. It's too bad that we're wasting such vast sums on environmental research, especially on climate. For all the rhetoric, there's no such thing as an anthropocentric impact on global climate. It's all a scientific illusion."

"Those are rather strong words. What about all the geologic evidence . . . the ice core samples . . . the seabed samples . . . the measured drop in heat-retaining atmospheric gases?"

Tidok's gesture waved away Maertyn's words. "Most of it's mere coincidence or largely irrelevant. Fluctuations in methane and CO_2 have been around as long as there's been a biosphere on Earth. Human beings just don't have the ability to make the kind of impact all the theoreticians postulate. The ancients didn't create global warming, and the reactions of later cultures didn't create the cycles of global cooling and warming. We just have to adapt to it."

"You seem to be ignoring a fair amount of data . . ."

"It's all modeled data based on too few verified historical points. You know as well as I do that you can manipulate any data set to get the results or trends that you want." Tidok smiled more broadly. "The midcontinent canal's a bit of a fraud, too. You and I both know that it's not what's been claimed for it."

"How so?" asked Maertyn smoothly, wondering exactly where Tidok was headed. "The canal exists. It's been examined. It's been measured. How can that be a fraud?"

"Oh . . . I'm not denying the canal's existence. I'm just highly skeptical of the idea that it contains anything unusual or valuable. It's clearly an artifact, but an anomalous one. Call it the great accident of the ancients. They did something. It didn't turn out the way they expected, and the backlash hardened a massive but primitive waterway into the canal. After all, what civilization, what true civilization, would expend the resources for a highway for water-borne vessels? Totally anachronistic. Anachronisms don't happen, not in high-tech cultures. Therefore, it was an accident, nothing more, that people have been reading more into for eons." Tidok laughed.

"I find a two-thousand-kay-long accident extraordinarily unlikely," Maertyn replied.

"Not any more unlikely than human manipulation of climate, certainly. Or the idea that human intelligence just evolved from microorganisms or the like."

"A physician who recognizes genetic coding and who has reviewed his share of recoding, but who denies evolution?"

"Genetic codes of great complexity require a coder. They don't happen by chance. Manipulating and using those codes merely recognizes the codes."

Maertyn attempted a thoughtful nod.

"Some manipulation, of course, verges on the attempted creation of life," Tidok continued. "There are ancient legends about the dangers of that. We recognize the validity of what lies behind those legends, of course, in the legal structure. That is why the use of cloning is so restricted and why full-body cloning cannot be used for medical purposes, or for any purposes without the consent of both the Council and the Judiciary. But then, I'm certain you're most aware of the legalities there."

"That's a very interesting point."

"I thought you might find it so."

Maertyn managed a laugh. "I'm certain you didn't trek over here merely to lecture me on the validity of ancient legends and their application to current law. What did you have in mind?" *What indeed?*

"Actually, I had forgotten that Josef was on an extended tour of various universities. I was almost here when I recalled that. So I thought I'd say hello. I'd come to discuss the matter of transferring any funds that might be left in the Environment Research budget at the end of the year to Medical Research. Such decisions do have to be made before long."

"You obviously know where there might be such funds . . ." Maertyn raised his eyebrows.

"Climate research is one area. With the closure of the northern ice laboratory, it would appear unlikely that all those funds would be spent."

"No, but I wouldn't be surprised if Josef had plans for transferring the funds elsewhere within the subministry."

"That is true. But the preliminary transfer recommendations are due this coming threeday. They're not binding, needless to say, but . . ." Tidok shrugged.

Maertyn understood fully. If he, as acting assistant minister, recommended a transfer of some of those "excess" funds to Medical Research, Josef would have to provide a detailed rationale for any subsequent change and argue to Minister Hlaansk for a change in reallocation already proposed by his own subministry because the latter change was a better use of funding. Given some of Josef's priorities and his known association with Tauzn, doing so publicly would definitely create some difficulties.

"I haven't looked into it, I'd have to say. I've just received the current accounts with potential unspent funds. Those are on my schedule, but I will consider your advice when we go over accounts redirection then."

Tidok rose. "I couldn't ask for more. Thank you, and do give my best to your wife."

"I will." Maertyn held the smile until the door closed behind Tidok.

Had Hlaansk any part in Tidok's scheme? Maertyn shook his head. Hlaansk would have known what Tidok wanted. There wasn't any reason for the Minister of Science to say anything to Tidok. If Maertyn wanted to thwart both Tauzn and Josef, he well might have to consider reallocating funds to Medical Research, if only to keep some funds from falling under Tauzn's control, however indirectly.

Was there some aspect of Medical Research that Maertyn could support that went against Tidok's predilections? Anything at all?

Maertyn hated the thought of providing Tidok with even the smallest increase in funding. More than anything, he needed to read what Hlaansk had sent him on the reallocation earlier that day, but, what with one thing and another, he hadn't gotten to it. He sat down at the desk.

He might as well start, interruptions or no interruptions.

Once he returned home that evening, he needed to write Maarlyna again. The fact that there was no direct comm access to the station had been fine when the two of them had been there together, but with her there alone, he worried about her. A hundred years earlier, it wouldn't have been a problem, because broadcast radios had still been common, but geosat frequencies were monitored and controlled . . . and comparatively scarce, by Unity design.

He took a slow deep breath and began to read through the accounts projected on the desk screen.

23

❖   ❖   ❖

O nce she searched and buried the dead RF "inspectors," Rhyana
came up with a combination of netting and fabric that approximated the color of the canal stone and moved the RF wheeler so
that it was next to the east side of the station. She reported to Eltyn
what she had found on the bodies and in the wheeler. None of it was
unique or even particularly useful, except for the additional stunners
and their charge packs.

A high-flying minidrone would show the apparent longer length of
the station, but Eltyn doubted that the RF minions of The Twenty had
immediate access to the image archives of MetCom for a comparison.
That assumed the archives still existed. Since there was no one sending
on broadcomm at all, there was a high probability that the MetCom records were currently inaccessible, if they hadn't been destroyed as a result
of The Twenty's power grab.

While Rhyana watched the trussed-up RF "inspector" and set up one
of the station stunners to be recharged, both Eltyn and Faelyna went back
to work on their efforts to discern the station's shadow-comm structure
and protocols.

Eltyn couldn't help but occasionally check the local system monitors for the approach of other agents of The Twenty, but neither he nor
the system detected anything. MetCom remained silent, as did the emer-

gency freqs. Had the RF forces or The Twenty shifted to another comm structure? How would he know?

He kept working on solidifying the linkages in his conglomeration of makeshift controls.

"Sir?" Rhyana's voice broke into Eltyn's concentration as he was slipping the last microsections of his makeshift control circuit.

"Yes?"

"The riffie is coming to."

Riffie? he pulsed to Faelyna. *Heard that before?*

Null. Sounds like the nonlinkers don't think much of the RF, either.

You want me to interrogate?

Yes^2! The fewer interruptions the better.

Eltyn turned. "I'll be right there."

Right there turned out to be a good quarter hour later, because easing the microsections into place took longer than he'd thought. His sigh of relief died away as he realized that he'd spent hours cobbling together something that might not work—because he hadn't had the right components.

He stood and walked over to the side of the main level where the captive sat secured to a chair. Rhyana sat several yards back, a stunner aimed at the man, whose pale cream skin and washed-out gray eyes suggested a northern heritage.

"Who sent you?" asked Eltyn conversationally.

"I don't have to answer you. You're a murderer."

"I have to dispute that. Killing in self-defense isn't murder."

"Killing servants of the Ruche who are only carrying out their duties is murder. You are murderers."

"You were observed destroying or greatly diminishing the mental capacities of everyone at the logistics center in Apialor. That's murder, whether their bodies survive or not. Intelligent entities have the right to protect their existence."

"Anyone who opposes the Ruche threatens the health and welfare of all citizens. They need to be restrained and controlled."

"That's an old, old argument, and it was an excuse for tyranny when it was first used. The logic behind it hasn't improved with age."

"You can't get away with this sort of individualistic and self-centered behavior."

"We already have," pointed out Rhyana.

"Only for the moment. The Ruche will return you to the Meld."

The Meld? Eltyn pulsed Faelyna.

Another dubious[4] attempt at shared consciousness?

Eltyn continued. "Melding minds hasn't ever worked in the past."

"The Meld is different. Dissidence is suppressed prior to juncture. All share the common goals and values of the Ruche."

"What about common communications?" asked Eltyn. "Is it brain-range concentration limited?"

The would-be inspector looked blankly at the scientist.

"Do you know what you're thinking when you're apart?"

"There is no need of that. We all share the values of the Ruche."

"Do you report those thoughts on minicomms all the time?" asked Eltyn. None of those attacking the station had carried one. "Or didn't they trust you with one?"

"Private comms lead to private thoughts," asserted the inspector. "Unsupervised private thoughts can lead to error."

"You can't tell me that no one has a comm."

"Those of The Twenty do; they have been found worthy and beyond reproach. So have some of the regionals."

Eltyn nodded. That meant that the three of them had a little more time, since the two inspectors who escaped would have to either make their way to Apialor or be discovered or rescued. None of those alternatives would be quick. *They're maintaining control by restricting communications.*

Ironic[4] . . . keeping everyone isolated by declaring they all share the same values, and therefore need no private comm channels. Creates the impression that private comms equate to subversiveness. [disgust]

Immediately after they've subverted The Fifty.

Subverted? More like executed. Let me know if you discover anything of interest.

Unlikely[5]. Eltyn returned his full concentration to the captive. "How many of you were sent to the south side of the canal?"

The captive said nothing.

"Refocus the stunner to a narrow beam, as tight as possible," Eltyn said to Rhyana.

Her brows knit, but she made the adjustments.

"Aim it at his crotch."

"You can't do that," protested the riffie.

"Oh?" Eltyn looked to Rhyana.

"Twenty. That's the optimal number."

"Symbolism yet." Eltyn refrained from snorting. "How many stations or facilities were on your list to be visited?"

"All of those on the south side." After a glance at Rhyana, he added, "Seven."

"Were we the first?" Eltyn knew that was unlikely, because the desert research station was midway between Apialor and the west end of the canal.

"The second."

"What happened at the second station?"

"There was no one there. All the stores and all the water were gone. So was one vehicle. I don't know what kind. It had wide tires."

The desert researchers might just have a chance . . . for a while. They had a sand-rover, which Eltyn and Faelyna didn't. "Did you try to chase them?"

"No. We barely could reach the station. It was three kays south of the canal."

"Why were we and the research station targeted first?"

"Researchers are more likely to be dissidents."

"So you've wiped out TechOversight also?"

That question only elicited a puzzled frown.

"What other researchers have you targeted?" asked Eltyn.

"There aren't any others in the region."

"Is another twenty on the way to reinforce you?"

"I don't know."

From that point on, most of the captive's answers were less and less useful, not because the man was being obstructive. He was just uninformed. Finally, Eltyn shook his head and stepped back.

"What do you want me to do with him?" asked Rhyana.

"Keep him tied up. He could come in useful when his compatriot subversives arrive."

"We're not subversives," protested the captive. "The Fifty subverted the values of the Ruche. We seek a return to the true way of the Ruche."

If forced brain conditioning represents the true way of the Ruche, pulsed Faelyna, *we're doomed. [cynical sarcasm]*

"Suppressing intelligence at a time when creativity and new ideas are vital to survival is about as subversive as you can get." Eltyn managed to keep his voice level.

"You're the subversives. You've turned your backs on tradition."

"Gag him," Eltyn added. "We don't need to hear more of that." *Even if that's more like their techniques and views.*

It's not the same, replied Faelyna. *Citing tradition, and demanding even more rigorous adherence to it when it's failed, is what distinguishes all too many fanatics.*

"Yes, sir," replied Rhyana. "My pleasure."

"You'll all go to nihil when the Ruche becomes transcendent. You will . . ."

The riffie's words were cut off by the application of Rhyana's heavy makeshift gag.

"After all that, almost wish I'd shot him too," said the delivery woman.

Eltyn nodded. He could understand that.

"Better you get back to what you're doing, sir," suggested Rhyana. "Won't be that long before more of 'em show up."

Eltyn walked back to his work space, abruptly realizing that because he'd been interrupted, he'd never informed Faelyna. *Completed possible control circuit alternative.*

?????

He opened the link wider and let her see the schematic and his view of the assemblage.

Cumbersome . . . appears workable . . . what counts. Interrogative alternative for power modulator? Nanosecond level . . . current equipment works on millisecond intervals. She pulsed more details.

I'll need to see . . .

[laugh] Be my guest.

Eltyn turned and walked up the ramp. Would the mods she needed be easier than what he'd had to do for the control circuitry work-around? He doubted it.

24

❈   ❈   ❈

16 Siebmonat 3123, Vaniran Hegemony

Two days after the abortive attack on the station, Duhyle was walking up the ramp into the main area of the station. There the two junior officers and Helkyria were standing and talking. Duhyle froze and concentrated on the interchange.

"... showed you the images. Most of the entire world thinks the government killed three hundred peaceful protesters ..."

"They were only stunned, and the First Speaker had vids out in less than two hours showing the protesters awake and unharmed," returned Symra.

"It didn't matter. The Aesyr had the first images, and they even claimed that the Vanir government—that was the way they phrased it— would claim no one was hurt and would show false images of uninjured protesters." Captain Valakyr's words were bitter. "There were ten deaths. Those didn't help."

"In any government based on open representation, the majority wants to believe the worst about those in power," observed Helkyria. "The Aesyr are using that to their benefit."

"What will they do next?" asked Symra.

"They want something here at the station. They'll attack again before too long. SatCom is reporting magnetic anomalies consistent with a large submersible approaching from the west."

"Or do they just want to attack to prove that the government is hiding something here and will kill innocent protesters to keep whatever it is secret?" asked Symra.

"Does it matter?" replied Helkyria.

"Magnetic anomalies, I take it, are not proof?" asked Valakyr dryly.

"Not until attackers emerge and overrun us," replied Helkyria. "Or until we destroy and repulse them, in which case we overreacted in dealing with misguided Aesyr idealists." She turned to the subcaptain. "How many Aesyr are likely to be able to attack from the south?"

"We've been able to catch indications of comm activity, even with all their variable freq shifts. I can only guess, but no more than half a company."

Helkyria nodded. "That means they aren't likely to mount a diversionary attack prior to whatever they intend with the submersible. I've checked with Colonel-Marshal Dorja. With all the riots, they can't spare another company at the moment."

Not for a research installation, thought Duhyle.

"The only reason we're still here is that they can't spare the airships to come reclaim us for duty elsewhere," suggested Valakyr. "She's also afraid the Aesyr would attack them."

"They can make a scramjet available for a quick attack pass—nonlethal, of course," added Helkyria.

"It might help."

"One way or another, it will," replied Helkyria dryly. "For now, I'll use the equipment here to monitor world comms and developments, and keep you posted."

What about your work?" asked Valakyr.

"What I'm working on might prove helpful in time, but I'm not close enough to having anything useful that the next few hours of work will change anything."

Left unspoken was the point that unless they repulsed the putative Aesyr attack, she wouldn't likely be around to continue that research.

The two junior officers nodded. "Yes, ser. We'll let you know if we see any sign of attackers." They turned and left the station.

Only then did Duhyle make his way up to the main level.

"You heard the conversation," Helkyria said. "What do you think?"

"If you can't use the research to repel an attack in the next few hours, it should wait."

"A few days might be enough. I'm very close, but . . ." She shook her head.

"The control system?"

"I think so."

"Can I do anything?" Duhyle asked.

"Not right now."

"Then I'll see where else I can aid."

A faint tinge of deep blue appeared momentarily at the tips of Helkyria's short-cut hair, then vanished. "I'd appreciate that." She turned and headed up toward her work spaces.

Duhyle went to find Symra.

Two hours later, he was standing outside the canal-side door from the station, holding the looper he'd cadged from Valakyr. The close-range stunner that he'd gotten from Symra remained in its holster at his waist.

Two-thirds of the security troopers crouched behind the canal wall or behind sandbags stacked east of the station running from the wall southward. They waited for the Aesyr disembarking from the submersible that had moored almost a kay to the east of the station, out of range of the weapons carried by the security troops.

From that distance, Duhyle saw only glimpses of movement. Barely flickering forms of the Aesyr troops scrambled up the net ladders from the submersible and then re-formed on the flat stone of the top of the canal. He didn't even think about retreating to the station. The security troopers looked to need any help they could get, and the station was anything but a refuge. Either way, retreat would have been totally pointless.

Before long, the Aesyr began to move forward. Given the blend-in uniforms, close to the same as those worn by the security troopers, the impression was that the stone of the canal rippled westward toward the station. As the Aesyr advanced, the majority of security troops waiting behind the raised canal wall scurried into new positions behind the sandbags. Duhyle stepped back, so that the door opened. He stood in the opening, partly protected by the indestructible stone that formed the doorway.

The rippling of the stone was still half a kay from the sandbags when the high-pitched whining roar of a scramjet caught Duhyle's attention. He looked to the north, then back to the submersible. Although he couldn't see the entire vessel, a silvery streak flared from what he thought was the conning tower. In instants, the silver streak merged with the point that had to be the scramjet—and a brief flare of energy brightened the already bright northern sky. Then the streak seemed to return to the submersible, dwindling to a black point as it touched a square antenna protruding from the conning tower. The sky was empty, as if the scramjet had never been.

Duhyle had never seen a weapon like that streak. Nor had he read about anything or any technical development that would have foreshadowed it. It hadn't been a laser, because it had taken measurable time to reach the scramjet, but it hadn't been a missile either, not with the return pulse.

The dull rumble of the explosion followed, and then the Aesyr began to move more quickly toward the security troopers, fast enough that the stone itself seemed to sprint toward the sandbags. Duhyle felt that, again, the attackers outnumbered the security troopers, likely by two to one. From the blend-ins alone, the attackers were far better equipped than the demonstrators of the earlier attack. As the Aesyr neared the sandbags, where the security troopers remained, without firing, the flickering momentary images of the Aesyr looked like troopers in equipment and bearing. Like the demonstrators, they were large physical specimens, although Duhyle couldn't distinguish gender because of the blurring effect of the blend-ins.

Then, abruptly, with the Aesyr less than thirty yards away, all the security troopers opened fire, raking the attackers with interlaced stun bolts.

From the rear of the attacking force arched several containers.

Duhyle immediately closed his eyes and raised his forearm in front of his face—just before the vision-searing flash-blinders exploded. Even with his vision blocked and shielded, Duhyle felt his eyes watering.

After several moments, Duhyle blinked and opened his eyes.

Amazingly, the security troopers kept raking the lines of the attackers. Had they been wearing shield lenses? Or had they been trained to fire blindly, as directed by Valakyr? All officers had altered irises and retinas, one of the reasons for the silvery sheen and flecks to their eyes. Techs and troopers didn't.

Suddenly, as one, all the security troopers dropped behind the sandbag barrier.

Why? wondered Duhyle, but only for an instant before he stepped completely into the station and touched the stone beside the opening, willing it to close. His hands went to cover his ears.

He almost made it before the sonic nerve-ruptor slammed him to the floor. He lay shuddering for several moments, despite the protection afforded by the station. When he could move again, perhaps a minute later, he slowly climbed to his feet. He did wait for another two minutes before touching the stone to open the entrance.

He stepped back out into the late morning and surveyed the canal. His eyes still watered, but he could see the submersible was pulling away from the canal wall at high speed and submerging. Just before the conning tower looked to disappear beneath the gray-blue waters of the canal, a streak of brilliant green struck, and an enormous gout of water geysered skyward. Almost immediately, a second explosion followed the first.

The force of the explosions rocked Duhyle back and forth on his boots. He had to reach out and steady himself on the stone of the station wall.

For the next ten minutes, the security troopers remained behind the wall of sandbags, occasionally discharging stunners whenever there was a sign of movement. Then, when all movement among the fallen Aesyr had ceased, a squad of troopers moved out from the sandbags.

Still holding the looper at the ready, Duhyle moved forward. He glanced at the canal where the waves from the explosions had yet to fully subside, and then back at the stone expanse beyond the sandbags. The only movements were those of the security squad. By the time Duhyle reached the wall of sandbags, the security troopers had reached the rear of the bodies of the fallen Aesyr. How many were merely stunned, and how many were dead?

As Duhyle stood back of the sandbags, something flickered at the edge of his vision. He turned and loosed the looper. A projectile whined past him—only one. As the restraint loops tightened around a kneeling figure in blend-ins, a stun bolt slammed into the Aesyr, and he pitched forward onto the stone.

A security trooper hurried up toward Duhyle. "Are you all right?"

"I'm fine."

"He must have been lying low, pretending to be stunned, looking for a high-tech or an officer," she continued.

Symra joined the two of them, and the three moved toward the fallen attacker, less than thirty yards away.

The trooper knelt and turned the bearded man, still twitching, on his back. "Another big one. Big and stupid."

"Not . . . stupid . . ." gasped the man. "The Hammer will not fail the Aesyr . . ." The attacker's eyes glazed over, and he slumped.

"The Hammer?" asked Symra, looking to the tech.

Duhyle shrugged. "You'd have to ask the commander. I've never heard of it."

"After we make sure everything here is secure . . ."

"Are most of them dead?" asked Duhyle.

"So far. The nervous system isn't designed for multiple jolts, but one or two isn't enough to stop someone with the size of most of them, not when they're in berserker mode." Symra shrugged. "I can't say I have much sympathy for them. All the weapons they were carrying are lethal. Projectile guns, battle-axes for close-in, even razor knives."

Duhyle looked across the dead and fallen, possibly two hundred bodies, and nodded slowly. He'd heard that part of the Aesyr belief was that because chaos or the universe always triumphed, all that mattered was the struggle. The bodies suggested they really believed that.

Valakyr appeared behind them. "Once we have a count, we'll report to the commander." The captain moved away.

Duhyle made his way back to the station. He waited by the canal-side door so that he could accompany the two officers when they reported to Helkyria. Absently, he wondered exactly what had so preoccupied her that she had not come to see the results of the skirmish—since Valakyr and Symra had to have sent a quick report.

He debated asking by using private link, then decided against it.

He waited half an hour, studying the canal, the sky, and the ocean to the west. He saw nothing unexpected—and no aircraft or watercraft at all. Finally, the two junior officers appeared, and he followed them inside.

Helkyria rose from where she was sitting before the comm console and turned, waiting.

"There are twenty-three survivors among the Aesyr. They're all restrained," announced Captain Valakyr. "The other hundred eighty-one are dead. I regret the casualties. They won't make matters easier for the government or the First Speaker."

"When you're under attack, the enemies' casualties are secondary," replied Helkyria. "Particularly now."

"One of the fatalities claimed before he died that something called the Hammer would not fail the Aesyr," interjected Symra. "Do you know what he meant, Commander?"

Helkyria stiffened. "It is—or was reputed to be—a weapon based on Thora's Theorem."

"Ah . . . that's not exactly revealing to those of us without a technical background, ser," suggested Symra, ignoring the hard look from Valakyr.

"Freyja Thora was trained as a theoretical physicist, and also as an engineer. Her theorem states that, since all matter was once one, prior to universal inflation, with proper manipulation energy can be directed anywhere and then return, compressed and compacted and able to strike again, like a hammer. She left the Institute of Vestalte some ten years ago when the Bursar for Procurement denied her requests for equipment on the grounds that weapons development was against the charter of the Institute. Reputedly, she's been working at the Collegium of Asgard."

"That sounds very much like something for nothing, or perpetual motion, or any number of other frauds," opined Subcaptain Symra.

"It's not a fraud, and it's definitely not something for nothing."

"Ah . . ." Duhyle offered, gently, before continuing. "There was a silver pulse from the submersible. It destroyed the scramjet and then returned to the submersible. When it did, it dwindled to a black point. Whether it was that or another weapon, we likely won't be able to tell, since SatCom took it out. The fragments of the submersible are at the bottom of the canal, more than a kay down."

For a moment, there was silence.

"I was about to say," Helkyria replied, "that if you could build such a weapon, you'd end up drawing upon and possibly rending the very dark matter/energy that holds the universe together. Apparently, the Aesyr are ignoring such concerns. If such uses continue, before long the entire universe could be spiraling down like a giant snake into the icy entropy of Niflheim . . ."

"Not a world snake, then, but a universe snake?" suggested Duhyle dryly.

Helkyria's sidelong glance was cold enough to freeze him into not wanting to make any more comments, not in public.

"Did you see what Duhyle saw?" asked Helkyria.

Valakyr shook her head. "No, ser."

"I saw the silver pulse and the destruction of the scramjet," replied Symra, "but I was watching the Aesyr attackers after that."

"There was an anomalous energy pulse surrounding the release of energy that destroyed the aircraft," said Helkyria. "That would suggest that Thora was correct . . . and that the Aesyr have weaponized the theorem."

"So that was why they used the submersible? They needed the space for the equipment?" asked Symra.

"I'd judge so. The weapon on the submersible may have been a prototype."

"Sweet father Njord . . ." muttered Valakyr.

"Oh . . . and one other matter," said Helkyria. "We don't have to worry about public opinion quite as much anymore. Asgard has declared its secession from the World Republic and issued a statement of independence."

Duhyle studied her face before asking, "What else?"

"What amounted to a suicide force attacked the Institute at Vestalte, and several other key installations have suffered damage."

"How much damage?" Valakyr's words were intense.

"They were repulsed and largely destroyed, but the weapons laboratories at Security's research center were nearly totally leveled." A wry smile followed. "That might not matter. Most conflicts are fought and won—or lost—by weapons already developed or produced."

She didn't state the obvious—that the Hammer was clearly already developed.

"What would you like from us, ser?" asked Valakyr.

"The same as before. Keep the station secure so that I can continue working. What may be here is likely to be more important than we thought."

"Because of . . . this Hammer?" Symra's words were strained.

"Exactly." Helkyria paused, then said, "If there's not anything else . . . ?"

"No, ser."

Duhyle stepped back to see if Helkyria would need anything else after the officers departed.

Once the two left the station, she looked to Duhyle. "I'll need some equipment and components from the storeroom . . . along with your assistance."

Duhyle nodded. He'd thought so.

25

❖   ❖   ❖

28 Ninemonth 1351, Unity of Caelaarn

Maertyn glanced up from the desk screen and out into the darkness beyond the Ministry, absently massaging his forehead with his left hand. He'd spent part of the twenty-sixth and a good portion of the twenty-seventh just going through the reallocation documentation. He was a scientist, not a bureaucrat, and the welter of weasel-worded footnotes and annotations to the various budgets—just within a single subministry—was close to overwhelming.

Outside, he could see the local tube-train station, barely outlined by the backscatter of lights that projected downward. There could only be a few Ministry employees there. Most had left a good hour earlier.

"Sir . . . ?" Marcent's tentative voice projected into the assistant minister's office. "Will you be needing me any more this evening? You didn't say, and it is past six."

"Oh, no. I'm sorry. I should have let you know earlier. I've been buried in the budget documents. By all means, leave."

"Thank you, sir. Good evening."

After a moment more, where he just closed his eyes and tried to relax tight muscles, especially in his shoulders, Maertyn forced himself to look again at the footnote to a subaccount in a submission from the Office of Water Research.

... the monitoring equipment expenditures projected for the final quarter of the budgetary year in this category have been allocated [as req. per MSci 231.b.3.a.], but may not be realized, in view of the longer than contracted lead-time in fabrication of certain key elements of the control-activation subassemblies [see MSci Procurement 1103], in which case said expenditures must be rolled over into the next budget cycle, in order to avoid the cancellation fees required by the manufacturer, as per CompDec 1103.1, and as approved by the comptroller in the specific case, because no other manufacturer possesses said manufacturing capabilities [defined in CompDec 511.A] ...

In short, reallocating the funds would cost the Ministry far more in the next budget cycle than would be saved in the present.

Macrtyn took a deep breath. He suspected that all too many of the footnotes, explanations, and annotations were less than perfectly legally sound in their assertions, but he had neither the knowledge to question most of them, nor the time to go over every suspect justification or assertion with both a procurement advocate and Amirella or one of the other comptrollers.

After reviewing the budget reallocation documents he'd finished so far and thinking about his meeting with the Assistant Minister for Medical Research, the more puzzled he'd become. Even if every questionable attempt to hang on to research funds within the Environment Research Subministry happened to be suspect, the total amount of funding that could be reallocated to other subministries—or to other ministries—was comparatively insignificant. While he didn't have access to current-year budgets of other ministries, the overall budgets for previous years were a matter of record, and the expenditures of the Ministry of Public Safety or of Transport truly dwarfed the total budget of the Ministry of Science. And within the Ministry of Science, the Subministry of Medical Research was second only to the Subministry of Protective Services Research. The smallest budget of all belonged to Environment Research.

So why had Ashauer warned him, and why had Tidok and Amirella pressured him? What else was involved?

He shook his head. Why was everyone that concerned about a few million credits? Another hour later and perhaps another score of pages later, he closed down his desk screen, no wiser than before, and stood. Another day or so and he'd be ready to formalize his recommendations for Minister Hlaansk, not that he was looking forward to that in the slightest.

He donned his jacket, this one maroon, and like the others, silver-trimmed and designed to protect him against less powerful weapons . . . and moderate vagaries of the weather. Then he left the office, maglocking it behind him, and headed down to the main level of the Ministry.

A single guard in the dark green and black of Unity Protective Services sat on a high-backed stool behind the security console and gate. Maertyn offered his hand to the scanner and the gate slid open.

"Good night, sir," offered the guard.

"And to you. I hope it's not too long or too late."

"Thank you, sir. The quiet doesn't bother me . . . sort of restful."

A cold misty rain drifted down from low clouds as Maertyn walked the hundred yards across the narrow bridge from the Ministry building out to the car park. Despite its biofoam coating, the bridge walkway was slippery, almost icy in spots, and ice coated the handrails. Maertyn reminded himself to be careful driving.

Once he was inside the vehicle, he checked the power. Despite the fact that the day had been overcast, the level was at eighty percent, considerably more than necessary for the ten minutes needed to return to his town home. He pressed the studs for the running lights and headlamps, then eased the small vehicle out of the car park and along the short drive that led to the avenue bordering the greenbelt.

When he turned onto the avenue, heading roughly southeast, he noticed a larger vehicle pull out of a turnout, as if to follow him. The larger vehicle was obviously traveling faster than Maertyn, without headlamps and showing only running lights, and was rapidly gaining on him.

Maertyn immediately increased his speed, and could sense a growing instability in the runabout, but his pursuer drew closer. He slowed, and the lorry swooshed up and thumped the bumper-bar of the runabout, rocking it slightly, although Maertyn managed to speed up just enough to mute the effect, despite his worries about spinning out on the cold-slicked road. Even the lorry skidded slightly, and dropped back momentarily.

Ahead, on the left was a loop drive that ran around a group of buildings housing various subministries of the Ministry of Infrastructure. Maertyn slowed and made the turn, wishing that the running lights hadn't signaled his intent.

The lorry followed him, but slewed slightly on the curves, and again had to slow down. Still, after he'd returned to the avenue, still headed southeast, the lorry began to gain on him, then slowed as several other vehicles passed them both coming the other way. With headlamps coming in the opposite direction, their light and sharpness hazed by the continuing chill mist-rain, the driver of the lorry maintained a distance of perhaps fifteen yards between his vehicle and the runabout.

Although Maertyn had no proof, he also had no doubt whatsoever that the driver of the larger vehicle—a small lorry-type, he could see in the rear display—wished to create a crash, most likely one fatal to Maertyn, given the lightness and smaller size of his vehicle.

Exactly what could he do? The lorry had better traction and more mass, and there was no local Gaerda station nearby. Besides which, if Ashauer happened to be correct, there was no guarantee that a Gaerda operative wasn't driving the chase lorry.

The Laarnian Martyrs' Memorial! That just might work . . . if the oncoming traffic kept his follower from attempting anything until Maertyn reached Memorial Park . . . and if he could accomplish on ice-slicked roads what he had done on a dare years before when he'd been too young to know the dangers.

He continued to drive onward, glad that it was still relatively early and that there was just enough traffic on the avenue to keep his pursuer from making another attempt. As he neared the park entrance, he eased his speed up as much as he dared before angling left into the narrower road. Ahead was the roundabout.

Behind him, the lorry accelerated, doubtless because there were no headlamps along the access road or on the roundabout.

Maertyn didn't even try to make the turn into the roundabout, but cut off all the lights and guided the runabout straight across the hand-high berm separating the pavement from the sidewalk. The runabout bounced, but settled almost straight on the narrow park pathway, and Maertyn let it decelerate, guiding it through the antique stone pillars, flanked by near-ancient golden oaks, that served as the south gateway to the memorial placed in the center of the roundabout. The runabout slid through the stone with little more than a finger's clearance on either side, and Maertyn let the vehicle slow without attempting to brake on the slick surface.

He'd decelerated to little more than a fast walk when he came to the right-hand branch pathway, which he took. Fifty yards along the path, he slowly eased his vehicle through another set of pillars and back down the eastern radial from the monument to the roundabout road. Gingerly, he added a touch of power to get the runabout over the berm. Then he continued around the memorial.

As he neared the entry road, through the darkness he could make out what had happened. The lorry had attempted the turn and slid into the trunk of one of the large golden oaks flanking the memorial entrance. The entire front had crumpled. He'd hoped for something like that.

What he hadn't expected was the larger black lorry and the men in black already dragging the damaged vehicle into the covered rear section of the larger lorry. None of them so much as looked in his direction as he eased the runabout onto the entry road back to the avenue.

He kept checking behind him, but if anyone followed, they were doing so at enough distance that he couldn't discern them. Even so, he left both running lights and headlamps off for the remaining distance to the house.

Once he had parked the runabout in the garage, he just sat there for several moments, his body not quite shivering while he thought over what had just occurred.

Ashauer had intimated that, while some people wanted him to succeed in his research, more than a few people wanted him dead or out of the picture. Maertyn still didn't understand why he posed a threat to anyone. As a deputy assistant minister, he served at the pleasure of Minister Hlaansk and the Executive Administrator of the Unity. If they wished his departure, all they had to do was ask. If he refused to resign, they could terminate his appointment immediately. His research on the canal could certainly be ended with the stroke of a pen, as Hlaansk had hinted merely by asking for a report.

Unless . . . unless there was actually some evidence somewhere that some sort of power that could be used lay within the canal structure. But . . . if that were so . . . why hadn't those who wanted him to discover how to use such a power found a way to let him know?

After a few more moments of fruitless speculation he eased himself out of the runabout, glancing at each side. Except for several golden leaves caught around the doors, he didn't see any signs that he'd actually scraped anything in his escape maneuver.

Rhesten was standing in the hallway between the kitchen and the breakfast room.

"Is there a problem with the runabout, sir?" asked Rhesten. "I noticed you entered without lights."

"I made certain that the charger was attached," replied Maertyn. "It should be fully powered in the morning."

Rhesten nodded. "I did take the liberty of preparing a light supper in case you might wish something to eat. I had thought . . . the breakfast room."

"That sounds excellent," Maertyn admitted. "I had an early lunch and didn't eat all that much."

The "light" supper consisted of cream of mushroom soup, with a touch of roast garlic, two warm biscuits, and a small green salad, accompanied by green-gold hot tea. Maertyn ate it all and had two cups of tea.

When he finished, he looked to Rhesten. "Thank you. That was excellent, and perfect on a chill evening." He paused. "Rhesten . . ."

"Sir?"

"I'll be assembling a number of items and packing them up in a crate. In the next day or so I'd like you to arrange shipping it to Lady S'Eidolon at the canal research station. It's nothing urgent. The crate can go as regular freight, but you'll need to have a second crate built around it. Some of the items for her comfort are fragile."

"Very good, sir. I'll take care of it."

Once Rhesten had departed to the kitchen, Maertyn made his way down to the lower workroom, where he had gathered and hidden various items before he and Maarlyna had left for the canal. He'd concealed them because he hadn't believed they'd be necessary at a research station. While he would retain several, such as the miniature stunner, the invisible knives, and the light-cloaking uniform he'd never returned after his stint in the Gaerda as a very junior ensign, the others would go in the crate.

That way, if a warrant should appear, they wouldn't be in the house, and they would be where Maertyn could make use of them, if necessary. The crate might or might not arrive at the canal research station, but if it did, Maertyn would feel far more relieved . . . assuming he also arrived at the station.

26

✦   ✦   ✦

30 Quad 2471 R.E.

Despite Eltyn's worries, no aircraft or other inspectors soon followed the first group of RF inspecting enforcers. Their sole captive lapsed into sullen silence. Eltyn had also been correct about the difficulties in changing the calibration settings for Faelyna's equipment. After another day's work by both of them, her modified assemblage was ready to test by late afternoon on sixday.

Once more the assembly was focused upon the upper-level north side window, except this time Eltyn was standing well back from both window and the projecting transmitter.

Ready . . . actuate! pulsed Faelyna.

The only sound was a faint hum—and the window opened, far wider than Eltyn had seen whenever he'd touched it to open it in the past. Outside, the sky was a hazy grayish yellow, an indication that another sandstorm was imminent, possibly why they had not seen another RF attempt to attack the station.

Eltyn looked back to where the window would have been on the south side of the chamber, but that space remained solidly closed.

!!!!!!!!!! Faelyna smiled broadly.

"You did it!" exclaimed Rhyana from the top of the ramp into the work space. "You didn't have to touch the window."

"Would you look down below and see if any windows or doors opened?" asked Eltyn.

"Yes, sir." Rhyana headed down the ramp.

That shouldn't happen. That command shouldn't affect any openings below.

Correct . . . but . . . sometimes . . .

Skeptic.

[rueful admission]

The delivery woman reappeared. "Tight as tight can be down below."

Faelyna arched her eyebrows. *[satisfied amusement]*

I concede. "So . . . we can now seal the entrances and windows?" Eltyn spoke aloud for Rhyana's benefit. "From one location? You won't have to cart the assembly to each place?"

"Possibly." *That comes next. Provided there's not something else locked into the shadow codes.*

????

Secondary control level beneath(?) direct physical controls for station.

Physical controls secondary to other layer?

Most probably.

Interrogative protocol? Similarity?

Structure appears the same. Greater[4] complexity.

"What are you two talking about?" demanded Rhyana.

"Whether we can learn to do more than open and close and lock windows and door openings," replied Faelyna. "We might need that if The Twenty sends a large force."

??? pulsed Eltyn.

"If they can't get in, what can they do?" Rhyana's pale brow furrowed.

"Starve us out," replied Faelyna. "They could surround us to the point where we couldn't get out, even if they couldn't get in."

"Couldn't you just make that stone window small enough to poke out a projectile rifle?" asked Rhyana.

"That's possible. We don't have unlimited ammunition or food, and they can sever the cables from the powernet."

"Best you keep working. I'll check on the riffie again." Rhyana headed back down the ramp.

Practical, observed Eltyn.

Practical[3].

Now what? he asked.

Follow Rhyana's advice.

He laughed. *Where do we start?*

Analysis of the shadow symbols on the next level linked to activation commands. If even possible.

That made what she'd accomplished so far seem like a very small step, indeed. He linked into her workplan.

Two hours later, they were just beginning to catalogue patterns/structures.

EEEE!!! The white emergency pulses were followed by a red flash, something Eltyn hadn't sensed on the CommNet before.

The Twenty have confirmed that all critical functions of the Ruche in Hururia and in regional centres have been restored. While a handful of isolated installations have not yet reaffirmed their loyalty to the Ruche, largely because of weather conditions, it is expected that full loyalty will be reported no later than threeday . . .

Full loyalty? [snort] Eltyn shook his head, although he knew Faelyna was not looking in his direction.

Full coerced loyalty was her reply. *Doubtful if true.*

Most doubtful . . . You think Chiental still resisting?

Most likely holding out. Otherwise The Twenty would be claiming great triumph . . . great triumph [irony].

Twenty may not even know location . . . in detail . . . isolated, Eltyn pointed out.

. . . but, once incorporated in the Meld [bitter sarcasm] . . . formerly isolated instances of disloyalty will result in de-Ruchement . . .

That sounds so much better than disminding or discorporation, pulsed Eltyn.

As intended.

Do you think they'll be here with enforcers by then?

Unless the sandstorms are still raging.

For the first time he found himself hoping for the mother of all sandstorms.

27

⚜   ⚜   ⚜

17 Siebmonat 3123, Vaniran Hegemony

Immediately after breakfast, Helkyria met with the junior officers and Duhyle in her work space. She stood, suggesting that the meeting would be brief.

"Ser?" offered Symra. "You requested our presence?"

"I did. You need to know where we stand. After yesterday's fighting, I doubted that it would be long before matters worsened. I'm a little surprised that it took this long. That suggests the Aesyr had a few matters to tend to . . ."

The three waited.

"The Aesyr have revealed that they have the Hammer. They're not calling it that, but it amounts to the same thing. They are threatening to use it to destroy any orbital installation that uses weapons against any Aesyr locale or force, or anything at all located in Midgard." Helkyria's smile was wintry. "At the moment, the government, or, as they say, the Vanir oppressors, controls Vaena and most of Vanira and the other continents, except Midgard, which is controlled completely by the Aesyr, and Niefl, which remains open, not that there are more than a thousand souls up there in the ice. The Aesyr are demanding the free passage of all Aesyr who desire it to Midgard. If the government delays, the Hammer will fall . . . somewhere . . ."

"They'll destroy the universe, beginning with Earth, unless we let them take over everything?" Symra's voice was not quite incredulous.

"They're not saying that. So far. I doubt that many even know of that possibility. I have conveyed my assessment of the weapon to the Magistra of Security. It did not make her particularly happy, but my assessment was not the only one reaching that conclusion."

"Can't SatCom take out the installations that have the Hammer?" asked Valakyr.

"I'm sure it could—if we had any idea which ones they were. But within a few moments of when SatCom launches anything, all those installations with Hammers will take out all satellites, and at least some of the missiles. The Aesyr immediately removed one of the smaller and less consequential relay satellites to prove their point. The Magistra of Security has pointed out that Security is limited in what can be done. Yes, she could flatten Asgard with missiles and kill almost a million of innocents. Within minutes, the world would be without communications, and the power grids would be shredded. Not to mention that the very space-time and dark matter and energy beneath what we think of as 'real matter' would begin to unravel."

"How can they even contemplate using the Hammers like that?" asked Symra.

"That's simple enough," replied Helkyria. "If you believe, as do the Aesyr, especially Thora and Baeldura, that intelligence always loses to the universe in the end, then what matters is not the result but the glory of the struggle itself, especially against great odds. Principle always trumps survival."

"That's sick . . ." muttered Valakyr.

Symra shook her head.

Duhyle understood the logic, but not the emotional acceptance of a belief that would doom hundreds of millions of people, if not life throughout the universe, to a far, far earlier death than necessary simply so that one group could control how life was conducted on one insignificant planet.

"No one has said anything," continued Helkyria, "but I have no doubts that a far larger Aesyr force is being readied, if not already being deployed, to seize the station here."

"Why now? Haven't they got what they want already?" asked Valakyr.

"The Aesyr don't have any compunctions about how they use force," said Symra caustically.

"They're not totally insane. Freyja Thora clearly understands the potential of the station and the canal, and the Aesyr would rather be in charge without having to rely on the threat of the Hammers. They'd prefer another form of power—"

"Pardon me, ser," interrupted Valakyr. "I don't see how this Thora physicist knows what you're doing, or what it implies."

"I've been reporting my findings to the Magistra of Science and the Magistra of Security. Apparently, the Deputy Magistra of Science was an Aesyr sympathizer—or is, since he is now what amounts to the director of military research for the Aesyr."

"Treachery is easier than research," offered Duhyle.

"It always has been," replied Helkyria.

The two younger officers looked at one another. They did not look at Duhyle or the scient-commander.

"How is the shadow-imaging coming?" Duhyle's voice broke the strained silence, although he knew very well how far Helkyria had gotten.

"I'll be able to lock the station doors and windows, once you help me finish building a last piece of apparatus. Otherwise, it's close to being finished."

"Then the Aesyr won't be able . . ." began Symra.

"Ah . . . will the station hold . . ." Valakyr's voice trailed off.

"We don't know either," replied Helkyria briskly. "First things first. If it comes to that, and it doubtless will, we'll have to see. There are . . . possibilities . . ."

Duhyle hoped those possibilities were very real indeed.

28

❊   ❊   ❊

1 Tenmonth 1351, Unity of Caelaarn

On the morning of the first of Tenmonth, which had dawned cold and clear, with frost over everything, Maertyn sat in the office that was not his and scrolled through all the routine communications on the desk screen. Among the memoranda was a reminder to all assistant ministers to include supporting documentation along with the reallocation recommendations. Maertyn had finished the reallocation recommendations for the Environment Research Subministry on the twenty-ninth of Ninemonth, well before they were due, but he'd already decided not to submit them until late on the second. His supporting documentation was voluminous, for reasons other than mere budget justification.

Cautious as he'd been in leaving the Ministry in the evening at times when others were also departing, and varying his times of departure, as well as taking other precautions, he continued to worry about the lorry that had attempted to run him off the avenue. Other facts tended to support his concerns. Not a single other assistant minister had suggested they eat together, nor had any old acquaintances contacted him. While part of that had been because he had contacted no one, he had run across several at a budget briefing held for all assistant ministers and a number of deputy assistant ministers at the quarterly briefing at the Executive Administrator's meeting hall. Everyone had been pleasant . . .

and no more. Amirella had also avoided him since she had stopped by his office over a week ago. That also bothered him.

Rhesten, in his quiet efficient way, had shipped off the double crate to the station. Maertyn hoped that it arrived and would be waiting for him, even as he hoped he would not need its contents. All in all, Maertyn was very much looking forward to Josef's return, and not because he had any desire to see the not-so-honorable Josef Cennen, although he hadn't been able to get a firm date on when that might be from the minister's office. And that worried him as well.

The comm chimed, automatically announcing, "Lord Ashauer calling."

"Accept."

Ashauer's image appeared on the desk screen. "Maertyn . . . I hadn't realized you'd be staying in Caelaarn so long. I just learned of that. I know it's rather short notice, but, by any chance would you be free for lunch today?"

Maertyn laughed, softly and briefly. "As it so happens, I would be."

"Then let me pick you up at a quarter past noon, and we can go to my club."

"I could easily meet you there."

"I'm driving in any case, and it's on the way."

"I bow to your common sense," replied Maertyn with a smile.

"Then it's settled." The screen blanked, to be replaced by the image of the last memorandum that Maertyn had read.

A faint chime announced that another message had arrived. Maertyn called it up. The message had been sent blind, with no originating address, and no text, only an enclosure. The enclosure was a news story. Maertyn read, and then reread, the part intended for him.

> . . . the advocate-inspector of the Ministry of Justice indicated that the Ministry is looking into what he termed "the abuse of privilege" in cases where close to full-body cloning had been employed to return victims of accident and disease to full function . . .

Maertyn deleted the message.

After reviewing his reallocation recommendations, then reading and modifying a number of replies drafted by subministry personnel in response to inquiries from the Council and the office of the Executive Administrator about various environmental research projects, Maertyn finally left his office and walked down to the main level of the Ministry and out across the bridge to wait for Ashauer—except Ashauer's official sedan was already there, driven by a stern-faced man whose bearing screamed "security."

Maertyn slipped into the sedan. "You're early."

"Better that than late," replied Ashauer with a smile.

Maertyn nodded as the driver eased the sedan back toward the avenue.

"You've been here in Caelaarn longer than anyone expected. I imagine you're looking forward to getting back to your wife and your research."

"Very much so."

"Do you have any idea when you'll be leaving?"

"Only in the general sense that it will be shortly after Josef returns."

"He's returning on the fifth, I hear."

"That wouldn't surprise me."

"I suppose you'll be planning to leave on the morning of the seventh, then."

Maertyn understood exactly what Ashauer meant. "Once his arrival is confirmed, of course. I'm certain Minister Hlaansk will want me to brief Josef."

Ashauer chuckled. "We both know that Josef may have other thoughts about such matters."

And, of course, what happened after that was another question, Maertyn knew.

"It's been a while since you've been to the club, hasn't it?"

"Quite a while." In fact, it had been years since Maertyn had been to Aesthica, and that had been as a guest of Maarlyna's uncle, Jaeryn S'Weryl, just before his untimely death.

"It hasn't changed much. Hasn't changed much since my grandfather's time, I expect, except for better power and climate control systems."

Before long, the driver turned off the avenue and up a long drive that wound through a park-like setting with tall evergreens and exposed boulders amid wild grasses that had largely turned to the autumn brown. The sedan slowed as it approached the raw stone archway that clearly dated back to the time of Ashauer's grandsire, if not before, and stopped behind another vehicle, from which two men in the blue jackets of the Transport Ministry emerged and walked toward the club entrance.

"Do all the lords in Transport belong to Aesthica?" Maertyn smiled as the driver pulled up to where a man in a singlesuit of Aesthica blue waited to open the vehicle doors.

"Both of us do, in fact."

Maertyn waited for the doorman and then stepped out of the vehicle. Once Ashauer joined him, the two lords walked through the oak door opened by another club servitor and into a long and narrow foyer, totally without decoration or adornment and walled in the same natural stone as the outside vehicle archway.

At the end of the foyer stood another figure in a pale blue jacket. "Lord Ashauer . . . Lord Maertyn," he offered before escorting them through the brass-bound double doors and down the left-hand corridor and into a small dining room with wide north windows overlooking the greenbelt and Lake Caela. Ashauer's table was at the far left end of the windows. No one was seated at the adjoining table.

"Thank you, Daulhaus." Ashauer took the seat closest to the side wall, paneled in time-darkened golden oak.

"My pleasure, sir."

The table linens were as Maertyn recalled them, of a blue so pale that it was almost but not quite white.

A server appeared, a woman in a tailored pale blue suit that neither accentuated nor concealed her femininely modest figure.

"Would you care to share a bottle of Alais, Maertyn?" asked Ashauer.

"I'd like that." Maertyn smiled politely. Alais was his favorite light white wine, but not that of Ashauer, who generally preferred heavier whites or reds.

"Then . . . the Alais."

"Yes, sir."

Ashauer barely glanced at the handwritten menu card set on the charger before him. "A cup of the trout bisque, with the Salade Selenian."

The server turned to Maertyn.

"The cream of mushroom, with the fowl risotto."

"The soups here are always excellent," offered Ashauer as the server slipped away.

"I've always found them so on the few times I've been here."

"Nothing better than a good hot soup on a chill day." Ashauer paused as the server returned with the wine and presented the bottle to him. The older lord nodded, then waited while she opened the bottle and poured the slightest bit into his goblet. He sipped the wine. "Very good."

The server filled both goblets just over the halfway point, then eased the bottle into the chill-cradle at the side of the table before again retreating.

"We're getting to the time of year when driving can be rather treacherous," said Ashauer blandly. "Are you still using that tiny runabout?"

"The sedan is in storage. I didn't see much point in getting it out for a few days, and then . . ." Maertyn shrugged.

"I can see that. Still . . . larger vehicles can have advantages. But then at times, so do smaller ones. I remember reading a report. It must have been years ago. It noted that a young lord had driven a runabout at high speed between the approach pillars of the Laarnian Martyrs' Memorial without even scraping the sides of the vehicle." Ashauer laughed. "You were always the cautiously reckless type."

"More reckless at times than cautious," admitted Maertyn.

"Someone must have remembered that. Last week someone did the same thing—the night when everything iced up. There were several accidents. Anyway, whoever it was drove through the stone pillars at the memorial, and a lorry went after the runabout and plowed into the oaks there. The lorry driver died on the spot. He must have had trouble seeing the road and followed the first driver blindly . . . until it was too late." Ashauer shook his head. "When I read the report in the news, I couldn't help thinking of you."

"I'm a little old for that sort of thing," replied Maertyn, "especially on icy roads."

"I thought as much. Oh . . . and that lorry driver, he didn't have any identification. He used to work for the Gaerda, but their personnel people said he was stipended off a month ago."

Maertyn understood. Whenever a Gaerda operative was killed in suspicious circumstances, somehow, in public notices at least, the operative was always a former employee . . . or a private contractor who was not currently under contract. "Amazing, isn't it, how many people who are killed in strange ways turn up not to have any identification, at least until much later, when everyone has forgotten the events surrounding their death?"

"Unless they're well known, and then everyone gets everything wrong, and by the time it's all straightened out, most people can't remember why they got so excited."

"The patterns are similar," Maertyn replied.

Ashauer laughed. "There are only so many patterns. It's only the young or the arrogant that think there's much new in the world . . . and they're the ones who most often repeat those patterns."

"They don't have the experience or knowledge, or they reject it. They don't understand that, unless they understand patterns and history, they'll repeat the patterns because human beings tend to react in the same ways." Maertyn took a sip of the wine. "At times, we don't have choices. If your house is burning down around you, the pattern says to run—and it's right."

Ashauer took another sip from his goblet. "This is a particularly good year for the Alais. I fear those years are numbered. The springs are later, and the falls earlier. You've seen the crop figures, I imagine."

"I have."

"So has Minister Tauzn. He's begun to make a point of them. There was almost a riot after he spoke to a group in Saenblaed. Some of the not-so-resettled marched on the local office of the Ministry of Environment."

"I hadn't heard that, but I can imagine it was . . . unpleasant."

Ashauer paused, then asked, "Do you think your research will make a difference?"

"That depends entirely on what I discover. That's why it's called research. You may think you know how it will turn out, but it may not. And there's always the chance that another researcher won't be able to replicate your results. I'd like to think it will make a difference, one way or the other, but . . ."

"Do you really believe great secrets are hidden in the canal?" Ashauer's words were direct, neither skeptical nor scornful.

"That's not the question. The fact that we can't even analyze the stone, let alone replicate it in any fashion, indicates great secrets are there. What lies beyond the stone itself, if anything, and whether we can determine that, remains to be seen."

"Interesting, the way you phrased that. 'Whether we can determine that . . .' Could anyone else? Who else might that be?"

"Ashauer . . . civilizations rise, and they fall. The canal appears to have been created by human beings. If we fail, and civilization again rises . . . someone else will doubtless try."

"You don't sound optimistic about our future. Some even might say that's not a good attitude for an assistant minister."

"Tauzn, for example?"

"The Minister of Protective Services does believe that all problems can be resolved by application of a relentlessly positive attitude."

"And by removal of all those without such an attitude?"

"Maertyn . . . I'm certain that the current Executive Administrator would scarcely countenance the implementation of such an approach by any of his ministers."

"I appreciate that, and it's clear that you do as well." What was also clear was that Ashauer was implying that Tauzn would be seeking election as the successor to D'Onfrio, and that more than political views would change.

"Of course, any positive results from your work could not but help influence the course of other events."

"Of course." In short, the EA needed every positive development he could find to derail Tauzn's bid to succeed him, and Tauzn really didn't want such developments, or at least not until he was the EA. Maertyn took a larger swallow of the wine. It suddenly tasted bitter, and he set the goblet back down on the pale blue of the table linen as the server neared.

"You always did like cream of mushroom. So did Maarlyna. Jaelora reminded me of that the other day." Ashauer smiled. "You've been very cautious. I imagine Maarlyna still does enjoy cream of mushroom."

"Of course." Maertyn smiled in return.

29

❀ ❀ ❀

Sandstorms raged all day on sevenday and through the night, but showed signs of subsiding on eightday. For the fact that the storm had lasted that long, and carried enough sand to totally cover the RF wheeler, Eltyn was grateful. For the fact that neither he nor Faelyna made any progress beyond the simple commands to open, close, or lock the openings in the station stone he was far less grateful. He was also relieved that Rhyana continued to deal with the riffie captive, although the man refused to eat and would only drink water.

That was the riffie's problem, Eltyn told himself, especially since he had no doubts that once the storms died away it wouldn't be that long before the next attack. In the meantime, Eltyn and Faelyna sat, side by side, in her work space, where the projector was trained on the window, and where they could both physically watch the screen that projected and tracked shadow images.

Faelyna had been able to capture the shadow images of the direct commands that floated "somewhere" in or beyond the stone, almost like a list, but there was no effect if she touched the image on her screen or if she projected a point of shadow at one of the symbolic lines. The door or window only opened or closed or locked if the correct symbols were replicated and projected into the stone near an aperture. Which aperture opened or closed depended on the second symbol. When any action occurred, another set of symbols appeared, a set that looked totally unlike the first set. While the first set appeared white, as did Faelyna's commands, the second appeared "black."

Interrogative depth of projection? inquired Eltyn.

Depth? It's not relevant. Not in the dimensions into which we're projecting.

Multidimensional multiverse? Disproven by Sancrataz's Theorem.

[snort] The stone of the wall measures less than a yard in thickness. From the energy used to project and return, it's more like a kay. Is the stone impossibly dense . . . or is the distance transdimensional? Or . . . ???

What about energy resistant?

Possible, but improbable, given the lack of subsidiary energy scattering or heat buildup.

Eltyn lowered his eyes from the screen, closed them, and massaged his forehead. *Treat as a differential?*

The door commands/language as a differential of the overall command structure?

Eltyn shrugged. *Or an integral. Something like that. Some linkage necessary.*

Linguistics as a calculustic structure?

Structurally deterministic is another possibility, he offered.

?????

Interrogative linkage trace from specific command . . . shadow under/ overstructure?

Faelyna opened her virtie-screen to him.

Eltyn studied it, then compared it to the real-time screen before him. Finally, he replied, *Color symbolism is culture-centric, but in most cultures, white and black are opposites, if linked.*

Some sort of inversion?

That's a guess^2.

More like guess^5! she replied. *Linguistic/symbolic inversion? How?*

Program the system to invert physical symbols?

Then compare?

Attempt worthwhile for reaction, suggested Eltyn.

Attempting [wry humor].

Eltyn shifted his attention to the images outside the station, where the last traces of the sandstorm were beginning to fade away.

After close to two hours of work, Faelyna offered an "inverted" command.

No reaction at all appeared on the real-time scanning screen.

Change color of command to black? Eltyn suggested.

Attempted already . . . haven't discovered operatives for color change within stone.

Interrogative change of energy levels? Harmonics? Overtones?

Would require additional modifications to projector.

Eltyn considered the possibilities, wondering whether varying the projected power levels of the signal would have any effect at all. He knew he was missing something . . .

FLASH! Urgent! Incoming missiles! The local system warning flared crimson through Eltyn's skull.

Retract and shield! Retract and shield! The repetition was unnecessary, Eltyn realized after the fact, but there was no harm done. *Report status.*

All shields in place.

Report damage in real time.

The system did not acknowledge the command. Systems didn't, unless programmed that way, and Eltyn hadn't bothered to reprogram it.

The two of them sat there without communicating for several minutes.

"The time for 'submit and all will be well' is over, it would seem," he finally said.

"The Twenty never meant that all would be well, only that they'd prefer not to use force."

"I wonder how many other isolated stations are receiving similar notification."

"We can't be the only one, I wouldn't think."

"No. Just one in a location where no one will see or hear the detonations."

Main scanning antenna inoperative. Local antennae and scanners operative. Power grid operative.

Unshield local one. Status?

One scanning.

Eltyn accessed the local input, conscious that Faelyna had linked in as well. The image of the area to the east of the station showed a slight cratering just south of the canal wall and roughly even with the east end of the station.

Interrogative scare tactics? pulsed Faelyna. *Or do they think we have a comm-link to what's left of MetCom or The Fifty?*

???? Does it matter?

The image from the local antenna abruptly shivered.

Lock all the doors and windows, suggested Eltyn. *Visitors before long. Unless they can't reach us immediately and want to disable comm.*

Eltyn thought, then pulsed, *Your alternative more likely, but . . .*

Locking station.

Shield local one. Unshield two and report.

Two scanning.

Eltyn accessed the image of the area to the west of the station. Again, the stone and station were undamaged, but a half crater radiated away from the stone south of the west end of the station. That half crater looked to be twenty yards across and at least five deep.

Directed monatomic hydrogen warhead . . . mused Eltyn. *What happens if the next one is nuclear?*

We lose all power except what's stored in the capacitor batteries below, because all the collectors and generations get vaporized, along with the cabling, and The Twenty loses its reputation for being merciful, and the whole world knows it.

Nuclear "persuasion" unlikely?

Unlikely[3] . . . for now.

They watched and waited for another ten minutes, but no more missiles or warheads arrived.

"Back to work," suggested Faelyna.

"I'll try to add variable power projection . . ."

"Thank you."

Abruptly, Eltyn recalled what had struck him just before the missile attack. "I was thinking . . . whoever set up the control system wanted someone to be able to decipher it. They just didn't want it to be easy. So what is it that they wanted us to learn?"

"I'd thought that, but I haven't figured out an answer yet." She smiled, faintly. "I wish I knew more about fermionic entanglement, something more than the basics."

"Maybe the whole universe is entangled."

"We already suspect that."

"Maybe all universes are entangled," he bantered.

"You might be onto something . . ."

Exactly what, Eltyn had no idea, but he smiled anyway.

30

✵ ✵ ✵

18 Siebmonat 3123, Vaniran Hegemony

At three minutes to ten in the morning, two days after the previous Aesyr attack, Duhyle and Helkyria were testing her "apparatus" on the main-level windows and doors. They had verified that the equipment did in fact open, close, and lock the exterior apertures when Captain Valakyr appeared.

"Commander, ser?"

Helkyria looked up. "I take it that some Aesyr force is approaching."

"Yes, ser. Two submersibles and a cargo vessel that is most likely a troop carrier." Valakyr's voice carried faint puzzlement, as if to ask why the vessels had been allowed to reach the western shore of Vanira. "They're likely two hours from reaching the canal."

"I've been in touch with the Magistra of Security, Captain. I see no sense in losing satellites and threatening the future over those attackers. Not yet, at least. Bring all your troopers and food into the station . . . and as much equipment as will fit with them comfortably. We can seal the station against them, and not even the Hammer can broach the stone."

"That's eighty-five security troopers in addition to the seven spec-ops techs, ser."

"There's room enough, isn't there?" replied the scient-commander. "They all fit in the larger lower chamber for your briefing."

"I beg your pardon, ser, but with only two exits, attacking them from inside the station might prove . . . difficult."

"Attacking them with conventional weapons would prove nothing and would merely give them the excuse to use the Hammer. None of your troops would survive that, and the use would push us that much closer to destruction. Now . . . if you would muster them in the lower spaces and inform me when everything is settled."

"Yes, ser."

Duhyle saw that the captain was less than pleased.

Once Valakyr had left the chamber, Helkyria added, "Knowing which battles to fight and when is often more important than winning the ir-relevant . . . or worse, losing it."

"How are you going to use the station? Beyond being a shelter?"

"At the moment, I have no exact idea, other than I think I've man-aged to mimic the upper-level command structure," admitted Helkyria. "I'm convinced it has other capabilities. At the least, the troopers will be safer inside the station, and we'll have postponed immediate disaster."

"What else about the upper-level command structure?"

"It branches into other . . . areas . . . I need to get on with looking into that. You and Symra might see how you can assist the captain."

"I can do that." Much as Duhyle wanted to know about those "other areas," he also knew there was no point in pressing Helkyria.

He nodded and headed out to find the subcaptain.

In the end, Duhyle's greatest help to the security captain was his understanding of where what gear and supplies could be stored, partic-ularly in the lower level. Even so, it took most of two hours before he, Symra, and Valakyr were satisfied that every possible space had been utilized.

"It's tight," declared Valakyr, "but we didn't have to leave anything of great value outside." She paused, then added to Symra, "Except for your vehicle."

"We extracted all the equipment and the shielding generator."

Valakyr looked to Duhyle. "If you wouldn't mind conveying to the commander . . . we're standing by for her orders."

"Certainly." Duhyle linked to the station systems to check the out-side monitors. The lead Aesyr vessel, one of the submersibles, was hold-ing position a kay or so to the northwest of the station, off the middle of the canal, apparently waiting for the others. "It might be a while. The Aesyr aren't in position to do anything yet."

Valakyr nodded.

Duhyle strode the ramp to the main level and to Helkyria's working area.

She did not turn from the screens before her.

"They're all mustered inside, and everything we could get inside is stored."

"Good."

"They're standing by for your orders."

"They'll be standing by for some time," said Helkyria. "The Aesyr will send a small recon force. They're looking for an excuse to use their Hammers. We won't give it to them."

"What do you want me to tell the captain?"

"Just tell her that . . . and to stand by and that, if anything changes, she'll be the first to know." The scient-commander paused. "Tell her that what I'm doing might result in . . . oddities."

"Oddities? She'll ask what kind."

"I don't know, but there's a mental aspect to the command structure. The system is partly anticipatory, and that suggests that it reads intent. I can't tell what else it reads, or how it may react. There might be strange sounds that aren't really sounds, or momentary illusions, or dead silence . . . or nothing at all."

"Is everything locked?"

"Not yet, because a total lock might sever the power and comm-links, but tell the captain and the subcaptain that no one is to leave because I may lock down everything at any time. Then you and Symra should come back here."

"I'll take care of it." *Dearest.*

The faintest pink suffused the tips of her locks. But she did smile. *Insubordinate . . . but appreciated, dear man.*

He'd really wanted to say the endearment aloud, but since his current position technically required a "Yes, ser," he'd compromised with a non-salutatory acknowledgment. Then he headed back down the ramp.

Once he'd delivered the messages to both officers, he hurried back to see what Helkyria was doing. He didn't wait for Symra.

A half hour later, he and Symra still stood behind Helkyria as she worked on the console that she and Duhyle had built, while she occasionally checked the eternal screens and monitors. Duhyle did his own observing, noting that a comparatively high-speed launch had left the cargo vessel that now waited offshore with the two submersibles and cruised swiftly toward the station. *Two more submersibles? How long have they been planning this revolt? Or were those research craft that they appropriated and converted?* He knew his thoughts were wandering, but all he could do at the moment was wait. Good techs, engineers or not, could.

Another half hour passed before the first of the Aesyr scrambled up a boarding ladder temporarily affixed to the canal wall. Given the height of the wall above the water, it was a long climb. Because the attackers wore blend-ins, Duhyle strained to determine precise movements, but it was clear that the first Aesyr arrivals were surveying the area.

Then, three figures moved toward the station.

"Locking the station," said Helkyria coolly.

The light seemed to change, although Duhyle couldn't have said how.

Then, he froze for a moment, because an image appeared literally before him—that of a couple. Both had short and curly dark brown hair. They were roughly the same height. The woman was closer to Duhyle. She had dark hazel eyes, a tan skin, lighter than his or Helkyria's, but darker than that of a northerner or an Aesyr. Both man and woman had strong but slightly pointed chins, and both wore identical formfitting singlesuits that left very little to the imagination. Each wore a patch or an insignia on the right shoulder, a design of intertwined and stylized lightning bolts that curved back on each other.

The man said something and gestured, and the image vanished.

Where did that come from? Who are they . . . or who were they? Had the canal captured images from all who had inhabited it? Would his image appear to some future inhabitant or investigator?

His eyes turned toward Helkyria. He wanted to ask her if she'd seen what he had, but he swallowed. Instead of the pale blue and not-quite shapeless uniform singlesuit she had been wearing not moments before, Helkyria stood before the controls of her equipment in a shimmering and filmy golden garment that left almost nothing to Duhyle's imagination. So stunning and inviting was the image that Duhyle found himself breathing faster and wanting to lunge forward, yet he knew it was an illusion.

The image vanished, and Helkyria stood there in her pale blue singlesuit. A range of colors played though her hair, golden light flaring from the tips and from her eyebrows. Duhyle glanced at Symra, whose hair was momentarily a dazzling blue.

Symra immediately looked down and away from Duhyle.

Then all the extraneous light vanished. The chamber seemed dim and lifeless, although the lamps remained lit.

No one spoke for several moments.

"That . . . was rather a profound side effect." Helkyria's words were a trace ragged, the first time in years Duhyle had heard emotion in public. A much fainter rainbow of light flickered through her eyebrows and hair before vanishing.

What, if anything, had Helkyria seen in him? Duhyle wasn't about to ask with Symra there. "Did you see an image of two people . . . a man and a woman?"

"No." Helkyria's voice was firm. "I was watching the console."

"Ah . . . I did," admitted Symra. "They had dark hair and tight suits, and they were so much alike that they might have been brother and sister. They were here for just a moment. Their image was, I mean."

"Let me know if you see anything else unusual."

Duhyle attempted to access the external comm-links. He expected them to be off-line, but they remained, as did the external monitors. The console before Helkyria continued to operate as well. He hadn't expected otherwise, since they'd linked it into stored power.

Helkyria frowned. "We're still getting power from the external system. I hadn't expected that with the locking, but the underlying control system is more sophisticated than I thought."

That worried Duhyle. Did that mean the locking wasn't as secure? Or that the canal and station walls harbored some form of energy-based intelligence? "What about ventilation?"

"The ducts are still working, but I can shut them down if necessary. I think it might be possible without losing access to the external grid."

Think? Duhyle did not voice the question.

"Ser . . . what are you going to do?" asked Symra.

"For now . . . we wait. I'm going to inspect the station. Later . . . we'll see."

31

5 Tenmonth 1351, Unity of Caelaarn

Maertyn stepped into the assistant minister's office early on the fifth of Tenmonth. Before leaving for the Ministry of Science he had packed his shoulder bag, but left it at the town house. Supposedly, Josef would be in the office early that afternoon. While Maertyn had advised everyone at the Ministry that he planned to leave on the afternoon of the sixth, he had no intention whatsoever of remaining in Caelaarn that long, nor of telling anyone that. Although he had not observed any more suspicious vehicles, to him all that meant was that he was being observed at a greater distance and that, as a result of Ashauer's quiet involvement, no one wanted his death to occur in Caelaarn itself.

The outer office was quiet, since he was early and since Marcent had not yet arrived. So he sat down at the desk and accessed the screen. The first memorandum was from Hlaansk.

From: Minister of Science
          Unity of Caelaarn

To: Maertyn S'Eidolon
          Assistant Minister [Acting]
          Environment Research Subministry

Subject: Funds Reallocation

This is to congratulate you for your work in drafting the preliminary reallocation recommendations for the Environment Research Subministry. You provided a solid basis for my final decisions, especially on short notice and in the absence of Assistant Minister Cennen.

I trust that your research will soon provide tangible results, and that there will be no necessity to call on the resources of the Ministry of Protective Services.

That was it. Maertyn studied the last sentence again and nodded.

After several minutes of reflection, he read through the few remaining memoranda and messages, then straightened as the comm chimed.

"Deputy Assistant Minister Olason Tedor," announced Marcent.

"Have him come in." Maertyn wondered what Olason wanted, since the man who'd married Tauzn's niece had studiously avoided Maertyn the entire time he'd been acting assistant minister.

"Greetings," offered Maertyn, standing to welcome the fair-haired Olason, who directed the Office of Waste and Recycling Research. "What can I do for you?"

"Not a thing, Lord Maertyn. I heard you will be leaving tomorrow, and I wanted to wish you well."

"I appreciate the sentiment." Maertyn smiled politely. "How are you and Berenyce doing these days?"

"Excellently, excellently. She was sorry she didn't have a chance to see your wife, but we both hope she is well and continuing her recovery."

"She is doing well. The quiet at the station suits her." Maertyn laughed softly. "In some ways, it suits us both."

"She is most fortunate to have such a devoted husband, and one who would go to such lengths for her."

"I'm fortunate to have her, just as you are most fortunate to have Berenyce . . . if perhaps for differing reasons." Maertyn paused just briefly, before adding, "I did send you a memorandum, but I'll tell you again that your budget submission was outstanding. Very clear, and very clean."

"Thank you, sir. I just came by to wish you well."

"I do appreciate it, and I wish you the best. Oh . . . and you might offer my regards to Berenyce's uncle, whenever you see him. He's conveyed a great deal of solicitude, and that's been very helpful."

For an instant, Olason's face showed a hint of puzzlement, but that vanished with a polished smile. "I will . . . although we do not see him that often."

After Olason left, Maertyn wondered why Tauzn had bothered, unless it had been to disarm Maertyn by the use of a veiled threat that was meaningless unless he returned safely to the station.

He checked the time. Only ten past nine, and Josef wasn't due in until after one in the afternoon. Then he stood and walked to the window, where he looked out into a cold, clear, and sunny morning.

He'd expected the day would have brief meetings such as the one with Olason. Doubtless there would be more. But he hated waiting.

Not quite an hour later, Marcent announced, "Assistant Minister Alaser Fancoyn."

First the nephew in marriage of the Minister of Protective Services and now the Assistant Minister for Protective Services Research—Maertyn didn't know whether to be flattered, amused, or truly alarmed. He stood and waited.

Alaser was a tall and broad-shouldered bear of a man, with a broad face and a generous smile at apparent odds with his reputed ability as a bureaucratic infighter, except that Maertyn had learned long ago that the most deadly politicians were the most personable. Alaser offered that smile as he stepped into the office. "Maertyn."

"Alaser . . . I hadn't expected to see you." Maertyn remained standing, but moved from behind the desk, stopping a yard or so short of the assistant minister.

"How could I not come when you are leaving? You are leaving tomorrow, are you not? That was what I heard."

"You heard correctly. It's a long trip, even by tube-train." Maertyn paused but slightly, before asking, "How are matters in your subministry?"

"As well as can be expected. Weapons research is dastardly expensive, more so than other research, and no research worth pursuing comes cheaply."

"All too true." Maertyn chuckled. "Nothing worth pursuing comes cheaply, whether it's research or power, or even peace and quiet."

"You may recall that I did inquire about whether your research was likely to discover what lies behind the material strength of the canal."

"I do indeed." Maertyn managed to keep his voice warm and interested.

"I personally wish you well in that effort. I feel that your success will benefit the Unity in many ways." Alaser offered a wry smile. "Success in anything sharpens both sides of the blade, and sometimes an impenetrable defense can be the best offense. But then, as an Indurate, you would know that."

"Defense is often underrated." Maertyn had studied the Indurate texts, and even attempted to put some of the teachings into his life and professional career, but he'd never actually been apprenticed to an Indurate Master. So who was spreading the rumor that he was? Ashauer? To spare him from interrogation techniques? Why? Just to thwart Tauzn?

"Do you really think you can discover something useful before your research appointment is over?"

"I've already discovered some unusual aspects to the canal." Maertyn shrugged. "It remains to be seen if they will prove useful, but that's what I hope to find out."

"Might I ask . . ."

Maertyn laughed gently. "You can, but you know that no true scientist wants to reveal something before he's certain that it's replicable. Right now, those aspects are very preliminary."

"I understand caution, Maertyn, but sometimes caution is equivalent to rashness."

"That's true as well, and I appreciate your pointing it out. As soon as I have a more solid basis for what is now speculative and preliminary, you will be among the first to know."

"I would indeed appreciate that." Alaser offered his wide and generous smile. "I won't keep you. I know you must have matters to finish up so that you can return to your lovely wife."

"I do miss her . . . and thank you." Maertyn walked toward the office door with Alaser, stopping short and letting the other leave.

Then he walked back to the window. Matters were far worse in Caelaarn than he'd thought, and they didn't look to be improving.

The next several hours were devoted to dealing with last-moment inquiries—and his own speculations—as well as a quick and solitary meal in the junior ministers' salon.

At quarter to one, Josef Cennen walked through the door into the office that was officially his. "I see you've made yourself quite at home, Maertyn."

Maertyn rose from the small conference table. "Actually, I've changed nothing and touched nothing except for the desk and table screens. Given the requirements of Minister Hlaansk, that was unavoidable."

"So considerate of you, but then, you've always been considerate."

"As have you."

"I do hope we don't have to go through some tedious business of you pretending to brief me, and me pretending to listen to you."

"I don't think that would be in either my interest or yours, Josef," replied Maertyn. "I will offer to answer any questions you might have."

"I do appreciate that, but then, as I just said, you always have been most overtly considerate, Maertyn." Josef paused, then asked, "Given the timing of the extension of my inspection tour of universities, I presume that you had no idea that you would be positioned as acting assistant minister."

"You presume correctly. I had thought to deliver my research report and to depart as quickly and quietly as possible."

"You did not think that Hlaansk's request for your return was unusual?"

"He has been known to insist on accountability and to make an issue of it by example. I had no reason to believe otherwise."

"I suppose not." Josef's tone was bland. "I also presume that you avoided reallocating any potential surplus funds to Protective Services Research."

"Of course. That was clearly Minister Hlaansk's agenda, and I presumed that he wished to spare you the . . . difficulty . . . of the differences between you."

"You put that so diplomatically, Maertyn, but you always have been that. I trust you understand that, in this time of fiscal exigency, there is little possibility of extending your research project."

"I never assumed there was any possibility of an extension, regardless

of any small success I may yet achieve. That was one reason why I requested additional equipment."

"And doubtless why a copy of that request went to Hlaansk?"

"I did wish to make sure he was informed."

"So very thoughtful of you, Maertyn."

"With so much at stake, I felt he should know."

Josef didn't even nod.

"Is there anything else?" asked Maertyn.

"I think not."

"Then I should leave you to catch up on matters. I doubt you'll find
any surprises at all."

"I expect not." After the briefest of pauses, Josef added, "You'll be
leaving before long, I assume." His smile was warm and solicitous, and
Maertyn distrusted it totally.

"Tomorrow afternoon."

"Give my best to your lovely lady."

"I will." Maertyn inclined his head just slightly, then turned and left
the office he had inhabited so comparatively briefly. No one said a word
to him as he made his way out of the subministry and then down to the
main entrance and outside.

The sky was clear, but the sun shone down without much warmth,
and the pale haze that was the Selene Ring barely sparkled in the winter
light as Maertyn made his way to the car park and the runabout.

For all his vigilance on the drive back to his town home, he could
detect no close followers. Once home, he picked up the waiting shoulder bag and then turned to Rhesten, who had come into the rear foyer,
possibly from his own quarters.

"Rhesten, I'd appreciate it if you'd come with me in the runabout.
I have a task that will take two of us. You won't be gone that long."

"Yes, sir."

Once they were in the runabout, Maertyn eased the vehicle out of
the garage and onto the avenue, heading for the tube-train station.

"You're departing, sir?"

"I am."

"Might I ask about your return?"

"I have a year and four months left on my assignment at the canal.
I can't say whether I'll be back again before then. That's largely up to

the Ministry. If I am called back, I'll let you know as soon as I'm informed."

"Yes, sir."

As he approached the tube-train station, Maertyn guided the runabout into the narrow private vehicle drive up to the drop-off portico. There he halted the runabout and slipped out, carrying his shoulder bag. "Thank you, Rhesten. As I said, I don't know when I'll be back, but I will keep you informed."

"Very good, sir. We'll keep everything the way you like it."

"Thank you." Maertyn smiled, then turned and hurried from the covered portico past the local tube transit corridor and then through the main archway across the pale golden surface of the main concourse to the public booking screens—hardly ever used, except by guards and others without full comm-links. *Or by lords who do not wish their intentions known until the comparatively last moment.*

The booking screen in the upper level of the tube-train station showed only lounge seats on the local to Semelin, leaving in less than an hour, but a compartment on the following express that went to Brathym and then, after an hour's delay, on to Daelmar.

Maertyn accepted those arrangements, although the waiting in Semelin and Brathym concerned him, and made his way to the ramp leading down to the platform from where the train to Semelin would depart.

32

❧   ❧   ❧

32 Quad 2471 R.E.

Eltyn spent another two hours working on the power modifications to Faelyna's projector . . . until his eyes burned. Since no more missiles had arrived, he decided to take a break and replace the main exterior scanning antenna with the remaining spare.

Heading out. Antenna replacement.

Attackers in the locale?

Negative. Local antennae = limited range.

Be careful³!

As possible. [grateful appreciation]

Eltyn left the antenna inside while he carried the collapsible ladder out and set it up just outside the door on the south side of the station. He positioned it so that he could climb right up to the flat top of the second level and replace the damaged antenna. Then he ducked back inside to get the antenna.

Rhyana stood there, projectile rifle in hand. "You need some cover?"

"There's no one out there right now. The only thing that could happen is another missile, and the rifle wouldn't help much in that case. I'm going to replace the scanning antenna before they let loose again."

"You sure you don't want help?"

"Not right now." Eltyn stepped outside, grasped the replacement antenna, and clambered up the ladder, the waist tool bag banging against the ladder. Once he was onto the flat surface of the top of the station, he moved quickly to the antenna assembly . . . or what was left of it. He laid down the new assembly, pulled out the pliers from the tool bag, and twisted away the first release clip. The second one caught, and it took him several attempts to wrench it free. Then he had to reset the base and replace another clip, before he could begin to slide the new antenna into place. The first of the new clips went into position easily, but the second, predictably, stuck, and he had to slowly wiggle it into place.

Then he wiped his steaming forehead with the back of his sleeve, trying to get the dampness out of the corners of his eyes because the combination of sweat and fine grit still in the hot air burned and blurred his vision.

FLASH! Urgent! Incoming missiles! flared the local system warning.

Retract and shield! Eltyn snapped as he grabbed the broken assembly and scrambled for the ladder. *Report status.*

All shields in place.

Eltyn tossed the broken assembly off the top of the station, then started down the ladder, half-sliding and half-climbing. He made it down and halfway inside the station doorway when the first missile exploded, just southwest of the station, by the sound, which was cut off by the stone closing behind him.

Status? [concern] pulsed immediately from Faelyna.

Fine . . . barely. He was touched by the warmth behind her inquiry. If only . . .

Riffies must have minidrone overhead somewhere.

Or control of the local geosat, he pulsed back.

"You all right, sir?" Rhyana's question was almost a demand. "Cutting it a little close, if you ask me."

"I'm fine. In a few minutes, I'd like to see if we can reclaim the ladder."

"You think they'll drop more bombs?"

"Missiles," corrected Eltyn, "they're using some sort of drone to target us. But there's a delay between observation and when the missile hits." He accessed the station system, trying to get an idea of whether more missiles were inbound.

The local antennae showed nothing. He decided to wait before deploying the newly replaced main scanning antenna.

"Sir?" pressed Rhyana.

"What is it?"

"Do you believe in spirits, sir?"

"Spirits? Discorporate entities? Why?"

"I've seen one. Here in the station. Around the time the first missile came down outside. It was a woman. She wasn't dressed like anyone I ever saw. She had amber hair and amber eyes, and she wore a long dress of golden cloth trimmed in silver-gray."

"Was she shadowy, the way they say spirits are?"

"No, sir. She looked right real. She looked sad, too. Then she was gone, like a video image that lost its signal or power."

Rhyana's seeing images, Eltyn pulsed Faelyna. *Or she did, when the first missiles came in. She's not the type to have hysterical visions.*

Might have been a projection harmonic, but we weren't projecting then.

Thought you should know.

Have to think about that.

"What is it, sir?"

"I was checking with Faelyna, to see if she did something different then. If you see something odd again, let one of us know."

"I can do that, sir."

"Thank you." *Unshield main antenna. Scan.*

Once the antenna was deployed, Eltyn tracked the findings in all directions. As he'd suspected, there was a blip almost directly overhead, at one point four kays—mostly likely the minidrone observing the station.

Confirming minidrone overhead. He could sense Faelyna's presence on the system even before he finished.

Noted. Too bad it's out of range of anything we have.

Agreed².

Eltyn turned to Rhyana. "Let's recover that ladder—quickly."

"Yes, sir."

Eltyn pressed the door and watched as the stone flowed back into itself, then crossed the four yards to the ladder, where he pressed the retraction stud. Nervously, he checked the system again, but there was no sign of anything out of the ordinary—except the minidrone overhead.

The ladder retracted into itself slowly, or so it seemed to Eltyn, and he shifted his weight from one foot to the other until it had compacted itself and he could finally pick up the handles of the heavy oblong.

Incoming missile! announced the system.

"Inside!" he snapped to Rhyana. *Shield antennae and report!*

All shielded.

In moments, the two of them were back inside the station. Eltyn moved back behind the wall, not standing in the opening as the door closed.

Less than two minutes later, the warhead arrived, close enough that even the shielded antennae recorded the impact.

We went out to recover the ladder. In minutes, we had an incoming.

The riffies want to keep us penned up.

Or pinned down, replied Eltyn.

"Sir?" asked Rhyana.

"We'll have to stay inside for now."

"Like to set the riffie outside and let him get the greetings the others sent." She shook her head. "Might as well check on him." She headed down to the lower level.

Since there was clearly no point in attempting any more ventures outside, Eltyn made his way to Faelyna's work space. She didn't look up as he entered the other large main-floor chamber.

"Any progress on the shadow operatives for color changes on the commands?" he inquired.

"I have some options in the structure and presentation of the commands. I need you to finish the power modifications to the projector."

[embarrassment] With all the missiles . . . forgot I hadn't finished them. He sat down at the adjoining table. *Shouldn't take long.*

We have some time. More than enough. [warm cynicism]

Because the riffies are trying to keep us inside?

What else?

"Have you figured out if the entire universe is fermionically entangled?" Eltyn resumed work on reassembling the modules for the projector.

"The entire universe is entangled, but that wasn't the question. You asked whether all universes were entangled."

"Are they?"

Immediate reaction = yes. Reason says no. Trust reaction, even without proof.

By that logic, with which Eltyn did not disagree, he suspected that Rhyana had indeed seen someone very real—real in some fashion— and that the ghost or image or whatever it happened to be was indeed linked to what he and Faelyna were doing.

33

❁ ❁ ❁

18 Siebmonat 3123, Vaniran Hegemony

While he followed Helkyria on her inspection of the station, Duhyle kept himself linked to the exterior monitors. Doubtless, she was doing the same, although neither spoke of it. Her scrutiny of the upper levels was slightly more than perfunctory. Once she headed down the ramp to the lower level, where the kitchen and the assembly area and storage chambers were located, she paused every yard, looking at what she held in her hand—something that resembled a personal comm.

At one side of the bottom of the ramp stood Captain Valakyr, trying to conceal an expression that mixed puzzlement and irritation.

"Captain, the Aesyr are attempting to break into the station. They will fail, but it will occupy them for a time. That will allow me to inspect and measure the lower level to see if we have more options than are apparent. You may accompany us for the moment."

"Yes, ser."

Helkyria continued her examination of the lower level, scanning—if that was what she happened to be doing—every part of the outside walls. Finally, she reached the small storeroom at the eastern end of the station on the lower level of the station, the only one with an actual interior door. She turned to Valakyr. "Please step back, Captain. I'm about to try something. If it fails, you will be in command."

Valakyr started to speak, paused, then said, "Yes, ser." The blue of puzzlement flickered at the tips of her hair. She stepped out of the store-room.

Helkyria added, to Duhyle, "Close the door."

He didn't question her, but touched the door.

After it closed, she stepped up to him, put her arms around him, kissed him gently on the lips. Duhyle could feel as much as see the warm gold of love flowing from the tips of her silver-blond hair. Then she stepped back, showing him the small oblong box with a miniature screen. "I modified a personal comm. Let's see if I'm right."

For several minutes, she stood there, manipulating images on the screen.

Abruptly, the eastern wall irised open, but in a hexagonal shape. Beyond lay what looked to be a long straight corridor, dimly lit as if by a radiance from the stone walls and stretching eastward into the distance. For a moment, Duhyle could have sworn he saw a rainbow, but when he blinked it was gone.

A faint smile crossed Helkyria's lips. "Good." She touched the screen again. The hexagonal door vanished. Then she looked at Duhyle.

He understood perfectly. "Does it extend the length of the entire canal?"

"It should. There's no way to tell. There may not be any exits any-where near, either."

Duhyle nodded. "Are you ready for me to open the other door?"

"Please."

On the far side, in the long assembly room, stood Valakyr. The cap-tain's eyes fixed on Helkyria, but Valakyr did not speak.

"For the moment," said Helkyria, "you and your troopers will stand by, but in stand-down status. It will be some time before you'll be needed, and I will give you advance notice—as I can."

"How long do you anticipate our remaining confined within the station, Commander?" asked Valakyr.

"As long as required to keep the Aesyr occupied and to keep you and your forces intact, Captain." Helkyria offered a pleasant but cool smile. "Also, we're trying to minimize the Aesyr use of the Hammers. It doesn't make sense to win a battle and lose the world . . . and the uni-verse."

"Would overuse of the Hammers lead to . . . immediate . . . destruction?"

Helkyria shook her head. "The effects might not be felt for decades . . . here on Earth. Centuries elsewhere in our galaxy, and perhaps eons in the farthest reaches of the universe. That is one of the greatest dangers of their use." She nodded to the captain and headed toward the ramp.

Duhyle followed.

When they were relatively alone at the top of the ramp before turning toward Helkyria's work chamber, Duhyle cleared his throat and asked in a murmur, "Now what?"

"I keep working, and you keep checking the monitors. The Aesyr will attempt various assaults on the stone itself. Those will fail. Then they will attempt something else. When it appears as though they will, let me know."

"And you will be doing . . . ?"

"Attempting to determine the best fashion in which to use the station's capabilities to counter what the Aesyr will try." She turned back to the array of screens before her, but set the converted personal comm just to one side of the central screen.

Over the next half hour, Duhyle sat at the small table in the corner, using his direct links to the station system to keep checking the external systems. He glanced occasionally toward Helkyria or Symra, who had returned and stood well back, only a few steps from the archway. As he observed, one of the submersibles and the cargo vessel moved inshore and took up station in the middle of the canal almost due north of the station, but closer to the far side of the canal, more than two kays away.

Why the cargo vessel?

Before that long, Duhyle thought he knew as he watched a crew begin to work on an apparatus on the raised fantail of the ship. Some sort of weapon, but one unlike the odd-shaped antenna that had heralded the earlier use of the Hammer. The ships were that far away in order to have a better angle for focusing an energy weapon on the station.

Finally, he spoke. "Check the north observation monitor. They're setting up a weapon to fire at the station."

After several moments, Helkyria replied, "It's likely a high-energy particle beam. Thora knows that the stone of the canal walls simply reflects even the highest-energy lasers. They'll try something that will attack the subatomic structure of the stone."

"Will it work?"

"No. She should know that, but she'll study the results before allowing them to use the Hammer. Let me know if anything unusual occurs."

Duhyle continued to follow the outside monitors. The Aesyr forces in blend-ins retreated southward, leaving no one in the area around the station. The high-speed launch that had landed them pulled away from the canal and took up station a good kay east in the middle of the channel, beside the second submersible.

Abruptly, the monitor covering the area to the north went blank. Duhyle cross-checked the others, then reported, "We lost the north monitor. There was a large energy surge consistent with a high-energy weapon."

"SatCom reports a similar energy discharge," Helkyria replied.

"What if they destroy all our scanners and antennae, ser?" asked Symra.

"They'll leave one . . . if only to try to communicate with us."

Duhyle had his doubts about that.

Three more intense blasts of energy, each several minutes apart, followed. Then, ten minutes passed. The eastern, western, and southern monitors showed no movement of Aesyr toward the station. Using the eastern monitor, Duhyle could just barely catch a view of the submersible to the east, but neither it nor the launch moved.

"They're about to try the Hammer," predicted Helkyria.

Duhyle watched all the system indicators, but over the next ten minutes, they showed nothing.

"SatCom reports that the submersible to the north initiated two Hammer strikes. They wish to know our status," Helkyria added dryly.

"What next?" asked Symra in little more than a whisper.

"I'd imagine they'll have decided that we have a ventilation system, and they'll attempt to attack us in that fashion."

"Will you have to cut off power to block the ducts?" Duhyle studied the land to the south of the station, but the Aesyr remained under cover and out of sight or heat-scanning.

"Not unless they try to put a power surge through the power net. We'll be able to see that . . . unless they take out the rest of the system sensors." Helkyria turned and looked to Duhyle. "They'll most likely lob in shells with some sort of antipersonnel or nerve agent first. They'd rather not destroy my equipment and anything I've discovered, and trying to destroy our systems through a power overload might compromise what they hope to find."

Duhyle forced himself to concentrate on the remaining monitors. While the north monitor was gone, the proximity of the station's north wall to the canal proper would make dropping a shell in the uncovered area difficult, if not close to impossible. Even if the Aesyr could do that, the impact and seismic registers from other sensors would indicate that something of force had struck.

Close to a half hour passed before a shell exploded to the southwest of the station, on the open ground beyond the stone of the canal. Immediately a greenish mist rose and drifted northward with the light breeze.

"Ser! Agent attack!"

Helkyria did nothing overt for a moment, then snapped, "Kavn, move under the duct vent to your left. Do you feel the airflow?"

Duhyle winced, but stood and moved to stand under the vent. The outside air was cooler as it flowed over him. "Yes."

Helkyria entered something on the small screen before her. "Has the airflow stopped?" Cold silver light from hair and eyebrows wreathed her face.

Her voice was so commanding that he replied, "Yes, ser."

"Good. We're protected from whatever that gas might be."

"How long will the oxygen in here last?" asked Symra.

"We'll have to see. It's better than breathing whatever nerve agent is in the mist-gas."

"With nearly a hundred people here . . ." ventured Symra.

"Why don't you go down to the lower level and monitor the air quality there?" suggested Helkyria. "If you sense any deterioration, report back here immediately."

"Yes, ser."

Once Symra had left, Duhyle moved back to where he had been sitting. From there, he continued to check the monitors. Several more shells dropped around the station, and before long, the entire area was shrouded in a greenish mist.

There was no noticeable change in temperature in the chamber, although Duhyle thought the air seemed slightly more moist. Was that because of exhaled water vapor? Yet the air in the chamber, if anything, seemed "fresher." Duhyle continued to monitor what he could and to look occasionally at Helkyria, who was totally absorbed in whatever she was doing. While he wanted to ask, he decided against it. She wouldn't tell him anything until she was ready to do so.

Within another hour, the light breeze that had swirled the first hints of the mist/nerve/whatever agent around the station had dispersed the remaining traces of the mist. Symra finally returned.

"Yes?" inquired Duhyle, when he realized that Helkyria wasn't about to say anything. "How is the air?"

"Ah . . ." Symra glanced toward the scient-commander, then finished, "It smells different, more humid."

Surprisingly, to Duhyle, Helkyria responded, even if she did not lift her head from what she was doing. "It should. What you're breathing most likely mimics what the canal's creators breathed. There's a diffusion process going on."

"Then . . . we won't be forced to leave because of the lack of oxygen?"

"It would appear not." Helkyria paused, then added, "If that is all, Subcaptain, you may remain here silently, or rejoin the captain and her troopers."

"Yes, ser." Symra did not leave and moved closed to Duhyle, but remained standing, murmuring, "That still doesn't deal with the longer-term problem of food, or water, especially."

"How much is there?" asked Duhyle in a low voice.

"Two weeks . . . three on short rations. Water . . . who knows?"

"We'll have water unless the Aesyr want to embark on a rather large engineering project," Duhyle replied, keeping his voice down. "The water comes from an aquifer south of here, and it's fed through one of the underground ducts that's something like fifty yards below ground. The biggest problem will be the sanitary facilities. They can handle the numbers, but it's likely to be very crowded."

"We've already noticed that."

"You might want to pass the water information on to Captain Valakyr," Duhyle said.

"Perhaps I should." Symra eased away from Duhyle and headed down the ramp.

Duhyle kept tracking matters, but another hour passed before a squad of blend-in concealed Aesyr appeared to the south of the station, crossing the open space cautiously. "The Aesyr are returning."

"They'll attempt to open the station," predicted Helkyria. "When that fails, they'll contact Asgard for instructions. Thora or whoever's in charge will suggest locating several power cables, but not trying to create power surges. That interchange will take a good hour. It may well be dark before they decide. Then they'll have to arrange the equipment, and that will take even longer."

"And then?"

"Let us hope that we're ready to deal with them." Helkyria looked down at the makeshift assembly and instruments before her. "We might even get some sleep."

Duhyle went back to his monitors.

Helkyria's assessment of the situation proved to be accurate. The lower edge of the sun was touching the waters of the Jainoran Ocean before a crew of Aesyr re-appeared with long narrow tanks and hoses. One of them wore black goggles on the top of his forehead.

Symra leaned forward to look at the image Duhyle had projected. "What's that?"

"Old-style gas cutting torch," replied Duhyle. "They're headed for the junction box where the power cables all join."

"They need to burn through the cables? Isn't there a switch or something like that?"

"There is. There are switches from each power subsystem, and then a main switch beyond the conformer. But the doors and walls to the chamber are steel. Thermasteel, in fact." Duhyle smiled.

"A chemical torch won't cut through that. Most lasers won't."

"No. But by the time they discover that, they'll either have to bring in lights or wait until dawn to backtrack the cabling subconduits so that they can find where they can cut through."

"Aren't there plans . . . schematics?" asked the subcaptain.

Duhyle nodded. "Over there, in the second chest. I had to install the power systems before Hel—the commander—could start her research. We never sent them to Vaena . . ."

"Mother Skadi . . ." Symra looked down at Duhyle sitting before the small worktable, then lowered her voice. "You're not just a tech . . ."

He smiled. "I was . . . before I went back to university." He waited a moment, then went on. "Doctorate in electrical engineering and electronic theory, but I always liked building things better than theory. I've enjoyed creating what Helkyria said was impossible."

"Oh . . . you're that . . ."

"For better or worse." Duhyle watched as the Aesyr assembled the cutting gear next to the squarish steel doors set flush with the stone of the south end of the canal wall.

Less than a quarter hour later, the Aesyr abandoned the effort and began to disassemble the torch in the long shadows that were almost indistinguishable from the twilight of late summer.

"Kavn," said Helkyria quietly but firmly, "I need some help here."

Symra stepped back as Duhyle rose and walked over to where she was juggling multiple inputs on multiple physical screens.

Helkyria looked toward the subcaptain. "Symra . . . it's likely that nothing will happen soon. If you would convey that to Captain Valakyr and suggest that the troopers might need a decent night's sleep. Tomorrow could be quite long."

"Yes, ser."

Once Symra had left, Duhyle looked at Helkyria and raised his eyebrows. "You have something drastic in mind."

"Only if it succeeds. If it fails, we'll have to retreat along the tunnel, and I have no idea if there are even any exits before the eastern end."

"Retreat?"

"After destroying the equipment. I wouldn't dare leave any of it for Thora."

"What do you have in mind?"

"Opening up the incomprehensible levels."

"That means making them comprehensible," he said lightly.

"Exactly."

He waited.

"The shadow symbols have a temporal component, not just a command structure. I could be wrong, but I think that's why the canal is impervious to anything here. I need what amounts to a temporal synchronizer . . . so that all three command levels are at the same temporal frequency. That's a crude way of putting it. Look." She pointed to the screen, then added a line of equations. "You see . . . if . . ." Another set followed.

Duhyle watched, listened, and finally shook his head. "I can do what you want. I don't fully understand, but I can convert them all to the temporal equivalent of direct current. I hope that will work. We can't go the other way because of the cycling."

"How long?"

"Two hours if I'm lucky. I won't be. Before midnight, I'd hope."

She reached over and squeezed his hand. "I'm sorry. I didn't expect things to turn out this way."

"I know." He squeezed her hand in return, then bent down and brushed her cheek with his lips. "I'd better get to work."

He felt her eyes on his back as he headed for the equipment storeroom.

34

❖ ❖ ❖

5 Tenmonth 1351, Unity of Caelaarn

The lounge car of the tube-train to Semelin was close to two-thirds full, but the man—a mid-level Environment Ministry functionary from his pale green and blue singlesuit—who would have been seated next to Maertyn took one look at the silver-gray trim of his maroon jacket and slipped away to another vacant seat.

Maertyn didn't sense any special scrutiny from the others in the car, but when the train was less than a half hour from Semelin, he stood and walked from his seat to the facilities in the middle of the car. Once inside a stall, he eased the special stunner from his shoulder bag into his jacket pocket. The weapon, except for the standard power pack, was totally biologic in construction, and assembling it years earlier had proven both expensive and time-consuming.

After finishing in the stall and then washing his hands and face, he returned to his seat to wait for the arrival in Semelin. He had no doubts that someone would be waiting for him. In fact, not finding someone awaiting would have been quite a surprise. Continuing to wear a lord's colors certainly made Maertyn more obvious, but it also allowed him to discover who was after him—and the jacket and undervest offered more protection than could any more proletarian garb he could have obtained while in Caelaarn.

Maertyn did not stand immediately as the tube-train glided to a halt at the platform at Semelin. Had he done that, all those in the car would have deferred to him. So he just sat and waited with a smile.

"The train has arrived at Semelin," announced the car speakers. "All passengers must depart."

Most of those on the train rose immediately as the doors opened, although several glanced toward Maertyn. He nodded to them politely, then gestured for them to continue.

As the last passengers began to leave the car, Maertyn rose and moved quickly, so that he was directly behind a large and muscular woman who wore the blue of the Transport Ministry, if with thin red piping on her jacket, a woman who moved with a grace more athletic than feminine.

His eyes went immediately to the bottom of the moving ramp leading up to the main level of the station. In the dimmer light to the right of the ramp was a man garbed as a maintenance or sanitation worker who was doing something to a duct in the side of the base of the ramp. He had to be a local agent, because Protective Services would not have had time to dispatch an agent from Caelaarn and because only emergency maintenance was scheduled in the early evening. Regular maintenance was handled in late evening and in the hours after midnight, not that most travelers would have known that or cared.

As Maertyn approached the ramp, using the muscular woman as a concealment shield, he eased his hand into his jacket pocket, then moved just enough to his right to trigger the stunner. The false sanitation worker toppled forward and a dull black dart-gun skittered across the lichen-carpeted surface. None of the other train passengers seemed to notice, except for a nervous-faced thin woman, who looked away abruptly and resolutely.

Maertyn stepped forward and onto the ramp, as if nothing had occurred, keeping close to the Transport functionary. The surveillance videos would have the Transport security people rushing down the descent ramp in minutes.

For Maertyn the greatest danger at Semelin lay ahead. He doubted that the single Protective Services agent was the only one waiting. If Tauzn wanted him dead, there would be more than one agent. For all that Ashauer had said, and all that Hlaansk's actions had hinted, Maertyn still found it hard to believe that so many people wanted to dispose of him, but searching for those reasons would have to wait.

At Semelin, as in many tube-train stations, the main platform served as access to two lower platforms, and the other lower platform was the one from where the much later tube-train to Brathym and Daelmar would depart, but Maertyn had no intention of descending to the other platform immediately, even if he could have, which he couldn't because the kiosk and the top of the down ramp wouldn't have permitted it until any trains scheduled prior to his had arrived and departed.

As he neared the top of the ramp and the main platform, he scanned the area. He still did not see any Transport security personnel, but in moments, he sighted two men in dark business singlesuits, one green and one gray. Both carried thin cases and appeared to be talking animatedly, although they both were facing the ramp carrying travelers up from the lower level. Casually, they turned and began to walk in Maertyn's general direction, although neither seemed to look anywhere close to him.

Maertyn anticipated that the two would swing around behind the group of passengers, then come up and flank him, half-stunning him right there and "walking" him out of the station. Ahead, he could see three figures in the red and blue of Transport security moving quickly toward him, more precisely toward the ramp behind him, since they were clearly headed down toward the false maintenance worker.

The two "businessmen" split to move past the first of the passengers, one going to the right and the other to the left, apparently unaware of or unconcerned with the security officers. Maertyn slipped his hand back into his jacket pocket, while remaining behind the muscular woman until the "businessman" to his right neared and looked toward Maertyn, smiling coolly.

Maertyn triggered his stunner, but directed the blast toward the man's knee and leg, so that he stumbled and then toppled forward.

"Help!" yelled Maertyn moving out to the side and kicking the stunner from the fallen man's hand. "He's broken his leg!" The stunner slid at an angle until it came to rest at the base of an alcove displaying a series of commercial scenes.

Two of the Transport security officers immediately turned and moved toward Maertyn. Most of the passengers continued onward, but the muscular woman did not, stopping and turning. Maertyn could see the other "businessman" quietly turn and join the passengers headed toward the short upper ramp to the street-level exit.

The agent started to sit up and reach for his waist.

"I wouldn't," said Maertyn, kneeling down, if far enough away that the man couldn't reach him. "You're alone. All you have to do is claim that you had a leg cramp . . . which you do, by the way. They'll help you leave the station without questions, and you don't want any. You can report that you couldn't act without giving yourself away to Transport. Your superiors won't like it, but you and they would like the alternatives less. If you try anything else, I'll point out your stunner and suggest you have other weapons." He smiled, then rose, beckoning to the Transport security officers. "Over here. I think he had a very severe leg cramp."

The lead officer took in Maertyn's maroon jacket, trimmed in silver-gray. "Sir?"

"Lord Maertyn. I'm headed to Daelmar on short notice. I couldn't get a direct train. He was walking past . . . and he fell."

The officer frowned.

"That's exactly what happened." The deep feminine voice came from the Transport functionary, who had continued to wait. Her eyes went to the man who still sat on the lichen-carpeted platform floor. "He's very fortunate that Lord Maertyn is a thoughtful and generous man."

"Yes . . . sir."

The muscular woman had continued to stand not quite beside Maertyn, and the two security types looked at her warily before helping the injured man away.

"Very nicely done, Lord Maertyn," she said in a pleasant voice. "Lord Ashauer will be pleased."

"Convey my appreciation, if you will."

"That I will, sir. You might wish to recover the agent's stunner. It might come in useful later. Transport has no security jurisdiction in Daelmar. Good evening." She offered a pleasant smile, then turned and followed the two security officers.

Maertyn didn't see the third officer, presumably dealing with the false maintenance worker. He did follow the woman's suggestion, glad that the security types had not recovered it first, but suspecting that they had been ordered not to by Ashauer's agent, as he picked up the stunner and slipped it into his other jacket pocket. He also continued to puzzle over why Ashauer was so interested in his survival. Or was it just that Maertyn's survival frustrated Tauzn's ambitions and schemes?

The platform was largely empty, given the lateness of the hour, and the only commercial establishment open was a small bistro at the south end. The faintly lit sign above the open door read DHOOREN'S. Maertyn saw no one else on the platform between him and the bistro. Nor did anyone appear as he walked to its open doorway and then inside, where he stopped. He counted the tables. There were eleven. A man and a woman, both in the gray of sanitary services, sat at the only other occupied table. Both glanced at him, then quickly looked away.

"Anywhere you want," announced the sole server, a stolid-faced woman perhaps his own age in the cream and white of food service.

"Thank you." Maertyn nodded politely.

After he seated himself at an empty corner table, facing the door, the server moved from behind the short counter that separated what passed for a kitchen from the rest of the bistro. "You'll be having what, sir?"

"Do you have a cheese and mushroom kalzeon?"

"Best I can do is lamb and cheese."

"I'll take it . . . with hot tea."

"Be but a few minutes, sir." There was a pause. "You'd be traveling late, sir."

"Last-moment change of plans." Maertyn let wryness creep into his voice.

The kalzeon was adequate, better than merely passable, and filling. Given that Maertyn hadn't eaten in more than eight hours, he didn't have trouble eating it all, although he took his time and had four mugs of slightly bitter tea in the process.

He also thought about the agents sent to detain or murder him. Why? There were any number of possible reasons, although most of them made little sense to Maertyn. The only one that held any semblance of reason was that Tauzn wanted media interest and publicity generated by the case of a murdered lord who was researching the secrets of the great canal in order to call attention to that research. But was that because Tauzn wanted Protective Services in charge of the research or to call attention to the "waste" of Unity funds on "worthless projects" in a time of crisis? The latter, Maertyn suspected, probably because no one in the media cared about a lord-scientist with an excellent reputation conduct-ing slightly unusual research on what amounted to a very low budget. But . . . if Maertyn were dead . . . he couldn't defend himself, and then there would be more digging into Maarlyna's illness and "treatment" and charges of waste and favoritism . . . as well as violating the medical ethics laws.

There might be other plausible reasons for the attacks, but Maertyn couldn't think of any. The fact that he couldn't also confirmed his wor-ries about the future of the Unity and his feelings about Tauzn's utter ruthlessness.

After almost an hour, the other couple, clearly also waiting for a train, rose and left the bistro. Maertyn watched them walk northward and then descend the ramp to the platform from which he had come.

Would anyone else appear in the hour or so before the tube-train to Brathym arrived?

No one else did, except for a contingent of Reserve guards, whom Maertyn followed down the ramp to the other platform. When his train did arrive, the small compartment he had reserved contained no sur-prises, although he did affix his own additional interior lock to the door before leaning back on the couch that was barely long enough to be a bunk.

For the next several hours, he dozed, if fitfully, then woke and waited while the train stopped in Brathym to take on more passengers. After that he dozed even more restlessly.

By just after what would have been dawn on the lands above the tube-train, on the sixth of Tenmonth, Maertyn sat in his compartment in the second car, looking at the image projected on the wall, a view the-oretically to the west. Powdery fine snow sifted back and forth across the barren flats between the stands of pines that marked the Reserve. Each autumn, the snows, light as they were, fell earlier than they had in the year before, and by spring, the snows were three yards deep on the ground above the tunnel where the train sped northward on the last leg of its trip from Semelin to Daelmar.

He had hoped to have returned to Maarlyna far earlier, but with all that had happened in Caelaarn, and especially upon his return, he was fortunate to have gotten as far as he had . . . and he'd still have to worry about what might await him at Daelmar.

He stiffened out of a semi-doze when the compartment speaker announced, "The train is arriving at Daelmar. All passengers must depart." For a moment, Maertyn wondered why the system had not addressed him as "Lord Maertyn" . . . until he remembered that he had not used his priority codes in booking the journey, not that his restraint had helped much, it appeared.

When he stepped out of the car onto the platform, the pewter finish of the tube-train and the fixtures of the Daelmar station felt cold, almost lifeless, although Maertyn could sense that the temperature was the same as it always was. He followed the Reserve guards, if by a yard or so—until he walked past the gate and kiosk toward the ramp up to the street level of the station.

Abruptly, Maertyn could feel a different chill, despite the solar and geothermal heat radiators in the walls and roof of the station . . . and something else, more like the warning or the call he sensed when an iceberg was about to calf and drop into the waters of the canal. Why would he feel that when the station was half a kay south of the canal?

"Your fortune, honored sir . . . your fortune?"

The woman who called to him from the dimness beside the ramp upward was the same slim figure, attired in red, that almost accosted him upon his departure. For all that she looked girlish, her hair was silver-gray and she held the same silvery oblong as before.

As she neared, not repelled or startled as she had been when he had been traveling to Caelaarn, Maertyn realized that he had never seen anything like the metallic rectangle. He also realized that she appeared . . . somehow . . . too sharp, as if outlined in some way . . . and he had the impression that another figure somehow accompanied her, but could see no one behind her . . . or to either side.

"Why did I startle you before, lady?" he asked, gently preemptive.

"You were not what was expected . . . after all these years, but that matters little. You are the husband of a lady with amber eyes and hair, and your entire future lies in her eyes and hands."

There was something about the way she spoke, a clarity at odds with the softness of her words. But he couldn't place it. "My entire future? And what of my . . . work?"

"You will find answers, but they will not aid those you believe to be your allies, nor those who are your enemies. The man who seeks you

stands outside the archway and wears a worn blue winter jacket. His part-
ner is the loader on the canal-runner." The young/old woman smiled . . .
and vanished.

Maertyn swallowed, then glanced around and back where the woman
had stood. Nothing changed. He was alone on the platform. Holographic
images? Yet he'd never seen an image that sharp and real, and with no
sign of any projection equipment and no other light sources. Had he really heard and seen her?

After a moment, he took a deep breath and started up the ramp,
putting his hands in his jacket pockets as if they were cold. By the time
he reached the upper level, the Reserve guards who had accompanied
him on the tube-train had all dispersed, and the inside upper level
of the station between him and the entrance was empty, except for a
bearded man leaning against the archway.

With his hands still in his pockets, Maertyn walked deliberately toward the arch.

The bearded man in a faded and mottled blue ice-jacket stepped
away from the arch, lurching toward Maertyn and smiling broadly. "Sir!"

"I'm sorry. I don't know—" As he said the word "know," Maertyn
pressed the stud on the stunner in his left pocket, hoping that he wasn't
acting on false information, yet *knowing* he was not.

The would-be beggar toppled.

"Medical aid! Security!" Maertyn yelled at the top of his voice. He
did not approach the fallen man.

Within moments, a squarish woman in the olive brown suit of a Reserve guard—since the Reserve guards were also security in Daelmar,
even for the tube-train station—hurried toward him and the fallen figure sprawled facedown on the lichen-carpet. She looked at Maertyn, taking in his garb, and then at the man lying there. "You're Lord Maertyn?"

"Yes, officer. I was just returning from Caelaarn. This fellow hailed
me and stepped toward me. I started to tell him that I didn't know him,
and he fell over."

The guard glanced back at another guard, younger and male, who
had wheeled a medicart up behind her, and then at the handful of by-
standers who had begun to gather. "Just stand back." She started to turn
the man over, then paused and lifted his right hand. From it fell a dark
gray object.

A single-jolt nerver, Maertyn suspected, the kind that would have produced an instant heart-stoppage.

The guard's eyes narrowed. She looked to Maertyn, and the faintest of sad smiles appeared. "I don't think there's any more you can do, Lord Maertyn. He's had some sort of seizure, and we'll find out why it happened. If there are any more questions, we know where to find you."

"You do . . . and thank you."

"Not a problem, sir." She eased the nerver into an insulated bag that she slipped from her belt, then turned to the other guard. "He'll need to go to medical confinement. He was carrying a proscribed weapon."

Maertyn stepped back. There were some benefits to being the only lord in at least two hundred kays in any direction, he reflected, as he walked through the archway to the main street, angling away from the space where the canal-runner would appear in the next half hour, and crossing the street on his way to Haarlan's Victualary. He was vaguely surprised to see that the Outfittery was open, the first time he'd seen it so in months, if not longer.

When he entered the victualary, he noted that Eylana was behind the counter.

"Lord Maertyn . . . what can we do for you?"

Maertyn smiled politely. "What would it cost me to request a number of special items for delivery today and to accompany whoever drives them out to the station?"

Her eyes widened. "Lord Maertyn . . . that is most . . . unusual."

"Humor me, if you would."

"I will have to check with Uncle Haarlan."

"Please do." Maertyn turned so that he could watch the entry as she linked to Haarlan, wherever the proprietor might be, listening as she relayed his request, but trying not to be too obvious about it.

". . . yes . . . yes, sir. I'll tell him . . . and see what he says." She looked up to Maertyn.

"Yes?"

"Two hundred more than whatever the order is . . . and he can't drive out for another hour and a half."

"That's fine. Done."

Eylana's mouth opened.

"Not a word to anyone, except your family, if you please."

"Yes, sir." Eylana cleared her throat, and added through her link, "Lord Maertyn says that is fine." She paused. "Yes, sir." Then she looked to Maertyn. "What would you like to order, sir?"

"Enough so that it's worth your while, your uncle's, and mine." Maertyn grinned.

After a moment, she finally smiled.

35

Eltyn and Faelyna worked, with little success, for the few hours remaining in eightday before finally retiring for the night. He did rig the alarms to wake them if anyone approached the station. Nothing did, and they resumed work early on oneday, after forcing down a breakfast extracted from ration paks.

The minidrone—or its replacement—was still circling overhead. When Eltyn took a brief break from helping Faelyna and went outside to inspect the antennae for damage, in less than three minutes, the system was reporting an incoming missile. The explosion to the southeast of the station didn't damage any of the exterior equipment, but Eltyn decided that any more excursions would only increase the odds of a warhead finally doing some serious damage to the exterior components of the scanning and power systems. And the riffies just might get lucky and time something so that he wouldn't get enough warning to return to the station.

No more outside work for a while, he pulsed as he headed back to rejoin Faelyna.

Good³ idea!

Glad you approve. [mild sarcasm]

Interrogative comm-links? [concerned curiosity]

In a moment. From the time Eltyn had isolate-blocked the comm system, he'd checked the incoming messages periodically, but the quarantine file had only contained general grand pronouncements similar to what had come in on the emergency system. Still . . . he hadn't checked lately.

Besides several more declarations from The Twenty asserting authority, there were two other text messages. They were identical.

All research activities previously conducted by members of the Ruche under the auspices of the radical organization termed TechOversight will now be assumed by Ruche Research Central. Any researchers who fail to preserve and protect such work will be treated as traitors to the Ruche and terminated. Those who preserve such work will have their efforts reviewed with a more lenient view, despite their previous allegiance . . .

Eltyn copied the text and flashed it to Faelyna.

Lovely choice. Immediate termination or brain-wipe. Doesn't change anything. That's all?

Except for more pompous[4] pronouncements.

The insanity of the Ruche as end-all and be-all . . . as bad as hysterical religiosity.

Worse.

Another reason to find a solution before they bring more force against the station.

Agreed. Eltyn walked up the ramp to her work area. *Status?* He sat down at the table adjoining hers.

Derivative and inversion approaches not viable, Faelyna pulsed.

????

Attempting commands in those formats results in return feed = frozen projector controls. Nanosecond response. Requires shutdown and power-up.

Less obvious alternatives?

Such as?

At that moment, Eltyn couldn't think of any.

They sat there silently.

Finally, Faelyna suggested, "Time to eat. Low blood glucose doesn't help with thinking."

"It's better than sitting here."

They walked down to the lower level, where Rhyana had already set up three places at one end of the plastene table that could have held ten. A rice and cheese casserole of a variety that Eltyn didn't recognize sat in the middle of the table with a rounded dome that looked to be hot bread beside the casserole on a square plate.

"Thank you," said Faelyna, "but you didn't have to . . ."

"Not much else to do right now. Can't go out without having missiles shot at you. You two need more than rations." Rhyana's voice was mock-gruff.

"We appreciate it," said Eltyn with a laugh.

"We really do," added Faelyna.

Eltyn had to admit that the casserole tasted far better than it looked, and he found himself taking seconds. "You're a good cook, and we don't have that much to work with here."

"Can't think on an empty brain. Got sweet fritters for dessert," offered the delivery woman. "I'll feed the riffie once we're done."

After finishing the last of the casserole on his plate, Eltyn took a bite of what looked to be a barely baked dough-strip, only to find that it was a light and flaky pastry that nearly disintegrated in his hands. "Good . . . very good . . ." he mumbled as he guided the remaining pastry flakes toward his mouth.

Alert! Possible Intruders!

At the warning, Eltyn immediately swallowed the last of the flaky fritter and shifted his attention to the monitors, noting first the surface-effect vessel skimming from the east toward the canal, holding a position midway between the north and south walls. In addition, there were five large trucks moving along the canal walls. All the trucks were hard-sided and roofed, with a shiny plate-like material on the outside that appeared to have been added recently.

What was it about the station that commanded so much interest from The Twenty and the riffies? No one had seemed to be interested before TechOversight had slipped Eltyn and Faelyna into the MetCom system in a quiet effort to research the station. Then, abruptly, the entire Ruche system had imploded, and the RucheFirst extremists and The Twenty had taken over in a coup. Since then, the station had been under continual, if intermittent, attack. Except, he corrected himself, none of the attacks had really involved major forces. It could just be that The Twenty were handling what opposition that remained as swiftly as possible.

Ship moving westward in the canal. Headed toward station. Several vehicles following on the canal road. Eltyn reached for the mug of cold *café.*

All entrances to the station already locked, Faelyna pulsed, swallowing the last of her dessert and rising from the table.

[affirm] Appears trucks retrofitted with armor. Driven all the way from Hururia? Eltyn stood.

They think we've discovered something special . . .

. . . and they want it.

[affirmation . . . sadness]

"What is it?" demanded Rhyana. "You both jumped up. You have those looks again."

"There's a surface-effect ship in the canal, probably with weapons, and five recently armored trucks rolling toward us," replied Eltyn. "Faelyna has made sure the station is locked. They can't get in, but we can't leave, either. Not without being terminated or brain-scrubbed, depending on the leniency of The Twenty."

"Death either way," said Rhyana, her tone almost matter-of-fact. "We got enough food for a good while. Might last long enough for you two to figure a way out for us." She gestured. "Go do what you have to. I'll come up after I clean this mess. See if there's anything I can do. Riffie can wait."

While Eltyn had his doubts about their figuring out a way out, he hurried after Faelyna, checking distances as he did. *Nearest truck is two kays plus. Estimate arrival in five minutes.*

Interrogative obvious weapons?

Nil obvious.

Once he was on the upper level, Eltyn sat at the worktable and began to check the monitors methodically. The trucks were slowing, and the first came to a halt more than half a kay to the east. All of them had been coated with a shiny golden brown polymer or something similar, but the coating didn't conceal the slightly uneven alignment of the thin plates that covered the panel siding and top of the cargo area. All five vehicles had stopped, and small dome-like turrets rose from the cabs of the first two.

No one emerged from the truck cab or from the rear. He checked the north monitor. The SEV remained stationary in the middle of the canal. From what he could tell, there were no comm-links, either.

Five minutes passed.

What are they doing? pulsed Faelyna.

Nothing. Nothing I can discern anyway. You?

Nothing. Don't dare to freeze the system. Shutdown and restart will unlock everything.

They continued to wait. Rhyana joined them, standing well back and saying nothing.

Eltyn kept scanning the monitors. When his virtie eyes locked on to the image of the area to the south, he blinked. An entire line of enormous bearded men swinging what looked to be battle-axes marched across grass—with pine trees behind them—toward the station. Where were the low dunes and sweeping sands? He blinked again, but the scene didn't change.

Check the south monitor. You see that?

Armored warriors with axes? No sand? pulsed back Faelyna.

That's what I see.

"Now what?" asked Rhyana.

Eltyn moistened his upper lip. Could he project the image he was seeing beyond the mental virtie picture? He shrugged. Either the system could or couldn't. He switched the scanner feed from virtie to projection.

The three stared as the full-sized image appeared between them and the south wall of the station.

"Who are they?" demanded the delivery woman. "Where are they?"

"That's what the south scanner shows. Maybe they're your ghosts," replied Eltyn. *Some sort of jamming . . . interference? That what the riffies are doing?*

Abruptly, a light of blue-green light scythed through the axemen, but the laser from the second truck had no effect. A second beam joined the first.

"The riffies think they're real," said Rhyana.

"They're not exactly ghosts," offered Faelyna. "I'm getting shadow signals or symbols."

Interrogative use/understand?

Negative. Totally different symbols. Different structure.

"Funny-looking images . . ." Rhyana's voice died away.

"They must be ancients, or images of ancients projected by the canal," said Faelyna. "Men haven't been that big in ages, and they're carrying antique weapons."

"It must be an image from the past that the canal captured. Some sort of defense, do you think?" Eltyn frowned. "Do you have any idea how?"

Faelyna shook her head.

The image vanished, and a white misty oblong hung in the air before them. Then the scene flicked, and the three were again looking at the familiar stretch of dunes and sand to the south of the station.

You think . . . the projection equipment and locking the station . . . together? Eltyn pulsed to Faelyna.

Improbable[5] . . . but possible.

How else?

Eltyn switched to the east monitor again, where the trucks began to ease slowly forward.

Between the trucks and the station, the stone seemed to ripple, as if it were moving.

The trucks stopped, and the lasers swept the undulating stone, with no effect.

Eltyn concentrated, trying to isolate something from the movements. For an instant, at the edge of the image, he saw a figure, a man silhouetted against a tree, except his uniform looked to be made of canal stone for an instant before it shifted into the green of grass and trees.

"What's that?" demanded Rhyana. "The stone's moving."

"There was a man there, a soldier," added Faelyna. "Then he vanished."

"They're wearing camouflage uniforms of some sort," offered Eltyn. "They blend into the background, so that each soldier looks like what's behind him or her, but they ripple some when they move. Or when the suit or uniform can't change fast enough."

"The ancients had those?" asked Rhyana.

"They must have. The canal somehow captured those images." *Why?* he pulsed to Faelyna. *It's not a defense.*

Surveillance triggered by lockdown and shadow-projection? Playback as side effect?

Slowing the riffies down.

For now . . .

Can you do anything?

Not without making us vulnerable.

[*sigh*] "The Twenty are novices in warfare," mused Eltyn, not knowing what else to say.

Both Rhyana and Faelyna looked curiously at him.

"They didn't seem to have much trouble in deposing The Fifty," observed Faelyna.

"That's because The Fifty didn't even think in those terms." He gestured vaguely. "Uniforms that blend with the background. That's hardly a revolutionary idea. As soon as I saw them, I understood why they'd work and their advantages. If the riffies out there report what they saw, I imagine The Twenty could come up with something similar, if they wanted."

"They won't," replied Faelyna. "They wouldn't want people who are opposing them to get their hands on something like that."

"Still," mused Eltyn, "we haven't thought that way in a long time. With just a little time and support, we could build something to drop that minidrone out of the sky." He paused. "Maybe more time and support, but it wouldn't be that difficult."

"We don't have either," pointed out Faelyna.

"No . . . but they can't get in."

"And we can't get out."

The stone stopped rippling, and Eltyn studied the riffie trucks. They didn't move. Neither did the SEV to the north in the middle of the canal.

A long afternoon, he pulsed.

Longer than that, replied Faelyna.

He suspected she was all too right.

36

❖   ❖   ❖

19 Siebmonat 3123, Vaniran Hegemony

Duhyle finished the synchronizer before midnight. It wasn't a temporal synchronizer, properly speaking, but a device to synchronize three command levels to "real time," although it could have been adjusted to any temporal base. That was, if he'd had any way to measure another such base. He'd installed it where Helkyria wanted. She insisted that they'd done enough and persuaded him to go to bed and get some rest.

Although that was what she had said, Helkyria held tight to him, and sleep was postponed for a bit. That alone concerned Duhyle, or would have, had he not been both tired and relaxed, but the concerns surfaced immediately when he woke—alerted by Helkyria sitting up on the side of the bed and beginning to dress. The orangish light diffusing through the "window" indicated it was barely after dawn.

"You're tense again." He rolled over and sat up. "This could be more dangerous than you said." He grinned. "Or last night."

The slightest hint of pink suffused the ends of her disarrayed hair. But she did smile before she replied. "Much more . . . but not so dangerous as not doing something to stop the Aesyr from continuing to use the Hammer as a weapon."

Duhyle scrambled into his tech uniform, then accessed the monitors while he waited for Helkyria to finish washing up in the small chamber that served as a bathroom. The operating monitors showed no sign of the Aesyr. The cargo vessel or the submersibles could have been moored directly to the north of the station against the canal wall, where Duhyle would have had no way of knowing—except indirectly, but there were no vibrations or electronic emissions on any standard frequency.

Helkyria waited for him, and they hurried down to the lower compartment that served as a mess room.

Captain Valakyr was waiting.

"The Aesyr haven't returned yet, but they will," announced Helkyria before the captain could say anything. "Most likely, they'll devote the day to severing our power connections. In the meantime, we'll be working on another way to thwart them."

"Ah . . . you *will* be working?"

"We worked late into the night, Captain. Determining how to operate trans-temporal shadow control systems requires a certain amount of mental acuity, which tends to fade when one operates with no sleep at all . . . and no food."

"Yes, ser."

"You should eat, too. One way or another, food won't be an issue." Helkyria took a ration kit and sat down at one end of the table.

Duhyle thought about taking two. Instead, he followed her example, then sat to her left.

They ate quickly, but when they returned to Helkyria's makeshift laboratory, the Aesyr had lifted a mechanical digger onto the canal wall. Two older figures were consulting handheld screens, and a crew prepared the digger. Several squads of Aesyr, each squad bearing both stunners and what looked to be projectile rifles, were positioned facing the station. Each squad directed weapons at where the doors and windows were.

"They're beginning to trace power flows," Duhyle said. "They've also got sniper squads targeting doors and windows. What do you want me to do?"

"Give me five minutes warning before it appears as though they'll sever a power cable."

"I can do that. Anything else?"

"Answer Symra's questions when she appears." *Please!*

Duhyle smiled, but he wiped the expression away as he heard the sound of Symra's boots on the stone behind him.

"Might I ask what's happening, ser?"

"She's occupied, Subcaptain," replied Duhyle. "The Aesyr have brought a power excavator. They're tracing power flows to find where they can dig and sever cables. The commander is working to thwart them. She'd appreciate not being interrupted. You might convey the situation to Captain Valakyr before you return to convey future developments as they occur."

"Yes, ser." Symra turned, a bit stiffly, and headed back down the ramp.

Duhyle doubted the honorific had been addressed to him, even though he'd been the one speaking.

Helkyria said nothing.

Duhyle glanced to the side at her, noting the fine sheen of perspiration on her forehead, partly, but only partly, a result of the higher humidity in the station. He transferred his attention back to checking the surviving monitors, one after the other.

The Aesyr finally completed their preparations, and the digger moved across the stone at the west end of the station to the southeast. It stopped just south of the sunken thermasteel compartment that shielded the power cables feeding into the station conformer.

More consultations between the digger operator and the two Aesyr with tracer screens followed. Then the digger moved farther southwest. Duhyle kept that monitor screen as the one physically projected into the chamber. He did not look up as Symra returned and stood back, midway between Helkyria and himself.

After the digger turned and the operator repositioned the digging blades, he said, "I'd say we're looking at five to ten minutes before they sever the cables from the cliff turbines."

"Thank you."

Duhyle quickly checked the other screens. Nothing had changed.

"Let's try this . . ." murmured Helkyria.

The light in the chamber became sharper. That was the way Duhyle would have described it if anyone asked him. No one did.

Symra didn't notice. Her eyes were chained to the image that appeared short of the Aesyr's digger—that of a golden ring, hanging in midair, about head high.

"Frig . . ." muttered Helkyria, almost under her breath. "Not there . . . too circular . . ."

The golden ring expanded, then shrank, dwindling, dropping, and vanishing into the stone of the canal.

Duhyle wanted to comment on how Helkyria's efforts might lead to treasure-hunting along the canal . . . or stories about hidden gold created by the ancients, or even golden rings linked to mysterious powers. He refrained. The single muttered curse—and the flickers of purple-black from the tips of her silver-blond hair—was enough to tell him that she was worried and struggling.

"This . . ."

Both Duhyle and Symra stiffened—and so did the Aesyr. A tall stern woman appeared before the mechanical digger. Her hair was silver-blond, and her garb was fitted and silvered armor comprised of small diamond-shaped plates that ran from her wrists to her neck and then down to shimmering silver boots. She held an upraised sword whose blade comprised flickering rainbow lightnings. The warrior woman was Helkyria.

"What . . . ?" Symra choked off the exclamation.

Duhyle said nothing, but concentrated on all the monitors and the reaction of the Aesyr. They all appeared as stunned as he was . . . for several moments.

Then one of the snipers turned and fired at the Helkyria image.

The projectile exploded a half-yard short of the image, and fragments dribbled from midair to the ground. The "projected" Helkyria touched the mechanical digger with the tip of the rainbow-fired blade, and the machine and its operator disintegrated into a pile of granules, but those granules were heavy enough that the light breeze raised no dust at all.

Then the image vanished.

Duhyle turned toward Helkyria. She wasn't there, yet he'd heard no movement at all.

"Where did she go?" demanded Symra.

"She can't have gone anywhere." *Not in the way we know it.* Duhyle checked all the monitors and all the systems. There was no sign of Helkyria. Then he focused on the south outside monitor. The Aesyr were looking at the pile of granules and small fragments of metal and who knew what else.

"Duhyle . . ."

At the sound of his consort's voice, Duhyle turned. Helkyria was sitting where she had been.

"Where . . . what . . . ?"

"We were right. There's a certain . . . temporal displacement associated with the canal and the station." A wry smile crossed her face, and vanished, along with the greenish tints to her hair that signified a sardonic outlook. "There need to be certain . . . modifications to the synchronizer. For now, anyway."

"How did you do that?" Duhyle asked.

"Do what?"

"Destroy the digger."

Helkyria looked at the monitor. "It's gone."

"We know. Someone who looked like you destroyed it with a rainbow-flamed sword."

"I didn't do it. For a moment, I was somewhere else, surrounded by flashing silver lights. It had to be some sort of temporal displacement."

Symra looked to Duhyle.

Duhyle shrugged.

"What about the Aesyr?" asked Symra.

"The ones outside are the least of our problems, I fear. Baeldura has threatened to loose the Hammers on Vaena if we do not surrender the station."

"Tell the First Speaker to threaten to turn Asgard into slag if a single Hammer is loosed on Vanira," replied Duhyle.

"She already has. Baeldura has reconsidered . . . for the moment. The First Speaker is pressing for us either to use the secrets of the canal in a way to stop the Aesyr or to allow a negotiated settlement where both the Aesyr and the Vanir share the discoveries."

"She doesn't want much," said Duhyle

"That 'negotiated' settlement would be a surrender, ser," added Symra.

"You're both right," replied Helkyria. "That doesn't change things. We don't have that much time."

"Can't the Aesyr see that using the Hammers will destroy them as well before all that long?" asked Symra.

"They believe that they and all life are doomed anyway, that the ice will sweep down and that the entire Earth will turn to ice, and that the

Frost Giants will rule. What matters to them is the glory of the struggle."

"But we're not those mythical or metaphorical Frost Giants," protested
Symra. "We're fighting the ice as well. That's why you're here."

"Facts are always irrelevant to true believers," interjected Duhyle.

"No," corrected Helkyria gently, "just those that conflict with their
beliefs. The others they use like hammers."

"Or the Hammers," returned Duhyle. *What now?* he private-linked.

"You'll need to make those modifications to the synchronizer. They
don't look too difficult, but I'm not the engineer. The Aesyr are doubtless reporting the destruction of the digger and requesting instructions."

Duhyle checked the outside monitors again. "The Aesyr look as
though they're pulling back . . . and rather quickly."

"That's not surprising," noted Helkyria.

"How . . . if I might ask . . ." ventured Symra.

"You can . . . they have reinforcements coming, and they don't want
to destroy their own forces unnecessarily. As for what we will be doing,
I'd tell you if I had time. It's connected with the canal's control system.
Tell the captain that it remains unsafe to leave the station." Helkyria
stood.

Symra did not flee. She did depart as if from unquestioned authority, not even looking back over her shoulder.

Duhyle realized his consort had acquired something . . . an additional presence, strength. She embodied what he'd seen in the warrior
image.

"We'll need to work as quickly as possible," Helkyria said. "SatCom
has relayed images. There's a vessel that dwarfs the *Skadira* headed our
way." Helkyria referenced the link.

Duhyle picked the locator up and focused on the image. He swallowed. The dark-hulled warship—for it couldn't be anything else—
looked to be almost a kay in length. "Where did they get that?"

"From the ice in Niefl, I suspect. It's been refitted, but the lines
aren't Aesyran or Vaniran."

"We aren't the only ones trying to decipher the past, are we? Do you
think that's where Thora came up with the idea for the Hammers?"

"It's possible. It's also possible that ancient vessel is only a platform that happened to be convenient. Or that something on the vessel led her to develop the theory and the Hammers."

"That ship has to have been time-protected . . . like the canal."

"I didn't tell you that." Helkyria smiled and raised her eyebrows, showing the cerise of amusement.

"That's the only possible explanation. For both that monster vessel and the canal."

"There's more than that . . . but we need to get to work."

After seeing the satellite image of the massive dark vessel speeding toward Vanira—and the station—Duhyle had to agree, although logically the size of the ship shouldn't have made any difference.

37

✵   ✵   ✵

6 Tenmonth 1351, Unity of Caelaarn

Haarlan and his freightrunner didn't reach the canal station until after sunset, although the sky was only light purple and not full dark. Before Maertyn stepped out of the cab, he slipped his personal credpass through the vehicle's portable recorder and added a hundred to the total.

"Sir . . . you didn't have to do that," protested Haarlan.

"Your victuals, your company, and your transport are all worth the extra . . . and I want you to be profitable enough to continue in business."

"Thank you, Lord Maertyn. I do appreciate it."

"As do I." Maertyn smiled. "I'll open the station door, since I doubt anyone's expecting me this early."

"I'll be along with the first cartons in a moment, sir."

"Don't hurry."

Maertyn stepped out onto the damp blue-gray stone of the canal wall, setting his boots carefully. South of the stone, the snow was close to knee-high, signifying more than a few storms over the past few weeks. He glanced to the north, where more dark clouds were massing. Then, he walked to the station and pressed his hand against the stone, waiting as the south side door opened.

"Hello there!" he called loudly and cheerfully.

Shaenya appeared immediately. "Lord Maertyn! You're back. We were wondering when you'd come." She half-turned and called, "Lady! He's back!"

"So I am, and so is a large load of provisions from Haarlan's. From the look of the snow and the sky, we'll be needing them."

"That we will be."

"Is that you, Maertyn?" Maarlyna rushed forward and flung her arms around him. "I'm so glad . . . I worried . . . we all worried . . ."

"I'm here, and I'm hale and healthy, if a little hungry." He kissed her gently on the cheek, then eased away, much as he wanted to wrap his arms around her tightly. "With that storm coming in, we need to let Haarlan unload everything and be on his way." Maertyn set the shoulder bag beside the door and walked back to the freightrunner, where he picked up one of the remaining cartons and carried it inside the station and down to the lower kitchen area.

He made one more trip carrying provisions, as did Haarlan and Svorak, who had hurried over from the square building that housed the power modulation equipment, before all that he had purchased was unloaded. Then he stood in the station doorway to see Haarlan off.

"Thank you again, Haarlan."

"My pleasure, Lord Maertyn." The wiry victualer smiled and nodded. "Good evening."

Once the freightrunner was headed back eastward, Maertyn closed the door and recovered his shoulder bag.

"I'll have a right regular supper for you in less than an hour, Lord Maertyn," said Shaenya.

"Not just for me, I hope." Maertyn smiled at his wife.

"No, sir. I wouldn't be forgetting Lady Maarlyna."

"She never does," added Maarlyna. "She's very good to me."

"You deserve it, dear." Maertyn looked to Shaenya. "And I can't tell you how much I appreciate it."

Shaenya flushed slightly, then nodded. "Best I be getting on with supper." She scurried down the ramp.

Walking beside Maarlyna, Maertyn carried the shoulder bag up the ramp to their chamber, where he set it beside the armoire. Then he removed both stunners and slipped them into the top drawer of his dresser, a family heirloom that had originally come from Norlaak. Although it had been an expense he had borne personally, he didn't regret in the slightest the cost of bringing familiar furnishings to the station, or what he knew it would require to return them all once his research term was over.

"How was your trip?" Maarlyna perched on the end of the bed.

"Long . . . tedious . . . difficult. The Ministry wants more concrete results from my research, or they'll allow the Gaerda to test weapons on the station and canal. I had to fill in for Josef while he was visiting universities . . . and that meant I had to handle the budget reallocations . . ." He went on to give a brief summary of all the "official" events and duties, but he did not mention the incident with the lorry or the events that had led to his taking the "local" tube-train from Caelaarn to Daelmar or anything that had transpired along the way northward. ". . . and then I stopped at Haarlan's to order supplies . . . and I came home."

"You've left out more than you've told me," said Maarlyna with an amused smile.

"Of course. I'll fill in the details after dinner."

"You promise?"

"I promise."

"I'll hold you to it, you know."

"I know."

"Oh . . . the crate you had shipped arrived last week. I had Svorak put it in the corner of your laboratory. It seemed rather heavy."

"It is. It has a number of items that we may need in the next few months, and I thought it would be easier to have Rhesten ship them while I was in Caelaarn."

"Those will fit in with what you haven't told me."

"Yes, they will." Maertyn walked over to the bed, eased Maarlyna to her feet, and held her tightly for a long, long time.

Neither said much in the time before Shaenya rang the chimes for dinner.

After dinner, the two of them settled into the section of the upper level that served as their sitting room, each taking a matching but ancient Laarnian Modern chair of the pair that flanked a low ebony oblong table.

"Matters were very bad in Caelaarn, weren't they?" offered Maar-lyna.

"Why do you say that?" Maertyn replied, keeping an amused tone in his voice.

"Because you were so cheerful when you arrived here. You're still doing it."

"That's because I'm glad to see you."

"Maertyn . . . I know that, but I can tell the difference."

He dropped the smile. "They weren't so bad as they could have been, but they weren't good. Ashauer met me at the tube-train station and warned me to be careful. He's never done that. Tauzn . . . the Minister of Protective Services—"

"I know who he is."

"He wants to succeed D'Onfrio as EA, and I'm guessing that he wants to make a political issue out of my research."

"He can't do that very effectively, can he? Your project is very low-budget. There must be hundreds larger and more wasteful. Besides, you're good at defending . . ." Her words dropped off.

For a moment, there was silence.

Finally, Maarlyna asked, "You couldn't defend matters . . . or me . . . could you, if you were dead? How many . . . ?"

"Three . . . four times . . ." he admitted.

"That many? How did you . . . did you kill anyone?"

"I managed not to kill anyone. One Gaerda operative who tried to force me off the road in an ice storm died when he lost control follow-ing me and crashed into an oak tree."

She raised her eyebrows.

"I . . . drove the runabout through the Laarnian Martyrs' Memo-rial."

"Oh . . . Maertyn . . ." Her voice was soft, yet warm. "Is it because you're a lord?"

"Because I'm a lord?" He laughed gently.

"Tauzn is courting the rabble. His type always does. If he can prove something involving D'Onfrio's appointees, especially impli-cating a lord, then that will strengthen his support, especially among them."

"Yes, lords must be above reproach, yet be able to get away with anything unscathed." Maertyn regretted the cynicism as soon as he had spoken.

"And their ladies . . ."

"You are above reproach," he said.

"Many might not think so."

He frowned. "How can you say that?"

"Maertyn . . . I'd like you to answer a question."

"If I can." He offered a smile, although the seriousness of her tone worried him more than he could have said.

"I'm not me, am I?"

"Of course you're you. Who else would you be?"

"I've never been that precise with words." A sad smile crossed her face. "Of course I am who I am. My name is Maarlyna, but I am not the Maarlyna who once was. I read the journal, the one in script, in your armoire. The writing could easily be mine, but it's not quite the same, and I remember the events written there, but my memories are as though I'd been told of them, and the way the words fall on the page is not quite the way I would write them."

He laughed softly. "I wouldn't write what I wrote five years ago in the same way I would now. None of us would. Why would you be any different?"

"Maertyn . . ." Her deep amber eyes focused on him, warm and intent.

He stood, then moved over to her chair, where he lifted her into an embrace, wrapping his arms around her for a long time. Then he stepped back, still holding her hands. "What is it? What has upset you so much?"

"You've had some disturbing things befall you . . . dangers . . ." She paused, then continued. "So have I. It's different . . . but I worry. I've worried more than I've told you."

"I've sensed it, but I never wanted to press you."

"I know that, and I appreciate it." After the slightest pause, she went on. "I never said much when you suggested you heard or sensed things about the ice calving or tsunamis striking the canal walls. At first, I just thought I was imagining things, or that it was because of all the medical procedures . . . but they didn't fade away. Instead, they got stronger as I did."

"You sensed them as well? I wondered."

"Not exactly. I saw shadowy figures . . . not shadowy, really, because they were more than shadows. They weren't at all white and ghost-like . . ."

"Was one of them a woman in red who was neither young or old?"

Maarlyna's mouth opened. "You saw her and didn't say anything?"

"I saw her just a few hours ago . . . when I got off the tube-train in Daelmar. She warned me about the Gaerda assassin waiting for me. Then she vanished." Maertyn saw no point in mentioning the earlier brief glimpse of the woman in red.

"The assassin . . . ?"

"I stunned him in a way that everyone thought he'd fainted or had a seizure. The Reserve guards found a nerver in his hand. No one said anything, except that they didn't see any reason to detain me."

"People here respect you . . . unlike in Caelaarn."

Maertyn didn't want to explore that. There wasn't any point in it. "What about the woman in red . . . or the others?"

"She showed me . . . how to lock the doors and the windows. Just from the inside. They can't be locked from outside. I can't do that, anyway."

"How . . . ?"

"I can't explain it. I can only do it." She eased her hands out of his and walked to where the window was.

That had to be from memory, thought Maertyn since it was well after dark, and he certainly couldn't see the window from any light being passed through the stone.

Maarlyna touched the stone and the "window" appeared and opened, with the cold air from the north sweeping into the chamber. After a moment, she touched the stone again, holding her hand there for several moments. "Now . . . you try to open it."

He stepped forward and stood beside her, reaching out to place his fingers against the stone that was neither hot nor cold to his touch.

Nothing happened. The stone did not change.

"You see." Maarlyna reached out and pressed her hand against the wall, then quickly pulled it away. "Try it now."

Maertyn did. The stone flowed back on itself, and cold air rushed past them strongly enough to disarray Maarlyna's hair. He touched the wall again, and the window closed.

"Well . . . if anyone tried to attack us here, you could keep them out."

"That . . . that was what she said."

"She talked to you. What else did she say?"

"Not really talked . . . it was more like I heard her words in my head."

Maertyn pursed his lips. Had he just thought he'd heard the woman in red speak to him? Had her words really been spoken? He'd thought her words so clear for being so soft . . . was that because he'd heard them in his mind?

"Maertyn?"

"I think I heard her in the same way . . . I just hadn't realized it." Should he tell Maarlyna what else the ice-sport or ghost or . . . whatever she was . . . had said? "She said that our fates were intertwined." That was close enough without putting pressure on Maarlyna. "Did she say who or what she was?"

Maarlyna frowned, tilted her head to the left, then finally said, "No . . . not exactly . . . but I had the feeling that she belongs here."

"Here?"

"To the station . . . the canal. How else would she have known how to show me the locking and unlocking?"

How indeed? "Can you show me?"

Maarlyna shook her head . . . sadly, it seemed to Maertyn. "It's not like that. It's inside my head, my thoughts. It's like she put a pattern there. When I think of that pattern and touch the stone, I can lock or unlock the doors and windows."

"Can you do anything else with the pattern?"

"Not that I know of."

Maertyn embraced Maarlyna again, murmuring in her ear, "That's all right. She must have given you that ability for a reason, and, from what she told me, it's for both of us. I just wish we knew why."

Maarlyna hugged him back. "I'm so glad you understand."

"How could I not?" He lowered his head and kissed her neck. "How could I not?"

Even so, later in the darkness, as he lay there beside her in the bed that had been his great-grandsire's, he couldn't help but wonder and worry.

Why had the silvery woman in red sought out Maarlyna? Why?

38

✦ ✦ ✦

33 *Quad 2471 R.E.*

For a good quarter of an hour, the armored trucks remained motionless while the Ruche surface-effect vessel moved in a tight circle in the middle of the canal.

"Why are they waiting?" asked Rhyana.

"They're probably calibrating a weapon on the SEV," replied Eltyn. "Or they're waiting for another kind of attack."

Calibrating . . . [incompetence], pulsed Faelyna.

"Not too bright. They didn't even notice the RF wheeler," added Rhyana.

"It is covered in sand," Eltyn pointed out.

Seeing only what they want to . . . or can, suggested Faelyna.

Several more minutes passed before a reddish gold point of light struck the north side of the station, barely caught by the monitors, then vanished. Another followed from the SEV in the middle of the canal. It was equally without effect.

Lasers ineffective[4]. Idiots, pulsed Eltyn.

Ignorant. No one left from TechOversight or MetCom who knows the MCC parameters.

One of the armored trucks rolled up alongside the south wall of the station. The cab opened, and a woman in gray drab scrambled out and pressed her hands beside where the stone door was. The small mini-turret atop the cab swiveled and a single-barreled weapon focused on the door. The door did not respond to the woman's touch.

Locks holding. Eltyn knew the comment was redundant. Faelyna was accessing the monitors as well. But he felt he had to acknowledge her success.

The woman kept holding her hands against the wall. The truck turned and headed back to join the other four, leaving the woman alone. Finally, she lifted her hands from the station wall and ran back toward the five vehicles. Eltyn continued to watch her, the trucks, and the SEV. After several minutes beside the lead truck, the woman trudged back westward, this time in the narrower space between the raised seawall and the north wall of the station. When she reached the point where the canal-side door was located, she again pressed her hands against the stone, to no avail.

Eltyn did his best to focus the monitor on her more closely. From what he could tell, her face was fixed in concentration, yet her eyes seemed . . . off. He projected the image.

Brain-scrub and conditioning, suggested Faelyna.

"They don't care if she gets killed," said Rhyana. "Poor thing."

"Just so long as she serves The Twenty." Eltyn didn't bother to mute the raw sarcasm.

Yet . . . he certainly hadn't questioned the The Fifty or any of the higher officials of the Ruche before the coup . . . or had he? He and Faelyna had embarked on a secret project for TechOversight, one that certainly wouldn't have been considered favorably by The Fifty—and hadn't been. But The Fifty hadn't been brain-scrubbing anyone who disagreed. They just hadn't approved their projects.

Where was the line between ethical disagreement and being a traitor? Was it killing? If so, he was now a traitor. But . . . there was a difference between killing to avoid being killed and killing others because they didn't agree . . . wasn't there? Eltyn didn't have time to ponder that point and what led to and from it. The emergency signal flashed.

They want to communicate.

You talk, pulsed Eltyn. *Might say what I think. [wryness]*

I won't?

You always think before you speak.

I'll remind you of that later. Faelyna pressed the stud to acknowledge the emergency transmission, using the manual override, rather than admitting that the station still had full internal communication systems. "Yes?"

"Regional Inspector Welkyr here. You have not opened this installation to inspection as required by The Twenty. Why have you not complied?"

"When your inspectors arrived, they came bearing arms," replied Faelyna. "They also followed reports that they had brain-scrubbed almost everyone at the Apialor station. The one inspector we captured threatened us with the same. Under those circumstances, would you have opened the station to anyone?"

"The Twenty are fair and just."

Faelyna did not reply to Welkyr. *How can I answer that without lying or infuriating him?*

"He's lying," muttered Rhyana.

You can't, pulsed Eltyn.

For several minutes, the three in the station waited.

Finally, Welkyr spoke again, his voice smooth coming from the comm speaker. "Despite your actions in failing to comply with the law of the Ruche, Ruche Research is prepared to offer you leniency if you leave MCC (W) with all equipment intact. There is no need to prolong this . . . inconvenience. Just be reasonable, and all will be well."

"Exactly what do you mean by leniency?" replied Faelyna.

Ask about whether The Twenty will abide by whatever agreement Ruche Research reaches, pulsed Eltyn.

Not yet, she pulsed back.

"You will be treated as any other nonviolent member of the Ruche who has not yet seen the way of The Twenty."

"That doesn't sound lenient after what we've seen so far." Faelyna's voice was totally matter-of-fact.

"It is most lenient for those who have defied the very principles of the Ruche."

"It's not lenient enough for us. We'd like to keep both our minds and bodies intact."

"The Ruche will not harm you. You will have long and productive lives."

As little more than barely sentient vegetables, suggested Eltyn.

"We're looking for long, productive, and thoughtful lives," pointed out Faelyna.

"We can offer no more," stated Welkyr.

"Then we must reluctantly decline your most kind offer," replied Faelyna.

"Then you must deal with the consequences that befall all who refuse the mercy of The Twenty."

Mercy? If that's mercy, we don't need to hear what they believe is justice or retribution, pulsed Eltyn.

"No mercy there," said Rhyana.

The emergency comm went dead. Shortly, all five armored trucks turned, one after the other, and drove eastward from the canal, raising a faint haze of sand and dust.

Eltyn increased the size of the image, so that Rhyana could see it clearly as well. *Retract and shield. Report status.*

Retracted and shielded.

The projected image vanished.

"What happened?" asked Rhyana.

"As soon as they're out of range, the SEV will start firing, either lasers or projectiles, or both," suggested Eltyn. "The lasers won't do anything, unless they hit an antenna or a scanner, and from where they're situated, they can only take out the scanner and the antenna on the north. Missiles or projectiles could take out the other scanners and even the power cables—although those would take lucky shots. There's no point in leaving anything unnecessarily exposed."

"The tidal generator is underwater," added Faelyna. "It's not the primary power source anyway. The solar grid is spread over kays to the south, and most of the cabling is buried deeply."

"Some of the sensors are shielded anyway, and we can get an idea of what they're doing."

A spike in temperature on the north side of the station confirmed that the SEV had focused at least one laser on the station. Several other beam strikes registered. Then, for several minutes, nothing happened.

"Projectiles are likely on the way," Eltyn said dryly.

Seismic sensors began to register impacts, more than a few.

Shelling us in earnest, Eltyn pulsed to Faelyna.

Nothing like a believer scorned.

Eltyn tried to get an image through the local antenna on the south side of the station, but all it revealed was sand and dust swirling around the station, with an occasional gout of dirt and sand, mostly sand, geysering into the sky south of the canal stone.

Then one warning indicator came up, and another.

The main antenna is out again . . . we've lost seventeen percent of the solar grid.

Eltyn waited as the impacts continued, but the system did not indicate any more warnings.

A good hour passed before the shelling stopped.

The emergency comm flashed again.

Faelyna looked at Eltyn.

He shrugged.

"Yes?"

"Are you ready to reconsider and accept the mercy of The Twenty?"

"Not unless you guarantee long, prosperous, and intelligent life," replied Faelyna.

"We have promised that."

"Then you're lying, and that's even more despicable."

"We only want you to embrace the Ruche so that you will not be lost to the Meld."

"We'll remain lost, thank you."

In less than five minutes, the shelling resumed, and continued for another half hour. Then the SEV began to move eastward, slowly at first, before gaining full speed, from what Eltyn could determine from the east-facing local antenna/scanner.

"How bad we hurting?" asked Rhyana.

"We've lost twenty-three percent of the solar grid and the main scanning antenna. We don't have another spare. Even if we did, being outside any time soon wouldn't be good."

Not at all, pulsed Faelyna.

"Now what?"

Eltyn shrugged again. "Their pride is hurt. They'll try something even more powerful."

"They wouldn't be stupid enough to use a nuclear device, would they?"

"Unless they've got more scientific expertise than we know, they couldn't have built one since they took over, but they'll come up with something."

Eltyn was afraid he knew exactly what that was . . . but they'd have to evacuate the area on the north side of the canal before they did, not that there were all that many people there.

You really think they would? Faelyna looked to him.

You think they wouldn't?

She shook her head.

"Is there any of that casserole left?" asked Eltyn, offering a smile he didn't feel.

39

✤　✤　✤

Duhyle had only made the first of the changes to the synchronizer before the arrival of the Aesyr's monster vessel, its hull and superstructure of a brown so dark that it was almost black. The warship turned sharply a kay off the west coast of Vanira and came to an immediate stop, sending a miniature tsunami shoreward. That cascade of water shot upward at the ocean wall of the canal and sent spray across the stone of the station. The warship was indeed nearly a kay in sleek length, yet lay low in the water, with the top of the single Hammer mast rising less than fifty yards above the surface of the Jainoran Ocean. Immediately forward of the bridge was a single turret with two stubby guns or launchers. A similar massive turret dominated the area forward of the fantail. Duhyle projected an image, hoping to gain a better view.

The entire superstructure of the vessel was angular and shiny. While the overall impression was that of a shimmering brownish black, colors rippled from the surface. A single Hammer streak flared from that mast—striking the sea cliffs to the south of where the canal wall ended. Dust flared into the midday sky.

Just as quickly, the Aesyr vessel vanished.

"Where did it go?" demanded Symra, who had returned to the

chamber so quietly that Duhyle hadn't noticed her. Blackish purple darkened her lashes.

Duhyle knew the ship was still there. It couldn't have moved, but it had become invisible to scanners at any frequency.

"Energy-shielded," observed Helkyria. "A laser would bend away from it now."

"They could have approached unseen."

"Not at that speed. The waves its mass created would have given it away. Besides, Baeldura wanted us to know what the ship can do. Let's see if . . ."

Abruptly, the light around the three *shifted*. The illumination wasn't more intense or less so. It was subtly, if fundamentally, different.

The chamber in which Duhyle sat changed as well. Before him rose a bank of instruments, or equipment, reaching from floor to ceiling. Yet he could make out none of it in detail. The dimensions or the properties of what he beheld shifted even as he tried to determine what lay before him. He squinted, trying to focus on the narrow console in front of him, only to see it widen, and then shrink to half its height before turning from a bluish silver to pewter gray, and then to silvered gold. A row of strange high-backed chairs stretched out beside him. He saw and felt that he was sitting in one, his arms lying comfortably in armrests, with controls under his fingers. A silver-haired woman sat beside him, except suddenly she was a dark-haired man with a square beard.

Duhyle opened his mouth to speak, and strange and incomprehensible words echoed in his ears.

Then, as suddenly as it had all enfolded him, the visions vanished.

He glanced toward Helkyria. The tips of his consort's hair had flared silver, then subsided as he watched. "What—"

"That couldn't be . . . equipment like that . . ." Symra's voice died away.

"Intersection of conflicting shadow harmonics," Helkyria said. "I'm judging that they bend time, or fragment it, or fragment our understanding of it. I'm still having trouble calibrating some of this."

"Did you see . . . was this a control room of some sort?"

"It was a control room of many sorts, probably for years. That was then. Right now, we still need to deal with the Aesyr ship out there."

That might be so, but the stark and spare space where Duhyle sat was alien in comparison to what he had experienced, if only briefly. He took a deep breath, massaged his forehead, and returned to studying the monitor images.

From the angle of the station scanners, he could see that the Aesyr Hammer strike had carved from the stone ramparts of the western coast a semicircle a good kay across. The scanners could not see how deep the damage went. From the stream rising from below, Duhyle judged that a new bay lay at the base of the reconfigured topography.

"The Hammer strike was aimed at us," Helkyria said, her voice even.

"What are they trying to do?" asked Symra.

"The same thing as all true believers—use force to remake the world to fit their views," replied Helkyria. "Like all believers, they feel that they've been wronged by others' inability to see that only they have the answers and the way."

"People aren't like that," protested the subcaptain.

Not all people, thought Duhyle, *but all too many. If no one stands up to those who want to force their views on others, then everyone suffers.*

"Quiet. We're getting a message. It's Baeldura."

An image appeared on the reception monitor. Duhyle projected it so Symra could see.

The woman who stood before them was tall, with neck-length flaming red hair, and silvered black eyes. She wore a plain black singlesuit with no insignia. No background projected with her, suggesting that she did not wish to reveal the details of wherever she was—or the equipment.

"Commander Helkyria . . . I presume. You might grant me an image."

Helkyria nodded to Duhyle, and he used the internal scanner to capture her.

"Much better." A warm and broad smile appeared on Baeldura's face. "You've been working hard, and more effectively than Scient-Marshal Thora imagined possible."

Duhyle had to admit that the Aesyr leader was breathtakingly beautiful, if in the cool and cruel manner he'd observed in other powerful women, usually politicians.

"I find that difficult to believe," replied Helkyria. "Thora has always had a broad and wide imagination. What did you have in mind, Baeldura, now that you've determined that the station is not so easily taken?"

The redhead nodded. "Not by force, it would appear. That may be for the best. It would be a pity to destroy what lies within. I am requesting that you surrender the station, for the good of all Earth."

"The good of all Earth?" Helkyria repeated the phrase almost without inflection.

"You believe that survival outweighs principles. We believe principles outweigh survival. Therefore, the maximum good for all comes if you surrender. Everyone survives—or most everyone—and principles reign supreme."

"Your principles, I believe."

"Come . . . let's not quibble, Commander. Will you surrender the canal and the station to us? Or will you watch as we destroy Vaena and the Vanir?" asked Baeldura.

"If you use those weapons, you'll destroy yourselves as well in a very few years," Helkyria pointed out.

"The universe will end, Helkyria. Better it end sooner in freedom than drag on eternally in the mind-numbing and subtle tyranny imposed by the Vanir."

"I'm not even in charge of Security, Baeldura."

"I won't even quibble about that. I'll give you twenty-four hours to consult with the Magistra of Security before you decide. If you don't come out and surrender the station intact to us then . . . then the Hammers will begin to fall. As you may have seen, I have already withdrawn the Aesyr from around the station." Baeldura's image vanished.

For several moments, none of the three in the chamber spoke.

"What are these principles that she keeps mentioning?" asked Symra. "Why are they worth destroying everything for?"

"They started out as self-government for Midgard, but self-government meant government by the Aesyr with no vote for any Vanir living there," Duhyle said. "Then, they wanted freedom of genetic choice. That translates, I think, into building bigger, stronger, and more intelligent Aesyr in order to maintain order, order being control over anyone lesser—"

"The issue of principles, per se, is secondary," interrupted Helkyria.

"She has to be bluffing," insisted Symra.

"Would you bet the universe on that? When the Aesyr have done exactly what they said they would do?" Helkyria looked at the subcaptain.

Symra looked down. "It's not right . . ."

"I doubt the universe cares what is right," replied Helkyria calmly.

Duhyle couldn't help frowning for a moment. Was the universe that . . . random? Was whatever its organizing principle might be so biased against . . . ? He shook his head. He couldn't frame the vague concept that lurked just beyond his mental reach.

He checked the monitors. As Baeldura had promised, he could detect no Aesyr group anywhere within range of the station. "What do you have in mind?"

"Fragmenting time . . . or at least the station's place in it. If we can." She looked to Duhyle. "I have some ideas about more changes to your synchronizer. They shouldn't take that long." Her eyes went to Symra. "You can tell Captain Valakyr about the Aesyr ultimatum. Also tell her about the rather permanent alteration to the cliffs . . . and that we are attempting a way to avoid making that rather unpleasant choice. All the troopers need to remain within the station. We will likely need them."

Puzzlement crossed the subcaptain's face. "Yes, ser." She turned and headed down the ramp.

"What do you need me to do?" asked Duhyle.

"Everything." Helkyria's smile was both affectionate and wry. "Starting with a way to double the power the synchronizer can take. Knowing you, it's overbuilt. I do hope it's overbuilt . . ."

"Mostly, but that will be stretching it."

"Then . . . stretch . . ."

Duhyle found himself smiling.

40

✵   ✵   ✵

7 Tenmonth 1351, Unity of Caelaarn

By the time Maertyn and Maarlyna woke the next morning, snow was falling heavily enough that even the blue-gray stone of the canal walls was covered, not that such a covering would last, but with heavy snowfall and bitter cold, several days often passed before the snow fully cleared from the stone of the canal and station. After waking, Maertyn took his time, enjoying the moments spent with Maarlyna, both dressing and in eating breakfast.

As she finished sipping the hot cocoa she enjoyed so much, Maarlyna looked to her husband. "You're worried about what is happening in Caelaarn, much more than usual. Can you tell me why?"

"All sorts of little things. Too many. Crop yields are down across the world. The re-settled are causing demonstrations. Food prices are up. Political maneuvering and accidental deaths among the well-connected in Caelaarn have increased . . . and I've told you about the attempts against me."

"They're trying to blackmail you with me, aren't they?"

"Why would they do that?" he asked. "You haven't done anything."

"Except survive when I shouldn't have." Maarlyna smiled sadly. "How did you manage it, dearest?"

"You know that. I arranged for the best doctors and regeneration specialists possible."

Maarlyna shook her head. "You did more than that. I know who and what I am, and I've read enough medical articles to know that there was only one way I could have survived." Her eyes brightened, not quite enough for tears to appear. "You risked everything, didn't you?"

Maertyn wanted to deny that, but denying it wouldn't have been true, and yet agreeing was almost as false. "That was never the question. What else could I have done? I hadn't given you enough of me, especially after . . ."

"After I lost all chance of having children?"

Maertyn's eyes were burning, but he shook his head. "I hadn't fully understood how much you meant to me, and I hadn't shown it. Then . . . merely telling you would have been but words, and there are times when words are anything but enough." He didn't know what else he could say, except that he loved her, and those words would have seemed trite at the moment.

"Oh . . . Maertyn . . ."

The silence was broken by the whine of the wind as the south side door of the station opened. Svorak stepped into the main room, stamping his boots, and shaking snow off his jacket. "Sir, Lady . . . canalrunner just came. Didn't think they would with the snow, but it's not so heavy to the east. Two envelopes, one for each of you."

Maertyn rose from his chair, walked toward Svorak, and took the letters. "I'm surprised as well. Thank you."

"You're welcome, sir. Best I be checking the light. Might be a ship or two needing it in the storm." The light-keeper smiled, then touched the stone, and slipped back out into the snow.

Maertyn looked at one, then the other.

The first heavy envelope was addressed to Lord Maertyn S'Eidolon, in care of the station, and bore the extra delivery fees . . . and an address he did not recognize. The second he did recognize. "One for me, and one for you. Yours is from your cousin."

"Lycinna?"

"The very same."

"You open yours first," said Maarlyna with a smile.

Maertyn just enjoyed her expression.

"Go ahead," she prompted.

He walked back and handed her the one envelope, then broke the seal on the second, scanning the letterhead. He frowned as he finished the short missive. "It's from Ashauer."

"Might I see it, dear?"

"Of course." Maertyn handed her the elegantly written missive and moved behind her chair, where he read it again, this time over her shoulder.

My dear Maertyn,

I learned from various sources that you took a rather circuitous route to return to your dear wife and your duties, just to arrive a few hours early. But then you've always been good at surprising people, yet leaving them discomfited and unharmed. Why should your journey back have been any different?

You may not have heard the sad news about Hlaansk. The fuel cell in his official sedan caught fire and the electrical malfunctions locked the doors. Of course, all government vehicles have now been inspected, but it is a pity that it wasn't done earlier. Minister Hedelin had recommended more preventive maintenance for the Unity vehicle fleet months ago, but the Council had rejected the funding as frivolous, given the higher priorities outlined by Protective Services. There was some question over his successor, but after consulting with other concerned ministers, the EA appointed your superior, Josef, as acting Minister of Science. As acting minister, of course, he will continue as Assistant Minister for Research . . .

I forgot to tell you that Jaelora also sends her best and trust you will not have to venture far from the station with a cold northern winter coming in.

The elegant signature was that of Ashauer.

"Matters are getting much, much worse," Maarlyna observed.

"There's no need to talk of those more at the moment." He smiled. "Read your letter." Then he sat down and watched as she read, just enjoying watching her.

When she finished and looked up, he asked, "What did she have to say?"

She leaned forward and handed him the two sheets. "You can read it yourself?"

"Thank you." He smiled and took the letter, noting that Lycinna's script was similar to Maarlyna's, not so surprisingly, since they'd both had the same tutor as children.

Dearest Maarlyna,

I've been so remiss in my correspondence, but with Elyna's acceptance at Hytaan, and getting her off, and Neulan's studies for admission to the University of Caelaarn's School of Medicine, time has just slipped away. It's so hard to believe that you've been buried in the frigid north for almost two years and that the summer evenings when we sat up and talked most of the night were so long ago. I don't feel that much older, but I must be. I suppose we all are, but at times I do long for those carefree days.

All is well with us, although Daerix is having to spend more and more time at the factorums, something about the change in baseline ambient temperatures requiring more careful adjustments and more training for the technicians . . .

I must confess that I've never seen so many Protective Services trainees as seem to have come into Oxara in the past few months, although we only see them when we leave the estate, and only on weekends, at that. Daerix's workers have told him that at times their houses shake because of all the explosions out at the training center . . .

These days we don't get to Caelaarn often, and I suppose that is for the best because I'd want to stop and see you, and you wouldn't be there. Is it as cold as everyone says up on the great canal? Please write and tell me all about it.

Maertyn handed the letter back to his wife. "She wants you to write back."

"She's lonely," said Maarlyna. "She's always had the children, and now they're leaving. Daerix has his work, and the estate doesn't require that much supervision." She paused. "I don't care much for the idea that the Unity is training more and more Protective Service troopers."

"Agents . . ." Maertyn said dryly.

"Troopers." She shook her head. "Are you going to work today?"

"No. I'm spending the day with you. We could even play in the snow."

Her smile warmed him all the way through.

41

Surprisingly, Eltyn slept decently. He couldn't help wishing he'd been sleeping closer to Faelyna, rather than on the narrow pallet in the corner of his own workroom. He woke early, at the first sign of diffused light coming through the stone "windows" on twoday. A quick check of the system and the outside monitors showed no one and no vessels nearby. He washed and dressed quickly, only to find Faelyna waiting for him by the ramp down to the lower level.

"I couldn't sleep any longer," he said. "I keep wondering what The Twenty will do now."

"I couldn't sleep longer either." She looked at him directly for a moment. "I'm glad you're here." Then her eyes dropped. *We need to do something. We can't just stay trapped inside the station.*

Options? he pulsed.

Such as?

?????

Exactly. Nothing else gets us beyond the first command levels . . . except freezing the system. Not good now.

Eltyn had to agree with that. *Exactly. Still . . . someone told me, Eat first. Think later.*

Faelyna did smile as they walked down to the lower level.

Rhyana was waiting. "Thought you two might be up early."

"Don't you ever sleep?" asked Eltyn.

"Not late. Delivery schedules are—were—always out early." She pointed to the table. "Sit. Eggs . . . what passes for 'em . . . are almost ready. Pastries . . . sort of, too."

"Thank you." Both Eltyn and Faelyna spoke almost simultaneously.

"No need for thanks. You both are doing what you can. Least I can do is feed you. Without you two, I'd not be thinking . . . or not much except what the riffies wanted."

"We still appreciate it." Eltyn slipped into one of the chairs, before which was a platter, and across the narrow table from Faelyna.

As he ate more of the egg-like omelet than he thought he could, Eltyn had to admit that food preparation had improved immeasurably since Rhyana had joined them, especially with the flaky pastries.

"Anyone out there?" asked the delivery woman.

"Antennae don't show anyone, but the locals are only good for a kay or so."

"Riffies'll be back. They want everything their own way."

Eltyn stiffened at the warnings coming from the system. *Trouble . . . seismics and locals showing something . . . coming our way . . .*

They couldn't . . . how could they evacuate . . .

All the lights went out, except for the emergency beacon . . .

Eltyn immediately accessed the station systems and scanned all the indicators. *Readings show temperatures . . .* Eltyn swallowed. *. . . sensors . . . vaporized . . . Entire outside power grid gone, even the tidal pump.*

Thermonuke? No . . . there aren't any . . . are there?

Eltyn checked the last readings, frozen on the system. *Radiation . . . but not weapons . . . superheated[3] steam . . .*

. . . steam . . . ?

Abruptly . . . the two exchanged glances. Eltyn checked the ventilation system, but something had shut off all the ducts, and the ventilators had cut off. He closed down the internal net, and the nonessentials, leaving just basic lighting for the moment. They'd need all the power in the inside storage system, and they certainly wouldn't be leaving the station any time soon. Before long they might have to worry about air quality, but with only the four of them and the size of the station, that wasn't an immediate concern.

"They wouldn't . . . would they?" asked Faelyna. "The area to the north . . . hundreds of kays . . ."

"Maybe they evacuated the people."

"The Twenty? Do you think they'd bother?"

"What happened?" asked Rhyana. "Something bad, from the look of you."

"Exactly? We don't know," replied Eltyn.

"Eltyn . . ."

"The Twenty dropped—we think—a chunk of nickel iron or something like it out of orbit and aimed its re-entry at us. It looks like it hit water, probably to the west and north of us. That's just a guess from what information the sensors recorded before they all vaporized."

"Vaporized? Turned to gas?"

"That's an educated guess, too. None of the sensors are registering, and the temperatures outside were hot enough to melt, if not vaporize, most metals and composites."

"You sure? We didn't feel anything."

"Inside the station you don't. We didn't feel any of the shelling. The whole Earth could fall apart and you wouldn't know."

"Can't we open a door or window and look out . . ." Rhyana glanced from Eltyn to Faelyna. "It's too hot?"

"In more ways than one." Eltyn stopped, then glanced around. Something else had changed, although he couldn't quite determine what.

"Do you notice something?" asked Faelyna. "The light . . ."

"It's sharper . . . or different . . ." Eltyn stood, moving away from the table, his eyes going to the ceiling, then to the walls.

Banks of instruments appeared, shimmering as if shrouded in transparent silver, but crisp and solid. They lined the walls of the chamber, but as soon as Eltyn tried to concentrate on a single area, one console or equipment bay was replaced by another, different but appearing equally solid and crisp, and the rate of change varied from moment to moment.

"They keep changing," said Rhyana.

"We're seeing all the equipment that's been here . . . or will be . . . Do you think?" Faelyna slipped from her chair and moved until she was beside Eltyn.

He wasn't certain what to think.

Echoing from the adjoining chamber came a moaning that rose into a thin and piercing scream. "No, no, NO!!!" Then there was silence.

Rhyana hurried to the archway, then turned. "Everything's changing in here, too. Riffie's passed out." After a moment, she added, "There's a door here now . . . a real door. Except it's got six sides. It's open. Sort of."

Faelyna started forward immediately. Eltyn joined her as they stepped through the archway. He glanced at their captive, who slumped forward in the chair where he'd been restrained, and then at the hexagonal opening at the east end of the small room. The door didn't look like an illusion or a projected image, and beyond it stretched a corridor—except that some ten or fifteen yards beyond the opening was another hexagonal door, and it was closed.

Rhyana stepped toward the slumped riffie, reached out, and touched him, looking toward the two scientist-techs. Her mouth opened, but she did not speak.

At that moment, three figures appeared, stepping through the nearer open door. Two of them had short curly brown hair and wore identical shimmering brown singlesuits with the intertwined lightning bolt insignia on their shoulders. All three wore almost resigned expressions, and the man shook his head. Then they vanished.

"They were us!" exclaimed Rhyana. "They were."

"It could be that means if we go through the door we'll come back," suggested Eltyn.

"Or someone wants us to think that," replied Faelyna.

"What else are we going to do? Stand here and wait? We won't even be able to check outside for a good day or so, not safely."

"Sometimes . . . waiting isn't a bad option."

"Where can we possibly go?" asked Eltyn. "The station's been around for thousands and thousands of years, and no one's been trapped inside yet."

"Not that we know of."

"There would have been traces."

"What's the harm of going through a door?"

"A hexagonal door that no one's ever seen before," she replied.

"That we know of," he countered.

That brought a momentary smile to her lips, a smile he appreciated.

"What about the riffie?" asked Faelyna.

"You don't have to worry about him," said Rhyana. "He's dead. Was about to tell you when . . . all that happened."

"How could that occur? No one touched him," Eltyn pointed out.

"Not physically," countered Faelyna. "But he's been brain-conditioned at least some, and . . ."

"You think what he saw . . ."

"We don't know what he saw, but you heard that scream."

"Saw that happen at the Apialor station," said Rhyana. "Serves him right."

Eltyn wasn't totally sure about that. What choices did someone have once they were brain-conditioned? Then he shook his head. "We might as well try the door."

Faelyna raised her eyebrows.

"More in favor of errors of action than errors of inaction." Eltyn reached out and took her hand. The two stepped through the hexagonal opening together, Rhyana close behind them.

Eltyn turned to look back, but the door remained open.

"Eltyn . . ." murmured Faelyna.

He looked forward.

The entire corridor before them was fragmenting into branches and pathways, seemingly an infinite number that shifted and twisted. He swallowed and looked back . . . only to find that there were at least scores of overlapping hexagonal doors . . . and all of them were closed.

He turned to Faelyna.

"Only a door?" she asked.

"Do you pick the way or do I?"

She squeezed his hand and started forward . . . toward the corridor directly ahead . . .

42

❈ ❈ ❈

20 Siebmonat 3123, Vaniran Hegemony

Duhyle didn't quite use the "bigger hammer" theory to rebuild the synchronizer. He did calculate exactly how much power each component in the current assembly could take without failing, melting down, or otherwise malfunctioning. Then he started modifying. That resulted in subassemblies angling off from the body of the device.

At one point Helkyria looked up from her makeshift console and at his table.

Duhyle grinned at her. "You did tell me that speed and reliability outweighed compactness and efficient design."

She smiled back, warmly, and went back to work.

Twilight was dropping across the canal by the time he checked the last connections and cleared his throat.

"You're finished, Kavn?"

"I hope so. And you?"

"I've done what I could. I've been waiting for you. I didn't want to break your concentration. Is it ready?"

"As ready as I can make it. I never asked what you had in mind."

"No, you didn't. For that, I'm grateful. There's a pattern in the systems, but what exactly completing it will do . . . of that I'm not certain."

"You must have an idea."

Helkyria nodded. "If Thora's correct, and she seems to be, then gaining full control of the system might grant us access to the canal's internal systems."

"Ah . . . what does Thora have to do with that?"

"Time . . . There's no way the canal can exist as it does. Therefore, it doesn't."

Duhyle shook his head, then abruptly stopped. "The ancients did something to place it somehow outside of time?"

"I don't see how that's possible, but if she's correct, it might be possible to anchor the canal across a continuum of time, not all time, but at points across hundreds of thousands, perhaps millions of years, perhaps at so many points that it would seem continuous."

"But the energy . . . ?"

". . . had to come from somewhere."

"Where, ser, if I might ask?" asked Symra from where she stood at the top of the ramp.

"There are a number of possibilities, but we won't know which one unless and until the synchronizer works."

"What do you want us to do? Captain Valakyr—"

"Like all good junior officers, she wants to do something. The question is what will be most effective. We will find out shortly." She looked at the subcaptain. "If you'd have someone bring us some rations and something to drink . . . ? We need a break before we test this."

"Yes, ser."

After Symra left, Duhyle asked, "Have you thought what we do if this doesn't work and we get to Baeldura's deadline?"

"I have."

Duhyle waited.

"We refuse to give up the station. Unless we can stop them, the Aesyr won't stop using the Hammers, even if we surrender. They'll just keep using them to get their way. Their actions already prove that. If they'd used just one Hammer strike and held back on the others, I'd be more inclined to trust Baeldura's word, but they've already used the Hammers here several times, and we have no idea where else they've employed them."

"Isn't that playing turtle?" he asked.

"Unfortunately, but the First Speaker agrees."

"I thought she wanted us to negotiate."

"That was before she discovered that Aesyr mobs in Asgard cut down forty Vanir with axes. Now both she and the Magistra of Security see no reason to negotiate. None of us trust the Aesyr, and certainly not Baeldura, for all of her public reputation for honesty. She may be beloved, but it's only by the Aesyr."

"You knew that before Baeldura made the ultimatum."

"I did. We needed the extra time."

Neither spoke.

Duhyle started to say more, but then heard Symra's boots on the stone of the ramp.

"Ser . . . I brought the ration paks and some tea. It's only warm . . ."

"That's fine. Thank you," offered Helkyria.

Only after he'd eaten the entire ration pak did Duhyle realize just how hungry he'd been. Then he stood and stretched, looking for somewhere to put the carton because the cycler was down on the lower level.

"I'll take those," offered Symra.

"Thank you." Duhyle handed her the carton and the mug.

"It will be a while before everything's powered up and checked," said Helkyria. "You should be here."

"I'll be right back, ser." Symra headed down the ramp with the empty cartons and mugs.

"She'd be watching and listening from the ramp anyway," Duhyle pointed out.

Helkyria nodded. "Let's start powering up. If this works, we won't have that much time to figure out how to manage what we discover."

"You were rather effective with that flaming blade," Duhyle pointed out. "Couldn't you try something like that?"

"Kavn . . . I told you. I didn't do that. At least, I don't remember doing it, and I have no idea how to replicate that. I'm hoping that if we can get to the next level of commands, we might be able to use the canal for directed forces that way . . . but I don't know." For a moment a combination of off-black and green colored the tips of her short hair. "System power . . ."

"System power on."

"Disabler one . . ."

"Disabler one . . . removed . . ."

By the time Symra hurried back up the ramp and stood behind them, they had the system fully powered and were ready to employ the beefed-up synchronizer.

"Beginning search probe . . ." Helkyria pressed the stud.

The work space/laboratory exploded into a brilliant silver light so bright that Duhyle could see nothing, nor could he access any of the systems. He closed his eyes against the intensity that was far more than mere glare. For several moments, he thought that the light would dim. It did not. Instead the brilliance increased so much that his closed eyes began to tear.

Then the light vanished. A darkness as intensive and as intrusive as the light had been enfolded him. He wanted to protest that darkness couldn't behave like light, that it didn't have a wave form or photonic behavior.

That was before both heat and chill shook him so that he was burning and shivering . . . and plunged him into depths that were neither hot nor cold, light nor dark . . .

43

❖   ❖   ❖

8 Tenmonth 1351, Unity of Caelaarn

When he woke, lying next to Maarlyna, Maertyn knew that he had to get back to his research. Yet, in some ways, the whole idea felt futile. Maarlyna, simply by being receptive to the image or the ice-sport, or whatever the woman in red happened to be, had uncovered more of a novel nature in a few moments than he'd discovered in more than a year and a half. Even before he moved, Maertyn smiled, if ruefully. He'd already enlisted her aid. Why not bring her into the research more fully? With that thought, he eased out of bed, looking back at Maarlyna, who opened her eyes at his movement and smiled sleepily.

The rest of rising, breakfasting, and beginning the day was uneventful, until Svorak appeared just after midmorning, stepping into the station and holding two items. "No messages today, excepting a letter from Shaenya's sister, but the canal-runner driver thought you might like to see the morning newsheet from Daelmar." He handed the single sheet to Maertyn. "Strange doings in the capital."

Maarlyna reached out and took Maertyn's arm. He held the sheet at a slight angle so that she could read it as he did.

. . . Minister of Protective Services announced that the Gaerda had discovered a wide-spread conspiracy to undermine the Unity government . . .

recent deaths of several ministers and assistant ministers only a small part of a vast plot . . . Minister Tauzn petitioned the Executive Administrator to declare a state of emergency throughout the Unity . . .

. . . EA D'Onfrio rejected the petition, but Tauzn has appealed the rejection to the Unity Council . . . expected to consider the matter in emergency session . . .

Maertyn looked up from the sheet. "Very strange. Thank you, Svorak."

"We just thought you should know. Will you be needing anything, sir?"

"Not at the moment. Perhaps later."

"Yes, sir. I'll be working in the shed for a time if you need me."

"That's good to know." Maertyn smiled, but did not say more until the lighthouse-keeper had left the station.

Maarlyna released her hold on Maertyn's arm. "The Council will overrule the Administrator, won't they?"

"Why do you think that?"

"Tauzn wouldn't have made the appeal unless he had the votes."

"You're likely quite correct, dearest, but there's little we can do from here. Perhaps we should don winter jackets and walk out and observe the ocean."

Maarlyna glanced toward the ramp leading down to the lower levels and nodded. "I'll be just a moment. I'll get your jacket, too. The green one?"

"The dark green one, please."

Within a few minutes, the two were walking toward the lighthouse overlooking the canal and the ocean. Each breath created a faint ice-mist in the still air of late morning, and an icy corona wreathed the pale early-winter sun.

"You didn't want to say anything in the station," Maarlyna finally offered.

"No. I don't see any point in getting Shaenya and Svorak upset. Not yet, anyway."

"Do you think Tauzn will come after you?"

"He might. He's known to be vindictive."

"He wouldn't like the way you escaped all his agents . . . is that it?"

"He's the kind who'd regard that as a personal affront, especially the fact that I managed it without killing anyone."

"What about the lorry driver?"

"I doubt the accident killed him. The lorry wasn't that badly smashed. I think Ashauer's men did when Transport cleaned up the accident." Maertyn stopped short of the worn bricks of the lighthouse and glanced northward across the canal. All he could see beyond the icy gray waters and the gray-blue stone of the far walls were the whites of ice and snow. After several moments, he turned westward, where a few whitecaps dotted the swells of the ocean.

"I never met Tauzn," Maarlyna said, "but the few times we encountered Administrator D'Onfrio, he seemed more concerned, more accessible."

"D'Onfrio's just as political, but not quite so ruthless, and the way things are now, that might be his undoing." Maertyn continued to look out over the ocean, not really seeing it.

"What does Tauzn want?"

"Power."

"Why can't he just wait? Isn't he likely to win the election for EA?"

"He's the most likely candidate, but that's more than a year away, and matters could change. Right now, people are worried and concerned. If he can use his power to convince everyone, especially the returnists, that action against subversives is necessary, and that the restrictions against geo-engineering are foolhardy in a time of crisis, he'll create the illusion of action when everyone else is seen as doing nothing, and that will insure his election."

"It will also insure the loss of civil freedoms . . . won't it?"

"Their curtailment at the least, and perhaps more. He'll justify it by making the remaining lords the scapegoats."

"You're the most visible . . ."

"And that's a sad commentary—a deputy assistant minister of science as the great opponent of change, who stands in the way of progress in a time of crisis." He shook his head and turned, looking back at the station and then to the south. There was something . . .

In the sky to the southeast, above the pines and the south, he caught sight of a long black shape with thin longitudinal red stripes and a black gondola snug on the bottom of the midsection. Behind it was another.

"Maertyn?" Maarlyna turned and stared. "Maertyn!"

"Ashauer didn't know the half of it," he said. "Those are Gaerda dirigibles, and there's only one reason they could be heading this way." He looked to Maarlyna. "Can you lock everything in the station against them?"

"I could . . . but we can't go anywhere. We can't stay there forever."

"I'm hoping we won't have to," he replied. "I don't think they can fly around here for days without someone noticing and looking into it. They think they can just walk into the station and take me away. They don't know you can lock the station. In thousands of years no one's been able to do that. But Shaenya and Svorak need to leave. Send them to the Reserve station, the one to the south on the coast. It'll be hard going through the snow, but if they try to take the canal back to where the road leaves it, the Gaerda will catch them."

"Why would they hurt them?"

"The Gaerda wouldn't want any witnesses around. I do think they'd hesitate to wipe out a Reserve station as well, especially if they don't know whose tracks are leading there. Now . . . get them out of here. I'm going to set the lighthouse beacon on emergency."

Without another word, Maarlyna ran toward the station.

Maertyn took several hurried steps, then pressed the numerical code into the lighthouse lock. He opened the door and stepped inside, moving to the small control board, where he pressed the orange EMERGENCY stud.

As he left the lighthouse and re-locked the door, Maertyn could hear Maarlyna's voice.

"Svorak . . . Shaenya! You have to leave! Now! Just pull on your boots and jackets and go! Run for the Reserve station to the south. The black-shirts are coming. The guards are only three kays away. You'll be safe there."

Maertyn hurried toward the station, looking to the southeast through the clear air, but the dirigibles were still a goodly distance away, perhaps even as much as twenty kays.

Maarlyna was shifting her glance from the two airships to the station door and back to the airships when Maertyn joined her.

"I told them to hurry."

"I heard you."

Svorak was the first to join them, running from the maintenance shed, his eyes also taking in the airships as he halted short of Maertyn. "Sir . . . you sure you won't be wanting us here?"

"The best thing you can do is get to the Reserve guards and tell them what's happening. You can't help here."

"Please . . . go," added Maarlyna.

"Lady?" asked Shaenya as she stepped out into the chill, struggling into a heavy gray jacket.

"You need to go . . . and hurry. You need to get into the trees before they can see you."

The older couple hurried across the gray-blue of the canal wall and then began to follow tracks in the snow, doubtless made earlier by Svorak in checking the wind turbines. Before long they had reached the low pines and were out of sight.

Maertyn studied the dirigibles. They looked to be slightly more than ten kays away. "We need to get inside. They may well have long-range weapons." He took Maarlyna's arm.

"You think they'll shoot at a distance."

"Probably not, but I'd rather not tempt them." He reached out and pressed the stone, since the door had already closed. Once they were inside, and the stone was resealing itself, he turned to her again. "Can you lock all the doors and all the windows except the upper one on the south side? That way we can watch what happens."

"I think so . . . but then what?"

"We'll just have to see, but it will be obvious fairly soon what the Gaerda troopers have in mind. I think they intend to march in and take over the station. They'll have some pretext for taking me. They're sending two dirigibles so that they'll have enough men to keep the Reserve guards from stopping them."

Maarlyna stepped up to the wall and held her hand there. Then she crossed the main chamber and did the same on the north side. "They're both locked."

"Good. Now, let's go up."

Maarlyna stepped away from the wall, then paused, looking down at a sprig of greenery. She bent and picked it up, slipping it into the small chest pocket on her jacket when she straightened.

"What's that?"

"Mistletoe. Shaenya must have gathered some for the year-end."

"She is superstitious that way, but I suppose it's harmless."

Maarlyna only smiled as she walked beside him.

Maertyn had the feeling that she'd seen something he hadn't . . . again.

Once they were on the upper level by the open south window, after Maarlyna had locked the north window, they watched the black airships slowly descend as they neared the station.

After a moment, he touched her shoulder. "I didn't ask . . . you could have gone with Shaenya and Svorak."

"You didn't have to ask. You can't lock the station. How could I let them take you? They'd kill you and stage it so that you looked like you were trying to escape. After what you did to escape Tauzn's agents before, who could dispute a story like that?"

Maertyn had to admit that she was most likely right about that.

"You never abandoned me. I should leave you?" she said gently. "And . . . somehow . . . it also feels wrong. This is the only place I've felt I belonged since . . ."

"I know . . . I've known that from the time you walked in . . . even before, I think. I don't know why, but it was important that we . . . you . . . have familiar furniture."

She reached out and squeezed his hand.

Shoulder-to-shoulder, they continued to watch as the first airship dropped to within yards of the stone of the canal wall less than a hundred yards to the east of the station. Black-jacketed troopers began to slide down lines into the snow bordering the stone of the canal. All of them bore rifles in slings.

A deep voice boomed from a speaker on the dirigible. "This is a custodial mission. No one will be hurt. I say again. No one will be hurt. Under the emergency authority of the Unity, Protective Services is taking possession of this government facility. If you do not resist, no one will be harmed . . ."

Despite the language, Maertyn couldn't help but note that once the troopers landed, they immediately had their rifles at the ready as they moved toward the station.

Maarlyna reached out and touched the stone, stepping back slightly as it slid from itself to re-form as a solid surface. "They didn't look peaceful to me."

"They always start out with weapons ready," Maertyn pointed out. "What bothers me is the number of troopers and dirigibles. If it's a mere custodial issue, why does it take as many as hundreds of troopers to handle one lord, his wife, a lighthouse-keeper, and a staff woman?"

"They were expecting you to resist, dear, because they know what they're doing is wrong, and they know you'll resist wrongdoing." After a moment, she asked, "How long do you think we should wait before checking to see what they're doing?"

"I'm guessing at least a day. The lighthouse is flashing on emergency and its transmitter is doing the same. The Reserve guards have a satellite comm-link, and they'll report, especially after Svorak and Shaenya reach them."

"Why is the Council letting them do this?"

"I don't know . . . unless Tauzn has them all terrified that they'll have some sort of fatal illness or accident. We might as well go down to the main level and have some tea . . . or something."

As they turned from the locked stone of the window, a figure appeared—the woman in scarlet. She stepped toward Maarlyna and spoke.

"You are the key."

As the words came from her mouth, Maertyn could not hear them so much as see them in his mind. And . . . again . . . he had the sense of another figure. For just a moment, he thought he glimpsed a figure in silver . . . or was it silver-gray? He blinked, and the second figure vanished.

"The key . . . ?" murmured Maarlyna.

"The key to what will be . . . and is . . ."

"What about the black-shirts?" asked Maertyn, hoping the woman might offer more information, as she had at the tube-train station.

"They are but one shadow of many, and the shadow you must oppose."

Exactly how? wondered Maertyn. "Who *are* you?"

"You see but a construct of the past and the future." The woman turned once more to Maarlyna. "Find the door and go through it."

"If I don't . . ."

The woman/construct vanished.

Maertyn looked at his wife. "The door? There isn't a single door in the station . . ."

"There wasn't . . . but there wasn't anyone else but us here, either. We're not doing anything else right now. We might as well start looking to see if there is a door."

"She's been right about other things," admitted Maertyn, although he could hear the doubt in his voice—and disliked it.

"The assassin . . . and didn't she say that we were linked?"

"She did." He smiled in the dim light. "Let's see if we can find a door where there wasn't one before."

They inspected their bedchamber and sitting room and the rest of the upper level, and then the main level. As they did so, Maertyn couldn't help but wonder exactly what the Gaerda troopers were doing . . . and thinking.

After discovering nothing, they stood at the top of the ramp to the lower level.

"It must be down there." Maarlyna started down the ramp.

Maertyn followed, absently wondering what might happen if the troopers cut off the power from the turbines and battery banks. From the bottom of the ramp, he glanced toward the kitchen area, where Shaenya had hurriedly covered her preparations for dinner. He saw several more sprigs of the mistletoe in a glass vase filled two-thirds of the way with water.

After inspecting the chambers on the west end, they moved eastward until they reached the small chamber off the largest lower room.

"There!" Maarlyna pointed at the blank east wall.

"Where?" Maertyn saw nothing.

"Can't you see, dear? There is a door here. It's six-sided, but not hexagonal, and it's open. It looks like there's a long passageway beyond it."

For all of Maarlyna's description, Maertyn could still see nothing. "Do we really want to go through it?"

"Why not? We can stay here for days, perhaps weeks . . ." Maarlyna said. "But we're like a turtle. It can't go anywhere unless it sticks its neck out."

Maertyn had to admit that she was right about that.

"Maertyn . . . dear . . . I needed to be a turtle for a time. I needed to recover and discover who I am. I'm not the Maarlyna you lost. At times, I've wished I were." She smiled sadly. "But I'm me, not her."

"I know that."

"Do you?" Her voice was soft. "Take my hand, and close your eyes."

Maertyn couldn't help but hesitate.

"You asked me to do that for you. I did. Do the same for me. Please." After a pause, she added, "I may not be the Maarlyna you lost, but I love you every bit as much as she must have."

Maertyn reached out and took her hand.

Together they stepped forward . . .

. . . and blinding silver light swirled around them . . .

You cannot see what you cannot comprehend.

44

From high in the sky, the city appeared as a giant hexagon. From orbit, its hexagonal shape remained clear, if greatly diminished in size amid the surrounding fields and forests of more conventional rectangular dimensions. The roadways radiated in straight lines, either from the points of the large hexagon, or at times from the smaller hexagonal cells that comprised the larger hexagon of the city proper.

From the center of the city, in the middle of the hexagonal main square, a kay on a side, rose a golden structure, also hexagonal in shape, crowned by a shimmering golden dome, a perfectly rounded surface bearing no adornment whatsoever. Some of the adjoining hexagons contained buildings, and those were of close to uniform height, if varying in size and function, while others held parks or exercise fields or even occasional schools.

Some few scattered clouds dotted the sky, but only a few, and that was why all those who had glanced into the blueness of the heavens paused, not to view the pale silvery trace of the Selene Ring, but because a rainbow arched across the sky from the arid south of sun and sand and was descending toward the golden hexagonal structure in the center of the city. While there might have been a trace of blue-gray in the distant south where the far end of the rainbow was anchored, neither clouds nor rain surrounded the colors of the heavenly bridge.

In moments, the end of the rainbow caressed the third level of the golden-domed hexagonal building. Those in the central square watched, and the minidrones, whose surveillance had replaced that of the satellite facilities, scanned the bridge of light.

Moments and then minutes passed.

Abruptly, dust and haze billowed up from the central square, high enough to shroud the golden dome . . . and the rainbow shivered along the thousands of kays of its length . . . and vanished . . .

Those others in the city and beyond gaped at the disappearance, and the plume of dust, then shook their heads and returned to their industrious businesses.

45

20 Siebmonat 3123, Vaniran Hegemony

The blinding intrusive darkness flared and waned, waned and flared, until Duhyle had no idea whether he was blind in the presence of brilliant light or seeing nothing amid darkness. Slowly, he became aware of a coolness that became an icy chill. Was this death, the chill of Niflheim, the old and discredited idea of the depths of an afterworld where even the flames of fire had no heat?

Amid that darkness, he became aware of Helkyria, and a soft silvergolden light that radiated from her. He turned and opened his mouth to speak, but there was no sound. Yet there were words, as if upon a neuralnet of some sort. *You're silver-gold.*

So are you, came her calm reply.

Where are we? Or when? Or if?

We are . . . because we're thinking. As for the other questions . . .

Abruptly, the darkness vanished, and they stood in the chamber where they had activated the synchronizer. Yet it was not the same chamber, because banks of instruments lined the walls, each clad in a soft silver light, each displaying symbols that changed, and with each change, words ran through Duhyle's mind. He didn't understand the words.

Do you know the language? he asked.

I don't, she replied. *I'd judge it's that of the builders.*

Builders? Someone had to have built the canal, but to think they might encounter them after millions of years? That was improbable, since time travel had long since been proven impossible.

Even before Helkyria's words faded in Duhyle's mind, a figure appeared before them, midway between them. At first, Duhyle thought that a man stood there, then a woman, but features and physique shifted. All that remained common was the fitted scarlet singlesuit.

You keep shifting. What else could Duhyle have said that wouldn't have revealed even greater ignorance?

. . . no shifts . . . perception . . .

Behind the figure, whose appearance continued to change, one image/figure/persona replacing another in flicker-fashion, the instruments also changed—at the same time as the figure did.

Are we seeing all possible futures? Duhyle finally asked.

I don't think time works that way, replied Helkyria. *There's something else . . .*

Duhyle took a step forward, and everything swirled around him so violently that vertigo and nausea left him trembling. He was barely able to hold himself together. After a long moment, if they were where time existed, and he had his doubts about that, he straightened up slowly and carefully. *Don't move . . . very painful . . . disconcerting. So dizzy . . . vertigo . . . disorientation.*

Thank you. After a pause, she added, *It was painful and disorienting to watch you. You seemed to fragment . . . but you didn't.*

The figure in scarlet seemed to speak. *. . . all event-points . . . all at once . . .* Then he/she became an indistinct shifting shape.

Duhyle thought he'd understood what it had said or projected. *Did you get that—about all event-points at once?*

That could be a suggestion that sequence or causality exists independent of perception, replied Helkyria.

Or? You don't sound all that certain.

There's always been a debate about whether time exists independent of space. Most theorists say it doesn't . . . or that it doesn't exist at all. Rainbows, or something like them, flickered around Helkyria.

How can time not exist at all? questioned Duhyle, slowly beginning to feel the last of the vertigo and nausea subside.

More than a few people have asked—

All the silver vanished, and the darkness returned.

46

❖ ❖ ❖

34 *Quad 2471 R.E.*

Faelyna took only three steps before the corridors beside and overlapping the one that she, Eltyn, and Rhyana had taken began to contract and expand, getting dimmer and then increasingly brighter with each expansion . . . and each step. After another few yards, the glare was blinding.

Eltyn squinted so that his eyes were barely slits. He had no idea where they were going.

Faelyna slowed and stopped. So did the other two.

The light dimmed, slowly, and until the three stood in a long corridor that stretched ahead of them, disappearing into the distance as a silvered point of light.

Eltyn turned and glanced back over his shoulder, past Rhyana. The hexagonal door through which they had stepped was now open. He blinked, but nothing changed. "Do we go on?"

"Let's see." Faelyna took another step forward, and the corridor twisted, and light flared. She stopped.

Eltyn turned around and took one step, then another, past Rhyana and toward the still-open doorway. Nothing happened. He looked back at Faelyna. "I think we head back."

"For now," she agreed, turning and joining him.

They retraced their steps and made their way through the hexagonal door. Eltyn shook his head, almost resignedly. He couldn't help but wonder exactly what had happened and where the corridor led—to the eastern end of the MCC, some two thousand kays away?

The dead riffie was in the same slumped position where they had left him, and the images of equipment on the walls flickered in and out of focus, shifting colors now and again.

Eltyn looked back again. The door to the long corridor was still open. "Let's go up to the equipment and see if we can figure out what it shows."

Rhyana sniffed. "The air smells different. Sort of damp."

"The ventilators aren't working," Eltyn said. "The station closed the ducts, or the debris did, and I shut down the system right after the impact."

"It does feel more humid," acknowledged Faelyna. "We're still seeing equipment around us." She stepped toward the silver-flickering images, then stopped and fumbled in her belt pouch, extending what looked to be a folded scrap of something.

The scrap touched the edge of the image and passed through it, then seemed to double, and the second ghostly folded scrap flared instantly, and dust sifted down toward the stone floor.

Faelyna still held the first scrap. Her brows furrowed.

"Real and not real?" Eltyn's words sounded inane, at least to him.

"I wonder," replied Faelyna. "We might as well see if our equipment is still there." She started up the ramp.

All three of them stopped at the top of the ramp. Everything had changed. The main chamber was filled with silver light, but dark rust-brown consoles seemed to be everywhere, leaving corridors to the ramps and to where the doors were—or had been.

Yet as he watched, Eltyn could see the consoles shifting, and, abruptly, they were all dark gray, and the intensity of the light increased once more.

Where are we?

That Rhyana's voice came to Eltyn in the same manner as a private comm pulse stopped him from asking an almost identical question.

It might be when . . . not where, replied Faelyna. *We were just on the main level. That can't have changed.*

Doesn't look the same to me, replied Rhyana.

A swirl of gray and scarlet appeared before them, momentarily coalescing into a figure in a scarlet singlesuit of some sort, only to be replaced by a figure in silver and gray, and then by one in pale ice-blue, before returning to the scarlet-clad figure.

Eltyn swallowed. *Who . . . what . . . are we seeing . . . ?*

The figure's mouth moved. *. . . all event-points . . . all at once . . .* Then he/she returned to an indistinct blur of fast-shifting shapes.

All event-points at once, mused Faelyna. *That sounds like a theory of time.*

No sequence or causality? Hasn't that been discredited?

Politically, because the Ruche is founded on certainty and causality. The feeling of a laugh followed Faelyna's words. *There are a few theoreticians who might not think the universe is that certain.*

What about universes? asked Eltyn, looking for the smile he knew he wouldn't see amid the increasing light and shifting images.

That's more likely in a multiverse—

A flare of light brighter than a nova and simultaneously darker than the depths reserved for unbelievers in the Ruche swept over Eltyn . . . and the chamber . . .

47

8 Tenmonth 1351, Unity of Caelaarn

The blinding silver light lessened and then dimmed, and Maertyn opened his eyes, only to find that scores of corridors swirled before him. Vertigo and nausea wrenched at him, and he immediately closed his eyes again.

Are you all right? As it had been with the woman in scarlet, Maarlyna's voice was clear in his thoughts, not his ears.

I'm better . . . now. I opened my eyes . . . very disorienting. Where are we going? Maertyn grasped her smaller hand more firmly, holding on to the warmth of her presence.

To the center . . . or something like that.

The center of the canal? That's a thousand kays to the east . . .

The sense of a soft laugh bathed him. *A control center, I think. I can't read the inscriptions on the wall . . . yet they're familiar . . . and I feel as though I should.*

Maertyn concentrated on holding her hand and trying to follow her lead, not that such was difficult, because she was walking in a straight line.

We're going to stop and turn here. We're almost there, I think.

Where?

Maarlyna didn't answer, but guided him through what must have been a door or an archway, because the sleeve of his shoulder brushed against stone. Then she stopped.

Maertyn took another half-step, then halted as well.

You can open your eyes, dear. It shouldn't be too bad.

Maertyn did. He found himself in a small chamber, no more than five yards by three, standing beside Maarlyna and facing a whirl of scarlet and gray that coalesced into a solid figure in a scarlet singlesuit, except that before the image or person solidified, a man in silver and gray stood there . . .

That . . . it was you . . . Maarlyna's surprise went beyond the words in his head.

. . . only to be followed by a woman in pale ice-blue, before returning to the indistinct scarlet-clad figure.

Words echoed in Maertyn's mind, but they were not directed at him. That he could sense.

The battle . . . not fought in one time . . . the choice . . . yours . . . to be key . . . keeper . . . of all those . . . choose fate . . . the universe . . . this event-point . . . only you . . . so few . . . ever . . . able to see . . .

For all his concentration, Maertyn could only grasp fragments of sentences or phrases, words clearly directed at Maarlyna, a conversation to which he was party only in the sense of a partly deaf man trying to understand a rapid exchange between two others in an ancient tongue.

Wait! That preemptory command was Maarlyna's. She turned to face Maertyn. Even though her mouth opened, he could hear the words only in his mind. *You need to know . . .*

Know what? He offered a wry smile. *I have the feeling I'm not going to like what I'm going to hear.*

It's not as bad as it could have been, dearest.

But . . . ?

Would you want everything to end?

What do you mean . . . everything? Life? The world?

Slowly, she nodded. *And I saw what I might be . . . and the awful emptiness that will happen if I don't . . .*

Can't you . . . or this power you're being offered . . . can't you just deal with the Gaerda? he pressed.

When I've asked you about politics and the government, sometimes, you've said to me . . . it doesn't work that way. This doesn't work that way. If I choose . . . what I feel is right . . . things . . . between us, they'll change.

How?

I'll never be able to leave the station . . . I told you once that it was like coming home. I didn't know how true that was . . .

Maertyn just stood there, his eyes burning, and not because of everything shifting around him. Time seemed to freeze, as though he could not move. *But . . . why?*

Everything affects everything else . . . She swallowed.

Maertyn could see that, and the tears flowing from her eyes.

*If you **knew** that Tauzn would destroy the world, what would you do?* she asked after a time.

I still wouldn't want to lose you. Yet he knew that those words were not an answer, not with the Gaerda waiting outside the station, and not with the tears in her eyes.

Neither one of us will die. Things will be . . . different.

Different? How? He paused. *Can we be together? Can I touch and hold you?*

If you wish . . . for as long as . . . we can.

What do you mean . . . if we wish?

I'll be different. I'll know more . . . I think. I'll see things that will be hard for you to see.

Maertyn moistened his lips. *Like the corridors that shift? They don't for you, do they?*

No. Not in the way you mean.

He just stood there, trying to think, looking at the woman he loved, and for whom . . . He pushed that thought away. He'd done what he'd done as much for himself as for Maarlyna, and she'd hung on to him even when she hadn't understood. And now . . . it was his turn. "Where you go so will I go . . ." Those words were cribbed from somewhere in the past. That he also knew. He also understood that while no feeling was truly new, that lack of novelty did not mean lack of truth . . . or love. And yet . . . how could he let go . . . ?

How could he not . . . when she had already been through so much?

Finally, he looked at her again. *I love you. I trust you. Do what you feel is right.*

I love you . . . more than you know.

Maarlyna turned slightly and stepped forward. So did the indistinct figure . . . and they merged. Just as suddenly, Maertyn and Maarlyna stood alone in a small room. Thin consoles sheathed in golden-silver light lined the walls. Several panels on the consoles displayed stylized digits he could read, and letters he could not. At the same time, he had the feeling that the consoles were both there . . . and not there . . . although they did not flicker in and out of existence.

"What happened?" Maertyn swallowed.

The woman before him had Maarlyna's features and slim figure, but the amber eyes were now silver, and her hair was a shade that somehow combined gold and silver without appearing old. And she wore the scarlet singlesuit.

"You . . . you're the one, now, who appeared in the tube-train station?"

"Not exactly. That was a probability construct of the . . . canal." A sad smile crossed her lips. "I have a faint recollection of that, just as my memories of the Maarlyna who was before you healed her are faint."

"Why you?" asked Maertyn.

Maarlyna looked at him. "Why me? Did you hear what she said?"

He shook his head, trying to concentrate on his wife . . . if she were any longer just his wife.

"She said that I have less knowledge than others, but that knowledge can be learned. What cannot be learned is to see things as they are . . . as once in ancient times, a poet said, to see them played upon a blue guitar . . ." Maarlyna offered an embarrassed smile, one that recalled the woman he loved. "I couldn't make up words like that, you know?"

Maertyn had liked the flow of those words, and the feeling they evoked, but could only guess at the instrument to which they referred. "But . . . what was she? . . . and you?"

"She was the construct . . . the . . . pattern . . . the knowledge . . . of the last keeper of the Bridge . . . the canal." Maarlyna took his hand, and hers was cool, but still warm enough for him to know that she was indeed still there. "We need to go back. I . . . we have some things to do."

"Where?"

"Back in the station. It's easier there, or it will be for them."

"Them? Are the black-shirts in the station? How could they—"

"No. These aren't the Gaerda. I can't explain yet, not exactly, because I'm still two people, except I'm not, and I'm afraid if I don't do what I must while I still know what it is, I won't be either." Maarlyna began to walk back along the corridor, now lit in the pervasive silver-gold, but without any consoles.

"What are you going to do?"

"Prevent the unraveling of eternity . . . in our universe. If I can . . . The keeper . . . the pattern . . . said I could . . ."

The unraveling of the universe? Maertyn wanted to shake his head. In the space of a few days, his once-quiet wife had gone from someone he thought he knew into someone very different, more confident . . . and someone or even something possibly far more powerful. And he really didn't understand why or how, all because he'd maneuvered himself into getting assigned an obscure research project, as much to protect her as anything.

He found he had to walk quickly to keep up with her as she walked through what was, or had been, the lower kitchen area and up the ramp to the main level and into his laboratory. There she glanced around. So did Maertyn. All his tables and equipment were there, but overlying them were colored but more than ghost-like images of consoles sheathed in light.

Maarlyna kept looking, although Maertyn had the feeling she was looking somewhere he could not see.

Then the light shifted again, and Maarlyna seemed to shimmer, as if she were there, and not quite there, except she was. Before her, as if through a shining veil or a misty mirror, stood two indistinct figures, although one was apparently a tall woman clad in pale golden armor, or something similar.

Maarlyna said something, but it meant nothing to Maertyn. He concentrated, realizing that the little he "heard" was in his mind and thoughts.

. . . face the end of eternity . . .

Why . . . nothing fixed before? asked one of the ghost images.

You could not see it . . . needed key and keeper . . . no time . . . You perceive . . . continuity as . . . temporal . . . no time. There are only . . . event-points.

. . . something you're doing for us?

That is what a keeper does.

With those words, Maertyn sensed sadness . . . melancholy. He wondered why and lost his concentration on what was going on before him.

. . . universe . . . a pivot point . . . battle . . . that will decide whether all continues.

What about you?

I am the keeper . . . last keeper fought . . . the ring in the heavens . . .

Maertyn tried to follow the seemingly mental interchanges, but lost much of what Maarlyna was saying. He did get a sense that whoever she addressed faced a far bigger problem than he and she did, and that the political machinations of Tauzn were almost trivial by comparison.

Suddenly, the light changed, and the two of them stood alone in the workroom.

Maarlyna looked very tired.

"Are you all right?"

"We need to eat."

"Can you tell me what all that was about?" Maertyn rubbed his forehead, trying to massage away the headache he hadn't realized that he even had.

"After we eat. Doing . . . that . . . is harder than I thought."

"Doing what?"

"Talking across time. But time doesn't work that way." She turned. "I have to eat something. I'll tell you then."

Her face was pale. He didn't say another word, just took her hand and walked out of the laboratory and down the ramp to the kitchen area.

48

20 Siebmonat 3123, Vaniran Hegemony

The darkness vanished. Duhyle and Helkyria stood in her workroom—or what had been her workroom. The worktables and equipment were there, untouched, but over and around them were ghost images of consoles sheathed in silver-gold light. Behind them, Duhyle sensed Symra, but he did not look back because between Helkyria and Duhyle stood a woman in a scarlet singlesuit. Her hair was silver-gold. Her eyes were silver, her features fine on an oval face. Behind and to her left was another figure, in silver and gray, barely visible, an image as insubstantial as those of the consoles.

You face the end of eternity. The words filled Duhyle's thoughts.

That's possible, replied Helkyria.

Why was nothing settled or fixed before? asked Duhyle.

The woman in scarlet smiled, apologetically. *It was as fixed as it ever was. You could not see it as such.*

Why can we now? Helkyria's words were hard.

The woman in red glanced to the silver-shadowed figure to her left, as if inquiring, then finally spoke. *You needed key and keeper.*

Who or what are the key and keeper? asked Helkyria. *Why would the canal need that, since it stands independent of time?*

Not independent, warrior woman, not independent. The scarlet woman tilted her head, as if listening, then nodded. *There is . . . no time . . . You perceive . . . continuity as . . . temporal. The canal . . . Bifrost Bridge . . . is linked to all event-points in this universe over which it was . . . constructed.*

Duhyle frowned. The keeper sounded hesitant, as if she was having trouble explaining. Were the Vanir that backward? Or . . . Why hadn't the keeper appeared at first? Or was it simply a linguistic problem?

Time is a mere perception? interjected Helkyria. *Then the synchronizer would not work . . . and we would not be here, wherever or whenever here is . . .*

There is no time. There are only . . . event-points. The experience of those event-points creates the perception of time in all intelligences.

Duhyle slowly turned his head and looked at Helkyria, simultaneously wearing the ice-blue singlesuit and formfitting armor running from her neck to wrists and ankles and comprised of small diamond-shapes of silver-gold light.

. . . might be said to be the . . . commonality . . . behind all intelligence . . .

How did we get here? Helkyria's question was as direct as a stunner bolt.

You are where you always were. The locking of the entrances to the Bridge was the first step in breaking the perceptual links to your event-points. Your . . . device . . . was the second. You can see all the event-points simultaneously . . . or you could if your perceptions were not conditioned to a limited set of points . . .

Who are you? How can you communicate with us? Why now? Earlier all we could make out were fragments.

With the range of all event-points, the systems attempted to address all possible inquiries . . . but you were not equipped . . . to limit . . . your focus on a unique set of points.

Are we now? asked Helkyria. *Or is it something you're doing for us?*

That is what a keeper does.

Duhyle felt a sense of sadness . . . and yet of muted triumph.

The universe, the keeper went on, *our universe—is at a pivot point— at two other times, the same struggle is being fought, but your battle is the one that will decide whether all continues.*

What about you? demanded Duhyle. *Where do you fit in?* He could sense Helkyria's irritation at his interruption, but the idea of an outside force or keeper or whatever dictating what they did bothered him.

I am the keeper. There have been other keepers. The last keeper fought the same battle that you must fight. There was a long pause. *When you look at the ring in the heavens, you see a portion of those costs . . . as the Bridge is also a remnant of that battle and a cost . . . and promise.*

Promise? asked Helkyria. *How can you help us? Can you destroy the Hammers?*

"I" am not truly where you are. Our event-points do not coincide. Yet there are possibilities. Another pause followed. *Tell me exactly what you face and where.*

The Aesyr of Midgard have revolted and are threatening to use a weapon that will, if used often, unravel the dark matter of the universe. They have a ship, from the past, fitted with this weapon . . .

Duhyle listened as Helkyria gave a summary of the situation, followed by a description of the Hammers and the threat they posed.

The keeper said nothing, her eyes focused totally on Helkyria until the scientist paused. *There is only one Hammer. It can be made to appear at multiple points but can only force intersection sequentially, not simultaneously.*

It can strike in the future, then? asked Helkyria.

The keeper shook her head. *Not even the Bridge can do that. It can only reach any point with which it coexists and only at that point. There is no future, just as there is no past. There are only infinite sets of points of existence. Each coherent set of infinite points traveling through space can be said to be a universe . . . and not all points intersect naturally for all of that journey. Observation of those intersections is experienced by those with intelligence as time. All living organisms have some intelligence.*

Duhyle thought he knew why Baeldura and Thora wanted to control the canal station, but wasn't certain. *The Hammer—or Hammers— can only strike at one . . . location . . . one event-point . . . before it can proceed to another?*

In a general sense . . . yes.

So where is the Hammer, its physical locale? asked Helkyria.

There was another long pause before the keeper replied. *Physically, it is located on the large warship to the west of the canal.*

You said there were possibilities that you could help. How? pressed Helkyria.

What you call the great canal is a Bridge to anywhere equal to its length. Each of you can only depart it at the moment you left the event-point you inhabited and you can only leave it in an event-point congruent to your past/present event-point . . .

You're saying that the canal can touch anything anywhere within two thousand kays and at any time? asked Duhyle.

Almost simultaneously, Helkyria inquired, *You can let us depart somewhere near, but only at the same time as when we sealed the station?*

That is essentially correct.

Duhyle knew that "essentially correct" translated into "grossly over-simplified."

Is there any limit to those who can leave? asked Helkyria. *Could all the troopers leave at once?*

They could.

Do you have any weapons to support them?

None that would not make matters worse. Far worse, and far sooner.

Duhyle watched Helkyria, but his consort only nodded before asking, *Can you provide a view of the inside of the warship?*

Another long pause followed. *We can see the outside, and there may be plans of the vessel, but I cannot transfer those to you. I can only describe . . .*

Our event-points are not congruent, said Helkyria dryly.

No . . .

We will have to determine how to attack the ship, Helkyria said. *Give us some time . . . or continuity of event-points . . .*

As you wish . . .

The keeper vanished, as did the shadowy silver figure, but the light-shaded "ghost" machinery did not. Nor did an indirect and diffuse illumination that seemed to come from the stone itself. Duhyle discovered that he had a slight headache, possibly from straining to see what amounted to two sets of images occupying the same space. "You're going to invade the control centers of the warship?"

"That's where the Hammer is. Do you have a better idea?"

Duhyle didn't. "What if she—or it—isn't what she says?"

Helkyria smiled wryly. "Let's see."

"What do you mean?"

"If I understand what she said, or the implications, she can only communicate with us so long as the station is locked. Let's see if we can unlock one of the windows."

"You don't think we can, do you?"

"Let's say I have my doubts." Helkyria walked toward the synchronizer, then stopped. "All the outside screens are frozen, with the last images on them."

"How . . ." Duhyle swallowed. "When we used the synchronizer . . . did that put us outside of time?"

"I think the keeper would have claimed that we're outside our event-point . . . or something to that effect," said Helkyria dryly. "That's a good indicator that we probably can't open things."

Duhyle realized that the synchronizer was still powered, but running off the stored system, not off the grid.

Helkyria bent over and touched the screen. "We're locked out."

"What if we depower?"

"It shouldn't make any difference."

Duhyle cut the power to the synchronizer.

Nothing changed, nor did the light from the stone diminish.

He walked over to where the window was and touched the stone. It remained immobile. He looked at Helkyria.

"I'm inclined to believe her," said Helkyria. "It appears as though we don't have much choice."

"Ser . . . ?" offered Symra. "Aren't there any other . . . ?"

"Options? Can you think of any with a hundred of us locked inside here?"

Symra looked away.

"I'll need to work out how we'll do this." Helkyria gestured toward the nearest wall. "We'll have to use one of the existing doors, and that only will allow three fully equipped troopers at once." She turned to Symra. "We'll need to talk over what you and Valakyr need." Then she looked back to Duhyle. "We'll need you, too."

"I do have some biotherm," he said with a slight grin.

"That will come in useful, more than I'd thought."

Duhyle nodded. He'd have to work out detonators, but he could manage that . . . somehow.

49

8 Tenmonth 1351, Unity of Caelaarn

Maertyn didn't even try to ask Maarlyna any questions until after he and she had each eaten a healthy portion of the still-warm cheese, potato, and lamb casserole that had been left on what served as a pantry table. Then they had walked back up to what had been their main-floor study, and Maertyn poured two goblets of a Zaendan red that he'd been saving for a special occasion that had never come. The Voharan carpet looked the same, and so did the ancient chairs from Norlaak . . . except Maertyn could see/sense the light-sheathed consoles that seemed to be everywhere and yet not there at all.

Only when Maarlyna had seated herself and taken several sips from the monogrammed crystal goblet did Maertyn finally ask, "Can you tell me what it is that you're doing? What you were doing with those people I could barely make out. I could only sense and understand a little, and it didn't make much sense to me."

She frowned, then pursed her thin lips for a moment, setting the goblet on the side table. "I didn't really understand until it happened. It's something that . . . no one else can do. The ancients, the ones who built the Bridge, they thought there would always be some people who could see . . . the universe . . . as it is, or maybe they thought that there were ways to train people . . ."

"Maybe they didn't even think about the future."

"They did fight to make sure that there was one . . ." Maarlyna picked up the goblet and took a small swallow, rather than a sip. "They set up the Bridge to seek keepers."

"You say that there's no time, or that time doesn't exist, and that would mean that across all time there's no one but you who can do this . . . whatever it is? That seems . . . strange . . ."

Maarlyna shook her head. "They have to live in a time—one of the event-points—contiguous to the Bridge . . . and no one else ever has . . . or will, not so far as the last keeper and the Bridge systems could determine."

"How close—physically—do they have to be?"

She did not speak, and her now-silver eyes darkened for several moments, before she finally answered. "The Bridge systems can detect anyone with such abilities on the same continent, farther under some conditions."

"You're saying that in thousands of years . . ." Maertyn broke off.

"Hundreds of thousands . . . it could be millions of years." Her eyes brightened, again almost to tears. "How could I say no? How many people would not come to be . . . to know love and joy?"

". . . and fear and disappointment," Maertyn added dryly.

"Maertyn . . ." Her voice was soft.

"I know that sounds cynical, but I'm feeling a little that way with all of this." More than a little, but he wasn't about to voice that. "I'd like to concentrate on a few things more immediate. We're still trapped in here. What about us? And the Gaerda?"

"Oh . . . they've just left a group of soldiers in a portable hut of some sort. There's more snow falling, and I almost feel sorry for them . . ." She shook her head. "I forgot. All this seems so natural, and it's not. It's like I know things that I didn't know I knew until I do them. It's very strange."

"You can see or sense beyond the walls?"

"Farther than that. I don't know how far. I haven't tried, except a ways out into the ocean to find the warship. Not inside buildings or things, except inside the Bridge."

"What warship?"

"The one threatening the Vanir. That's not now."

Maertyn took a solid swallow of the Zaendan. His wife was talking about warships he couldn't see that existed in other times. "But you can't use weapons . . . did I understand that correctly? So how will we deal with the Gaerda? What about things like power and food? You do need to eat, don't you? You must, after all you just went through."

"If I'm . . . awake."

"Why wouldn't you . . . The canal has some sort of life-suspension?"

"It's more just being out of time . . ."

"I thought time didn't exist," he teased, trying not to sound forced.

"The keeper would say that it's being separated from event-points so that continuity is stopped."

"The keeper would say?" he asked with a grin he didn't totally feel.

"I'm still two people . . ."

"In one body."

"I was going to say that . . ." She shook her head again. "It's not so much two people as me and another person's skills and memories."

"Who told you to run off before you knew what had happened to deal with some problem? You just dragged me . . . as if you weren't quite you . . ."

"It wasn't like that. I was the one who decided. I was afraid that I wouldn't remember. I still didn't understand time. That was because I needed to integrate . . . a lot of things . . . and I was worried I'd lose hold of . . . aspects of things, especially with the Vanir."

"You're simplifying for me, aren't you?"

"Yes. We don't have words for some of it. I have to think in the old keeper's language . . ."

"You learned another language . . . like that?"

"I didn't have much choice, dearest. It just happened. Does it bother you?"

"What about the . . . Vanir? Did you learn their language?"

"No. The Bridge structures do that."

"Are they ancient, too? The Vanir?"

She shook her head. "We're ancient to them. I haven't told them. I think their leader—she's something like a soldier-scientist—knows that."

"Did you say something about not having weapons to help them?"

"I did."

"So you don't have any way to deal with the Gaerda?"

"Not without causing a disaster. The Bridge is a weapon. Even the keeper's memories were not clear. What is clear is that to use it again as a weapon will destroy Earth."

"Of course." Maertyn nodded. He did have a feel for that, from all his studies. "It's somehow outside of time. That means that its mass and energy are as well. To have an effect on matter, it would have to become real, and if it destroyed the ancient moon the first time . . ."

"There's great horror around those memories." Maarlyna's face and eyes stiffened, almost as if she were retreating into some past distance. "Almost no one and nothing survived, except for the few in the Bridge."

"That was a long time ago," ventured Maertyn.

"It was." A trace of a smile appeared. "Now I know I won't forget."

"Forget what?"

"The others. The ones I haven't dealt with yet. They're in their own event-point, and I don't have to hurry. Right here is the only place where I can't wait if something has to be done."

"Does something have to be done here?" Maertyn frowned.

"In a little while, after we talk some more." She lifted the goblet again.

For several moments, the chamber was silent.

"I still don't understand. Why you? How?"

"The keeper sensed me. There's a field . . . something . . . around . . . me . . . or there was after the operations . . . the procedures. You were drawn to the Bridge . . . to the canal . . . there are images of what was, is, and will be . . . they reverberate through time and through minds . . ."

Maertyn thought back. He really hadn't even considered the canal research project before . . . not until Maarlyna was recovering and it had been clear that she would recover. It had been one of a number of proposals stacked up in his console. But he still couldn't say why he'd picked it. "How can the Bridge . . . the keeper . . . do that?"

"It can't make anyone do anything, but it can amplify images . . . feelings . . . and sometimes people respond. Most times they don't."

"And I responded, all because of you?" Maertyn asked.

"Yes." She stood, took several steps, until she stood before his chair, and held out her hands.

He took them and rose, as her arms went around him, and her lips touched his.

50

34 Quad 2471 R.E.

The light and darkness split . . . or shivered . . . and flaked away, leaving Eltyn, Faelyna, and Rhyana standing in the same chamber. This time the equipment consoles had diminished in size and were sheathed in silvered-gold light. Before them stood a tall woman in a scarlet singlesuit. Her hair was silver-gold. Behind her stood an even taller figure so shadowed in silver that Eltyn could not make out his face—if he were indeed even a man.

Who are you? Eltyn had spoken the words aloud, but they came out as if pulsed on the private net.

She said something, but the words made no sense . . . not at first, but after a moment, he could hear them, as if they had been pulsed to him. *I am the keeper of the Bridge . . . what you call the canal.*

Why couldn't we communicate before? asked Faelyna.

I was not prepared. What disaster threatens you?

How were they supposed to answer that? Eltyn glanced to Faelyna, who did not show any expression. Finally, he offered, *The Ruche government has been overthrown, and we took refuge in the canal station where we were doing research. The usurpers tried to destroy the station with a nickel-iron meteorite.*

Eltyn looked to Faelyna.

She added, *The fall of Hururia and the Ruche to barbarism . . . and the sand and heat, it would appear.* After a moment, she went on. *Who are you, and why are you responding to our attempts to gain control of the functions of the canal?*

I am the keeper of the Bridge . . . the canal.

Why have you never appeared before?

I am not in what . . . you would call . . . your time.

What we would call time? Is not time . . . time? asked Eltyn.

"Time" does not exist. Intelligences perceive the continuity of interactions within their event-points as time . . .

Eltyn didn't know what to say.

We experience time, Faelyna replied, *and there is a temporal component to the controls of the doors and windows of the station.*

The controls that govern the Bridge are in levels, linked to degrees of event-point continuity.

Time by any other name, Faelyna insisted, following her words with an equation.

In response came an equation, and then another.

Eltyn and Faelyna exchanged glances. He didn't understand the second equation, but it was clear that Faelyna did.

What's happened outside the canal? interjected Rhyana.

An object from beyond the atmosphere struck the western end of the Bridge. The energy was transferred to the water and the seafloor. Nothing living remains within . . . a kay(?) of this terminus of the Bridge.

Can you help us? Besides keeping us alive inside the canal? asked Faelyna.

The woman in scarlet was silent for a time, and she looked back at the shadowy silver figure. Then she seemed to sigh. *Tell me more.*

The riffies took over and The Twenty overthrew The Fifty . . . began Rhyana.

The world warming threatens the Ruche . . . Eltyn stopped.

The keeper laughed softly. *One at a time, please . . .*

51

✤ ✤ ✤

9 Tenmonth 1351, Unity of Caelaarn

Maertyn and Maarlyna sat the Laarnian chairs in the chamber he had once come to think of as the study. Before she'd begun to explain what she had learned from the second group she'd "visited," he'd turned his chair so that it faced hers more directly. That way, he could almost ignore the light-sheathed ghost consoles that haunted the room . . . except that when he looked at Maarlyna and listened, the silver-gilded light extended itself around her, emphasizing her, like some ancient monarch, and her eyes and hair held a strange luminescence. Or was that just the interpretation of his own senses? Would he ever know?

"The Ruche people . . . they sound like they live in almost a hive culture," he finally said. "They all look alike—"

"The ones I saw did. They all might not, but I think you may be right," replied Maarlyna.

"They don't have even the weapons we do, from what you've said, and almost all the people just went along like sheep with the new tyrants."

"Do most people in the Unity really care if Tauzn becomes the next EA?"

Maertyn paused. Her voice was calm, almost gentle, but . . . He decided to go on. "They'll support Tauzn because they believe that D'Onfrio isn't getting results, and they're frightened . . . even when they're the ones who've elected people who are cautious."

"What if The Twenty are just like Tauzn? What if they gained power because those in control weren't solving the problem?"

Maertyn paused before replying. "From what you said, their problem is worse than ours. We're fighting the ice, and they're fighting warming so great that where our fertile lands are they have desert, and where we have ice, they have forests and cropland. And because whatever this Fifty is or was couldn't stop the desertification, there was a coup, and some sort of tyranny took over. At least, we don't have the Earth burning up on us." He paused. "Are they in the future, too?"

"Yes. Not so far as the Vanir."

"How far are the Vanir, then?"

"I can't tell. I don't see things that way . . . but it's far. They're different, physically, especially the women. They're bigger than the men, and their hair actually changes color, almost as if each strand has tiny lights in it, and they can consciously focus their eyes, I think. Well . . . the Bridge systems made that observation."

Maertyn found himself fingering his stubbly chin. "With all those changes . . . did they come from the Ruche people or from us? Could it be that Tauzn gained control and forced both genetic changes and geo-engineering . . . ?"

"And when the solar cycles changed, the Ruche ended up facing a runaway greenhouse effect?"

He shook his head. "I don't know. It takes time for a society that rigid to evolve from the ruins of another, and anthropogenic warming builds faster than that. Then again, it might not, if there were significant depopulation." He paused. "These three want you to help them?"

Maarlyna nodded. "They were part of a team that was trying to learn more about the canal station. Whatever the political change was, the results make Tauzn look moderate. This Twenty group either kills people or alters their brains, and they do it on the scale of thousands of people."

"Do you think they're telling the truth?"

"The systems help. I can tell that they believe they're telling the truth, and there is a large and very recent crater in the seabed northwest of the station—in their event-point locale. The water was still boiling."

"That's very recent." Maertyn winced. "I thought Tauzn was cold-blooded."

"In a hive culture, only the hive as a whole truly matters. Only survival . . ." Her voice caught for a moment, and she stopped. "Then . . . it could be that all human societies have more of the hive in them than we'd like to admit."

"What are you going to do?"

"I have to help the hive people and the Vanir. Both of them were well on the way to deciphering some of the station controls. Can you imagine what would happen if this Twenty gained control? Or Tauzn? Or those Aesyr?"

Unfortunately, Maertyn could, but her question raised several others. "Could you help them to operate the station . . . the Bridge . . . in their time?"

"From what the Bridge has gathered about the equipment they used, it would take years."

"Does time really matter?"

"There's elapsed time. That means it would take years of my time. They also don't have the right equipment, and I don't know how effective I would be in trying to explain, even with the help of the systems. There's also the resonance problem."

"Resonance problem?" Every time Maertyn thought he understood a bit more, something else came up.

"All the event-points in a universe are linked, some more strongly and directly than others. When similar events occur they resonate across the whole. If I can resolve our problems, those of the Ruche people, and those of the Vanir, while they are still linked, the end result will be better. If it takes more of my elapsed time . . . then it gets harder, and the Vanir solution won't have the same effect. Because I'm nearest the one event-point that has the least impact on the resonance, I have more leeway in elapsed time here. If I can help the Ruche people first, before the Vanir . . . that would be better."

Maertyn had the feeling that Maarlyna wasn't telling him everything. "What are you leaving out?"

A brief rueful smile was her first reply. "It's harder that way, but if I can make it work, things will be easier for you . . . us."

"A great deal harder?"

She shrugged, not totally convincingly. "I don't know how much harder."

He wasn't going to get a better answer. From experience, Maertyn knew that. So he asked the other question that had nagged at him. "Why was the station left open? The one at the other end was locked. Is it like this one?"

"They're the same," she affirmed. "The records don't say. The keepers' memories don't, either. I think the last keeper might have stepped outside . . . and died or . . . Whatever happened, she or he didn't lock the station."

"Maybe they knew the only way to find another keeper was to leave it unlocked."

She nodded thoughtfully. "That's possible, too."

"You've told me how you're going to help the Vanir. What about the Ruche people?"

"I'm not sure. That's why I wanted to talk to you before I promised anything to them."

Maertyn almost said something about being glad to be of some use, but he bit back the words. "How far will the Bridge reach—outside the now . . . the event-point, I'd guess, of each time?"

"It can reach a distance of its length from any point along its course—except it's not actually penetrating the event-points." Maarlyna smiled, almost ruefully. "That's something that takes getting used to. The old 'me' still doesn't understand that. The 'new' part of me . . . that's silly in a way, because everything I've learned and felt from all the keepers' memories is much older—"

"*All* the keepers' memories? Plural? How many memories are there?"

"It's all one memory, but the part of each one back is fainter than the one nearer to me. The past few years are clear and sharp, especially since we came to the station. The memories of the Maarlyna I was are hazy, but I can remember most things, I think, even if they don't always feel real. The previous keeper's memories are hazier than that . . . and each one is fainter than the one before. It feels like that, anyway, even if the ones I think of as later take place earlier. That's why I can't remember much about the terrible disaster when the ancients actually used the Bridge . . . there are images of the sky being filled with fire, and massive things falling everywhere . . ." Maarlyna's voice faded, and she shuddered. "But the feelings of terror . . . and desolation . . . they're still there."

Maertyn wasn't quite sure what to say to that, and he waited.

"Why did you ask about the reach of the Bridge?" she prompted.

"I wondered if the capital city happened to be in reach?"

"Hururia? That's what they call it."

"How can you remember all that?"

"I really don't. The Bridge does, I think." She paused, then said, "Hururia is . . . well, it will be . . . eleven hundred thirteen kays to the northeast of the station."

"So the Bridge could reach there?"

"Yes. What do you have in mind?"

"I don't know, not exactly, but I have an idea. You'll have to talk to them again. We need to know more about the Ruche and how their government is set up, and if there are any symbols that have special significance . . . things like that . . ." As he talked, Maertyn couldn't help but feel that he needed to think about similar issues himself—because the Gaerda outside the station weren't likely to go away any time soon.

Not now that Tauzn had proof that Maertyn had gained some control over the station, although that control was totally Maarlyna's.

52

❈ ❈ ❈

Eltyn, Faelyna, and Rhyana sat around the end of the table where they ate in the pale luminescence now exuded from the blue-gray stone of the station itself, a light slightly dimmer than that cast by a few antique candles, yet an illumination so diffuse that it cast no shadows.

"Who . . . or what is she?" asked Rhyana.

"The keeper?" asked Eltyn. "She obviously controls the canal and the station."

"How do we know that?" persisted the delivery woman. "Just because she can appear and change what we see?"

Eltyn looked to Faelyna. "What do you think?"

"What would be the point of deceiving us?"

"To keep us from learning how to control the canal?" suggested Eltyn.

"If that happened to be her aim, couldn't she have killed us when we were blind and immobile?"

"Not if she's really not in our time, like she said," Rhyana pointed out.

"If she's communicating across time, wouldn't that suggest she's telling the truth?" asked Eltyn.

"What if she's not?" countered Rhyana.

"Do you think we're just dealing with a programmed intelligence that we woke up when we closed the canal?" He looked to Faelyna.

"That's possible. That raises other questions. She/it can communicate through our minds...in our language. If she's from what amounts to our future, why would she bother? If she's from the past, how does she know how we speak? None of the ancient tongues are like Hururian."

"It bothers me," declared Rhyana.

"We don't have too many choices," Faelyna pointed out.

That concerned Eltyn. None of their choices were good.

The light intensity in the lower level brightened, and the three turned to see the keeper standing there, with the same silver-shadowed presence behind her. *I need to know more if I am to help you.*

Why did you contact us? asked Eltyn. *Why do you want to help us?*

The keeper did not answer immediately, as seemed to be the case, Eltyn thought, whenever a difficult question was posed. Was that a sign of an artificial intelligence?

By closing the station, you contacted ... me. The Bridge has great power, but using all but the smallest fraction of that power will destroy the Earth. If we help you, that power is less likely to fall into the hands of those like The Twenty.

Why don't you show us how to operate things? asked Rhyana. *That way we can decide for ourselves.*

The keeper laughed, yet there was a sadness behind the soundless gesture. *You cannot operate the Bridge the way I do. If you had more time and more ... advanced equipment, with help, over years you might discover those means. For many reasons, that is not practical.*

Not practical for us ... or for you?

For either of us. You do not have the supplies, and there is no way to get them to you. If you do not act soon, in terms of your own event-point, the chances for success decline.

How do we know that all of this isn't just a way to get us to leave the station? pressed Rhyana. *To keep us from finding out how it works?*

If that were my intention, all I need do is nothing. All I need do is wait. Your food and water will not last forever.

We can unlock the station, Eltyn replied.

The keeper smiled sadly. *Not any longer. You should try. I will wait.*

Eltyn glanced at Faelyna. Then the two of them stood, followed by Rhyana. They eased from the table, made their way to the ramp, and walked up the lower ramp and then the upper one to where their equipment remained. At a distance, the keeper followed.

"Do you think it's safe?" Eltyn looked at the makeshift assemblage, which appeared cloaked with the ghost consoles that represented, he thought, equipment from another time.

"I'm not going to open anything," she replied. "I'm just going to un-lock one of the windows. The stone will still protect us, and there can't be anyone outside looking to get in. The riffies will be watching by minidrone, if they're watching at all."

"Do we have enough power?"

"We should, and we need to know if she's telling the truth." Faelyna addressed the screen before her. "We'll try the south window." She frowned. "There's no response."

Rhyana walked to where the window had always opened and pressed her hand against the stone before either of the others could say a word.

The stone remained immobile.

After several moments, Eltyn turned to the keeper. "You . . ." As he started to speak, his words went from spoken to thought. . . . *seem to have us where you want us.*

I would not wish where you are upon anyone. I do understand.

The almost plaintive honesty of her response went through Eltyn like a blade.

The three exchanged glances.

Finally, Faelyna asked, *What do you need to know?*

Would you tell me more about The Twenty . . . where they are lo-cated . . .

We don't know too much, but they represent themselves as upholders of tradition . . . began Eltyn.

Before long, he had lost track of all the questions posed by the silver-eyed keeper, but he did notice that she often glanced at the silver-shadowed figure that always seemed to follow her.

Much, much later, the keeper finally said, *Thank you. We must think of the best way to deal with your problem.*

Then she vanished.

Eltyn used the back of his sleeve to blot away the dampness on his forehead.

"She asked a lot of questions about The Twenty and Hururia," said Rhyana.

"She asked as many about what people believe," mused Faelyna. "And about traditions."

"And why the questions about the rainbow?" Rhyana wrinkled her brow.

Eltyn had to admit that he'd been puzzled about the keeper's inquiry about legends dealing with the rainbow. Then, he'd also been puzzled about her questions about what she had called politics. Even after her explanation of the term, it hadn't made that much sense.

53

❉ ❉ ❉

20 Siebmonat 3123, Vaniran Hegemony

Duhyle required less than an hour to rig capacitor-jolt detonators for the biotherm. Then he reshaped the explosive into ten makeshift grenades around which he formed thin metal/composite fragments, wrapped in another metal sheath. For the detonators and the casings, he cannibalized much of his own equipment, since he had no doubts that, one way or another, it would be unnecessary in the future. He was finishing sealing the last grenade when Helkyria walked up from the lower level.

"Are those . . . ?"

"Grenades of a primitive sort. They've got impact/timer detonators. They should go through most impact-resistant uniforms. Even if they don't, there are likely to be broken bones and other injuries." He completed the last seal and looked up. "How are the techs and troopers taking it?"

"They're more than ready." Her smile was crooked and rueful. "They don't like being cooped up."

"It hasn't been that long. It only seems that way. Think of what it must have been like when the ancients sent military forces to Mars and the Belt. Or farther."

"Farther? We don't know that. In any case, that's old, old history. You might as well ask them about using spears."

"What about the officers?"

"Valakyr doesn't trust the keeper, not surprisingly, and Symra worries that we're being double-crossed."

"And you?"

"We're not being double-crossed, but we're likely to be very expendable. The keeper doesn't want the Aesyr to use the Hammer any more than we do. Much less, in fact. I'd judge that she—or it—is more worried about Baeldura than we are." Blackish purple light glowed from the tips of her hair and was reflected in her silver irises before fading into a faint blue.

"We're the handy tool to take care of the problem," replied Duhyle. "Do we really have any choice?"

"That was the point I had to make to Valakyr. It didn't seem to occur to her that, if the universe collapses, even the canal—the Bridge—will go with it. That doesn't benefit the keeper. Symra at least understood that."

Duhyle frowned. "I might be wrong, but I think there's more at stake than that for this . . . keeper."

"More than what?"

"Survival, either of her or the Bridge."

"I'd have to agree, but I don't think we can count on finding out."

Duhyle stood and stretched. "You might ask her. You're the only one who has a chance of understanding the answers."

"You might be better than I am at that," she replied.

"I doubt it, but that doesn't matter. The keeper and the officers are both more likely to listen to you."

Helkyria sat on the stool facing Duhyle. "Kavn . . . what do you think the keeper is after? You've had a chance to watch her."

"I think she's new at her job. Or she hasn't done it for a long time, and she's faced with something she didn't anticipate."

"I had a thought or two along those lines, but . . . some of the technical jargon . . . she speaks it without hesitation. Expert systems, you think?"

"Very expert systems. That's another problem. I worry that she may be a captive of those systems."

"What do you suggest we do about it?"

"We can't do anything about the systems. We've already tried."

"So you want me to try to find out more from her?"

Duhyle shrugged. "What else can we do? Except prepare to wreak whatever havoc we can on the Aesyr."

"Grenades or no grenades, you aren't going in first."

"No . . . but there's no point in my being behind everyone, and I know how they'll work. I'll follow the spec-ops types."

"Kavn . . ."

". . . and some of the security troopers."

She looked at him.

"Mimyra, if we don't stop them, we don't have a future. And I was combat-trained first."

She nodded slowly. "I don't have to like it."

"Neither do I."

She reached out and took his hand. They sat in the ever-changing light, waiting . . .

54

❊   ❊   ❊

9 Tenmonth 1351, Unity of Caelaarn

Maertyn set the platter of cool casserole in front of Maarlyna, then seated himself across from her at the lower-level table next to the kitchen area. "What are the Gaerda troops doing outside?"

"Trying to stay warm. The wind has picked up, and it's bitter out there." She looked at the sprig of greenery and then replaced it in the side pocket of the singlesuit. "Hardly what we expected for the holidays."

"I don't know that we expected anything, except being together."

"I'm so sorry, Maertyn. You've tried so hard . . . and now . . ."

"You couldn't let everything end . . ." he said softly.

"I could have. Perhaps I should have. Everything will end, sooner or later." She shook her head. "Except so many people would never have the chance to laugh . . . love . . . live . . . and . . ."

". . . enjoy whatever holidays they might have?" Maertyn kept his voice light, hard as it was.

"I was looking forward to the holidays, spending them with you."

"We still can, can't we? They're more than a month away." He smiled. "All we have to do is save three civilizations. Oh . . . and find a way to remove our guards before we can save our own."

"Dearest . . . what do you think we should do about the Ruche people?"

Maertyn almost smiled at her avoidance of his indirect question. "If you can send them weapons, even a few of the ones I sent here, have them stage a counter-coup."

"With three people? Isn't that unrealistic? Besides, I can't send anything . . ." She paused. "Nothing substantial."

"What do you mean . . . nothing substantial?"

"Just a moment." Her once-amber eyes turned an almost blank silver.

Realizing that she was "consulting" with the Bridge systems, or dredging the memories of past keepers, Maertyn hoped she might come up with something.

After a time, her eyes refocused on him. "If I used all the energy available for the event-congruency the Bridge touches and they leave, I might be able to send fifty grams to the Ruche, and a fifth of that to the Vanir."

"That little?" he asked. "For all the available energy? How much does the Bridge generate or hold?"

"The amount is so large it's meaningless, but most of that is used to maintain it, as you put it, out of time. If the Bridge drops into time, more is available, but its mass is no longer shielded and the effects . . . that's what happened the last time, when the moon fell . . . was dragged . . . toward Earth and was fragmented." She paused. "It was the only time the Bridge occupied a single specific event-point, and it was very brief. It also was almost the last time."

Maertyn let out a low whistle.

"That's why the Bridge has been seeking a keeper. The systems can only monitor, not act. Things are stable, but the Aesyr have enough knowledge to make them very unstable if they get hold of the station. The Vanir don't want to give up the station for that reason, but they know the Aesyr would rather bring the universe to a very premature death than allow the Vanir to remain in control of Earth."

Maertyn shook his head. "I don't understand. If there is no time, only these . . . event-points, don't all events essentially happen at once? And if that's so, why couldn't earlier keepers know what would happen and do something about it?"

"Time is the way intelligences perceive the entropy of events. Events do succeed each other. No one has ever resolved with certainty the degree of causality involved, or if strict causality even exists." Maarlyna shook her head. "Those aren't my words, and I'm not sure I got them quite right. They don't translate into Laarnian."

"So events do somehow follow each other?"

"Yes."

"All right. So you can't send anything explosive back—or forward . . . or to their event-point—with the Ruche people."

Maarlyna smiled, brittlely. "Anything I did send would be highly explosive, but most of it would have to be shielding. If I didn't shield it, it would explode instantly in their time period."

"Like antimatter?"

"With event-point separation along continuity, energy differentials do build, and it takes more and more energy . . ."

Maertyn nodded, a slow smile spreading across his face as she—or the Bridge systems through her—explained.

". . . but the nature of the event-point penetration limits what the Bridge can do, in direct relation to the event-point separation from the event-point locale of the keeper . . ."

"You can do more here than for the Ruche, and more for them than for the Aesyr?"

"It's more complicated than that. Here there's no energy differential, but . . . yes, that is, for the Ruche and the Aesyr."

"Maybe you should just leave the choice to the Ruche people. You can extend the Bridge out of time, so to speak, anywhere. Let them choose where they want you to put them down."

"I can't put them just anywhere. No more than the length of the Bridge from any point on its apparent geographical location." Maarlyna made a wry face. "I don't talk that way, but it's like I don't have any choice when I try to explain some things." She frowned. "I might be able to do something else, though."

"What do you mean?"

"If we leave the Bridge out of the event-point, but open a door . . . and leave a present from here . . . and then set the Ruche people down where they can find allies . . ."

"Leave a present from here? I thought you said you couldn't put them in two places or . . ."

"I can't. But I could expel fifty grams from here . . . without having them leave the Bridge . . ." She shook her head. "I'm sounding like

Tauzn might. What's happening to me? I'm not like that . . . I wasn't."
Tears oozed from the corners of her eyes.

He stood and walked around behind her chair, where he leaned
down and put his arms around her.

"Why . . . why, Maertyn?"

"Because it's much easier to be compassionate when you have no
power. When you have power, no matter what you do, someone gets hurt."

"That's . . . that's not the only why. Why am I feeling it now . . . and
not earlier?"

"I can only guess." He waited, but when Maarlyna did not speak, he
went on, "When you . . . merged . . . or became the keeper . . . some of
what is you got submerged. You're strong, stronger than most people realize, but it took a while for you to get . . . your mental balance. You have
now . . . and you're asking the questions you always did."

He could sense her nod as he kept his arms around her.

There was another period of silence before she spoke again. "The
Ruche Twenty . . . they've killed thousands. Would hitting them be that
bad?"

"You've asked twice about the Ruche people. You don't have much . . .
elapsed time to work with, do you?"

"There's some."

"But not much." Maertyn's back began to cramp and twinge from
the awkward position, and he eased his arms from around her and
straightened. "No . . . it's always a risk when governments are attacked,
especially if the attack is successful. You never know if the new government will be even worse than the old one. Much of the time, it is."

"Are you saying I shouldn't do anything?"

"No. I'm saying that I believe you should. But you should, knowing
that it might not work out."

"How would you make it more likely to work?"

"Can you tell if people are in a building?"

"Not really."

"Then we'll have to guess . . . and hope. I'd say that, since it's not a
tropical culture, even if it's warm temperate, The Twenty are most likely
to be present in early afternoon. Even if they're not, if your present can
destroy whatever the capitol building is at a time when the most people
will see it . . ."

"Do you really think that will work?" asked Maarlyna.

"The odds of the three of them fomenting a successful counter-revolt aren't good," he admitted. "But they're essentially dead if they stay in the station or if they try to leave it where it's located geographically, or if they attack the capital directly." He paused. "Can you lock the station for at least a few years after they leave?"

She stiffened, ever so slightly. "I think so. Actually, that will happen anyway. I don't know that I could unlock . . . Why? Oh . . ."

"Just to keep the Ruche honest for a time. I don't know that I . . . we know enough about causality or what was it you said . . . 'the entropy of event-points.' Do you need to talk to them quickly?"

"Fairly soon . . . I just feel it. I can't explain it."

"Then we should eat, and you should do so." He stepped back from behind her chair and moved around the table and settled back at the table, looking at her and then at the casserole.

55

35 Quad 2471 R.E.

The keeper returned to Faelyna's workroom in the station less than half an hour after she had vanished. That was the way it seemed, but all of the station equipment that indicated time was nonfunctional. Eltyn had tried not to look too hard at the images of equipment that continued to shift and mutate moment by moment. He did wonder just how many eons those changes represented and how long the ancients had actually operated the station in the fashion represented by those images.

You weren't gone that long, offered Eltyn as the woman in scarlet appeared.

It was long enough to consider the possibilities. Do you know of a place where you have friends who will help you?

Why? asked Rhyana.

I can transport the four of you there, if it is no farther than Hururia. We can also create . . . a disruption . . . in Hururia that will make seeking you . . . less of a priority.

Eltyn glanced to Faelyna. *TechOversight?*

She shook her head.

He should have realized that The Twenty and the RF would have targeted all the known TechOversight Facilities.

Chiental is possible, offered Faelyna.

The keeper glanced back at the shadowy silver figure that Eltyn had not seen appear; then toward the three. After a moment, a map of the continent appeared, projected into the air, with dots in places where there were no cities. *Point out where this place is.*

Eltyn stepped forward and studied the map, finally locating the Fhranan Peaks. *About here. Against the western cliffs in a valley opposite the tallest peak in the range.* He paused. *Most of the installation is under the mountain, except for what looks like a log lodge.*

We should be able to locate it. We're already shifting the Bridge toward Hururia. It won't intrude into the event-point, but it will be visible in a way, just below the reality horizon. The Twenty will see it. It won't be a Bridge, though.

What else could it be? asked Rhyana.

The most glorious rainbow they have ever beheld. We should go down to the main level. That's from where you'll be leaving.

So soon? asked Eltyn, almost involuntarily.

There are advantages to operating outside the event-points. The keeper turned, walked to the ramp, and headed down to the main level.

As he followed, Eltyn wasn't certain that her boots actually touched the surface of the ramp. He also tried to sense whether the station or Bridge was moving, but he felt nothing. He looked to Faelyna.

She shook her head and shrugged.

Rhyana slipped ahead of them and continued down the ramp to the lowest level.

Eltyn frowned, then nodded when he saw the delivery woman return carrying the projectile rifles and two stunners. There wasn't any guarantee about what might be waiting for them, and the weapons would be useful even if they were welcomed with open arms, although he doubted that was too likely. He was hoping for skepticism, rather than out-and-out hostility, if and when they reached Chiental.

Rhyana set the weapons on the floor, along the outside wall, but away from the door, then straightened.

The keeper stopped short of where the south door was—or used to be—and turned back toward the three. She extended a small round pebble to Eltyn. *When the south door opens, throw this out. Make sure that it strikes the dome. You have only one chance. Do not let your hand or fingers or any part of your body extend into the door opening or beyond.*

He fingered the tiny stone she had dropped into his palm. It felt like the walls of the station, except that his fingers did not quite touch the smooth surface of the pebble. He frowned. *A stone?*

It will do what is necessary.

Why can't he lean out? asked Rhyana.

Then you will all have to leave at that moment . . . or remain in the station for some time. The fall to the stone pavement around the building would likely kill you all if you tried to leave. You might not be able to depart the station until you were out of food if you did not leave then.

Might? pressed Faelyna.

I would not be able to open the station again for some time. How long would depend on too many matters to calculate now.

Could you allow us to open the doors? asked Faelyna.

I could . . . but not if you want to attack The Twenty and leave the Bridge in a location other than where you entered it.

That's not much of a choice, snapped Rhyana.

To move the Bridge, even outside your event-points, requires energy. Opening the doors at a geographic locale other than in its moored orientation requires energy for shielding. There is only so much energy.

None of the three spoke.

Do you want to attack The Twenty and then reach this place . . . or not?

Eltyn sensed something behind the voice, but whether it was anger, impatience, or frustration . . . that he could not tell.

We'll attack and go to Chiental, said Faelyna firmly.

I'm glad you finally made up your mind.

There wasn't much humor in those mental words, Eltyn realized.

The keeper turned toward the south wall. The stone slid open wide.

Eltyn blinked, because the opening in the wall was surrounded by a coruscation of colored light, as if the Bridge/station were in the center of a brilliant rainbow. The keeper had told him that would be the effect, but hearing her words hadn't conveyed the incandescence of what lay between him and the gold-gilded rounded stone of the Ruche dome.

The smooth and unmarked top of the dome was a good ten yards below the opening before him and no more than five from the station wall. For a moment, he just looked, wondering how it was possible that they were where they were.

Throw it!

He grasped the small stone and threw it at the top of the dome, but not too hard, knowing that excessive effort was all too often counter-productive. Once the pebble passed through the station opening, the stone wall of the station began to close. Eltyn kept watching as the door narrowed. Just before the small dark rock was about to strike the dome, it flared, and then accelerated into the structure. Light flared every-where, bright enough that he couldn't see, even after the Bridge/station sealed itself off.

What happened? demanded Rhyana.

The building is in ruins. The keeper's tone was matter-of-fact.

With all those people in it? asked Faelyna. *Just like that?*

They ordered the killing of all those who opposed them, didn't they? They destroyed the ability of thousands to think, didn't they? Or did you lie to me?

No . . . but . . .

But what? Never in our long history has anyone who used such meth-ods been stopped without the use of force and more killing. With almost no break in her words, she went on. *Before long the Bridge will reach the locale you indicated.*

The keeper glanced to her left, where the shadowy figure in silver had appeared. For a moment, she blurred, then resolidified.

An image appeared in midair, showing a valley.

That's not it, said Faelyna. *The western cliffs should be higher, and there should be a small lake to the south.*

Two more images appeared before Eltyn said, *That's it. The entrance is through the log building below that cleft.*

The image vanished.

You need to take the body of the dead man when you leave. You can drop it once you're outside the Bridge.

Rhyana looked to Eltyn. He nodded, and the two of them walked back down to the lower level, where she cut loose the bonds that held the dead man to the chair. His limbs were still stiff and locked him into a sitting position. That made carrying him back up the ramp awkward and slow. They set the body down next to where the door had opened, then straightened.

Can we just toss him out when the door opens?

Whatever you want . . . A wry smile crossed the keeper's lips, then vanished. *It won't be that long now. I cannot extend the Bridge into the cliff itself, except along the metal tunnel beneath the log building . . . and not that far.*

When the door opened, Eltyn stepped over to the dead riffie. Rhyana joined him. As soon as the opening was wide enough, the two of them swung the body outward, not as effectively as Eltyn would have liked, since the dead riffie barely tumbled past the edge of the stone and out through the rainbow corona, beyond which he could see only a hazy grayness.

He stepped back and turned.

Faelyna already held a long-barreled stunner. She eased toward the opening, but stopped short.

Eltyn immediately reached down and lifted the remaining projectile rifle, then straightened and turned to the keeper. *Why are you doing this?*

Because I must. You offer the hope of intelligence against the dead hand of a dead faith. Go! All of you.

Rhyana was the first through the doorway. Eltyn and Faelyna hurried after her.

Eltyn stumbled, and then righted himself as the rainbow incandescence quickly diminished. He blinked. The three of them stood in a metal-lined corridor with a ceiling less than a yard overhead. Behind them the last of the rainbow flared momentarily . . . and then vanished totally.

Toward them hurried a man in a drab brown garment that had been a TechOversight singlesuit before it had been subjected to far too many cleanings. He came to an abrupt halt. "Who . . . how did you get inside? What was that light?" He almost reached for the stunner at his waistband, then saw the weapons in the hands of the three.

"Tech Eltyn, Tech Faelyna," said Eltyn. "We were stationed at the MCC MetStation when the RF uprising started. We received the order for Contingency Three. It took a while for us to get here."

"How did you get in?" demanded the older tech, his voice bearing equal traces of anger and concern.

"The only way we could," replied Eltyn.

"How did you manage that rainbow effect? Did you burn . . . ?" He stopped speaking and looked past them toward the dead riffie, his brow furrowed in puzzlement.

"The riffie tried to kill us," snapped Rhyana.

"We'll be happy to explain that, as well as we can, when we're debriefed," added Eltyn.

"The only place you belong is in detention."

"I have a suggestion, Supervisor," Eltyn said pleasantly. "Along the way, we also blew the top off the Ruche dome in Hururia. We'll be happy to wait quietly until you get confirmation."

"Oh . . . and when did this explosion occur?" The supervisor's voice dripped with sarcasm.

"Just a few minutes ago."

"Most amusing."

"It's true. All you have to do is wait."

"I could brain-scan all of you."

Eltyn didn't mention that the supervisor was outnumbered and outweaponed. That wouldn't last long.

"That wouldn't make you any better than riffies and The Twenty," snapped Rhyana. "We've worked hard to get here. You might look over the riffie's body." She half-turned and pointed to the limp figure on the composite floor of the tunnel. "It might tell you something."

Eltyn frowned. Was there a pulse-net in Chiental? He extended a probe, trying to determine . . .

Authenticate! demanded the system.

Eltyn entered his TechOversight codes and ID.

Accepted. Level three.

Eltyn looked to Faelyna and mouthed, "Pulse-net."

After a moment, she nodded and smiled.

Interrogative access? demanded someone.

The supervisor glanced from Faelyna to Eltyn, then back to her.

Project Canal-three, MetCom cover, replied Eltyn. He had the feeling that the Chiental pulse-net was operating on individual segregation, except possibly on the supervisory level. They'd never needed that at the canal station, not with two people. How many techs and others were sheltered on the multiple levels of the redoubt?

Supervisor Tauryl . . . bring the canal techs to debriefing section. The net command conveyed absolute authority.

Even so, Eltyn wondered how well the speaker might do against the Bridge-keeper. He kept the thought to himself. No one else in the Ruche was likely to ever enter the station.

"How did you manage that?" asked Tauryl.

"Senior net access," replied Eltyn.

"You might as well come, too," Tauryl said, glancing at Rhyana. "Chief Interrogator Bernyt will want to know everything."

"What about the riffie?" demanded Rhyana.

"I've sent for a crew to pick it up. Now . . . let's go." He pointed deeper into the mountain tunnel.

Chief Interrogator? Exactly what had they gotten themselves into? questioned Eltyn.

Faelyna eased closer to Eltyn, murmuring, "Just tell them every-thing about the Bridge systems."

Eltyn didn't understand what she meant, but only for a moment.

"No whispering!"

"I was just telling him to make sure to tell them everything."

"You both will. The interrogators are quite thorough."

"We're both TechOversight operatives," Eltyn pointed out.

"You say you are. The interrogators will make certain."

Eltyn had no doubts of that, nor that the process would be painful to some degree. Still . . . what else could they have done?

56

❈　❈　❈

9 Tenmonth 1351, Unity of Caelaarn

The silvery shadows vanished from the main chamber of the station, and Maertyn glanced around, taking in the familiar furniture—and the still-unfamiliar ghostly light-images of unfathomable equipment. His eyes came to rest on Maarlyna, wearing the red singlesuit that remained an instant reminder of how much had changed so quickly between them.

"Dead hand of a dead faith?" offered Maertyn. "Where did that come from?"

For a moment, Maarlyna did not answer, her eyes and senses still somewhere else. Then she looked at Maertyn and smiled, wanly. "From me. Well . . . the words were mine, but it came from seeing everything the old keepers saw. Why do you ask?"

"The words seemed strange . . . that's all."

"Strange . . . or strange coming from me?"

"Both," he admitted.

"What I said is the problem in Caelaarn, too, dearest."

"There are more than a few problems in Caelaarn," Maertyn admitted, "but I don't see the dead hand of faith as one of them."

"Dead hand of a dead faith . . . that's what I said."

"What did you mean by that?"

"Why can't you or anyone else see what I see here in the station?

What I saw from the beginning and didn't mention because I was afraid you'd think I had lost my mind?"

Maertyn knew it had to have had something to do with the regeneration and partial recloning that had restored her. "Because you see things differently."

"Why?"

He shrugged.

"I had to learn to see all over again. You remember that?"

"Yes," he responded with caution.

"I learned then that we don't actually see the world around us. Our eyes scan constantly, relaying bits of information to our brains, and our brains interpret that information into a coherent whole. They also filter out anything that doesn't seem . . . relevant . . . I'm guessing, but seeing event-points outside or away from where we are makes surviving harder, not easier, and our brains have to process a great deal anyway."

"What does this have to do with faith, dead faith?"

"What you see is based partly on what you believe, even if what you believe is not truly the way things are." She shook her head. "The Unity . . . everyone believes that biological solutions are always the best. That's faith. The ancient ancients believed that technology could solve everything. That's another kind of faith. Their ancestors believed in deities who would put things right if one only believed. The Ruche believe common values will prevail. They're all faiths, and because they're incomplete, they're dead. Those who follow those faiths are chained by the dead hand—"

"Of a dead faith," he finished. "The only problem is that people won't accept that."

"That's why, I think, I felt better when I came here, even though I didn't know why."

Maertyn wasn't quite sure what to say to that. After several moments that felt endless, he finally said, "Can you rest for a bit before you deal with the Vanir? You're looking pale."

"Only a little while." Maarlyna stepped back and settled into the antique Laarnian chair, taking a slow deep breath, then another, as if what she had said to him had been an effort.

As he seated himself across from her, Maertyn half-smiled, reflecting that the chair had existed for little over a century and that he'd thought of it as almost ancient while standing in a structure that pre-dated his entire culture by hundreds of thousands, if not millions of years. The flickering of the ghost images reminded him of another nag-ging question. He cleared his throat.

"What is it?" Maarlyna's words were gentle.

"I see all these images of equipment lining the walls, and I'm guess-ing that they come from past times. The station still operates, but there's no equipment in our time, and there hasn't been for a long time. And I know time doesn't exist the way I've always thought of it, but . . . if the station still operates . . . what happened to everything?"

"I wondered about that, too." Maarlyna's lips quirked. "I asked . . . and searched. In the last years before the great catastrophe, the ancients changed everything and incorporated all the functions into the structure, the stone, itself, so that nothing could ever damage it."

"But they couldn't save themselves or their civilization?"

"How many times have you told me that finding practical solutions that could be readily implemented is easy, but that getting people to ac-cept them is almost impossible?"

He had to smile at hearing his own words from her.

"Before long, I'll need to talk to the Vanir."

"I thought you could enter their time right after you left . . ."

"It's not that simple. They need time to prepare . . . and there's the resonance problem."

"You mentioned that before. Why do actions now or with the Ruche or with the Vanir have any direct relationship to each other? They're in different times . . . event-points . . . as you call them."

Maarlyna sighed. "I'm not sure I understand enough to make it clear, and some of the words . . . some of the concepts . . . don't exactly translate. The universe . . . the multiverse . . . religious people, believ-ers, all tend to think that there is something beyond it. There isn't. On the other side, the rationalists assume that any universe is, I'd guess you'd say, limited and neutral. It's not. The confluence of all actions within its event-points determines its . . . flow. Actions by intelligences have a greater proportional impact as the universe . . . progresses . . ."

"Of course. Technology and biological sciences can affect more."

Maarlyna looked as if she might say something, but did not.

Maertyn waited.

"That's true," she finally said, "but it goes beyond that. Universes, like individuals, seek meaning."

"You're saying that a universe is alive?"

"I don't think anyone knows that. The ancients didn't. But universes progress from initial exploding chaos into structures that continue to evolve. Those that don't . . . they collapse." She shook her head again. "I can't make it clear, not in Laarnian. All I can say is that what they face is the negation of everything, and that if the Vanir defeat the Aesyr, if the Ruche can force back the negation they face, and you can halt the negativity Tauzn represents, the struggle . . . the evolution toward meaning . . . will continue . . ."

At that moment, Maertyn had no idea whether Maarlyna was mouthing nonsense, trying to translate the untranslatable . . . or whether he was incapable of understanding exactly what she was trying to convey to him.

"Maertyn . . . just let me have a moment . . ."

He could do that. Yet, as he sat back in the familiar comfort of the old family chair, a familiarity that no longer reassured him, he had to wonder if all the things he'd watched and heard were really just part of a grand delusion. He knew the canal existed . . . and the station. But what else was real? Did he know . . . for certain?

57

❖ ❖ ❖

35 Quad 2471 R.E.

As Eltyn had suspected, before they had gone another twenty
yards into the mountain, a half squad of techs armed with heavy
long-barreled stunners appeared. All wore TechOversight singlesuits, and each stood ready to fire at an instant's notice.

Relinquishing your weapons would be advisable, came the command
from the redoubt pulse-net.

Eltyn looked at Faelyna, then at Rhyana. "They suggest that we leave
our weapons."

"It's not as if we've got much choice," pointed out the delivery woman.
"Thought we'd get a warmer welcome."

Eltyn didn't comment, not in the face of that many weapons. He
handed the projectile rifle to the tech, but only after releasing and pock-
eting the magazine.

"You're not exactly trusting," noted the tech.

"Stunners don't kill. That does." Eltyn nodded at the rifle, noting
that Rhyana had followed his example and stepped forward with her
weapon. "I'd rather not have someone accidentally killed." Especially if
it happened to be one of the three of them.

Faelyna surrendered her long-barreled stunner without a word.

"Good." The tech handed all three weapons to one of the squad
members who had moved forward, then turned and began to walk, not

looking back. That showed he was linked to the redoubt's internal scanners as well as the pulse-net.

The three followed.

The metal-lined corridor still stretched more than a hundred yards farther westward when the tech turned into a small hallway that headed north. "This way."

Eltyn glanced back. The armed squad still followed, stunners at the ready.

Their escort stopped a few yards farther on. "Tech Eltyn . . . you go in there." He pointed to a featureless gray door.

Eltyn looked back at Faelyna, hoping it was not the last time he would see her—or remember seeing her. He smiled as warmly as he could, trying to convey more than concern. Then he turned and walked up to the door, pressing the lever and opening it. He stepped inside to find a woman standing there, clad in a gray-brown TechOversight singlesuit. Her oval face was not quite angular. Her brown eyes were flat, and her short brown hair was without highlights.

She did not smile. She closed the door behind him. "I'm Chief Interrogator Bernyt." She gestured to the heavy chair with the high headrest anchored to the floor in the middle of the small room. "Please take a seat."

"I'm not certain that's in my best interests. We've had to survive a great deal to comply with Contingency Three, and when we get here, we're treated like enemies."

"That's because you could be." Bernyt's smile was cool and professional. "Even with all the codes you have, it's possible that you're an RF plant. We intend to discover whether you are who you claim to be."

"What about DNA, gene maps, and the like?" asked Eltyn.

"If you're a deep plant, they'll match, because you'll always have been in the system," Bernyt pointed out.

Eltyn suppressed a wry smile. TechOversight had used similar means to get Faelyna and him assigned to the MCC.

Do not make matters more unpleasant than they have to be.

Eltyn didn't care for such reminders, especially from the pulse-net. He also didn't have much choice. He settled into the heavy gray chair gingerly. He even managed not to wince as the restraining cuffs clamped his wrists.

"We'll make this as painless and as quick as possible." Bernyt stepped back from the chair.

Eltyn had definite doubts about either aspect of that reassurance.

"Tell me your full name, your place of birth, and birth cohort."

"Eltyn CyanRed, Ascensia, Primia, Fal-233."

"Your occupation and current assignment."

"Senior Tech, MetOps, assigned to MCC MetStation (W), meteorological operations. Cover for TechOversight project CCS-3."

"Explain this project."

"The objective of the project was to determine, first, if higher-level technology was contained within the station and, second, if that technology could be accessed and developed . . ." Eltyn continued by repeating, as he remembered it, the official description of the work he and Faelyna had been assigned to undertake.

Before he finished a burning jolt ran through his entire body. "All you're doing is reciting. Explain the project in simple and direct terms."

"That was the description TechOversight provided—"

Another jolt burned through him, and his eyes watered.

"Stop stalling. Explain it without the jargon."

Eltyn swallowed, then began again. "No one's been able ever to even make any impression on the stone of the canal or the station. The doors and windows slide into the stone itself without leaving any openings or traces—"

Thud! Eltyn's head slammed into the back of the chair from the force of the nerve jolt.

"Do you expect anyone to believe that?"

"I've seen it," he replied groggily. "There . . . are books and monographs . . . describing it . . . Lasers have been fired at it . . . no effect." His entire head throbbed.

"How much progress did you make?"

"We'd been able to detect a response on the fermionic level—"

Another pulse of pain jolted him. "No jargon!"

"Not jargon . . . fermions are subatomic . . . have a detectable . . . shadow . . . with proper equipment . . . showed symbols . . ."

More pain slammed into him. "Symbols?"

He moistened his lips. "Symbols . . . when we duplicated them . . .

before the coup . . . just before . . . we could open doors . . . windows . . . without touching them . . . no one . . . done that before . . ."

"What happened after The Twenty announced their taking control of Hururia?"

"They didn't . . . announce it that way. First, there was an announcement demanding power reductions, and then an announcement on the emergency band saying The Twenty had superseded The Fifty in accord with some prime emergency directive . . ."

That brought another jolt. "Some emergency directive?"

"We'd never heard of it . . . thought it was an RF invention . . ."

Bit by bit, Bernyt led him through the attacks by the riffie inspectors, with only a few jolts, until he got to how they had "locked" the station.

Three stiff jolts in a row left him reeling in the chair.

"Explain that again. You're not making any sense . . ."

He just let his head loll there against the headrest. "I can't . . . not any better . . . could jolt me to death . . . but it's physics, fermionic theory . . . practical application . . . and things . . . they got stranger after that . . ."

Surprisingly, Bernyt didn't jolt him when he described The Twenty's efforts to destroy or open the station by the dropping of material from orbit . . . and the heat and the results.

He did get another series of jolts when he mentioned the manifestation of the keeper as a projection of the Bridge systems . . . that was the best he could do, because there was no other way to explain how the systems interfaced . . . but he wasn't certain he was making any sense.

"How did you get here? The station is on the south side of the canal."

"The Bridge systems . . . they curved the canal out of time . . ."

Another jolt. "Likely story. Try again."

". . . can't," he gasped. "Can't . . . how we got to Hururia . . . how the Bridge blew the Ruche dome . . ."

The jolt following those words brought blackness down on him.

When he regained consciousness, his face was damp.

"Do you want to try again?"

"You . . . can kill me . . . with that . . . won't change anything . . . no other way to get here. No boats. The wheeler . . . buried in sand . . ."

Pain coursed through every nerve in Eltyn's body, and, again, blackness swamped him.

When he slowly struggled through grogginess, a slow thought crept through his mind. Was there that much difference between the methods of TechOversight and those of The Twenty? Except he still had his mind. So far.

"Try again."

"I told you. The Bridge systems told us . . ." Behind the pain, he kept telling himself that the keeper was only part of the systems.

From that point on, he wasn't even certain what he was saying.

Then, abruptly . . . another darkness swept over him, and the pain ended.

58

❖   ❖   ❖

20 Siebmonat 3123, Vaniran Hegemony

Duhyle and Helkyria—and all the others in the station—ended up waiting hours, although Duhyle doubted that any time had elapsed outside the station, not that he had any way of telling. The outside monitor screens showed the same image as they had ever since he and Helkyria had triggered the synchronizer. Helkyria had gone down to the lower level to go over the assault plans with the two officers, while Duhyle had fashioned a chest harness for the grenades, placed the grenades in it, and considered how best to use his makeshift weapons. While he knew they would explode as designed, how much damage they would do inside the refurbished antique Aesyr warship was another question entirely.

For all the time he had pondered, he wasn't certain he'd accomplished all that much when he finally stood and eased his way down the ramp, far enough that he could hear Helkyria.

"... and remember ... the control center for the Hammer has to be located directly behind the bridge on that behemoth. We can't get there directly. At the single point the Bridge can touch the ship and we can cross, the only hatch open is one a level down and twenty yards aft of the ship's bridge. We'll have to fight our way from there. Subcaptain Symra and the spec-ops team will take the hatch and hold it, and Captain Valakyr's troopers will spread and secure the superstructure, especially the ship's bridge and area just aft . . ." When Helkyria had gone over the rest of the plan, she looked to the two junior officers. "Form up your techs and troopers. The keeper will return when we're ready."

Duhyle hoped that was so, but how would they know?

"How do you know we can trust this . . . keeper, Commander?" asked Symra.

"I don't," replied Helkyria. "The probabilities favor trust, but they're far from absolute. I don't see any other options. Do you?"

"No, ser."

Duhyle slipped back up the ramp and waited for Helkyria in the large main-floor chamber. When she returned from the lower level, he asked, "Are they more settled?"

"As settled as they can be."

"If the Bridge is out of time—or out of this event-point," asked Duhyle, "why can't the keeper just have it open inside the Aesyr ship?"

"There's a layer of something that's similar to the stone of the canal in the armor of the ship. That's why it survived so long. I'd guess that the Bridge, even if it exists out of what we call time, can't penetrate anything that's existed for a long time, either, like a mountain." She paused, then went on. "If we're actually out of time, or suspended where time doesn't exist, that will give us the advantage of surprise."

"Because we'll appear sooner than Baeldura would expect?"

"That's the hope."

The two looked at one another, waiting, when the silvery radiance began to build, almost directly before Helkyria.

"Tell Symra and Valakyr to muster everyone for action. Then have the two of them join us."

Duhyle hurried to the ramp and down to the lower level.

The two officers jumped up from the bench where they had been sitting.

"The commander said to muster your forces and then join her on the main level." Duhyle immediately turned and strode, at not quite a run, back up to rejoin Helkyria.

Behind him, Valakyr ordered, "Stand by for deployment!"

Duhyle supposed that was as good a command as any, and better than "Be ready to go through a stone door of an ancient canal station into the hatch of a slightly less ancient warcraft." When he reached the main level, Helkyria was listening to the keeper.

The keeper stood less than a yard from the scient-commander . . . *ready to move against the Aesyr?*

Before we go any farther, I'd like a few words with you, Keeper. Privately. Helkyria stepped forward.

We can do that. A silvery curtain flowed from somewhere around the two women.

"How did she do that?" murmured Symra, as she hurried up on Duhyle's right. "Why now?"

"She's bargaining for knowledge," Duhyle said in a low voice. "That's my guess. The keeper isn't in our time, and we're fighting her battle as much as our own. The commander wants some payback, and all that's possible is knowledge."

"Let's hope it's worth it," murmured the subcaptain.

Neither of them mentioned that the knowledge would be useless if Helkyria did not survive the attack on the Aesyr warship.

After a time—and Duhyle wondered what time was when people were out of time and whether they aged—the silvery curtain vanished.

Helkyria stepped back and pointed to the space where the southern door of the station had always opened. "Spec-ops, forward!"

Symra strode down the yard or so of the upper ramp and stood at one side. Duhyle moved back to the bottom of the ramp leading to the upper level, then halted as the seven remaining spec-ops techs positioned themselves directly behind the southern door of the station.

Once the spec-ops techs stood ready, the first of the security troopers moved up the lower ramp to form a tight column that doubled back on itself and then ran down the ramp to the lower level. Captain Valakyr stationed herself behind the first three troopers.

The keeper looked at Helkyria. *Are you ready?*

We're ready.

Surprisingly, the keeper moved across the main chamber to where Duhyle stood. She extended her hand. In it was the tiniest sprig of greenery. *When all else fails against the Aesyr leader, affix this to your last grenade before you throw it. The grenade itself may not suffice, but the mistletoe will not fail.*

Mistletoe . . . how could that help? Duhyle did not voice the question, but accepted the sprig. Anyone who controlled the canal . . . or the Bifrost Bridge, as she had termed it . . . might know more than he did.

You think you are blind and slow compared to all the others, she went on. *You will see what they do not.* A sweet smile followed.

Duhyle felt that sadness lay behind her expression, or perhaps a lifetime or an eternity of sadness. He fingered the green sprig, barely the size of his thumb, realizing as he did that his fingers did not actually touch the greenery, as if an invisible shield surrounded it. There was more to that greenery than met the eye. But why had she given it to him?

The keeper in red had already headed back toward Helkyria. She stopped just to the right of the first spec-op techs. *The Bridge is almost in position.*

"Spec-ops!" called Helkyria. "Stand by for insertion!"

Duhyle fumbled in his waistpak for the stiktite, easing out a strip and holding it and the mistletoe in one hand. With the other, he levered out the cylindrical grenade from the topmost strap holder on the right side of his makeshift harness. Then he pressed the sprig against the stiktite and wrapped the strip across the surface of the grenade, before carefully slipping it back into the strap holder.

"Spec-ops . . . stand by!" ordered Symra.

There was no feeling of movement or anything else, yet when the south door to the station opened, what Duhyle saw over the heads of the fast-moving spec-ops techs was a brilliant rainbow of light, so bright that it hurt his eyes . . . and beyond that a wall of blackish brown metal.

Two massive and red-bearded Aesyr stood on the narrow metal platform before an open hatch, their mouths agape. The techs surged forward, and both Aesyr fell. In moments, the techs were inside the hatch, and Valakyr and the first of the security troopers were pouring onto the platform and through the hatch.

Duhyle moved across the chamber to a position near the open door. There he waited until several groups had left the station, then jumped in front of another threesome and hurled himself through the opening. Landing on the hard metal platform deck sent a shock up through his boots, almost as if the Aesyr ship carried one sort of charge and the station another. He staggered, then righted himself and followed the troopers into the passageway beyond the hatch, its dark brown metal bulkheads two yards apart. The overhead was also metallic, a smooth silvery cream that emitted a cool and indirect light.

He'd taken only three steps before something like a jagged lightning bolt flared down the metal passageway, striking some of the techs and missing others, crackling and leaving the acrid odor of seared flesh, fabric, and equipment.

Duhyle started to catch a falling trooper, then let her slide past him to the deck as he realized that the charcoaled face held no life. He swallowed and followed two troopers who were dodging toward a ship's ladder up to the next level.

"Boarders on the bridge! All marines midships! Second deckhouse level!" The announcement reverberated off the metal bulkheads with such volume that it almost deafened Duhyle as he followed the pair of troopers toward the ladder.

More of the lightning-fire flared down the ladder toward a trooper at the bottom. He lifted a small shield, and the electroplasma flared harmlessly around him.

Duhyle flattened himself against the bulkhead to let another three troopers rush past him, then followed them closely. All four of them stopped short of the area at the foot of the ladder.

While the trooper at the bottom of the ladder continued to deflect electroplasma bolts, the force of the bolts froze him in place. No one else would have been able to climb the metal stairs in the face of that barrage, either.

"Marines midships! Midships on the double!"

The announcement reminded Duhyle that they didn't have much time to reach the deck above, especially with Aesyr marines swarming toward them from all over the enormous vessel. He eased out one of his grenades and made his way past the troopers near the open space at the base of the ladder. He stopped just short of where the electroplasma bolts could reach him.

There he pressed the detonator, then waited a slight moment before taking a quick two steps. He leaned forward and flung the grenade underhanded and up the ladder—before jumping back before another electroblast streamed downward.

The explosion of the grenade was thunderous within the metal-enclosed space, but when the trooper with the shield started to move up the ladder, another jagged plasma bolt flared downward, forcing him back.

Duhyle pulled another grenade from his chest harness, waited for the next plasma bolt, then pressed the detonator, jumped forward, and flung the second grenade. This time, the return bolt passed close enough to his arm that he could feel the heat and power.

But . . . no more bolts followed the second explosion, and a wave of troopers flowed up the ladder. Duhyle was more than glad to let them. He followed after a good squad's worth of troopers had scrambled up the metal stairs to the bridge level.

Once up the ladder he followed the cross passageway toward the center of the ship, keeping low to avoid the occasional and intermittent projectiles and electroplasma bolts that ricocheted off the dark metal walls or the well-lit overhead.

Ahead of him, the midships passageway intersected a fore-and-aft passageway, predictably enough, in the middle of the superstructure. Several troopers hung back from the fore-and-aft passage, even while snapping fire around the corner because of the fire coming from the direction of the bridge.

Why hadn't the Aesyr closed the hatch to the bridge? They'd had enough time. Or was there something preventing them?

Duhyle pulled out another grenade as he moved forward, pressing aside several troopers and stepping over one who had fallen. As he neared the corner, he dropped to his knees, then took a quick look toward the bridge, then jerked his head back. The passageway was strewn with bodies, but one of the dead or immobile Vanir troopers had jammed something in the hatch, and the Aesyr were struggling to remove it, and several bodies that blocked the hatchway as well.

Taking another grenade, Duhyle tabbed the detonator and then leaned forward and hurled it toward the hatch, ducking back and reaching for another grenade from the harness.

The first grenade bounced down the passageway and stopped short of the hatch, caught on something, before it exploded.

Immediately after the explosion, Duhyle let go of a second grenade, hurling it toward the opening in the hatchway. His aim was off, and the cylinder ricocheted to a halt just short of the hatch. Duhyle dropped back around the corner and readied a third grenade as the second exploded.

Beside him, Valakyr grabbed one of the small shields from a trooper, clearly waiting for Duhyle to throw his next grenade.

Duhyle did, and as soon as the explosion echoed down the passageway, Valakyr sprang clear, ordering "Forward!" as she sprinted the ten yards or so toward the hatch.

Troopers surged after her.

Duhyle let them. The Hammer control section had to be aft, and he looked to his right, down the fore-and-aft center passageway. Bolts of force flared from an open hatchway some fifteen yards away, dropping a trooper.

Duhyle didn't move. There was something odd . . . wrong. The trooper had bounced away from the hatchway—before being struck. The forcebolt had held a reddish shade. Duhyle had never seen that before . . . ever, and he'd seen every kind of weapon used by the spec-ops and security forces.

He watched the aft hatchway more intently. Another trooper fired a stunner bolt at it, and the energy angled away from the open hatch as if reflected.

Symra drew up beside Duhyle, gesturing toward the open hatchway. "That's where Baeldura is."

"I thought so." Duhyle glanced at Symra. "Where's the commander?" He couldn't bear to use her name, not when he feared what the subcaptain might well say.

"She's still on the lower deck. Part of her leg got torn up some by their flechettes, and we can't get her up here. She said to tell you she'll be fine, but that it won't matter if we don't stop Baeldura. She's on a portable comm with Baeldura."

Duhyle understood that the "we" mostly likely meant him. He just nodded, then eased around the corner into the fore-and-aft passageway and flattened himself against the metallic bulkhead. Whoever was firing from inside the compartment couldn't quite hit the space right next to either bulkhead.

From behind Duhyle, Symra fired at the open hatch, and the heavy flechette shattered against . . . nothing.

Duhyle moved quickly, keeping his back against the bulkhead and nearing the seemingly open compartment hatch. Once closer to the hatch, he could hear words, from a voice he could not help but recognize, even from the few times he had heard it.

"The very walls, the very air turns away anything your troopers can fire at me!" A manic energy infused Baeldura's words. "If you do not withdraw all of your forces immediately, I will loose the Hammers all across Vanira."

There was a silence.

"Don't tell me you can't . . ."

Duhyle reached for the topmost grenade in the harness, the one with the mistletoe strapped to it, knowing that he was almost out of time, hoping that the keeper's "gift" would make the difference.

Standing just in front of Symra, Duhyle pressed the detonator stud, waited, and then stooped and turned, pitching the makeshift biotherm grenade toward the open hatchway.

A bolt of reddish energy grazed Duhyle's sleeve, destroying the fabric and searing a patch of bare skin. Duhyle almost didn't feel the pain.

At that flash and motion, Baeldura looked from the console before her, catching sight of Duhyle. "You . . . bitch!"

Those words were directed at Helkyria, doubtless, but the Aesyr commander said nothing more, her mouth open as the grenade passed through the barrier that had repulsed all other energies and projectiles. Her hand jabbed at the console before her.

"So much for Vaena—"

The grenade exploded. So did Duhyle's world, and he was bathed in fire and ice . . .

59

❋　❋　❋

9 Tenmonth 1351, Unity of Caelaarn

Maertyn stood by the northernmost of the Laarnian chairs, trying to sense the words and the actions of Maarlyna through
the silvery veil of time. At moments, he thought he could also
make out a woman in silvery armor, although sometimes she appeared
to be wearing a pale blue singlesuit. Maarlyna moved across the chamber several times, and once she walked *through* the low table that had
also come from Norlaak. That, more than anything, told Maertyn how
much things had changed.

When she finally reappeared, she sank into the other Laarnian chair
without speaking.

After seeing the tiredness in her eyes, without speaking, he went
down to the lower level, cut some hard cheese, and rummaged around
until he found some biscuits and wine. Then he brought up a plate of
cheese and biscuits with two goblets and a bottle of wine. He set the
platter and one goblet on the end of the low table nearest her and filled
her goblet two-thirds full. "This might help."

"Thank you, dearest."

After pouring the wine into his own goblet, he settled into the
matching chair and took several sips of the Boulena he'd chosen because
Maarlyna preferred white, although he would have opened a red, had
the question been one of his preferences. He watched as she slowly ate

several slices of the white cheese and a biscuit . . . and as the color returned to her face.

After a time, she looked at him. "You haven't said much."

"I've been thinking."

"About what?"

Maertyn took another sip of the Boulena before replying. "About
Tauzn. About me. About us."

This time Maarlyna was the one to wait for him to explain.

"After hearing and half-watching all the others risk their existence
to stand against . . . I guess you'd call it nothingness . . . how can I not
do the same?"

"Do the same? What do you mean?"

"Tauzn sent assassins after me. He dispatched two dirigibles filled
with Gaerda black-shirts. No one said a thing, I'm certain. No one did anything to stop him. Am I supposed to let him tear down a good civilization because no one else will take a stand against his fear-mongering?"

"What do you think you're going to do? The Vanir had over a hundred troopers. There's no one else to help you."

"There were three Hu-Ruche . . . and I'm not alone. I have you, and
you can put me exactly where I need to be." He offered a smile, knowing it was false, and knowing that she knew it was false. Yet what else
could he do?

"I can't help you once you leave the Bridge. You know that, don't
you?"

"I do."

"You'd leave me?"

He wanted to point out that, in many ways, she'd already left him.
Instead, he said, "I think I'd find it hard to live with myself if I didn't do
what I could. Besides, the Gaerda won't leave, and with them stationed
outside, sooner or later, our food will run out. I can't step outside of
time—or the event-point—the way you can."

"I could do it for you," she said.

"Then what? Will I wake and fret that I did not act when I could?
How long before I go truly mad and self-hating? With you and the
Bridge, you can open his office . . . or at least his balcony to me, to place
me inside most of his guards."

"The Bridge can do that," she admitted. "What will you do then?"

"I do what I must, and, after that, if I can, I make my way back north to the station and pray that I can enter it and find you. If not . . ." He swallowed. Finally, he spoke again. "We had each other for more and better years than would otherwise have been. If Tauzn becomes EA . . . then few indeed will have years like that. I could not spend eternity . . . or however long it might be . . . knowing that I had a chance . . ."

"You will always have that chance . . . you know?"

He shook his head. "The chance I will always have, but will I have the will? With each passing day or month or year or eon, or whatever, will it not become easier not to act? And as I see it, time within the canal flows the same for us. Is that because you're the keeper . . . or because it's necessary while I'm here?" He looked across the low table to her.

Her only response was a wan smile.

"Either way, that means that with each day, Tauzn gathers more strength." He paused. "What time is it outside?"

"Well past midnight."

"Then we have the night . . . and tomorrow . . . we each will do what must be . . ." He stood.

So did she . . . and both their eyes were bright.

60

❋ ❋ ❋

35 Quad 2471 R.E.

When Eltyn finally emerged from darkness, he found himself on a pallet stretcher in a cool room. He turned his head. It throbbed so much that his eyes burned. He could see nothing, except that the light level was low. His lips were so chapped that they felt like he'd been amid the sands for days, but when he tried to moisten them, he couldn't. His mouth was like dry cotton, and his tongue felt swollen.

"Easy . . ." said a voice. "Just be still. I'll give you some Revive. That will help."

Eltyn didn't recognize the pleasant male voice, but in moments a tube was in his mouth.

"Sip it slowly."

That was all that he could do at first.

Before long his mouth felt more normal, and the splitting headache subsided into an unpleasant but bearable throbbing. The worst of the burning in his eyes died away, and he could make out a man in a pale green med-tech singlesuit.

"What . . . about . . . the others?" Eltyn finally managed.

"They're here, too, but you're the first to wake. That's because you were the first to be interrogated and scanned."

"Does it . . . do any good? People . . . say anything . . . that much pain."

"It seems to work. It's not what they say, but how their brain reacts."

Eltyn barely managed to avoid coughing and decided to stop trying to talk.

"Just lie there for a while longer. You'll know when you can sit up."

A little while longer turned into a doze, from which he was awakened by voices, and one of them was that of Faelyna.

". . . might work . . . but barbaric . . ."

"Tech," replied the man who had given Eltyn the Revive, "it might be barbaric, but I'm not in charge, and no one tampered with your mind. The RF doesn't care what happens to people's minds so long as they're obedient and subservient."

Eltyn slowly sat up and glanced at Faelyna, who was sitting sideways on the pallet stretcher holding a beaker. She looked better than he felt, but he was very glad to see that. He offered a smile. "Quite an interrogation."

"Torture," snapped Rhyana from where she sat on a straight-backed composite chair against the wall. "Might be better than the riffies, but it's still torture."

The medical tech stepped toward Eltyn, holding a beaker. "You might want more of this."

Eltyn accepted the beaker and took a swallow. The taste was bearable. That was all he could have said for it.

The door to the chamber opened. Chief Interrogator Bernyt stood there. "Now that you're all awake with your identities verified, the Administrator would like to begin your debriefing by explaining a few things. This way."

Eltyn saw that Bernyt wasn't the type for politeness or apologies, even when it would have smoothed things over. He took another swallow from the beaker, before handing it back to the med tech. "Thank you."

"You're welcome." The man did smile.

Bernyt walked swiftly down the metal-walled corridor—not either of the ones through which they had entered Chiental—to the second side corridor and then to its end, where there was a blue door. She opened it.

On the other side was a conference room with a table long enough to hold five chairs on a side, all upholstered in pale gray.

"Take any chair you want, except for the one at the end." Bernyt stood behind the chair to the right of the one at the far end. "The Administrator will be here shortly." She sat down.

Eltyn took the chair across from the one claimed by the interrogator, and Faelyna settled in beside him. He did reach out under the table and took her hand for a moment, squeezing it gently.

While she didn't look at him directly, there was a faint smile, and she squeezed his hand in return until he released her fingers.

The four sat in silence. A wall panel on one side of the room slid open, and a small muscular older man in a pale gray singlesuit without insignia stepped into the conference room.

Eltyn leaned forward as if to rise, not that he wanted to.

"Please stay seated. You've been through quite a bit," offered the newcomer.

Bernyt nodded to the speaker. "This is TechOversight Administrator Solano. He can explain why we had to put you through so much."

Solano slid gracefully into the seat at the end of the table. "I regret the depth and pain of the interrogation. I can assure you that the effects will pass . . . if not immediately." He offered a regretful smile. "We've had five deep RF plants attempt to infiltrate over the past few days. Fortunately, they made contact with outlying stations so that Chiental's location was not compromised. Then when you three arrived, everyone feared the worst. That was why Senior Tech Bernyt's efforts were necessary." He nodded toward the brown-eyed and unsmiling interrogator.

"You two are who you claim to be." Bernyt gestured to Eltyn and Faelyna. "Your records and responses and genetics check, and your brain prints match. The pain and nerve jolts were absolutely necessary, because any brain overlay distorts in a clearly identifiable way under nerve pain. A non-overlaid brain print doesn't." She looked to Rhyana. "With you, we had a bit more trouble. We had to check consistency there."

The delivery woman glared at Bernyt, but said nothing.

Bernyt looked back at Solano as if to indicate that she had said all that was necessary.

"Now . . ." continued the Administrator, "I had to admit that your initial story . . . report . . . seemed more than fantastic. But we have been able to verify it from a number of unimpeachable sources—the chaos in Hururia alone suggests that you, or whatever entity aided you, managed quite a disruption. All the reports indicate that a brilliant rainbow arched from the south and touched the Ruche dome—which then exploded and collapsed the building beneath. Here we checked the outside scanners. They recorded a rainbow of light, magnitudes brighter than a natural rainbow, also arching from the south over the peaks and down onto the lodge. When we compared the data from our back-channel snoops, the spectra match what happened over Hururia just before the top of the Ruche dome exploded. Many of The Twenty appear to have been inside, but we won't know who for a time. What we'd like to know is how you accomplished that."

"We didn't." Faelyna's voice was resigned. "I told your interrogator that."

"You both told the same fantastic story, and it matches the data, but it would be most useful if we could obtain access to that technology."

"I don't think that's likely," answered Eltyn. "The Bridge systems indicated that future access to the canal station—or the Bridge—would not be possible." The keeper hadn't said anything like that, but she also had been very clear about their departure, even to their taking the dead riffie.

"You couldn't learn anything about the systems?" asked the Administrator.

"We didn't say that," Faelyna interjected. "I can give you the design and specifications for the equipment we used to control a few things in the station. I can even give you the practical and theoretical basis for the first-level control system. There are several difficulties, though. The control system is multilayered, and we never deciphered the other levels. The main problem is that we brought the systems on-line by what we did, and they took over, and locked us out. The Bridge systems even challenged us to try to unlock things. We couldn't."

Eltyn nodded. Faelyna had thought out, better than he had, how to explain what had happened in a way that would be understandable to TechOversight. Whether it would be acceptable was another matter.

He added, "In the end, we didn't have much choice. The systems did blow off the top of the Ruche dome. We hoped that, and the rainbow, would create a symbol that TechOversight could use as a rallying point to restore The Fifty . . . or to topple The Twenty and replace them with a system that is less tyrannical."

Faelyna didn't even blink at his statement.

Solano looked to Bernyt.

The interrogator nodded.

"That's emotionally rationalizable enough that it might work." Solano paused. "We'd need something that would generate that more frequently."

"A set of tuned lasers might do it," mused Eltyn. "You might be able to focus them on aerogels or water vapor. That's not my expertise, but I think it would be feasible."

Solano nodded slowly. "It might at that." After another moment, he said, "Tell me more about these Bridge . . . systems . . . and how you discovered what you did."

Eltyn looked to Faelyna.

"You start," she said.

"We knew that the doors and windows opened to human touch," began Eltyn. "That's something that's been known for years . . . centuries. No one has ever known how the stone resists all energies or how or why the entry systems worked. We were assigned to see if we could determine that . . ." From there he went on to describe all their efforts through his failed attempts, finishing with, ". . . based on that, Faelyna decided on another approach. It was more successful." He looked to her.

"The key seemed to be recognition and intent . . ." Faelyna continued.

More than an hour passed, between their reports and the Administrator's questions, before Solano leaned back slightly in his chair. "Very interesting. We will likely have other questions, but that will do for now."

"What do you expect from us now?" Eltyn shifted his weight. Despite the padding in the chair, every movement still hurt, and probably would . . . possibly for weeks.

"From you three?" The TechOversight Administrator smiled warmly. "We could very much use your and Tech Faelyna's technical skills in the laboratories and workshops here. We lost all too many of our higher-level techs."

"No fighting?" asked Rhyana.

"If you want to, you can, but Tech Eltyn and Tech Faelyna are too valuable to hazard." He paused. "Besides, I don't see how you could contribute more to the reformation's military effort than you already did, and it appears likely that we will be incorporating the rainbow as the symbol of the reformation."

"How is the . . . reformation . . . going?" asked Faelyna.

"We've already regained control of most of Primia, except the immediate area around Hururia, but after the destruction of the Ruche dome by the rainbow, and the probable death of a number of The Twenty, we'd be very surprised if we didn't have The Fifty reestablished by the end of the year . . . with a few changes . . . of course."

"Such as?" asked Eltyn warily.

"We're going to have to widen the forum for discussion and disagreement and change the idea that questioning equates to rebellion or that uncertainty, particularly with regard to science and public policy, means weakness . . ." Solano rose from the chair. "If you will excuse me and the interrogator. There are a few other demands on my time." He smiled. "One of my assistants will be with you shortly to work out quarters and provide you with passes and codes . . . and the other details of life here in Chiental." With a last smile, he turned and departed.

Bernyt followed Solano, but without a backward glance or a smile.

Eltyn did note that the wall panel, presumably to the Administrator's office, remained open after the two had left.

In some ways, reflected Eltyn, none of it made sense . . . and yet it did.

He turned to Faelyna. "We suffered more at the hands of TechOversight than at the hands of The Twenty, although The Twenty certainly tried harder to destroy us and the station. After everything we've been through, we accomplished more by throwing a pebble than by anything else either of us did."

"You wouldn't have been able to throw that pebble if it hadn't been for everything else we did," she said with a smile.

"Everything else you did," he corrected. "My approaches didn't work. Yours did."

"We did it together."

He looked directly into her eyes. "I'd like to do far more . . . everything . . . together."

Faelyna leaned toward him, taking his right hand in both of hers. "So would I."

61

❈   ❈   ❈

10 Tenmonth 1351, Unity of Caelaarn

After a long and bittersweet evening with Maarlyna, during which he had not so much loved her as clung to her, Maertyn spent most of the remainder of the night fully awake . . . amid infrequent brief periods of dozing. He would have preferred to have left then, but there was little point in that, since he only knew where to reach Tauzn during the day.

They spoke little as they prepared for the day and dressed, but Maertyn kept looking at Maarlyna, wondering how it had all come to the point where all his efforts to save her had led inexorably to his having to leave her, possibly forever . . . if he failed.

Do you really have to do this? That he had asked himself more than once over the long night. But how could he not? He, and he alone, from what he knew, had the ability to stop a tyrant before matters worsened. How did a man live with himself if he refused that opportunity? He didn't want to follow the example of the Laarnian martyrs . . . but he had to do . . . something.

Arm in arm, they walked down to the lower level, where they shared tea and not-quite-stale bread slathered with sweet orange preserves. He wanted to say something more to her about how much she meant . . . and how he didn't want to leave her . . .

All of that would merely have repeated what he had murmured the night before . . . and made him seem somehow . . . pathetic.

So he smiled and looked at her, trying to create a lasting image in his mind.

Then, as the time drew near, they walked back up to the main level, where he checked the pair of stunners that had been in the crate Rhesten had sent so many days before. He also fingered the ice hammer, before putting it in the inside pocket of the formal ministry jacket he'd chosen to wear—a maroon and silver-gray lord's jacket for all of that.

"Is it time yet?" he asked "I want to be in his office just before he returns from his morning staff meeting."

"Almost. What if he doesn't have a meeting?"

"Then he's there . . . or he's not, and I'll work around it." He slipped the stunners into the side pockets of the jacket, then walked toward the south door of the station, where he stopped. "Let it be done . . . dearest. I will return . . . as I can."

"You know that if you leave the Bridge this way, you can't return . . . except by traveling back to the canal?"

"I know. I heard you tell the others that."

"And you know I can't leave? Ever?" The tears ran down the sides of her face, and she stepped forward and embraced him. "You deserve better . . ." she murmured.

"We don't always get what we deserve," he murmured back. "But perhaps we have . . . or what we wished for. I wanted you to be here forever, and I wanted the chance at great deeds." He tightened his arms around her for a moment, then brushed her lips with his, before easing out of her arms.

"Be as careful as you can, dearest," she said softly.

"That I will." He smiled and looked at her, taking a long look, one he hoped would not be the last, then turned toward the door.

"It takes longer here," she said quietly. "Or seems to. I'm not quite certain which."

"I know." He did not look at her, but kept his eyes fixed on the station wall.

When the stone did slide open, the brilliance of all the colors of the rainbow flared around him as he stepped through the opening and down from the railing onto the outside balcony of the office of the Minister of Protective Services, a balcony that overlooked all of Caelaarn to the south.

Maertyn did not look back but hurried to the glassine door between the covered balcony and Tauzn's private office. Inside, the office was empty, as he had hoped. The door was locked, but it only took three sharp blows with the ice hammer to break the lock. That wasn't surprising, since few would have expected a burglar or assassin to enter from an eleventh-floor balcony in the middle of a guarded complex.

He wiped the grip of the hammer with the fabric at the bottom of his jacket and dropped the hammer on the yielding flooring of the balcony, then took one of the stunners from his pocket before he stepped into the office.

So far as he could tell, his entry activated no alarms. At least no one burst through the door to the outer office, but that might have been because the brilliance of rainbow light still flared behind him, possibly distracting security personnel.

From his recollections, the offices of all ministers had private facilities for changing and other necessities. He tried the door on the left. It was a closet. The one on the left held the facilities and a robing chamber with a mirror. That would do. He left that door ajar and turned back to the wide and empty desk.

There he checked the comm system. He didn't even try to access anything in it. All he wanted was an open line with a delay to one other system. That took him only a minute or so, and he couldn't help but smile wryly as he thought about the idea that time didn't exist, only event-points on a continuum, or something like that.

Then he retreated to the small room, leaving the door barely ajar, and waited . . . and waited . . .

He wasn't certain how long he had waited when he heard voices.

". . . took forever this morning . . ."

"That's understandable, sir. There's been no success in entering the canal station, and with the inquiries about the Gaerda dirigibles . . . and that rainbow . . ."

"Ashauer's at the bottom of this . . ."

Although Maertyn had only heard Tauzn speak a handful of times, the minister's deep, resonant, and reassuring voice was distinctive enough that he recognized it immediately.

". . . Maertyn's just an expendable piece . . ."

". . . rather resourceful for being so expendable. How did he seal the station? No one's ever done that."

Maertyn had waited to see if anyone else would enter, but it seemed as though no one else would. Raising the stunner, he eased the private facilities door open a trace wider, then fired at the back of Tauzn's head, switching to the man on the left, Deputy Minister Aembit. The third man was someone Maertyn didn't know, but he immediately yelled, "Assassins!"

That was all he got out before the third stunner bolt hit him.

Maertyn pushed the door open wide, took three quick steps and thumbed the stunner up to full narrow beam strength, and placed the tip at the back of Tauzn's head, giving a double jolt. If the minister lived, and Maertyn didn't care one way or the other, he wouldn't have much mental processing power.

Maertyn immediately did the same thing to Aembit, then hurried across the room, flinging the door to the balcony wide open, and then moving to a position where he'd be shielded by the door to the outer office opening. As he took his position, he adjusted the stunner to a wider beam.

For several minutes nothing happened, and Maertyn wished he'd known that. He could have used the time to alert Ashauer. Then the door burst open, and three black-shirts sprinted into the office. All were wearing body armor and helmets.

That didn't stop stunner beams aimed at the back of their necks, and all three toppled.

Maertyn eased over to the door and kicked it shut, then twisted the privacy lock. He knew that would only slow them, but he needed a moment or two . . . or three.

Dashing back to the desk, he triggered the comm code for Ashauer, although the open line had been feeding to the deputy assistant minister. Ashauer's image came up, and Maertyn hit the override. "Ashauer . . . Maertyn here. I'm in Tauzn's office. He's been assassinated, and now everyone's attacking the office. Thought you might like to know. Do what you can."

There was no immediate answer.

Maertyn left the channel open, and retreated into the facilities room, leaving the door ajar.

Outside he could see another brilliant rainbow arching toward the balcony, but this time it did not touch the balcony. He smiled.

The rainbow continued to coruscate for several more minutes, and no one tried the door to the office.

He waited . . . and the rainbow vanished. He kept waiting, then checked the time. Almost half an hour had passed.

What was going on? Were they mobilizing a full assault team?

From somewhere, he heard sirens.

Then the door burst open, and more black-shirts poured in, fully armored, looking around.

Outside the balcony a flitter hovered.

Maertyn narrowed the stunner beam to a needle focus, and fired . . . without effect. The black-shirts looked around. Maertyn fired again.

One of the black-shirts turned toward Maertyn, leveling a high-impact projectile automatic at him and triggering it.

Maertyn felt himself falling, and he clutched at the doorway, seeing for a moment a fog that rolled away from the flitter and in through the open balcony door. One of the armored black-shirts staggered, but Maertyn lost sight of him as he toppled backward to land on the hard floor.

". . . least I got Tauzn . . . Maarlyna . . ."

Above, the ceiling began to spin around him—before darkness crashed across him.

62

❖ ❖ ❖

24 Siebmonat 3123, Vaniran Hegemony

How long the heat and cold, the rush of time, and the sense of time passing not at all, while he could neither move nor sleep, lasted Duhyle had no idea. He only knew that it ended, and darkness enfolded him. When he did wake, he was encased in a medical unit in a small chamber, with only his head and upper neck free. There was even some sort of cap on his head. Every appendage of his body, not to mention his torso, was a mass of pain, except that the medical nerve blocks kept him from feeling that agony, only letting a trickle through so that he was aware of how severely he had been injured.

Helkyria looked up from the small screen in her lap. She sat in a reclining medichair and her entire right leg, from mid-thigh to toes, was encased in a regeneration cocoon. "Welcome back into time and the universe."

"Am I going to stay here?" His voice was ragged and hoarse.

"The medical types weren't certain at first, but you're far more resilient than they could have imagined, and there's no doubt now."

"Symra said that your leg got torn up a little. A little? Was there anything left before they got you to regen?"

"Enough for the regen to take." Her voice was pleasant.

Duhyle could see the darkness around her eyes. "Barely, I suspect."

"You were in far worse shape, dear."

Duhyle wasn't about to argue. "Where are we?"

"In the medcenter in Vestalte. There's not much left of Vaena. That was the last Hammer strike."

"Did we stop her soon enough? What happened after I threw the last grenade?"

"You did. What did you have in it?"

"Not in it. On it. That was what the keeper gave me. Mistletoe. Mistletoe from the distant past, from the keeper's time. The insulation allowed it to penetrate Baeldura's time or event-point shields, and the grenade then shattered the insulation, I'd guess, and channeled the explosion toward Baeldura." He managed to stifle a cough. "I presume it was enough."

"It was."

"You . . . we . . . were incredibly lucky," he said.

She nodded. "We were, but we were lucky because the Aesyr rushed things. We couldn't have taken that ship against a fully trained crew. They would have sealed every compartment at the first sign of boarders. I was counting on that."

"How . . . did you know?"

"I didn't, not for certain, but things pointed that way. Baeldura, or her captain, didn't bring the ship all that close to the canal station, and the turns and maneuvers were sloppy. All their attacks on the station were rushed, and they were variations on strategies tried elsewhere. Baeldura and the Aesyr keep pressing for quick decisions. They were running out of time. They knew that if we could hold them off, their support would crumble. They had to win quickly, or not at all."

"They were willing to destroy the entire universe . . ."

"One entire universe," Helkyria corrected. "It does happen to be ours. That does make a difference. To us, anyway."

Duhyle wanted to nod. He couldn't. Not the way his head was restrained. He could only turn it slightly, just enough to see Helkyria. "Is it all over?"

"Mostly. When your . . . mistletoe . . . grenade exploded, there was some backlash to the other remote Hammer facilities. There's nothing much left of Asgard and more than a few other locations in Midgard. They'll have to be rebuilt. Thora was in Asgard, we think."

"What about Valakyr . . . Symra?" Duhyle knew he wouldn't like the answer.

"Valakyr's troopers took the Bridge. She didn't make it. Symra stepped in front of you."

"She didn't have to . . ."

"Yes, she did. She should have been in front of you the whole way."

Duhyle disagreed, but he wasn't about to say so. Finally, he asked, "Do you know *what* the canal—the Bridge—is?"

"The keeper called it a bifocused bridge—not a bifrost bridge," she said with a smile. "It was built to block an ancient version of the Hammer—except the hammer was being wielded from Earth's moon. The backlash of stresses pulled the moon closer to Earth and fragmented it—and a few billion human beings along with it—"

"How could they have built it without disrupting the entire planet?"

"It was actually built outside the local event-points, as the keeper would have termed it, outside of time, or what we'd call non-time, and anchored across from the time—or the event-point—of its building to the far future. It wasn't actually meant ever to appear on Earth when it did—that was another unanticipated backlash of the conflict, but the builders had to bring it into 'reality'—even if shielded—in order to stop the lunar bombardment of the world and to heal the rents in the dark energy web."

". . . and the cost of saving the universe was the destruction of their own civilization?"

"Essentially."

"So our little effort was nothing compared to that?" Duhyle didn't conceal the sarcasm in his voice.

Helkyria shook her head. "No. The way Thora and Baeldura had repeater Hammer stations across Earth, it would have been far worse. They might have even created such seismic upheavals as to wipe out all life entirely . . . except on the microscopic level."

"I know I've asked this before . . . and you've explained . . . but how could they?"

"Because they believed that their truth was the only truth, and that beside it, nothing else mattered. Hasn't that always been so with true believers?"

"So we stopped yet another group of true believers who believed that their 'truth' was so precious that the failure of us unenlightened types to perceive that merited the destruction of all Earth and the universe?"

"According to the keeper, we did more than that. The strain of the first conflict and ours reverberated or resonated through the event-points, or as we term it, through time. Those reverberations created images that receptive minds, dreaming minds, pick up on all event-points, even in those we'd call the distant past. Those minds only catch the images and sometimes the terms . . . and they become part of myths, of poetry at times, even cultural images." Helkyria laughed softly, ironically. "That's why so many myths are so illogical, and yet grip people, because there's a ring of verity behind them, but the people who catch the images don't know the context and fill it in with their own interpretations. I don't suppose we'll ever know . . ." She shook her head.

"And the canal, the Bridge is . . . what? The artifice of eternity?" he asked. "Or is that a phrase like the myths, one that resonates from the deep past to the future?"

Helkyria smiled. "Let's just say it resonates, and the resonance worked for us."

Duhyle almost snorted before asking, "And what of the keeper, the ruler of eternity? What resonates there?"

"Who can say? She doesn't rule so much as keep eternity . . . for us . . . at least for her reign, perhaps longer."

"Ruler . . . keeper . . . did you get anything of value from her?"

"Besides saving the universe?" Helkyria smiled, and her hair glowed warm gold. "Let's say that I have a few equations and a few ideas for us to work on."

"Oh?"

"They should allow us better ways to rebuild Asgard and Vaena . . . well enough that we can appreciate what lies, if you will, beyond the rainbow."

Duhyle did smile at that, even as he wondered why.

63

❀   ❀   ❀

16 Tenmonth 1351, Unity of Caelaarn

Fire burned along his left arm, and his lower legs were ice, and hot pokers stabbed into his body in too many places . . . Maertyn tried to turn, but found he could not move. Then he dropped back into a hot darkness . . . only to half-wake sometime later mouthing a name . . .

It was a beloved name, so beloved . . . and so much a part of him, but he could not remember it before another wave of darkness took him . . . and so it went, endlessly, dozing, fire, pain, darkness and light, and names and words coming from his mouth, none of which he recognized . . . until an even deeper and cooler darkness claimed him.

Then . . . he was awake

Slowly he opened his eyes, but he was alone in a small chamber—a hospital room, or a reasonable substitute for one. Equipment hummed, and some of it was centered on him, if only for the reason that he was the only one in the room. He was restrained in a bed, with regen pads clamped everywhere, it seemed, but only below the neck.

He was alive . . . but he was still tired . . . and his entire body ached . . . particularly places in his thighs and abdomen.

He tried not to think about what might come next.

An angular woman in the pale greens of healing walked into the chamber. "You're awake at last, Lord Maertyn. You're much better today."

"Could . . . I have . . ."

His mouth was so dry he could not continue, and she stepped over to the bed and offered a tube from a beaker. The liquid helped.

Finally, he completed the sentence. "Could I have been worse . . . still survived, Doctor?" Maertyn assumed she was a doctor because of the competence and the lack of badges and credentials affixed to her greens.

"Some have," she replied with a smile. "Not many. You have a visitor. He can only stay a few minutes, but he insists that it's important. Since the Executive Administrator of the Unity sent him, we had to agree to a few minutes. But if your vitals get disrupted, we'll be back to escort him out. Immediately."

Maertyn almost smiled at that, but he worried. Exactly who was the EA these days, and how long had he been recovering? Before he could ask, the doctor had stepped out.

The figure who stepped into the room and closed the door was not unfamiliar.

"Ashauer . . . I can't say as . . . I'm exactly surprised to see you."

"How could I not pay my respects to the hero of the Unity?" asked the older lord politely.

That certainly wasn't what Maertyn expected. He swallowed, then tried to gather his thoughts. Finally, he said, "My memory is a little hazy. Perhaps you had better refresh it."

Ashauer smiled warmly. "After all you've done and been through, that's scarcely surprising. I can't tell you everything, because your efforts to protect Tauzn from the assassins within his own bodyguards damaged several of the security scanners. The records we did recover implicated Aembit, not to mention Smaert . . ."

Maertyn had never heard of Smaert, but just nodded.

". . . Caellins, the head of the Gaerda, turned a stunner on his brain before he could be taken into custody. It's amazing what you uncovered, Maertyn."

"I just did what was necessary . . ."

"EA D'Onfrio has already made a public statement that your actions prove that Caelaarn still has heroes . . ."

Maertyn was beginning to get a very uneasy feeling.

"There are some matters unresolved. No one can enter the research station . . . and your wife is missing . . ."

Maarlyna . . . was she as lost to him as if she had died? Or he had? His eyes burned, and he shook his head, then swallowed.

"Another casualty of the renegade black-shirts?" asked Ashauer gently. "I do know how much you loved her."

Maertyn just nodded.

"I hesitate to ask . . . but the station?"

"Something happened . . . after everything. It's sealed. I don't know how, only that nothing I know how to do will open it."

". . . and then there's the matter of the rainbow." Ashauer looked at Maertyn.

"The rainbow?" asked Maertyn.

"While you were fighting off the assassins, a brilliant rainbow arched across Caelaarn, its tip touching the Ministry of Protective Services." The older lord shook his head. "It couldn't have been orchestrated more dramatically."

"I'm afraid I'm both tune- and tone-deaf," Maertyn managed, "and certainly no composer or orchestrator."

"All who know you agree to that. It's also what makes your efforts so much more heroic, Maertyn." Ashauer smiled once more, not quite ironically. "We also found records about all the attempts on your life. What the various media found most interesting was how you avoided so many without ever having to kill those who were trying to kill you."

"You made . . . all that public?"

"There wasn't any choice, Maertyn. If we hadn't . . ."

Although Ashauer hadn't completed the sentence, Maertyn knew exactly what he meant. One of Tauzn's remaining subordinates would have taken over where Tauzn had left off.

"D'Onfrio will endorse you, if you choose to seek his position."

"Me? I've never sought anything like that . . ."

"Precisely . . . and he will make that quite clear. He'll actually request that you seek the office of Executive Administrator because it is obvious that you have always put Caelaarn and others ahead of personal gain and power . . . and that you have lost so much in doing so."

"Ashauer . . . you—"

"Lord Maertyn," interrupted the older lord quickly, "I know that you are suffering great losses, but so is the Unity."

The formality of Ashauer's words stopped Maertyn's objections. He took a deep breath. "I see."

"I believe so."

"Still . . . a lord . . . there hasn't been an EA who was a lord since . . ." Maertyn started to shake his head, but the instant stab of pain down his neck stopped that abortive motion cold.

"Since Lestaat . . . and that was a bloody experience. But the people have seen that you were willing to brave the cold and storms trying to find a way to help them, that it is evident you lost your wife to the assassins, and that you avoided bloodshed as long as you could. The media are calling you a throwback . . . the last honorable lord . . ."

"I never . . ."

"No . . . but there are times when only one man can lead . . . and you are that man."

Thanks to Ashauer and D'Onfrio, Maertyn realized.

He also doubted he'd ever know all that had happened while he'd been recovering. Knowing Ashauer, no one else would, either.

"I can't stay long, the doctors say, but I did want you to know, as soon as possible." Ashauer inclined his head. "We all appreciate everything you did and look forward to your complete recovery." With a last smile, he turned and left the room.

Maertyn stared blankly after him.

EPILOGUE

The white dirigible hovered over the blue-gray stone of the canal, just to the east of the station and the dilapidated lighthouse, while a figure in a white cold-weather jacket followed two guards, also in white jackets, down a heavy rope ladder onto the stone. Two more guards followed the older man. Then, the five walked away from the airship, and the dirigible lifted fifty yards skyward, holding its position, hovering into the wind.

The man in white walked toward the station, motioning for the guards to remain behind.

He stopped short of where the south entrance was, or had been, waiting.

A silver haze appeared before him, a haze he knew would appear as mist or fog to the guards.

"I came back," he said quietly.

"In time," she replied.

"It would have been too painful, earlier." He offered a warm but crooked smile. "I couldn't have returned to you, not and have things except like this, could I?"

She shook her head, sadly. "I hoped you'd see that. Once you left the station . . ."

"You held the rainbow for me, didn't you?"

"I did. It took all that the Bridge could muster."

"Thank you, dearest. That may have saved Caelaarn."

"You saved it. I might have helped."

"More than you know." He paused, then went on. "You saw more than you've ever told me, didn't you? Well before it all began?"

The hazy silver figure in the red singlesuit nodded. "Then . . . I didn't know what it all meant. Even while I was recovering in Caelaarn, I'd seen the station. I saw us standing as we are now, except I didn't recognize me. I wondered who that striking woman you were talking to happened to be and why she was so ghostly." Her thin lips offered a smile both warm and rueful.

"You were always striking," he said.

"I owe you everything. You coddled and protected and saved me."

". . . and loved you," he added. "You were . . . you are . . . my empress."

"You did, and I still love you. Yet I belonged to you. That was my choice as well. But . . . I chose to do something that allows me to belong to me. Something . . . purposeful, with meaning. As you have found."

"Will you be lonely?"

"At times . . . but whenever you were not around, I was lonely . . . and without meaning. The Bridge, from it and what you . . . and the others . . . did, showed me that without meaning . . . there is no life . . . Even the universe will die if meaning departs."

"Will you see me if I come again?"

"Always . . . dearest . . . always . . ."

He stood there for a time, caressed by the silver mist, by his empress of eternity, before he turned.

The Executive Administrator of the Unity of Caelaarn walked southward toward the dirigible that would convey him to Daelmar and the special tube-train that waited for him.

Behind him, once the dirigible lifted and carried him eastward, a brilliant rainbow arched across the northern sky.